CHARLY BAY
BOOK ONE

Like No Other

C JAYE

ISBN : 9798547940484

Editor : sharpeyedshari.com
Cover design by : Getcovers.com

For Shari, Chrissy, and Shana, who have always believed in me. Thank you for helping me shape my story into the book it is today. I couldn't have done it without you. For the ones who have the courage to chase their dreams.

For the ones who embrace their quirky side and originality.

This one is for you...

*'The real lover is the man who
can thrill you just by touching
your head or smiling ointo
yur eyes — or just by staring
into space.'*

Marilyn Monroe, 1956

Prologue

"...I ...I ...I don't deserve you. I'm so sorry."
I gulp for air through the sobbing. It proves my heart feels different from my head. My mind keeps telling me that I need to let him go; that it is the right thing to do. But why is it tearing me apart?

"We're moving too fast... Please forgive me; I can't do this anymore...."

My arms lose all muscle, like they are just sacks of skin, hollow just like my soul. The phone slips from my grip, but I don't hear the clash and the smash. My eyes red raw reflect at me from the hallway mirror. My long blonde hair appears to be just as sad as my expression; the strands stick to my tear-soaked cheeks. My once ocean-like eyes look more like murky ponds than dazzling crystal blue waters. Who is this cold-hearted version of Charly Bay? Looking away, I am too ashamed to see myself. I slump into a mess on the floor. I hear footsteps thudding on the ground heading towards me as I fade out of the world.

What the hell have I done?

One

Sixty-six days, two hours and six minutes ago.

There is a new man in my life. He's so kind, so pure, so honest, and a perfect gent. 'Perfect,' in my head sounds so right, but said out loud has cliché written all over it.

After countless poor choices, my best friends Harper and Ashley convinced me to sign up for online dating. The columns after columns of smiling faces seemed so relentless to sift through. After a while, they merge into one. Mug shot after mug shot of James Bond wannabes. Do they think they can catch a girl with such a fake persona? Why big yourself up, be natural, just be YOU. No amount of Dwayne Johnson style arched eyebrow is going to reel me in.

At that moment, something caught my eye; you caught my eye. Big brown eyes are staring back at me. Short brown hair with a slight curl. Black casual t-shirt with an acoustic guitar laid across your lap. Something about your expression sings of shyness. A nervous tinge to your smile. I cock my head to one side as my eyes drink him in, surveying him, trying to figure him out. I am usually attracted to confident, borderline arrogant guys, but there's something different about Gareth81; I don't get an inkling of any of those traits in him, time for a change, maybe? My face starts to ache when I realise how broad my grin is. I let out an almost bashful chuckle as if he's sitting right here in front of me. I look away from the screen for a moment to compose, to think. I look back at his face; the kindness that radiates through his eyes mesmerises me into wanting to know him more.

Where on earth do I begin? I lean my face on my hands as self-doubt kicks in; exhaling sharply, I peer at the screen through my fingers. How can I introduce myself without sounding like a used car ad? Hello, this is Charly, five foot eight, curvaceous from every angle, two previous owners (both assholes hence why I am here!), damaged interior, in need of tender loving care. I shake away the silly thought with a chuckle and a toss of the head. Okay, focus, this is important. Deep breath, concentrate.

'Hello Gareth, my name is Charly; I'd love to get to know you.' No, no, too cheesy. Delete, delete, delete. Start again.

From: Charly88
To: Gareth81
Hello Gareth, how are you? x

Perfect! Short, sweet, and to the point. I click send, nerves chattering my teeth.

It felt like hours before I got a response. I must admit I squealed with delight when I saw Gareth's name sitting in my inbox. The already nervous butterflies playing the drums in my stomach suddenly launched themselves into a full-on cancan dance. Calm down, Charly; he might not even like you! In that split second, the butterflies are shot down one by one. 'Pow, pow, pow' ouch! With eyes closed, deep breaths easing the racing of my heart, squinting one eye open, I gingerly click on the envelope icon—the computer screen fills with his message.

From: Gareth81
To: Charly88
Hi Charly, I am well, thanks. How are you? x

Okay, short and sweet, just like mine. No hint of 'I fancy you.' But that's okay; I can dig a bit deeper. Time will only tell.

To: Gareth81
From: Charly88
Hi Gareth, yes, I am good, thank you. I cannot wait for Friday! It has been a busy week so far, and I am ready to chill! What do you do for work? x

The messages kept pinging back and forth all night. Before I knew it, it was past midnight. I reluctantly sent my goodnight wishes and headed for bed.

***

Lying in bed, I stare at my alarm clock, trying desperately to switch my mind off, but I can't help thinking how easy it was to talk to Gareth. He didn't hold anything back, just like an open book. He lives just outside the city, veterinarian by day, musician by night. I can't help but smile, hoping this is the start of something good.

Two

L.N.O. Publishing House on headed notepaper stares back at me, losing myself in deep thought as Gareth's face showcases in my mind's eye, a pile of papers slam down on my desk, propelling me out my blissful daydream. A slim waist dressed in electric blue blots my eyeline, my gaze reluctantly drifts up to meet Miranda. Her scowl is framed by her strikingly long dead-straight red hair. She looks so out of place here, like she should be H.R. for a fashion magazine, not a publishing house.

"These documents need filing away," she snaps.

'Don't react, don't remark, stay calm, just be cool,' my inner spirit says softly. I try my best to smile without an ounce of sarcasm as I scoop up the papers. No gratitude passes her lips, there's just a furrowed brow; she doesn't even give me eye contact, just turns on her heel and struts back to her desk in her fitted dress with a split up the back. A heavy sigh escapes from my chest as I make my way to the filing cabinets. A gentle caress meets my shoulder.

"Don't let her get to you," George whispers.

I turn my head as he draws closer to me.

"I heard through the grapevine... there's an opening across the hall at the end of the year... you should go for it, girl," he continues.

I beam with the best bit of news I've heard in ages. My hand overlaps George's, giving him a gentle squeeze.

"Thanks for the heads up... how are the retirement plans going?" I ask.

"The missus and I bought a campervan... just going to see where the road takes us," he says—gesturing like he's signalling on a runway.

"George, you are so rock n roll," I chuckle.

He does a little dodgy hip thrust, Elvis style, I think.

"Well, thank you very much," he smoothly says.

I can't help but laugh as he dances his way back to his desk; I'm going to miss him when he goes; he was the only one in this office, who took me under his wing and has stayed by my side ever since. Across the hall is where the publishing assistants are, and it's where I want to be, not some dogs-body for some pompous cow, with the most giant fucking chip on her shoulder. I only took on this role to get my foot in the door; now, I am so ready for that challenge across the way.

I mentally cheer when the clock finally strikes five; swiftly grabbing my jacket, bag, and phone, I dash out of the door before anyone can stop me. I fling on my coat and bag as I make my way to the lifts. I look down to put my phone in my bag; before I know it, I collide into a blue and white check shirt wall, forcing someone to drop their diary and papers.

"Oh shit... I'm so sorry," I blurt out.

I automatically squat down to help pick up the papers, along with a diary with the name 'Ben' on the front.

"There you go, Ben," I say as I hand over his possessions.

A look of confusion spreads across his features as he looks up at me.

"I saw your name on your diary," I continue.

I hope it's enough to reassure him I'm not some mad woman. As he gathers up the remaining papers, he gets to his feet and pushes his glasses back up the bridge of his nose. He stares at me, astonished, I think, like one of the cool girls has finally acknowledged him or something. His cheeks flush as he tries his best to clear his throat.

"Thank you... sorry, you took me by surprise there," Ben finally says.

"Yeah... sorry about that... I'm Charly, by the way," I reply.

"Nice to meet you, Charly... I better get back," he says hurriedly.

He smiles and gestures towards the doors that withhold my dream job.

***

On the way home I stop in the supermarket to buy some wine and chocolates. As I walk the last stretch home, I look to the sky and smile at the remaining sunshine. Even though it's the end of October, there's still an ounce of warmth in the air. Thoughts track back to Gareth, and a warm fuzzy glow of contentment rises within me that I have never felt before.

Soon as I step into the house, I head straight for my laptop. Just waiting for it to fire up feels like an eternity. Harper and Ashley find it hilarious that I haven't caught up with the 21st century yet with all the latest downloadable apps, I will one day, but I like my phone clutter-free for now. Gareth is up to date though, the first of many messages drops typically just after 6 o'clock when his shift finishes. I know it's too early in the day to expect a message from him, his work shifts are always so hectic, but I couldn't help taking a peek, you know, to be sure. Just as I thought, no new messages. I sit there for a few minutes, staring at the screen. Maybe somewhere in my brain, I could unlock the ability to make something appear, like some superpower. Then I realise I have not blinked; the dryness stings my eyes; this is silly. My stomach growls, reminding me I need to eat. I throw together a super quick pasta dish. So hungry, I inhale it. The hunger growls, now satisfied. Armed with my large glass of wine, I make my way to my makeshift office again, tucked away in the corner of my living room. A loud, tired sigh escapes from me as I slump down on my chair. Thank goodness it's Friday. Sore, tired aches run across my shoulders. I nurse it while I wait for the screen to wake up. Then there you are.

From: Gareth81
To: Charly88
Charly, do you like hiking? x

I slump back in my chair. I groan out loud.
"No, thank you."
I say my response aloud as if he is asking me in the flesh to pack myself up and leave right this minute. Batting the tired thoughts

away, I clear my throat as if I am about to say rather than type my words.

To: Gareth81
From: Charly88
I am not fit enough for hiking x

His reply pings within a blink of an eye it seems. Time seems to have no substance when it's just the two of us chatting away. I take a couple of sips of wine as I open the new message.

From: Gareth81
To: Charly88
Oh, that's a pity.

Oh crap, have I just blown it? Okay, think Charly, what can I say to turn it around, some sort of compromise maybe? I hold my head in my hands, letting out a deep sigh; come on, think. Then my laptop pings with another message.

From: Gareth81
To: Charly88
How about countryside walks instead? x

As I finish reading the message, my head instinctively cocks to one side. Trying to make sense of it through the tired fog. Even reading it twice does not help. Is he asking me out? It suddenly dawns on me that I have been staring at the screen. Wake up, Charly, wake up and think.

To: Gareth81
From: Charly88
Is that an invitation? x

A simple question suddenly feels so forward. Cheeky, for some reason. Was that the wrong thing to ask? Desperate? A flash of regret tugs at my stomach as soon as I hit the send button. I grimace as my eyes close, tilting my head backwards; I beg the darkness for good news. My eyes fly open in sync with the familiar new message ping.

From: Gareth81
To: Charly88
It is indeed. I have to work tomorrow, but only until three; maybe meet me just after. But if tomorrow is too soon, I fully understand x

Holy shit, I have a date. I am stunned at the words on the screen in front of me. So much sudden excitement floods my body from head to toe. My hands shake as I hit each letter on the keyboard. It seems like my fingers are refusing to function correctly. Can fingers go into shock? My inner spirit feels like she has frozen too. How can such simple everyday sentences and questions send me into such a giddy unresponsive mess?

To: Gareth81

From: Charly88
Sounds perfect to me, count me in. x

Before I could sit back in my chair, I hear a new message ping.

From: Gareth81
To: Charly88
Great! I'll meet you outside Starbucks near City Bridge. Maybe grab a coffee first? x

I don't hesitate to reply either; my fingers come alive, flying around on my keyboard at lightning speed, full of excitement.

To: Gareth81
From: Charly88:
Fine with me, see you then x

Three

Not sure if this pink and white striped jumper and jeans combo is first date attire, but what else can you throw on, suitable for a walk and still look good? Too late to change my mind now anyway as I stand trembling in the autumn sunshine. But that does not stop me from looking down at myself, making sure everything is in place. As I look up, there he is, wading through the sea of busy heads. He suddenly stops as he catches sight of me, but I can't read his expression. Second thoughts, maybe? Oh crap, a ton of doubt hits my stomach; I knew this bright pink jumper was a bad idea. Feeling cross at my terrible choice of wears, I glare down at myself as if the jumper were the one to blame. A moss-green grandad style jumper greets me and my gaze scales up to his face; his familiar nervous smile greets me.

"I'm so sorry to disappoint you with my choice of jumper," he says, a little embarrassed.

My face creases, trying to hold in a nervous giggle. Gareth looks at me with a confusing twist in his expression; he waits for me to explain. Come on, Charly, compose yourself.

"Funny... I was thinking the same thing," I finally say.

I step back and whisk my arm out in a 'ta-da' motion. In sync, we burst out laughing; a wave of relief washes over me. As we both compose into sensible people, we find ourselves just staring at each other in awkward silence. I feel myself blush first, as I realise he's everything I hoped he would be, funny and handsome.

"Shall we?" he says and gestures towards the café door.

I nod and smile coyly as he holds the door open for me; I'm not used to this. I must add chivalrous to that list too.

"Thanks," I say timidly.

As we enter, the familiar aroma of freshly brewed coffee hits my senses. I stare at the menu board above the counter, suddenly feeling lost, then the feel of a gentle hand on my shoulder brings me back and my gaze drifts to Gareth's face.

"I'm going to go for a cappuccino... what do you fancy?" he asks.

I watch as his face lights up when he looks at me. What do I fancy? 'I fancy you,' my inner spirit coos; my cheeks instinctively blaze and I look back to the board, quickly.

"I'll have the same," I reply.

I look back to Gareth, and our gazes lock until we hear someone shout 'next please!' It makes us jump.

"Find a seat... I'll get this," Gareth insists.

As I turn, I notice vacant seats next to the window, perfect. I take my jacket off and hang it on the back of my chair as Gareth carries two plates to our table.

"I could hear your stomach calling out for food; I hope you like chocolate croissant twisty things."

In automatic embarrassment, I clutch hold of my stomach.

"That's perfect, thank you."

Amongst all the chaos of getting ready earlier, I forgot to eat. The smell of dark chocolate sends my stomach into a growling frenzy, so much so all I want to do is stuff my face, but I remind myself to not act like a pig scoffing in a trough. I gingerly bite into it; oh my, it tastes as good as it looks.

"Oh, it's so good... I love food, especially something sweet, I have a sweet tooth," I murmur.

Gareth smiles at me, amused, probably pleased with himself that he made a good choice. He bites into his and mirrors my appreciative expression.

"You are so right," he says, smiling approvingly.

Handsome, chivalrous, pastry, chocolate, cappuccino, good humour, the boxes keep on ticking. Gareth's relaxed, calm nature puts me at ease; I feel myself warming to him more and more with every passing minute. So comfortable, I feel like I've known him for ages. I gaze out of the window at the world passing by with a contented sigh as I finish the last mouthful.

"You are so beautiful... sorry, I should have said it way before now," he says under his breath.

It sounded like he blurted it out as a thought slipped out, his cheeks flushed at the same time. My eyes widen as it takes me by surprise; I feel my eyes glisten as his compliment sinks in. My heart skips with joy. He watches me intently as the words process; when it does, my smile quite literally stretches from ear to ear.

"...and your smile... wow, it's something else... it brightens up the whole room," he continues.

My cheeks flush from warm to red hot, instinctively covering my mouth with my hand, but only for a moment, I let out a quiet, muffled giggle.

"Hasn't anyone ever told you that?" he asks, on the verge of horrified.

No, they haven't; I look down as the thought overtakes, forcing me to shake my head. The moment is interrupted by mugs noisily landing on our table. As I look up, Gareth is watching me intently, with that shy smile. He only breaks eye contact for a moment to say thanks to the barista, then his eyes dart back to mine. Where do I begin with explaining past relationships without it sounding like I am seeking pity? I sharply exhale when I realise I've been holding my breath. Just be honest, I guess, let everything out and then let him be the judge whether I am relationship material or not.

"Not by someone who truly meant it... I haven't had, umm, a serious relationship... they talked the talk... I got swept along thinking I meant something to them... one cheated on me... and I was one of many with the second one...." I murmur.

Gareth slumps back in his chair, astounded, I hope, his mouth is hanging like he is. He finally shakes his head.

"How can anyone do... ah," he tails off.

Before he can add anything more, I turn the spotlight round to him.

"What about you?" I ask.

He shifts and straightens up in his seat.

"I've had one serious relationship... lasted nearly five years... she too cheated on me... What made you choose me?"

Oh crap, tables turning yet again, spinning so fast it could have knocked me out.

"I was drawn to your eyes... there was something about them... kind and shy, I think..."

Oh dear, I should have said something along the lines of 'Your incredibly handsome face bowled me over'. For fuck sake, my inner spirit sighs and rolls her eyes. But as Gareth locks eyes with mine, he doesn't seem at all displeased, phew.

**

Six empty mugs, four empty plates and a dozen conversations later, I notice the evening starting to draw in; numerous shades of orange fill the sky. Gareth follows my gaze.

"Ah, looks like the walk is out of the question... Must have got too lost in you...." Gareth says.

I feel his eyes back on me; I peel my eyes away from the mesmerising sky to find his gaze again.

"Can I show you something instead?" he asks.

I nod and display my coy smile that he seems to like so much. Gareth gets up and flings his jacket on in a flash, zipping it up, hiding the mossy greenness. Before I know it, he's helping me into mine; he scoops my hair out with a quick flick of the wrists. His bare hands brush against my neck as he does so, sending the butterflies into a fluttering frenzy. My skin tingles from my neck down my spine. He offers me his hand.

"Ready?" he asks.

I just about manage to nod after the first thrilling feel of his hands on me, however brief. As we head outside, he guides me up to City Bridge. The pedestrian traffic is just as busy for the time of day; we weave in and out. He stops halfway across the bridge, out of everyone's way; Gareth gestures to the sky. As the sun starts to set, it fills the sky with such glorious blends of oranges and yellows, breathtaking in fact. I'd hate to admit that I've never actually stopped and admired it before. After a moment, he points to the right side of the river.

"Just beyond the Victoria Hotel over there is my practice," he says.

He walks round to my left, standing close to me and points to the other side.

"And that there is... nothing," he continues.

Huh? I look up at him, puzzled. There's a bashful glint to his eyes.

"I just needed an excuse for you to look at me," he says coyly under his breath.

I edge even closer to him, so much so, I can feel the heat from his body. I feel safe, he feels safe, he's not what I'm used to, but that's not a bad thing.

"You didn't need one," I reply.

He smiles with relief, yet he still seems hesitant. I gaze longingly at him, trying to send telepathic signals to let him know it's okay; kiss me, or shall I jump straight in? At that thought, I feel his hands cup my face, and his lips delicately find mine. I lean into him, my hands on his arms, not wanting to break the contact; we both relax into each other. The butterflies are forming into a hurricane type spin with every kiss. We reluctantly break away; he leans his forehead against mine.

"Can I see you tomorrow, Charly?" he asks.

My inner spirit jumps about, clapping her hands and whooping at the top of her voice; amused at the delight, I almost giggle.

"Sure," I smile.

**

Sipping my coffee, sitting on the sofa, in my pyjama's I recollect on this afternoon's events with a broad smile etched on my face. We stood and watched the sunset in front of us, I have no idea how long we were there, but the sky went from orange to navy. We watched as the city nightlife slowly came alive. When he put his arm around me for the first time, I felt safe, protected, wanted.

I retold everything to my mum over the phone as soon I could; she was delighted for me.

"Well, about time, darling... you're not getting any younger."

That is what she actually said, but I'd take that as she's pleased for me.

"I'm only twenty-nine, Mum," I had to remind her.

"Yes... well, I was married to your dad and had you by the time I was twenty-four."

I've heard it all before, so I got her to quickly change the subject to work instead. My dad left when I was four years old; I haven't seen him since. Mum never found anyone else after that, she didn't even date; I think she's happy doing her own thing in her little eccentric world with no added worries.

My thoughts make an abrupt U-turn back to Gareth. I remember his lips delicately on mine, so soft and polite. My fingers automatically feel where he has been. I feel giddy at the thought that he wants to see me again so soon; we're going for a walk like we should have done today. Talking to him was so easy, losing ourselves in each other's conversation; it's nice to have someone so interested in me, wanting to know everything about me. We had another tender kiss after he walked me home. Oh, shit, not concentrating, I spilt my coffee on my lap. Luckily, it was warm, not piping hot, but it still made me jump. Leaning my forehead against my palm, I shake my head as I restlessly giggle. What is this guy doing to me? I take a large sip of coffee as I compose myself. I gaze down at the mug in my hands and grin broadly, wishing tomorrow was already here.

Four

Bleary-eyed, I read 07:09 on my alarm clock. A loud groan escapes from me as I turn over and rewrap myself in the bedsheets. No, no, no, it is way too early. As I start to drift off again, my inner spirit gives me a gentle, nudging reminder. I bolt upright like a cartoon Dracula waking from his slumber. Flying out of bed, I start pacing, up and down the room, trying to get my brain into some order. I add things to my mental to-do list, which is pointless as it will more than likely erase itself within minutes, but I must make myself think that I'm orderly. I start trawling through my jumpers until I come across a deepish purple one, just like my favourite chocolate bar. Mm, I could go for some chocolate right now; the craving buzzes right through me, much like the excitement of seeing Gareth again so soon. Exhaling as I come down from the exhilarating feeling, I lay out my wears for today, ticking off my inner spirit's checklist as I go. I scrutinise each one until I am totally happy with my choices. A smile bursts its way through, followed by a skittish squeal and leap. I jump back into bed, burying myself in the sheets once again. Tightly closing my eyes, willing them to snooze for just a bit longer, but it is no use.

***

Excitement more than nerves drives me to eat breakfast this morning. I don't fancy flaking out halfway through the walk. I clutch my cereal bowl with the radio blaring. I do my best cat screeching in pain impression and a little prance around the kitchen. Hate to think what Doris next door thinks of that on a Sunday morning; but who cares? At least I'm having fun.

As time ticks on, the nerves start kicking at my gut like a punching bag. I sit and nurse a coffee at my kitchen table for what seems like hours. The second's hand on the clock seems to tick louder and louder; slower and slower, it's mesmerising. I feel myself falling into a daydream, visions of Gareth's face dance in my mind's eye, amongst snippets of yesterday's outing. Somewhere in the distance, I can hear a tapping sound. I jump up so fast; I knock over my stool. A concerned voice hums through the letterbox.

"Charly?... Charly, are you okay?"

I quickly straighten myself up.

"Yeah... I'm just coming."

Swiftly I scoop up my bag and coat as I go. I have so many bolts and locks on my door, like a medieval castle drawbridge; maybe I should have one of those hatches installed to peer through, so I can ask the visitor the secret code before entering. I chuckle to myself with the thought as I open the door.

"Oh wow... Hi."

It comes out more like a whisper at first. Gareth seems to glow in the morning rays.

"Morning, beautiful... ready to go?"

I beam with delight.

"Sure am!"

I grimace to myself as I turn round to lock the front door, cursing in my head for being and sounding too enthusiastic. But as I turn around, he does not seem fazed about my burst of excitement. Phew!

* * *

Right now, life is good. The journey from home to The Downs is a blur. As we park up,

I gulp as I clock the steep hill in the distance; Gareth follows my stare.

"Don't worry... there are other routes," Gareth reassures me.

As I climb out of the car, a chill in the breeze hits me; I am so glad I brought my coat. We follow the winding footpaths with hedgerows and brambles lining each side. Gareth picks the last of the blackberries as we go and suddenly stops and turns to face me. Holding a single blackberry, he gestures for me to try it; I'm not keen on them, but I'll eat it just for him. He pops it in as I open my mouth; as soon as I start to chew, the bittersweetness hits my tastebuds with a punch, forcing me to squeeze my eyes shut and pout. I feel the corner of my eyes prickle as the sensation takes its toll; my eyes water. I hear

Gareth snigger at my screwed-up expression. As I open my eyes, I free the tears. Gareth draws closer to me; he rests his palms on my cheeks, using just the tips of his thumbs to wipe the tears away. I gaze at him through tear smudged vision, blinking a few times until I can see him more clearly. I smile broadly when the fog clears; the autumnal sun bounces off his hair and features gloriously, framing him like some angelic portrait. His thumbs still linger at the corners of my eyes.

"I'm sorry," he says softly.

He holds my gaze as he says it and I long for his lips to meet mine. At that thought, his eyes drift down to my mouth, his right-hand shifts, one thumb brushes against my lower lip instead, parting them slightly as he goes, my breath catches in my throat with the surprise touch. His lips finally find mine and the intimacy fills my body with such a rush. It's like being swept up into a whirlwind. As he pulls away, my body almost loses its balance, mistaking the whirlwind thought for a natural phenomenon. Gareth steadies me by my waist; the feel of his tender touch reassures me that he's got me. I am filled with such good vibes that I feel like I can conquer anything. Out of the corner of my eye, the hill visible from the car doesn't look so daunting now that we are so close to it.

"I suddenly feel like I can conquer that."

I gesture over to the climb with a nod. Gareth smiles broadly, eyebrows raised like he's impressed.

"What made you change your mind?" he quizzes.

"Good vibes, I guess," I reply and smile coyly with a slight shrug.

Gareth steps round to my side, offering me his hand; I gladly take it. We follow the path until we come across a gap in the hedgerows. As we ascend, we pass avid hikers and dog walkers, all sharing good morning greetings. It isn't as tiring as I thought it would be, a little achy pressure on the knees, but nothing too strenuous. I could get used to this; my inner spirit smiles, looking like she's just as invigorated. I look down at our hands fondly clasped together; for once I feel special, I can already tell that he has a good heart, a kind soul, his career choice also reflects that. Just as we reach the peak, a Labrador Retriever startles me out of my blissful thoughts as he bounds up to us, its golden shaggy coat bounces in the breeze and the force of its expedition; it seems eager to get Gareth's attention. Maybe he senses that he's a vet? He lets go of my hand and fusses over the dog; it jumps up at him with such immense excitement that it takes him out. I almost shriek, but soon as I see Gareth laughing, a wave of relief washes over me. The owner comes running over, apologising profusely, her face crimson with embarrassment as she pulls her dog away, then reattaching the lead to its collar, she hurries away without any more conversation. I offer my hand to Gareth, helping him to his feet.

"That looked like fun... I almost joined in," I chuckle.

"There was room for one more," he says out of breath.

I step back as I pull him up, but my foot slips on something; it feels squelchy underfoot as I fall. I hope and pray its mud. The thought distracts me, and I forget to let go of Gareth's hand. Before I know it, I'm on my back gazing up at him. When I realise how close we are, I feel my heartbeat frantically against my chest. I feel him shifting to get off me, but I hold onto him.

"Don't go yet," I whisper.

His eyes dance with the sun and this moment.

"I'm not going anywhere," he whispers back to me.

He holds my gaze as he says it; it feels deep and meaningful. His lips find mine, but this time it's more ardent. Someone tuts very loudly as they pass us. We start giggling before Gareth pulls away; we turn our heads the other way, not wanting to meet the eye of the unimpressed party. He eventually rolls off and sits up next to me. As I follow, I can't help but notice mud squelched underneath my legs; 'It could have been a whole lot worse', my inner spirit shrugs. I distract myself by taking in the magnificent view for a moment, it seems to roll on for miles and miles, it's pretty breath-taking.

"I can see why you love the countryside so much... it's beautiful," I say, amazed.

I feel his eyes on me as I say it. I shuffle closer to him, out of the muddy spot. Lifting his arm, he gestures for me to come into his hold. As his arm comes down around me, once again, I feel safe, wanted. I lean into him, resting my head on his shoulder, my nose brushes against the crook of his neck. I inhale a deep breath and the dewy scent of the countryside mixed with his aftershave makes me feel content. So much so, I do not want to move from this spot. I am hoping that this moment will never end.

"You okay?"

There is an ounce of concern in his voice. I hope he didn't mistake my sigh for dissatisfaction. I lean back a smidge so that I can answer his question.

"Everything is fine... more than fine... it's absolutely perfect."

Soon as I say it, I can feel his body retract and completely relax. His arm wraps around my shoulder. Comfortable in each other's company.

Yes, right now, life is good, more than good; it's absolutely perfect.

Five

The number '3' shines brightly as I press it, I hear the familiar whoosh sound of the lift as it lands on the foyer floor, the bell dings and the doors open a little too enthusiastically for my liking. I step inside, pressing '3 'once again, then spin around to rest my back in the right corner. As the doors start to close, I take a deep breath in preparation for today; I let go of it sharply as a hand thuds against the lift doors, forcing them to bolt back open. I clutch hold of my chest as my heart leaps, trying to escape up through my throat with the shock. I see his glasses first, but no blue and white check shirt today; it's a plain teal one instead. My heart comes back down in my chest with a thud as the rush eases. He glances up at my wide-eyed expression.

"I think we're even now," he grins nervously.

I just about manage a slight nod and half a smile. Ben comes to stand next to me at the back of the lift, just as several other bodies cram into the lift with us. They force Ben to stand right against me, then a couple more holler to hold the lift for them. Ben shifts his body just as the space gets smaller, facing me now. Someone slams into his back, knocking his glasses down his nose; he steadies himself on the wall next to my head. He's only slightly taller than me, but it feels somewhat intimidating being this close; it's the first time I've seen him properly. He averts his eyes away from me nervously; he tries to push his glasses back up with his shoulder.

"Thank you for not letting them crush me," I whisper.

His eyes drift back to mine as I say it, he gives me half an embarrassed smile in acknowledgement and a brief nod. Reaching up between us, I push his glasses back to their rightful place. He has blue eyes that really pop against the colour of his shirt, his narrow-lensed glasses frame them nicely, his dark brown hair is a little on the long side, but swept back, stubble finishes off his look. I'm sensing a little geek chic going on here. The lift's doors finally squeeze shut, the lift screeches under everyone's weight as it finally begins its journey. We stop at each floor and Ben steps back to give me more space as the bustle slowly eases until it's just us exiting at level 3.

"I'll see you around."

It hangs off his lips more like a question than a plain and simple 'goodbye'.

"Sure... thanks again, for you know...."

Pointing towards the lift's doors, I don't know why I felt the need to do that. My inner spirit slaps her forehead in dismay. He smiles to himself as he turns and walks away. One day I'll be heading his way, fingers crossed it will be at the end of the year.

My good mood breaks as soon as I lock eyes with Miranda. An invisible fishhook has latched itself onto the back of my jacket collar, my inner spirit is holding onto the other end at full speed, reeling me in before I make a complete fool of myself. I haven't even reached my desk, and she's already scowling at me; it burns into me like I am someone from a rival gang trespassing on her turf or something. 'Just smile,' my inner spirit pleads with me as she throws down the rod; I do as I'm told. As I place my bag and phone down, George comes over to me.

"Good morning, my dear... how was your weekend?" he chirps. I am so thankful for his distraction.

"Really good, actually... I had two dates," I proudly announce. George raises his eyebrows in surprise, a little unsure how to respond, I think.

"Don't look so worried... With the same guy," I add.

As soon as I say it, I watch his shoulders relax.

"Oh well done, old gal... about time."

That's pretty much the same remark as my mum gave me; why's it so frowned upon to be single at my age? Before I even have the chance to ask, Miranda, summons him to her desk. I slip my jacket off and hang it on the back of my chair. Air from my chair and my lungs both make a whoosh sound as I slump down on the seat. Switching on my computer, I pick up my phone while I wait for the system to wake up; my face lights up as soon as I see his name on the screen.

'Have a great day at work Beautiful. Can't wait to see you again xx'

I realise then that we didn't set another date. Maybe I can put forward a suggestion? But then again, I wouldn't know where to go, or what to do when it comes to the countryside. Okay, so let's quickly go back to this message before Miranda starts cracking her whip and giving her orders out.

'Wish I could escape, and come and help you instead... I can't wait to see you again, hope it's soon x.'

As I hit send, doubt punches my stomach; did that sound a little too needy, pathetic? Oh crap, I gulp hard, tugging the back of my throat; I wince.

"Are you here to do some work today?" the voice bellows.

I don't even have to look up to know it came from Miranda. A pile of files slams down in front of me; it makes me jump, and my heart leaps, even though I was half expecting it. Without another word, she marches back to her desk. I hold my head in my hands for a moment as I let my heart resume its normal rhythm, exhaling long and shaky, my lower lip starts to quiver; nope, I can't let that bitch get the better of me. My inner spirit fist pumps the air and shouts, 'that's the spirit'.

***

My body falls heavily. I land sprawled out on my sofa. One arm dangles above the floor, the other is flung over the headrest, one leg hangs off the edge while the other drapes over the armrest at the other end. Not the least bit comfortable, but I'm so tired. The TV flashes and blares at me, but I can't concentrate, anxiety has a tight grip on my stomach. I may have put Gareth off, he hasn't replied to my message from this morning. 'He's just busy' my inner spirit tries to soothe me and my ever-increasing tension. I look at the time on my phone; it's way past eight. As I drag myself up off the sofa, I chuck my phone onto the cushions; I need wine. I shuffle in my slippers to the kitchen and grabbing a glass, I help myself to a large glass of rosé. Resting my behind on the counter, I take a large sip of it; it slips soothingly down my throat. I hear a muffled new message ping on my phone; taking another large swig, I shuffle back to the sofa. Thank fuck for that when I see his name appear along with his message.

'Hey, Beautiful... sorry I have only just got back from work... a hectic day... I want to do something with you this weekend, and it's probably going to be a bit messy x.'

Hmm sounds a bit ominous, but at least he's still talking to me.

'Are you going to enlighten me first before I say yes or no? x'

I sit on the edge of the sofa and switch off the TV, taking another glug of wine while I wait. Before I know it, the familiar sound pings.

'Trust me, you'll enjoy it... oh and you're going to need wellies x'

I smile at the mystery, but as he mentioned wellies, then it's more than likely something to do with the countryside.

'Okay, I trust you... long as we're not mucking out a pigsty ha-ha x'

I let out a loud yawn that fills the silence. I am so ready for my bed. Finishing off the last dregs in my glass, I drag my tired feet up the stairs.

As I crawl into bed, my phone pings with another message.

'That's good to know that you trust me... and don't worry, it's something fun... pick you up at ten on Saturday... goodnight Beautiful x.'

Six

To say that this week has dragged by would be an understatement. But then I smile at the thought of Gareth and his mysterious plans for tomorrow. Our relationship is blossoming day by day, I haven't seen him since Sunday, but the evenings without fail have been full of messages pinging back and forth. It feels so good to be in someone's company with no stress of trying to be someone you're not. He likes me for me. I cannot tell you how refreshing that feels.

I find myself just staring at my computer screen, 'you better wake up, Charly, someone isn't impressed 'my inner spirit gives me a nudge. I let my eyes drift to Miranda's desk; sure enough, she's on the phone, but that doesn't stop her from glaring at me. Oh my, if looks really could kill. Maybe she's hoping she had Medusa's powers, so that she could turn me into stone with her laser beam vision, hissing her commands at me like she has an inner serpent. Hmm, if I was a stone statue, that'd be a good excuse not to get any work done.

Just ten minutes to go until the weekend starts, and I am as free as a bird. George comes hobbling over to my desk with a bundle of files under his arm; he's had trouble with his hip, so no Elvis style hip thrusts this week. You can tell he'd be the life and soul of anyone's party when his body isn't giving him grief.

"Another week closer to retirement," he beams.

As soon as he says it, he clutches hold of his hip with his free hand and winces; pain tears through his smile.

"You must rest this weekend... no more gardening... listen to your wife too," I command, playfully wagging my finger.

"I know... I know," George mumbles.

He continues to shuffle his way to the filing cabinets. It's sad to see him this way, I know he won't listen to my instructions, but I hope he does; I don't want him to retire earlier than he needs to.

The clock finally strikes five, and I'm so out of here, making my way to the lifts, being careful not to knock anyone out as I go. Come to think of it, I haven't seen Ben at all this week. Quite a few people are waiting and no sign of my knight in shining armour, so I take the stairs instead, almost skipping down each one as I go. Down in the foyer, it's even busier; I let myself drift along with the crowd's flow until we all leak out onto the pavement.

As I make my way up to and across City Bridge, the scenery opens. I realise then how gloomy the skies are, but it doesn't stop me from pausing for a moment on the same spot I stood with Gareth. No ounce of gloominess can put an end to my smile and good vibes today. As I look up, I notice the different shades of whites, charcoal and greys airbrushed through the clouds; raindrops start to patter on my cheeks, but not even that can steal away my Cheshire cat grin.

***

I have been awake, showered, dressed, and fed since 8 a.m. I opted for a red and navy check shirt, a black camisole underneath with a pair of dark skinny jeans, and hair up in a high ponytail. Oh, and not forgetting the old boots, I couldn't find my wellies, so I had to wear these old knee-high boots instead, with a flat heel, of course.

Standing on my doorstep with my thumbs in my jeans belt loops, one knee angled outwards, I wish I had a cowgirl hat to finish off my look. It's surprisingly warm and sunny for October 31st, ah Halloween, of course. 'It's going to be messy' - that part of Gareth's message hangs in my mind; as long as it's not a killing spree, apple bobbing I can deal with, not a bloodbath, I shake the crazy thought out of my head.

I see Gareth climb out of his car. He starts to walk down the front garden path equipped with his khaki wellies, dark wash jeans, plain black jumper with a khaki jacket over the top, looking rather charmingly smart for a supposedly messy day. He stops mid-stride when he catches sight of me; he smiles big and bright.

"Howdy, partner," I call out.

Flicking my invisible hat as I greet him, trying my best to sound original, I can't help but laugh as soon as I say it. He seems to share my amusement with the greeting. With one arm above my head, I pretend to swing around a lasso, flinging the invisible rope around Gareth, then reeling him in with my hand gestures. He plays along, jolting like I've caught him, with his arms tightly by his sides as he shuffles closer to me; all the while we never cease our giggling. I throw my arms down, putting an end to the shenanigans, craving for him to hold me instead as he starts to tower over me.

"So, what do you think... do I pass for a country girl or cowgirl?" I murmur.

"Definitely a country girl," he says.

Gareth smiles with a flourish while admiring each of my features as he says it and I adore how his face seems to light up whenever he looks at me. His fingertips brush against the side of my neck as his palm comes to a rest, using it to pull me closer until his lips tenderly meet mine. His touch on my neck tingles my skin, the tiny hairs spring up, waking the butterflies from their slumber. My inner spirit dances around on her tiptoes like she's some pirouetting ballerina; like her, I couldn't be happier.

***

"Oh, my goodness... this is... this is amazing," I almost squeal in awe.

The air smells so sweet, it's enough to hit you with a sugar rush. There's stall after stall of fresh cakes, sweets like fudge and toffee, pastries, jams, cheeses, and all kinds of bread; you name it and it's all laid out so tantalisingly, so seductively, so inviting, I want to devour it all. On the opposite side of the walkway, there's an array of vegetables and fruits, all colourful and delicious in their own ways. As I draw closer to them for a moment there's an earthy smell mixed with tangy berries, like it's the heart-warming scent of autumn. The field squelches underfoot from yesterday's rainfall. I look down as I feel Gareth take hold of my hand, squeezing me gently as I look up again to find that shy smile of his; sure enough, it's on display.

"I can't believe you remembered that I love sweet things..." excitement fills my words.

I smile shyly with an ounce of embarrassment for my display of childish glee, but he doesn't seem disconcerted; he looks pleased with himself more than anything, phew.

"I'm sorry... I've never been anywhere like this before... I truly feel like a little kid in a sweet shop," I add.

I'm looking at everything like I'm seeing it for the first time. Everywhere you look, it's so picturesque. Beyond the row of small white gazebos, the hills seem to run for miles, it's hard to believe that all this beauty is on the city's doorstep.

"I can't believe no one has ever taken you to a farmers market before."

I'm not sure what I should reply to that. I seek help from my inner spirit, but all she does is hold her hands up and shrug; I mirror her reaction with just one free hand.

"No one has ever taken the time to listen to me... or show me this part of the world before... so thank you," I murmur.

'Thank you?' my inner spirit looks bewildered. What can I say? I am thankful for someone to treat me right. Finally, someone who listens to me, intently wants to know me, not the airbrushed fake version, the raw real me. I smile along with that thought.

"Do you want to try anything?" Gareth quizzes.

It's the most beautiful question to interrupt my train of thought with. I let go of Gareth's hand and veer towards the sweet stuff.

"Sure... but where do we start?"

I clap and rub my hands together as I say it, looking like I am ready for action, and I am so ready to dive in and swim in all this sugar. I feel a hand on each of my shoulders and a mouth close to my ear. The touch and closeness force my breath to hitch.

"How about you find somewhere to sit... and I'll surprise you with something."

I search for him out of the corner of my eye as he says it. I smile as he comes into view. I realise then that I was holding my breath, so I exhale slowly, carefully not drawing attention to it; I don't want him to think I'm anything other than ecstatic right now. Giving him a silent nod, I peel myself away to carry on walking down the pathway. It looks more like a bridle path, oh, I wonder if they have horses here somewhere. My eyes search the scenery for any sign of stables, but they catch sight of a beautiful tall tree in between the stalls instead. Autumn has begun ravaging the leaves, but I stand in awe of its grandeur; its drooping branches make it look sad, sad but beautiful, what an odd combination. Next to its trunk is a line of tree stumps and one overturned log. Another couple close by are using them to sit on whilst they admire the view. Opting for the overturned log, I take a pew, and let my eyes follow to where one of the couples is pointing. I am just as amazed as they are as the sun's rays bounce around on the hillside; there's a quaint standalone cottage right in the middle of it. How idyllic would that be, no city noise, just the hum of silence and maybe the odd birdsong? A pair of legs appear in my eye-line.

"Hey, daydreamer."

Gareth sits next to me, leaving a polite couple of inches of space between us. He hands me a large paper bag and even though it's folded closed, I can still smell the spices; pretty sure it's cinnamon. As we both open our bags, a little brown speckled bird flies down to sit on the grass, watching us. I am mesmerised by this man's kindness as he points and starts talking about it as he breaks off some pastry and throws it to the bird. I don't take in what he's trying to tell me, all I can concentrate on is his eyes, his smile, and the motion of his mouth as joy radiates through each one.

"I can't take my eyes off you," I murmur under my breath.

Oh crap, it was such a cheesy thing to let slip, but it was so true as I watch the passion swim through Gareth's features as he talks about his love for all thing's nature. But that doesn't stop the crimson flush bolting through my cheeks. I look away just as I take a bite out of my pastry. I don't hear Gareth adding to my accidental remark, so hopefully, he didn't listen to me, but then again, I can't hear him at all. I feel the heat in my cheeks begin to cool. 'It's fine... just look at him;' my inner spirit reassures me.

"This is... uh."

As I turn my head, his face is right there to meet me; his lips catch mine in a passionate embrace, like no other kiss we've shared before. His hand comes to rest on the crook of my neck, fingertips brush against my hairline, keeping me close. I drop my pastry along with the bag just so I can touch and feel his face, the few polite inches between us disappear. The thrill shoots from my lips, through my core; it flies right through the butterflies like a bowling ball colliding into pins, right down to the pit of my stomach; the feeling ignites my whole body in more ways than one. I keep my lips slightly parted between each kiss to welcome his tongue, he doesn't accept or seem to notice the invitation, but the delight outweighs any disappointment. All that matters right now is us and the connection building and buzzing with electricity; my entire body sings with desire with this notion. He pulls away just an inch, but keeps me close with his touch.

"Me too," he murmurs.

Ah, shit, I thought I had gotten away with it, but as I peer at him through my lashes, the look on his face right now is nothing other than content and adoration. I let out a shy giggle; it's all I can manage as words fail me. Gareth lets go of me, reaches down to pick up my pastry bag, and hands it back to me.

"I'm sorry I made you drop your cake... ah pastry... I thought... I couldn't pass the chance...."

The words bashfully leave his lips, and it's the first time I've ever seen him blush, hmm endearing indeed. Luckily my pastry wasn't spoiled and I don't hesitate to finish it off. We both sit in comfortable silence; my eyes skim the scenery as I eat the last mouthful. I notice rows of tables with several pumpkins on display. Children wearing aprons stand there silently giggling as they try their hand at carving the creepiest of faces; their glee makes me smile. Gareth follows my gaze.

"Are you any good?"

Gareth nods his head in their direction as he says it, but I am so lost in their excitement that the simple question sounded more confusing than anything. My inner spirit helps de-mist the confusion fog by giving me a gentle shake.

"I... ah... can't say... I don't think I've done it before."

He raises his eyebrows, surprised, I assume. He's probably beginning to think that I have had a very unfulfilled childhood. The truth is that Mum doesn't believe in Halloween, never had never will, so it wasn't so much of a big deal growing up. I don't ever recall going trick or treating either. Christmas was and always will be 'Mum's thing'. She loves that just like she's a big kid.

Gareth stands and offers his hand to me. I gladly take it as he helps me to my feet and leads me straight to the tables.

"This is what I meant by messy."

Well, at least it wasn't my dreaded thought of mucking out pigs.

"Choose your opponent... I'll get us some aprons."

He gives my hand a gentle squeeze before letting go. I turn to walk the length of the tables, surveying each pumpkin; deciding which one will meet its fate seems a bit mean. 'It's only a vegetable' my inner spirit slaps her forehead and shakes her head in dismay. One in the middle catches my eye; it seems taller and prouder than the rest, like a brave comrade offering itself up for the picking. I look up to see where Gareth is. I catch him chatting to a guy with salt and pepper hair and a beard to match. They look rather pally with each other. As Gareth smiles and taps him on the shoulder, then turns to walk away, he looks up in search of me. I struggle to pick up the nominee, holding it up to nose level is all I can manage; I peer around the side of it, which is enough to grab Gareth's attention, he smiles big and broad at my best efforts. He holds up the aprons, a bowl and carving tools for a moment, his grin never ceasing as he makes his way to me. I place the pumpkin back down on the table so I don't end up dropping it.

"Wow... you've picked a good one... I'm impressed."

He hands me an apron. I slip it on over my head and giggle when it falls into place. It's a little on the small side, I don't think this activity is intended for us adults. Gareth places the bowl and tools down on the table, ready for action. He giggles as he slips on his apron. He shrugs in an 'ah well' kind of way when it falls into place. I stand close to him as he gets to work, scoring a circle at the top of the pumpkin. He digs a bit deeper each time he scores full circle, it takes a few stubborn scores before it comes off like a lid. I peer inside; it seems like a million seeds in there.

"This is where it gets messy," he grins at me.

His hand dives right in and he pulls it out again; orange flesh hangs from the gaps between his fingers, then he dumps the veggie remains into the bowl. Gareth gestures for me to have a go. I gingerly roll the sleeves up on my shirt, unsure of what feeling lays ahead, and I take a deep breath as I delve into the flesh; it's cold, wet, slimy, and stringy. As I pull out my hand, I take one accomplished look at it before I throw it into the bowl. Gareth gazes at me, looking somewhat impressed, then I suddenly thought, I hope this isn't a test, preparing me for vet duties, like sticking a hand up a cow's arse; I physically shudder at the thought.

"Was it that bad?" he asks.

"No... I just had a thought,... well, hoping really... hoping that you're not preparing me for some sort of vet duty... like a cow's anal exam... or something."

I smile crookedly, on the verge of cringing. Gareth sniggers at first, then burst into full-on laughter, a real belly laugh, like no other laugh I've heard from Gareth before. It makes me feel triumphant that I can make him laugh and smile. I think that makes it a win/ win.

He takes a deep breath to compose himself and uses the back of his hand to wipe away the tears clinging to the corners of his eyes.

"Not unless you really want to," he finally says.

I screw my nose up and shake my head, trying not to smirk.

"No, thank you... I think I'll pass on that one."

I chuckle light-heartedly with my reply; I don't want him to think I disapprove of his job in any way, shape, or form. Looking down at the choice of tools, I notice a scoop like an ice cream one. I grab it and hand it to Gareth as it's his turn to gouge next.

"The old guy… a friend of yours?" I quiz.

Gareth uses the scoop to dig right down, deep in the depths, he tries to pull it back, but it seems a bit stubborn to break free. I can see from the strain running across Gareth's face as his cheeks flare that he's trying, his teeth gritted.

"Kind of… I look… I look after his… his horses… Ted owns this farm."

His voice strains as he gives the scoop another full-on pull; his hand flicks up as the scoop breaks free, like a catapult, orange flesh splats across my cheek and eye. It happened so fast there was no time to dodge the fleshy bullet. I gasp as the cold, wet, slop slides down my face and hangs off my lashes.

"Oh my god… I am so sorry."

He uses the cloth of his apron to wipe away the mush off my face. The other hand cups my jaw, steadying me. I close my eyes as he gently goes over my eye; his touch is so soft and gentle. I lose myself with the sensation, so much that I don't realise at first that he has stopped wiping, but his touch on my jaw remains. 'Please kiss me;' I hope and pray that his lips meet mine. 'Maybe you should pucker up your lips,' my inner spirit suggests. Is she mocking me? Before I can think or act on it, my wish comes true; his mouth meets mine, more tender than the last, but welcoming nonetheless.

***

The glowing crooked grin stares at me from my coffee table. Gareth let me take our ghoulish vegetable creation home. A kid probably could have done a better job at it, but all that matters is the fun we shared. Today I felt Gareth warming to me as much as I warmed to him; those kisses were evident of that. I touch my lips and smile at the memory. I close my eyes as my mind retraces the steps of his touch on me. His hands on my face, on my shoulders, how his fingertips brushed my neck and my hand in his. All these thoughts send my heart racing; the butterflies sweep up into a whirlwind spin, and my dreamy inner spirit floats up onto cloud nine.

Seven

The cold crispness of November has crept in early, adding a bite to this morning's air. As I make my way to the building of L.N.O. Publishing, I start to mentally prepare for the ice queen herself. Walking through the foyer, it's strangely quiet. Checking my watch, no wonder, it's only just after 8:30. Maybe I should grab a coffee first? My inner spirit just as half asleep doesn't respond. Turning on my heel, I see a flash of red as I collide into a black wall laced with white pearls. My bag falls to the ground with the impact.

"Oh my God, I'm so sorry."

I apologise instinctively to who I just drove into; my brain is slow to recognise. Slim bare legs and flat black pumps catch my eye as I pick my bag up and I stay fixated on the body as I get to my feet. I meet vacant red-rimmed eyes that match Miranda's hair. She's dressed all in black like she's fresh from a funeral or something; this is so unlike Miranda. She never fails to wear colours that are just as striking as her hair. Talking of her hair, it lays unbrushed in a hurried side ponytail. All she's missing is a black veil to finish off her dramatic makeup-less look, but somehow it does make her more humanlike. She does have emotions, after all. A pang of sympathy hits my chest for whatever she's going or been through. Do I ask what's wrong? She looks a little lost.

"I was just going to grab some coffee... do you want to come?"

I had no idea what else to say. It takes Miranda a moment or two to compute what I had just asked, like a 'closed 'shop sign flipping over to 'open 'as her brain opens up for business.

"Actually... yes... umm... yes I would like that... yes," she says.

She blows me away; I thought this woman hated me. She's never had time for me at work, let alone outside. The ice queen still doesn't smile, but I think I can break her out of her dazed self with a coffee and a little gentle persuasion, hopefully replacing that hard line for a smile. I'm not going to pry; not everyone wears their business on their sleeve, but if she wants to tell me, then I'll gladly listen. The way she looks at the moment, I think her feelings are hanging on by a thin thread that could snap at any moment. As she heads for the doors, I follow her with caution, unsure of what I am about to walk into. Outside, we stand on the curb; I look left then right where Miranda was standing, but she's vanished. Her red hair catches the corner of my eye.

"Miranda!"

I shriek her name at the top of my voice, but she doesn't even acknowledge me as she continues to glide across the road in a Sleeping Beauty like trance; hopefully, there aren't any spinning wheels to prick her finger on inside the coffee shop. I run after her as she forces the traffic to screech to a halt, narrowly missing being run over by a taxi, forcing the vehicle to slam its breaks on. I hold my hand up and mouth sorry to each driver as I pass. Not even car horns can arouse her from her spell. Oh my, how on earth did she make it to work without ending up in A&E? She's in no fit state to work, that's for sure. I hastily take her under my wing as I get to her, ushering her to the side of the walkway.

"What... what were you thinking... you nearly got killed," I splutter out of breath.

My voice is on the verge of being harsh from the shock. Miranda looks at me like a wide-eyed lost child. I watch her lip quiver and her eyes glisten with the rising tears.

"I'm sorry... you just really scared me then," I continue.

The odd tear falls down her cheeks; she uses the back of her manicured forefinger to wipe away the remaining ones from the corners of her eyes. She looks at me, then her gaze searches the scenery around us, the dawn finally rising within her like she's thinking, 'how on earth did I get here?' I don't utter another word as I put my arm around her shoulder and guide her into the coffee shop. First and foremost, I find her a seat at a tall table nearest to the queue. She just about manages to climb onto the stool, she's more than adequately tall enough just to slide and shuffle her behind onto it, but right now, she's scrambling like a kid on a climbing frame.

Finally seated, she clutches hold of her handbag on her lap like it's her one and only prized possession. Jeez, what on earth happened to her? She's like a shell; pale, detached and empty, not that she had much of a personality to begin with, but still. I don't think she could handle a simple question like 'what do you want to drink'. I watch her with concern for a moment as she drifts back into a trance, staring blankly at the door. Luckily there are only two people in the queue as I join it. I don't take my eyes off her as I shuffle along in line. One way or another, I must get to the bottom of this; this isn't healthy; she's one step away from a breakdown, I think. I order two large cappuccinos to takeaway when my turn comes up. I wait with my back against the counter, my eyes watching Miranda like a hawk; she hasn't moved an inch, her eyes still fixated on the door and holding her bag like her life depended on it. I glance up at the clock above the door; shit, it's five to nine, we're going to get a bollocking, but then our bosses only have to take one look at Miranda and waiver any disciplinary for our lateness, surely? I collect our coffees as soon as they hit the counter, practically swiping them from the barista's hands. I smile apologetically at him, but he still glares at me, oh dear, someone isn't a morning person. I walk back to the table. Miranda seems to stir from her daydream as I put one of the coffees down in front of her. She glares at the cup; oh dear, have I got it wrong?

"I can't... I can't... b-believe... he's done... this to me."

For a moment, I thought she was going to complain about my choice of drink. She places her handbag on the table, taking in an entire lung of air and letting it out shakily like anger is starting to fill her veins. I perch on the edge of my seat, watching her intently, feeling a little uneasy about what's about to unfold.

"The bastard has been cheating on me."

The words leave her lips bitterly, but clear as day. She doesn't take her eyes off her drink. I begin to worry that it's going to be a victim of her bubbling fury at any moment. She clutches hold of her cardboard coffee cup and I can see the sides starting to crease with her grip, so I take it from her before she scalds herself. Jeez, maybe she needs a whisky on the rocks instead? Cheating husband, boyfriend? No wonder she looks like shit. I probably wouldn't have gotten as far as dragging myself out of bed if I was her. Her eyes are still transfixed on the cup, her mouth now a hard line, but her jaw tremors like she's gritting her teeth. I patiently wait for her to continue, allowing her to spill the suspicions at her own pace; I am all ears. I turn my wrist slightly to see the time, few minutes after nine now, shit. Walk and talk, maybe?

"Do you want to talk about it on the way to the office?"

She just about manages to lift her head, and her eyes lazily find mine; I can just almost make out a smile, not even half a smile, let's call it a quarter, but still far better than the usual scowl. Her head bobs in the slightest of nods. Okay, let's do this. I waste no time hopping off my stool and asking the grumpy barista at the counter for a cup holder. I almost let a giggle slide as he tries to slam it down on the counter, but all that he achieves is a muffled tap sound. I thank him, luckily my face keeps straight, but as I turn away from him, I can't help but quietly snicker. I fling my bag on and place the cups in the holder. Miranda slides off her stool carefully like if she did it any faster, her legs would shatter like glass.

"Okay... we can do this... hold on to me."

I offer her my elbow and she gladly takes it. As we head towards the exit, a guy opens and holds the door for us with a cheeky wink. I glance at her to see her reaction and the act brings a slightly bigger smile to Miranda's face; okay, good, I think we are getting somewhere. I thanked the guy for his kind actions and carried on our way. Soon as our feet hit the pavement, we walk down to the traffic lights, not taking any chances this time. She doesn't say another word, she doesn't say anything more about her fears or any evidence she has of a suspected mistress.

As soon as we're back in the L.N.O. building, I breathe a sigh of relief. I usher Miranda into the lift, it feels like we are one step away from the finish line. She still clings to me like a vulnerable child, scared of the big wide world. Everyone's faces hit the floor as soon as we enter the office. George helps me get Miranda to her desk and soon as she sits, George pulls me to one side.

"Jeez, she looks awful... has she said what's wrong?" he asks under his breath.

I gesture to walk to my desk, out of earshot.

"She suspects her husband or boyfriend of cheating... she didn't say anything more than that... I didn't want to pry... never seen her look so vulnerable... I'm just glad I got her into the office in one piece."

George pats me on the back as I take the seat at my desk. "You did good, Kid."

Eight

Sitting cross-legged on my sofa, I can't stop thinking about Miranda. I never thought I'd say this, but I do feel sorry for her. Understandably she wasn't in today and I hardly got any work done as everyone kept coming up to me. asking if I had any gossip. Jeez, let the poor woman have a moment to herself; after all, her mind must be fit to burst with all sorts of unanswered questions and fears. The TV blares at me for attention, but it doesn't make any sense; the actor's mouth moves, but I just can't tune my ears in.

Right on cue, my phone pings with a new message. I haven't even read it yet, and I'm already smiling. Soon as I pick my phone up, it starts to ring. Gareth's name flashes on the screen, whoah, someone's eager. Grabbing the remote control, I turn down the volume on the TV to just a hum.

"Hey."

I say, with a little too much enthusiasm, scrunching all my features with the cringing pitch of my voice and mouthing the word 'fuck'. I hear a shaky intake of breath through the earpiece and gulp hard as I feel my heart plummet to the bottom of my chest; this is not good. No, no, no, please don't be something terrible. The long pause sends my heart beat into overdrive, like someone going crazy with a paddle ball. 'Keep calm... give him time... be cool' my inner spirit soothes.

"Hi-i... I... I just ah... really needed... to hear... your voice."

My heart pauses in mid-leap in my throat with every gap in his speech, soon as I hear 'voice', my heart falls back into its rightful place, slowly resuming its natural rhythm.

"What's happened?"

I ask it steadily, trying not to let the worry rip through my voice. All I can hear is the heaviness of Gareth's breathing, the whoosh of traffic in the background and his feet heavily pounding the pavement. I feel the urge to run to him, to hold him, be there for him in any way that I can. I suddenly feel helpless even though he isn't that far away, but with how I feel right now, he might as well be on the other side of the country.

"I... I ah... lost a dog... on the operating table today... a retriever... like the one who jumped all over me... and... picturing you... helped me... helped me get through it...I don't... I don't normally get like this... but it was... it was like... a part of our date died too... sorry I ah... didn't mean to bring down your evening."

My heart swells for this man's sensitive side; I feel his pain. I can see the situation through his eyes. I totally get it, even though I'm not emotionally attached to animals in the same way as he is, but he's right, it does strangely feel that way.

"I ah... have enough dinner here... if you want to come over."

Damn it, it was the only thing I could think of on the spot; my response suddenly sounds so insensitive, shit. Why don't I ever think before I speak? Where's a brick wall when you need one? I have a head here that needs banging. My inner spirit strangely quiet; I could use her wisdom right now.

"Thank you... I appreciate it... but I am still in my scrubs... I really need a shower... I'm exhausted... I can't wait to see you again, though, Beautiful."

Is it terrible that the only thing my ears picked up from that is 'need a shower?' Now, all I can think about is what he looks like with nothing on. But the thought has awoken my inner spirit, and now she's thinking the same.

"I can't wait to see you too... enjoy your shower... make sure you have a good rest... don't forget to eat something."

I can't help but smirk at the word 'shower' but somehow, I manage to keep it together as we say our goodbyes. I put my phone back down on the coffee table, the box's glow continues to glare at me. I pull the blanket down from the back of the sofa, shaking it open, I drape it over my shoulders. I'm not cold, but I suddenly feel like I need a hug and the closest thing to that right now is this tatty old blanket mum gave me years ago. I hope it will relieve the melancholy feeling that has just silently crept in over me. A weighted feeling hangs in my chest, forcing my smile to fade; the usual rush of butterflies from just hearing Gareth's voice has disappeared. I pull the blanket tighter around me and the cocoon comforts me, my eyes feel heavy. I'm just tired, that's all, just extremely tired.

***

As I walk into the office, the first thing I see is a pile of files already waiting for me, but I notice something next to it. I realise it's a takeaway cup of coffee along with a paper bag as I draw closer to it. Walking round to the back of my desk, I look at the gifts; must be from George, I look up to find him, but he's not at his desk yet, hmm.

"Call it an olive branch."

Her voice makes me jump and my gaze follows the sound. She smiles crookedly, like it still pains her to be nice to me, olive branch or no olive branch; I think I have finally cracked her. I force a smile. I am still wary that this surreal bubble could burst at any moment.

"Thanks, Miranda... how are you doing?"

Her makeup-less eyes look down as her manicured fingers start to fidget and lacing them together, she hangs her hands in front of her dark teal dress. For the first time, I notice a rather expensive looking wedding ring, diamonds, no doubt. How on earth did I miss that dazzling piece of jewellery the other day?

"Better... just an ah... a big misunderstanding," she murmurs.

She nods slowly, but it doesn't hide the fact that her eyes glisten and twitch at the last few words; I can tell deep down she's not convinced. Her husband is either an excellent liar or too handsome and rich to let go. I have a hunch that it's a combination of all three, but what else can I do other than just take her word for it? At least she's looking more like her old self today.

"Well... enjoy," she says hurriedly.

Gesturing to the coffee, she then turns on her flat pumps and makes her way back to her desk before I can add anything more. There's movement out of the corner of my eye; George grabs my attention. He smiles broadly at me, getting his fingers to do the dancing as his hip is still a little dodgy. I mirror his moves and we can't help but giggle at each other's silliness. He gives me his 'You did good, Kid' side nod, wink and corner smile as he gently lowers to his seat. A glorious contentedness fills my chest as I sit at my desk, and a deep satisfying sigh escapes from me as I switch on my computer. The ancient old system takes forever to wake up, so I take a sip of my coffee while I wait. I try my best not to let my expression show that it's lukewarm; there's nothing worse than a nearly cold caffè latte. I grimace at the computer screen as it struggles to boot, the password screen finally appears, and the system strains again with the demand. I leave it to do its thing as I stand and grab the pile of files, lugging them to the filing cabinets. As I start to place each one in their rightful place, George whispers close to my ear.

"A little bird has a message for you."

He nods towards my corner of the room, and yet I still look where he's gesturing to. Hmm, what has he been up to? My gaze returns to him for more clarity, but he doesn't add anything more; just a smile, then taps my shoulder and hobbles back to his desk. Intrigue gets the better of me, so I quickly file away the remaining folders and hotfoot it back to my desk. My eyes search all over my desk, yet I have no idea what I'm looking for. A throat clears loudly; I look up just as George taps his pen against his computer screen. Ah ha, emails, of course, I click on the inbox, and my messages fill the screen.

From: George Spencer

Subject: A little birdie told me...

There's just a link in the body of the message, but soon as I click on it, the screen fills with the L.N.O. Publishing House logo, and the seven most glorious words stand out below it.

'...looking to recruit a Junior Publishing Assistant.'

My eyes don't finish reading the whole advert. They just stare at the words in amazement. And, excitement buzzes right through my body, almost like finding the winning golden ticket in a bar of chocolate.

***

Leaning right over the edge, I watch the very last glimmer of sunshine bounce and ripple on the water beneath City Bridge, and as the bright sky fades, the chill draws in. Fireworks above me bang, crackle and whoosh above, making me jump out of my skin, a not so gentle reminder that it's Guy Fawkes Night. I look over where Gareth had pointed out where his practice is and then down at my watch; it's 17:38. Maybe I should go and surprise him? 'What are you waiting for... need to know if he's okay' my inner spirit urges me to put my feet in motion; they follow through on the command, taking me across the last stretch of the bridge. Turning left, then immediately across the road, I follow the footpath right to the entrance of the vet's office. I peer through the large window; I see Gareth in his teal scrubs handing over a small pet carrier to an elderly gent in the waiting room. They fondly shake hands, and a sympathetic smile stretches across Gareth's face, a regular client maybe? The old guy looks reluctant to leave as he keeps talking to Gareth even though his back is inching closer and closer to the receptionist desk. Gareth puts one hand up and mouths 'goodbye' as the old guy turns and heads for the front door. I quickly head down the short path, pushing open the door just as the old guy reaches it; I hold it open for him with a smile as he passes me.

"Oh, thank you so much, m'dear."

He gives me a debonair wink as he slowly passes, the twinkle of youth still apparent in his eyes, I bet he was a smooth talker in his

—

day. I let the door go, and it bangs as it slams shut. I'm not wearing heels, but my footsteps seem to audibly tap against the tiled floor as I walk through the entrance to the waiting room.

"I'll be with you in one moment," a cheery voice chimes.

No one is behind the desk, but I hear the same cheery voice speak in hushed tones.

"You're so brilliant with Mr Richards."

She has a sweet but flirty edge to her tone. I see Gareth and a long-haired glossy brunette, only her side view visible, through the narrow gap of the door at the back of the receptionist office. Her hand gently caresses Gareth's shoulder, but he doesn't seem to acknowledge her kind remark or the touch; he just carries on reading the file in his hands. Something sparks within me; I'm not quite sure what...

jealousy, protectiveness, suspicion. I know one thing for sure, I'm feeling impatience and it gets the better of me; I step right up to the counter.

"Gareth?"

I say it loud and clear, which makes the brunette's head snap towards me. Gareth emerges fully through the gap of the door. I see his face light up when he realises it's me, and chucking the file down on a nearby desk, Gareth flurries through reception into the waiting room like a desperate hurricane, almost sweeping me off the floor as he hugs me fiercely like he hasn't seen me for weeks.

"Hey Beautiful!"

He gazes at me tiredly, yet the delight still shines through as he loosely lets go of me, finding and holding both of my hands instead.

"Oh, so this is the famous Charly."

The voice is gravelly but still feminine. I follow it with just my eyes. They meet an older lady behind the counter. She has a silver beehive hairstyle and deep red lipstick that matches her red-rimmed glasses that hang on the end of her nose. She peers over them with that 'over the glasses expression' that someone gives you when you're not sure if you are in trouble or they are happy to see you; either way, I smile broadly but with a hint of uncertainty.

"Umm, hi?"

It comes out more like a question rather than a simple greeting. I watch Miss Beehive push her glasses back up the bridge of her nose, picking her head up as she smiles, now looking a little less intimidating. Miss Brunette comes to stand next to her, now I can see her as clear as day, she's beautiful, no curves but very slim. Her smile couldn't be more phoney if she tried though, someone isn't pleased to meet me.

"This is Suzanne and Megan... our hard-working reception ladies."

Gareth gestures to each one as he says it; Megan is the one not so happy to meet me. At that moment, another set of teal scrubs appears from one of the rooms at the back. They belong to a rather tall, broad and muscular guy with a jet-black crew cut, a backpack, and a jacket casually slung over his shoulder. He looks like he could crush a hamster rather than nurse it back to health with those arms.

"And this is Daniel... the head vet."

As Daniel approaches me, he formally offers his hand. I look up to him before taking it; he has really piercing blue eyes that glint when he smiles, which is infectious. I find myself mirroring him as he firmly grabs and shakes my hand.

"Nice to meet you, Charly."

His tone is not deep like you'd think it would be but still charming. I've clearly been a popular topic around here. I feel a little bit like a celebrity at this moment.

"Likewise," I smile.

Daniel nods in acknowledgement and smiles at me, then turns to Gareth handing him a set of keys, and pats him heavily on the shoulder.

"Right mate... I'm off... leave when you're ready... have a good evening."

He nods at Gareth and then cheekily winks at me. Does everyone know something that I don't? It sure as hell feels that way. I watch Daniel turn and smile warmly at Miss Brunette and Miss Beehive; I've forgotten their names already.

"Have a good evening, ladies."

He gives them a brief wave as he leaves swiftly through a nearby door. My gaze drifts back to reception, Miss Beehive, or should I call her Miss Cougar now as she swoons after Daniel, but then I notice Miss Brunette fixated with Gareth, peering through her lashes and choppy bangs. She starts nervously shuffling papers around when she catches me looking.

"Charly... can I show you something?"

Gareth's voice brings my attention back to him; I smile broadly and nod as my gaze drifts to his tired eyes, but there's still a sparkle left in them. He takes my hand and leads me down a long corridor directly opposite the front entrance, turning right at the end to join another passage, then through a set of double doors. Soon as we step through them, I hear very timid wounded cries. Cages line the whole of the wall on the left side. I stand in front of one and peer through the rails; tucked away at the back of it is a ball of fluff, paws and claws stretch out as I disturb its slumber.

"I have to check on my patients before I leave."

Gareth stands right behind me as I watch the ball of fluff come to life.

"And this one is going home tomorrow."

I step to one side as he lifts the latch-up, angling his body just in case we have an escapee. When I see Gareth's arms again, the little ball of tabby fluff appears even smaller curled up in his forearm, almost looking lost. My eyes grow wide at the extreme cuteness overload.

"Do you want to hold her?"

I almost don't hear Gareth's question because I've lost myself in the little kitten's eyes. My inner spirit shakes me awake.

"Yeah, sure."

My voice melts just as much as my heart does. The kitten lets out a little timid meow as she gets handed over to me. Her fur is as soft as it looks. My voice goes embarrassingly high as I crumble into a gushy mess. I can feel Gareth surveying me with every move I make; he's probably hoping and praying I will be as gentle as possible.

"I was planning to umm... ask you something yesterday... but I ah... got so distracted I forgot... it's Cassie's birthday on Saturday... we're all going out for drinks... do you fancy coming?... sorry I know it's ah... only a couple of days away."

Cassie has come up a few times in our late-night conversations, very close siblings with how he talks about her.

"Sure."

I say it without giving it another thought. Saying before I think yet again, I blame the kitten; if I hadn't got caught up in her adorableness, I would have had a moment to think. Or maybe that's why Gareth brought me in here. Distract me, then drop the question when I'm least likely to say no. My eyes grow wide when I realise what I had just agreed to; one giant step that I'm not sure I am even ready for.

Nine

I have been staring at the same page for about half an hour now; it could be more, I don't know. The words of Charlotte Brontë seem to blur in front of my eyes, my mind busy elsewhere. Cassie's birthday is looming, and I have never been so petrified in my life. This is a massive step that I have never taken before, so I'm trying to steer my mind elsewhere. The interviews for the Junior Publishing Assistant are commencing near the end of December. I thought I'd better start brushing up on my reading skills, hoping it might clear some of the anxiety fog. My feet begin to tingle under my crossed legs. I close the book, sorry Jane Eyre; this isn't working, it's not you, it's me, I snigger out loud as I chuck the book onto the coffee table. I should probably stick to the genres I'm used to. For now, give me a thrilling plot with a million twists, turns and red herrings any day. I know I should broaden my horizons; after all, I'm going to have to read whatever is put in front of me if I get this job, but I like to feel that edge of your seat feeling, teetering on the edge kind of stuff, so I'll stick to what I know for the moment. My legs come back to life as I stretch them out in front of me and wriggle my toes. My laptop sits next to me on the sofa; I haven't turned it on and checked my social media for a few days, so I open the lid and turn it on. I plump up the flat cushions behind me, then reach over and grab my glass of wine off the table, taking a few deep gulps just as my back melts into the cushions; I rest my feet on the table and sigh deeply and satisfyingly. Using one hand, I put my laptop on my lap and open my social media; there are a few unopened messages and one friend request. I click on the notification, and I recognise her name straight away; Cassie's profile fills my screen as I accept her. She has a picture of a little white dog for her profile picture, a family pet, no doubt. I go to my messages. There's a couple from Harper and one from Ashley, they are probably wondering where I am, I should call them sometime. At the top of the list is Cassie. I take a deep breath as I open it.

'Hi Charly, I'm so glad you can make my birthday drinks. I can't wait to meet you. Gareth has talked about you so much in the last couple of weeks. I think he really likes you.'

Oh shit, I know his actions have been evidence of that, but it still takes me by surprise seeing it in black and white. It feels odd that everyone seems to know me, but I don't know them. I find myself tapping my chin, hoping it will kickstart some kind of thought process of how to respond.

'Hi, Cassie... thanks for the add. Looking forward to it.'

I hit send before my inner spirit has a chance to add her opinion, closing the lid of the laptop so fast that it slaps shut without the soft click sound that is familiar; I wince at the slap like someone striking my cheek instead.

***

'Black Velvet' by Alannah Myles drifts from the speakers in my bedroom as I run the mascara brush through my lashes, my hips rock to its sexy beat ignoring the fact that I'm trying to do my makeup. My inner spirit, cheering them on regardless, only encourages them even more, so I screw the brush back into the tube before disaster strikes. Rummaging in my makeup bag, I opt for a pale pink lipstick. I force my hips to a standstill just so I can apply it in neat lines, rolling my lips together to even out the colour. Stepping back from the long mirror, I admire my handiwork, giving myself a nod of approval. I turn towards my wardrobe and snatch my skinny jeans off their hanger. I slide each leg in while they sway along with the rhythm of my hips that are beginning to rock side to side again.

The last couple of days have flashed by in a blur. Tonight, is Cassie's birthday drinks, and I'm trying my best to drown out the fears running through my head by singing along to some of my favourite tracks; although not very in tune, it's doing an excellent job at preoccupying me. I slip on a black camisole then an electric blue long sleeve blouse with a flare to the sleeves; just as it slides down my body, the track changes to 'All Right Now' by Free. My top falls and drapes loosely over the top of my jeans, freeing my trapped hair, it falls smooth and sleek. Whisky on the rocks waits for me on top of the chest of drawers; I roll onto the balls of my feet as I strut, spin and dance my way across my bedroom floor. 'One for the road,' as I pick up the glass and knock back the contents; the woody taste hits my tastebuds like a punchbag, forcing me to grimace in distaste.

***

I inhale the cool November air; it sweeps through my lungs, leaving a tingling trail behind. Gareth had offered to pick me up, but I thought my inner spirit and I could do with some fresh air and a chance to clear the nerves, besides the pub is no more than a twenty-minute walk away.

I recognise his khaki jacket from the end of the street, he stands by himself, and a tiny part of me hopes there has been a change of plans. He beams as soon as I come into his view; he starts walking towards me, eagerness written across his face.

"Hey, Beautiful."

He pulls me in before I can say anything, hugging me fiercely; I let out an 'oof' sound as his arms squeeze me tightly then free me.

"Hey," I say once my lungs fill with air again.

A rush of lightheadedness makes me feel giddy for a moment, but the feeling leaves as quickly as it had come. Gareth steps round to my side and offers his arm; I gladly take it.

"Ready for this?" he asks.

I smile and nod, but at the same time, my inner spirit is chewing through her nails with the rising panic like a beaver chewing through wood at a hundred miles per hour cartoon speed. We walk through the doors of The Elm and Barrel pub; the atmosphere is buzzing with chatting and laughter. The aroma of stale booze, vintage wood and pungent perfumes aren't the only things that hit my senses.

"Charly!" a voice shrills.

It's so loud that it pierces through the chatter. Before I know it, another pair of arms embrace me. Cassie welcomes me with the biggest smile as she lets go; her long curly auburn hair bounces along with her excitement. Before I can even say anything, do anything, she grabs my hand and pulls me towards a row of booths tucked away at the back; I look behind me to make sure Gareth is following us. I smile at him crookedly like a 'help me' kind of expression; I don't think it registers as he just smiles at me casually. There are two guys and another woman in the booth that Cassie drags me to.

"Hey, guys... this is Charly... Charly, this is Devon... Theo... and Reggie."

I feel like I've just walked in on an amateur dramatics meeting or something; each one greets me with as much enthusiasm and flamboyance as Cassie; I am half prepared for them to burst into a theatrical song.

"Hi-i."

The simple word catches in my throat, forcing my voice to crack and I wave in the most awkward fashion, my inner spirit hiding behind her hands, peering through the gaps of her fingers, waiting for the cringe show to end; I hope my features aren't mirroring her unease. Cassie pulls me into the seat next to her; within seconds, they all force my fears to melt away as I ease into their company like I have known them for ages. I am drafted straight into their conversation with no awkward 'getting to know you 'or 'ice breaker kind of questions'. Gareth leans down and speaks against my ear.

"Drink?"

I turn my head before I answer and peck him on the lips.

"Rosé please. "

He gazes at me for a moment; affection fills his eyes. He swiftly kisses me on the forehead and turns and heads for the bar as I rejoin the conversation, well, a debate so it seems, on 'the best thriller movie of all time'.

"How about you, Charly?"

Hmm, thrillers are my favourite genre, but which one to choose. My inner spirit is flicking through my memory bank at top speed.

"Has to be... 'Shutter Island'...but I prefer books... 'The Girl On The Train' is probably my number one read... I love how it keeps you guessing right until the very end."

Within a brief moment, the gawks on their faces morph into broad smiles, and a hundred miles per hour chatter follows, I knew then that I had been accepted.

***

REVERSE in neon lettering dominates the building's entrance. A club is not my usual scene, but a cheesy throwback tune is pumping through the air as we wait in line. As soon as we're inside, the drinks keep flowing, and I'm feeling the alcohol start to pulse and buzz through my body.

"I haven't had this much fun... in a while!"

I shout the words close to Gareth's ear, trying my best to compete with the bass, he grins at me, so I assume he heard me.

We find ourselves drifting towards the dance floor as the alcohol takes over. Soon enough, we get separated from Cassie and her friends amongst the sea of grinding bodies. I don't know if it's the alcohol coursing through me or the slow bass that is seducing me, but the music seems to swarm around me. I have never heard this song before, something about 'slow hands.' Closing my eyes as I succumb to its spell, my hips start willingly rolling. My wandering hands rest on my hips, then sweep across my torso, dragging at my top as they go, up to my neck; my fingertips continue upwards, combing through my hair until my forearms come to rest on top of my head. As the beats play on, my body relaxes, and my hips become more fluid with moves I didn't know I was capable of; I think the song has bewitched me. I didn't feel his touch at first, his hands guide my hips to move in bigger sweeps, he spins me round to face him. Unhooking my arms from my head, they don't seem to want to part ways; Gareth ducks under and up into my lasso arms and draws me in. I can't remember the last time I danced so close to someone; anxiety grips my stomach.

The thought, the fear, and the alcohol cocktail seem to morph into one massive confusion.

I have lost count on how many drinks I've had, but I have had enough to know that it's rapidly taking hold of me, so much so I'm not sure what I'm supposed to be doing; my body seems to be detached from my brain, it seems to have its own ideas. My lasso arms break as I feel myself relax into Gareth's touch; he looks down, drawing one of my hands up to his shoulder, the other laces with his, looking like we are about to step into the waltz. His expression breaks into a foolish grin, our minds in sync, we burst into drowned out laughter, relief slowly washes over me when I realise he doesn't know what he's doing either. We waltz to the utterly wrong genre, but it feels so right in this moment in time.

Ten

I wake in a black shirt that I don't recognise, just a few buttons done up. My head swims and spins as I sit up way too fast; the room feels like it is on its own axis. Sore feet ache within these crisp white sheets, a sign of a good dance session. Oh shit, where am I exactly? I look to my right, and nobody is lying next to me. My eyes automatically search the rest of the room. Last night's attire is neatly folded up on a chair in the corner; alternate blue and white walls surround me, chic and minimalist. I hold my head in my hands while I try to get my thoughts in order. I have no recollection of the journey from the club to this place... Gareth's place? My inner spirit shrugs her shoulders heavily, looking a little comatose. It dawns on me that I should investigate whose place this is and do they have coffee.

I lift my head up slowly; the room has finally stopped moving. Throwing the sheets back, I gingerly climb out of bed. The door is ajar, daylight streams through the gap. As I cross the bedroom threshold, I step into the hallway; immediately in front of me, rock band posters neatly framed, line the opposite wall. Following the light to my right, I'm unsure why, but I find myself tiptoeing until I see him emerge from an arched opening and then my heels return to the floor. He places a mug on a tall bistro table, the floor creaks beneath my feet, grabbing his attention, his head snaps up, and he sleepily smiles. He's dressed in a white t-shirt and grey sweatpants, his hair ruffled from sleep, he's still picture perfect. It dawns on me that I haven't checked my appearance; oh shit, I've probably got hideous panda eyes and cow licked hair.

"Morning, Beautiful."

My panic simmers down; maybe I don't look so bad after all. I walk past a mirror, catching a glimpse of myself, my worst fears confirmed. Not only severe panda eyes but a crazy '80s' rock hairstyle to match, matted hairspray making the top of my head flick in all directions. I gasp long and hard as the panic starts to overtake again. Using the end of the sleeve, I frantically try to wipe away the smeared makeup, but to no avail, frustration takes over, my skin reddens. Gareth swoops in and stops me, holding me at the small of my back; he spins me round to face him, my reflection hidden from view, his touch is enough to calm my annoyance. He draws me and the shirt up, right onto my tiptoes. His gaze locks with mine.

"But I look...."

His forefinger rests across both of my lips, instantly shushing me; within a blink of an eye, his lips replace his finger, warmly and tenderly. The sensation leaves me starry-eyed and I feel like I am dancing on air as he gently releases me.

"Coffee?"

Simply, the best question someone has asked me in a long time.

"Yes, please."

My voice is dry and hoarse; trying to compete with the volume last night has left my throat raw. Gareth disappears through the archway again. I take in my surroundings while I wait. I notice the tall ceilings first. It makes the apartment feel much more spacious. My eyes drift back down to a comfy looking sofa in the middle of the room, with a pile of pillows and blankets piled on top; it faces a grand looking fireplace. Hmm, I bet it gets cosy in here during the peak of winter. My gaze drifts to the rest of the room, the walls washed in a cream shade, dark pine wood lines the floors. I notice a tall window, I find myself drawn towards it, intrigued of what lies beyond the panes of glass. Wow, what a view, it's a typical village green, but it seems to roll on and on. It's so breathtakingly beautiful, no wonder he loves the countryside so much; I mean, you'd be crazy not to with all this on your doorstep. My eyes continue to drift along the landscape. A few houses line the edges of the green with a few trees scattered in between. I can feel myself slowly drifting off into a daydream as I watch the clouds drift by. I'd stand here all day if I could—a gentle touch taps on my arm.

"Coffee's ready... you look like you are a million miles away."

His voice is silky, still laced with sleep; it brings me back down to earth as I shake away the dreamy look on my face.

"Sorry... I just ah... couldn't help staring at this view... it's amazing."

I feel his presence move to my back as I say it, followed by the warmth of his chest and arms as he embraces me; my back melts into him and once again, I feel safe, wanted. The familiar sound of my hunger growls breaks the comfortable silence forcing us to snicker out loud.

"Breakfast?"

The second-best question of the morning. I smile, half embarrassed, half appreciative, as I turn to face Gareth. A kiss meets my forehead just before he turns and heads back to the kitchen. I follow him through the archway, but I stop abruptly, taken aback by how tiny his kitchen is; you don't have to stretch both arms far to touch the counters on either side.

"I wasn't prepared for this... I've only got bread and eggs."

He holds up a loaf of bread and a carton of eggs and shrugs apologetically. Anything will do at this moment to stop my stomach from falling out; the thought of food makes the growls even louder.

"Let me rustle something up for you... It's the least I can do... as you kindly let me crash in your bed."

I nod towards the pile of blankets and pillows on the sofa. Gareth flicks his head in that direction, then back to focus on me.

"Actually... I insist," I press.

I take the loaf and eggs from him, snatching them from his grip; his hands fly up in a mocking 'okay whatever you say Boss' along with the mouthed word 'okay' finishing with a flourish of his shy smile.

I get to work. Luckily the first cupboard I open is where the pots and pans live; I fish out a frying pan, which seems the only thing big enough for scrambled eggs. I can see he hasn't got a lot of space here and definitely lacks in the cooking essentials. I wonder how he manages to get by; survives on take-outs, most probably. Gareth switches on the radio, 'Old Time Rock & Roll' blares out, and I can't help but rock my hips to the beat. Peering over my shoulder, Gareth has taken a seat at the bistro table and is intently watching me in amusement. His arms semi folded on the table, he's resting his chin on his palm, looking pretty cute with his ruffled hair. A tiny part of me wishes he'd jump off his stool, sweep me up into his arms and take me to bed instead. I silently sigh when he doesn't notice the longing in my eyes. I turn my attention back to the frying pan, cracking several eggs straight into the pan, opening the cutlery drawer on the hunt for a wooden spoon or something similar; nope, there's nothing of the sort, hmm. My eyes seek out just a tablespoon, that will have to do. I watch the gloopy egg mixture swirl as I puncture the yolks and stir them in. The toaster sits solo in the corner next to the hobs; I fill it as my mind drifts back to the music. My toes tap to the beat, and my hips start to rock from side to side. I look down at the spoon as I stir the eggs again, contemplating using it as a makeshift microphone and breaking into a 'Risky Business' style dance scene. I smile to myself as my inner spirit wakes up and helps to consider my next move, but the ping of the toaster puts an abrupt end to the shenanigans. I plate up the eggs and toast and carry them over to the table.

"Hope you're hungry."

I beam triumphantly as I place the two piled high plates down on the table. My stomach growls loudly once again as the smell of freshly cooked food hits my senses.

"I'm ravenous! Thanks, Beautiful."

He leans over and kisses me softly on the forehead, full of gratitude. I take my seat and waste no time getting stuck in, but reminding myself to be graceful with the task at hand.

I think I ate a little too fast as my stomach starts to feel uneasy, the hangover buzzes to life again, washing over me like waves so I close my eyes before the room begins to see-saw. I don't realise I'm sitting here rubbing my forehead until I hear Gareth's suggestion.

"Come and crash on the sofa with me."

He strokes my arm soothingly; it feels so comforting. I gently nod at his question as he helps me off the stool and takes my hand, leading me straight to the sofa. Gareth chucks the pillows onto the floor, but keeps hold of the blanket; he turns on the TV, but turns the volume right down to just a hum. I let him lay down first, then I follow, just a bit lower so he can still see over my head. I help him lay the blanket over us both; the warmth from his chest and arms instantly puts me at ease. He holds me close to him, and I feel my eyes getting heavy.

"Do you need to be anywhere today?"

He whispers the question against the top of my ear; his warm breath sweeps across my cheek, I smile sleepily.

"Nope, you have me all to yourself... If you want me to stay, that is."

I quietly yawn, my eyes can't fight the heaviness anymore, so I let them drift closed, just as I feel a kiss meet the side of my head.

"That's good to know."

Eleven

I have no idea how long I had slept in Gareth's arms, but it was nice while it lasted. Standing right under the flow of hot water, he kindly let me use his shower, and it's one of those that pour like thundering rain; it beats against my back like a free massage. The showerhead is probably as wide as me; I haven't seen anything like it. I had hoped he'd join me, but he said he already had snuck in and had one while I was fast asleep, so what I thought was sleep ruffled hair earlier was actually the result of a towel dry. I struggled to hide the fact that I felt gutted when he told me this; my chest suddenly feels like it drags down with the recent memory. My heart feels heavy like it's lead. Instead, I struggle to sigh deeply, the uneasy feeling buried deep within my chest tugs at my emotions, and I fight back the urge to expel it through my eyes.

Snippets of last night's events start to dominate my train of thoughts and I instinctively smile as I remember our foolish dancing; the memory helps relieve the doubt hanging in my chest. I turn and lift my head to face the flow; it feels good to finally wash away the matted hairspray and the dried makeup. I reluctantly turn the handle anticlockwise, and the flow of water comes to an abrupt stop. As soon as I step out, the cool air hits me, forcing goosebumps to prick up all over my body. I snatch a towel off the hot radiator, wrapping it around me; I hug myself for a moment, relishing the warmth until it fades.

I walk through the entrance, straight into Gareth's bedroom, the two rooms sit adjacent to one another. A clean green and navy checked shirt, a comb, a hairdryer, and my jeans are all laid out neatly across his bed. I chuckle out loud when my eyes come across a clean pair of boxer shorts, the first time for everything. I dry myself and slip them on; the towel hangs in front of me and I pat my face dry just as I hear the door creak open; water from my hair trickles down my back as my heart begins to race.

"Sorry... I ah... I thought you were still in the shower... I just ran over to the shop for you... here..."

He stays shielded by the door, not wanting to violate my privacy perhaps; he holds out a deodorant, face wipes and a toothbrush; it's a thoughtful gesture. I go over to the door and open it fully, the towel only just covering my breasts. I hope and pray that he whips it from me, but my thoughts of any intimacy come to an abrupt stop as I notice his cheeks are flushed. Which makes me wonder if he's ever actually seen a naked woman before, but he had said that he'd had a serious relationship, so surely, he must have. 'Or maybe he's just embarrassed that I took him by surprise,' my inner spirit adds her wisdom.

"Thank you... that's really thoughtful."

I smile as I take the items from him, using my upper arms to hold onto the towel. I catch him glancing up and down my body, looking like he's fighting back an urge; he hastily takes a deep breath.

"I'd like to take you for a walk... if you feel up to it."

'How about you take me against your bedroom wall' the suggestive thought sends a fluttering sensation through my sex. I clear my throat as if it'll help clear the idea too.

"Okay... um... sure."

I flash him a flirtatious grin as I turn, hoping he'll follow me. I do my best to coax him in as I wriggle my behind while walking away from him, back toward the bed. I hear a click; as I turn around to face Gareth once more, I realise the click sound belonged to the closing bedroom door.

***

I decided to take myself off to bed early, I'm exhausted from the day-long hangover, but my eyes seem reluctant to close. I lay on my back, my gaze fixated on the ceiling. I let my mind retrace the day spent with Gareth. My thoughts are projecting onto it like I'm watching today's events on a film reel.

I had emerged from his bedroom with bouncy, naturally wavy hair and minimal makeup; all I had left in my handbag was my eyeliner. I must have lost the rest while we were dancing. I had to tuck the shirt into the waistband of my jeans loosely. Otherwise, it would have looked more like a nightshirt.

Any doubt that I had from Gareth not following me into the bedroom got swept away when my gaze fell upon him looking out of his living room window; the sunshine beating through the panes made his skin look luminous, and his smile seemed even brighter. He took me for a walk to take a closer look at the village green. As we stepped out of his building and walked down to the end of the gravel driveway, I turned around; his apartment was a part of a grand white Victorian house, probably split into about four apartments; it was stunning. The fresh air made me feel a bit better; maybe I should walk off a hangover more often. As we walked hand in hand, he told me that last night was the best night out he's had in a long time. I'm pretty sure I said something along those lines last night as well, the fragments starting to piece back together again. Gareth's gentlemanly ways are not something I'm used to; it's hard to get my head around it; respect still seems so alien to me.

I sit up and shuffle my behind up the bed, resting my back against the headboard. My phone sits on my bedside table. I lean over and grab it, the mysterious song from the club springing to mind. I need to know what it's called, filling the search bar with 'slow hands song' the first result that pops up is Niall Horan. I hit play, and instantly, I am back in the club, dancing like I never knew I could.

As the song fades and brings me back to my bedroom, I add it to my playlist. I stare at my phone for a moment and out of the corner of my eye, I catch Jayne Eyre waiting patiently next to me on the bed; I let out a hefty sigh without even picking up the book. It is you, not me, sorry, Jayne. I just can't bring myself to read any of it. Maybe I should give something else a go instead? I turn my attention back to my phone and start scrolling through an online bookstore. I pick a few at random from their chart lists and add them to my basket. I let out a massive yawn as I complete my order, which should keep me occupied in the evenings for a while.

Twelve

"Ahh... fuck!"

My back collides into a pillar belonging to the building of L.N.O. Publishing. I suck in air sharply through gritted teeth as the smarting shoots across my shoulder blades. Someone had grabbed my arm as I left work! Losing my balance as I instinctively pulled myself free, I had smacked right into the concrete. I close my eyes and shield my face, my heart beating hard against my chest, I'm on the verge of surrendering my handbag. 'Please don't hurt me', I want to yell, but my voice can't find the words.

"Girl... what the fuck are you doing?"

I could recognise her voice from anywhere, but my arms are still reluctant to retreat from my face as they slowly fall to my sides.

"I kept calling your name... jeez, what's up with you?"

She stares hard at me like she's trying to read my mind.

"I didn't hear you... I thought... I thought you were some crazy person trying to mug me or something."

She roars with laughter, letting me know that my remark was insane; she loops arms with me and pulls me along with her, going the opposite of my usual direction towards home.

"Girl... you crack me up... let's go get a drink."

Just when I thought Harper was suggesting coffee, she bundles me into the first bar we come across; it happened so fast I didn't even catch the name of it. Expensive aftershave, leather and 'Watermelon Sugar' by Harry Styles fills the air as we enter. The music is trying its best to breathe life and summer vibes into the dull atmosphere. We turn the heads of a small group of businessmen, no doubt that's where the overpowering scent of cologne and leather is drifting from.

We take the seats right at the end of the bar, out of sight, out of mind, as they say. But as soon as our behinds meet the stools, we're ascended upon. A guy, suited and booted, casually leans on the bar by Harper's side, she raises her eyebrow on my side, a telltale sign that she knows he's there, but he isn't going to get anywhere; she's ready with the pick-up line comebacks.

"Hi... can I get you, two gorgeous ladies, a drink?"

Harper flashes her engagement ring at him as she tucks her long glossy brown hair behind her ear and rolls her piercing blue-grey eyes without meeting the guy's gaze.

"We're quite capable," Harper retorts.

Her voice is so sharp, it instantly cuts the guy's ego in half. She puts her hand up and smiles for the barman's attention, completely ignoring Casanova.

"Thanks... but no thanks," I add.

I smile as I meet the guy's gaze, hoping it will soften Harper's blow. He smiles reluctantly, nods and turns away without another word, dragging his wounded ego behind him.

"I see you haven't lost your brutal streak," I chuckle.

Nudging her with my elbow as I say it, her eyebrow still arched, she smiles back at me triumphantly. This meeting has turned out to be a pleasant surprise; I can't actually remember the last time we did anything like this together, just the two of us.

"And what can I get for you, fine ladies?"

Harper gawks at me, both of her eyebrows now raised, and tips her head slightly to the side. I try to hold back my smirk, her 'what the fuck... really?' face on display.

"Two large Ros'és, please," I say hastily.

I just about got in there to shield the poor guy from the next bout of Harper's bluntness. Don't get me wrong, she loves the limelight of being hit on, but when a guy plays the flirtatious one-liners card, he'd better have his running shoes on because he won't be able to run away quick enough before her comeback slaps them on the back of the head. Harper exhales long and slow as the barman retreats.

"So what's been happening with you?... the last I heard from you... you were seeing some guy... and then you went totally off-grid... I've been messaging you... I was starting to worry... so I thought I'd come to your work to see if you were okay," Harper says.

I mentally wince at the thought of my laptop lid smacking closed before I had even read any of the other messages that were sitting in my social media inbox the other day; shit, I had forgotten all about it.

"I know… I know… I'm sorry… things have been one huge whirlwind lately… I'm still seeing Gareth… it's all going so incredibly fast… I can't catch my breath… but he's such a nice guy."

The clink of glass on the counter interrupts my jabbering. I take a large gulp of the pink liquid, letting it slip down my throat slowly, avoiding the sharp tang.

"NICE?… you have a NICE guy? …Charly… when have you ever settled for NICE?"

She couldn't emphasise the word 'nice 'more if she tried. My inner spirit has her hands on her hips 'you know she's right'.

"I know… I know… I do like him, though… Gareth does make me happy… I never thought I'd say that about a NICE guy."

Harper searches my eyes for any telltale signs of dishonesty. It takes a moment for her to be completely satisfied, like she was waiting for me to slip up or something. Her stern look finally breaks into a smile.

"Okay, I believe you… okay, so… nice guys don't actually finish last then."

***

My stomach screams out for food as I carelessly throw together a pasta dish with cheese on top. It was great to see Harper earlier, but I really shouldn't have had so much Rosé on an empty stomach. My head starts to swim through the booze-fuelled haze as I try to focus on the task at hand. But the sauce still seems to find its way onto the counter and down my blouse. Shit, I better take it off before it stains. My fingers clumsily find the buttons, and I wrestle with slipping off the material. I do my best to rinse it off under the tap.

Goosebumps prickle their way up my arms as I sit in just my camisole and skirt; I say 'sit' more like slump over my bowl of pasta, propping up my head with my whole hand. The radio D.J. announces the song coming up next and 'Sex on Fire' by Kings Of Leon starts pulsing through the air.

"What fucking sex?... I'm drier than the fucking Sahara Desert."

A long snorting sound followed by a deep belly laugh roars out of me; somehow, I land on my back on the kitchen floor, while visions of tumbleweed rolling across drylands fuel the laughter even more. Giggle pain holds my stomach muscles in a tight grip, but it still doesn't seem to cease the hilarity of it all.

**

"HOLY SHIT!"

There's a cheese and pasta massacre in my kitchen. What the fuck was I thinking last night? Sauce splattered across the counter, up the walls, my blouse soaking wet hanging off the tap. Shards of ceramics and pasta have exploded across the floor tiles. Maybe I should get a take-out next time.

Thirteen

I turn the collar up on my jacket as I make my way across City Bridge, looking like a Top-Secret Agent on a mission, a 'hope anyone doesn't see me 'kind of mission. Dark shades shield my tired eyes, completing my disguise. I left the house as soon as I had cleared up last night's devastation, leaving no time for breakfast or coffee.

"Charly!"

I hear my name as I approach L.N.O.'s building; so much for thinking I was invisible. I hear my name again, sounds slightly closer this time. I turn and search around me in between the busy commuter heads. My eyes fall on George waving with his free hand, a walking stick and bag in the other. He seems like he's aged so much in the past week. I head towards him, taking his bag from him and offering my arm; he takes it appreciatively.

"Rough night?" he teases.

He may be in pain, but that doesn't seem to stop him from playfully ridiculing me; I can't help but smile at him.

"It sure was," I groan.

Never again am I crashing out on the sofa; my neck still feels stiff. I couldn't make it up the stairs, so the couch was my only option. As we set foot in the foyer, George lets out a low stifled groan. It catches the attention of the security guard, who strides out from behind his desk and without asking, he carries a chair over for George then returns to his desk. I squat down next to him as he sits, pain hisses through his gritted teeth. I push my sunglasses up to the top of my head so that I can see better. I automatically focus on his eyes; they glisten with grief and sadness.

"The old doc says I have arthritis."

I can tell it pains him to say it out loud, pride tries to overtake, but the look in his eyes tells me he's on the verge of admitting defeat. I take his hands and give them a gentle, reassuring squeeze and I smile. Hopefully, it's enough to let him know that I'll help in any way that I can.

***

'SORRY WE MISSED YOU'

The red capital letters stare at me from the doormat as soon as I open my front door. The confusion screws up my face as I pick up the note and turn it over. It lets me know that my parcel is with a neighbour. I grimace at the thought of having to retrieve it from Little Miss Nosey. I walk back down the path and round to my neighbour's house. I remind myself all the way that her name is Doris, my inner spirit sounding like a stuck record as she keeps repeating it for me, 'Doris, it's Doris, Doris, Doris, Doris'.

"Doris... hi."

She gets the tail end of my inner spirit's reminders as she swings the door open. Her eyes search me up and down before any words leave her lips.

"Good afternoon, Charly."

Her greeting is stark with only a hint of a smile. She looks down at the card in my hand, without another word she turns and heads down her hallway, then disappears, leaving me stranded on the doorstep. When she reappears, she's carrying a box.

"It came for you about an hour ago... maybe you should stay at home next time."

Her remark leaves me stunned, forcing me to freeze for a moment. She starts to close the door on me; oh dear, someone is having a bad day. I bend my body so I can call through the ever-decreasing gap.

"Thanks, Doris."

I am trying my best to keep my tone neutral, putting all my best efforts into stopping the sarcasm from creeping in.

Hauling the box onto my kitchen table, I exhale sharply and stare at the brown cardboard and the sticker that bears my name and whereabouts. I turn and walk over to the kettle, fill it, then switch it on. While I wait for the kettle to boil, I pull the cardboard tab down the length of the parcel. It looks like a zip. The end flops down as the contents slide out. Books? The name of the online bookstore on the invoice kickstarts the bells ringing with my inner spirit, 'ah ha yes, I remember now.' I'm surprised by what I had selected though, what on earth was I thinking? Sci-fi, horror, romantic comedy, fantasy and erotica? I take a closer look at the last one; the unmistakable grey tie adorned on the front. I flick the pages like it's a moving pictures book, and the smell of 'new book 'wafts up; breathing it in deeply, it fills me with contentedness.

***

I sit cross-legged on my sofa in my pyjamas with the pile of new reads sitting next to me. The TV stands silent for once. I have opted for hot chocolate as my drink of choice this evening; best stay off the alcohol for a while, well, at least for tonight anyway, I smirk to myself as my lips touch the rim of the mug. The grey tie on the top of the book pile is doing its best to lure me in. I peer at it from the corner of my eye, then look away again. The mystery that is Christian Grey beckons for my attention, 'it's just research,' my inner spirit keeps telling me. I pick up the book to survey it for a moment and reading the blurb yet again, I find myself compelled to turn to page one.

Fourteen

"George isn't coming back... His retirement takes effect from now without further notice... He left this message for you...."

The words seem to leave Miranda's lips warmly but leave me feeling cold. She hands me a folded-up piece of paper as promised. The last nine or ten days have just barely been bearable without him. The days seem to all roll into one; I almost lose track, and now that I've learned that it is permanent it saddens me even more. It will be strange without my sidekick here, but at least Miranda and I are on better terms.

"Thanks, Miranda."

She nods with her signature quarter smile and heads back to her desk. I spin round in my chair to face the wall as if it will be any more private. I gingerly open the neatly folded note. My eyes start to brim when I see George's neat handwriting.

'Charly, it saddens me to leave sooner than I had anticipated. I now must obey the Mrs and you, to pack it all in and head for the open road on a new journey. I have very much enjoyed working alongside you. I hope you go on to new pastures across the hall next year.

I am keeping everything crossed for you!

You did good, Kid.

George x.'

Tears start rolling down my cheeks before I even finish reading. I find myself just staring at the paper, no words, in particular, just the whiteness, until the silent buzz of my phone brings me back. I wipe away any evidence of tears, with my sleeve, just as I turn my chair back round to face the desk. Just his name on the screen gradually washes away any sadness.

'Hey Beautiful, can't wait to see you tomorrow. I've really missed you x.'

I didn't get to see Gareth last weekend, as he had an emergency down on Ted's farm. One of his horses had fallen ill, and Gareth was brought in to help. But without fail, he's been calling and texting every evening. In between that, I have been reading until the late hours pretty much every night. The TV has remained silent for the duration; it has just been me and the kinky shenanigans of Mr Grey. I tap on the reply icon, my fingers hesitate over the mini screen keyboard, pondering what to reply.

'I'm really looking forward to seeing you too x.'

I heavily sigh as I place my phone back on my desk. George's note still opened in my other hand; I take one last look before I fold it back to its original neatness. Placing it in my blouse pocket for safekeeping, I tap it twice.

***

"Almost there."

My old boots slip and slide on what I am hoping is mud, but the overpowering stench of manure is making me think otherwise.

"Gareth... where are we going?" I try not to let the anxiety breakthrough in my voice.

Soon as I stepped out of the car, Gareth wrapped his scarf around my eyes as a makeshift blindfold. He reassured me that it wasn't anything 'vet duty 'related, but I'm not convinced as the smell gets stronger the further we walk. I feel him walking backwards as he keeps hold of both of my hands, steadying me all the way.

"Wait here."

I can hear him trying to suppress the excitement. He lets go of my hands, and I can no longer feel his presence.

"Okay... you can take the blindfold off now."

It's the phrase that I wanted to hear, yet I'm in no hurry to take the scarf off. My inner spirit is on her knees, hoping and praying it's not anything to dread. Just like taking off a plaster, the quicker, the better. 'Three- two- one,' whipping it off on the last count. I underestimated the glare of winter's haze, so it feels like it blinds me as sunspots blot my vision, but I just about make out Gareth's smile in between. I make myself blink several times until things become a bit clearer. Shielding my eyes as I walk closer to him, the sun disappears behind a tall barn, and it makes things a lot clearer. I notice reins in Gareth's hand; my gaze moves along until my eyes meet the muzzle of a beauty. The cold air clouds as she grunts and huffs. My hands automatically spring to my mouth. I can't believe what my eyes are seeing. Gareth smiles at my awe. He starts strolling towards me, and the beautiful horse willingly follows.

"Oh my... oh my goodness... Gareth... she's beautiful."

Gareth doesn't correct me when I call the horse a 'she', so I assume I got it right. I run my hand up and down the length of her muzzle, feeling the roughness of her coat.

"Ted said we could ride these two... a thank you for my help last weekend... I think he feels bad for taking up so much of my time."

He nods towards the tall barns, and I see a guy wearing a grey woolly hat and dark green farmers attire, unmistakably Ted, and I notice his salt and pepper beard. He waits patiently, nervously smiling and holding the reins of another gorgeous horse.

"She's saddled and ready to go."

Gareth gestures to the beauty in front of me; anxiety suddenly hits me hard, like taking a blow to the stomach, my muscles tense, and my eyes widen at the thought.

"Don't worry; I'll help you."

Gareth takes hold of my hand and the touch sends a pang of calmness throughout my being. 'You've so got this' my inner spirit gives me a thumbs up. I smile at her encouragement and at Gareth's hand in mine. I find Gareth's gaze; he warmly smiles as I start to relax. I let go of his hand to walk round to the side of the horse; my eyes assess its height, the placement of the saddle and the stirrups. Gareth hands me the reins then shows me where to place my hands. My left foot finds the first stirrup and Gareth supports my hips, swiftly pushing me upwards as I swing my right leg around, and my behind lands on the horse's back. The poor thing grunts and fidgets as I land on her.

"You're a natural," Gareth praises.

I nervously smile as I find my balance, then I realise that I'm gripping onto the reins so tightly, my knuckles whiten, my fingernails are embedded in my palms. 'Ouch,' my inner spirit winces as I slowly unfurl my grip. I'm only a few feet off the ground, but I feel like I am on top of the world right now.

"What's her name?" I ask.

I find Gareth's gaze again as I start to feel steady. The winter's sunshine beats down on him, making his skin look flawless, and I can't help but smile.

"Florence."

Florence grunts and trots just her two front hoofs as she happily hears her name.

"I think she's raring to go." Gareth chuckles.

"...and that over there is Colin... wherever he goes... she follows... equine soulmates I think," he adds.

I instinctively look away as Gareth says, 'soulmates', we have a good connection, but I think it's too soon to say it's something that powerful. Gareth gently pats Florence on the side of her muzzle then walks away towards Ted.

Her front hoofs excitedly fidget from side to side as Gareth and Colin breathtakingly trot towards us. Gareth guides Colin at a gentle pace, forming circles in the yard. Without hesitation or command, Florence dutifully follows her mate's every trot. I can see what Gareth meant by 'equine soulmates'. They are truly inseparable. The sight makes my heart flutter at the sweetness.

"You're a born rider... it suits you," Gareth compliments.

I smile bashfully and look away, focusing on the back of Florence's head and neck, watching the joints move with the rhythm of her trot.

I'm wearing the same outfit that I wore to the farmers market, my hair embracing its natural waves, so I'm starting to feel and look the part; all I'm missing is a cowgirl hat. My gaze is fixated on Florence and I realise that I haven't said anything since asking what the horse's name was. My inner spirit panics and starts to clutch at straws '...c'mon... think... think', I have nothing. I look up and take in my surroundings instead, desperately seeking a subject to prompt me. I have nothing but the sun beating against my face; I close my eyes and look to the sky as the coldness bites through the rays, but I can still feel an ounce of warmth now and again.

"It's a beautiful day for winter."

I say it without even having to think about it; it just slipped from my lips. I glance at Gareth and then back up to the rays; I peer out of the corner of my eye, capturing that he's doing the same thing.

"It sure is... shall we ride a bit further out?... don't worry, I'll be right here with you... every step of the way."

He reassures me with just his smooth tone, almost like the words didn't even matter. Opening my eyes slowly away from the sun, I find Gareth watching me intently, half smiling, half squinting, waiting for an answer.

"Umm... yeah, sure... okay... as long as we don't go galloping off into the wilderness or something," I nervously chuckle.

He mischievously flexes his eyebrows, and his smile reflects the same. Nerves force my stomach to plummet; my heart tries to escape up to my throat. I instinctively hold tightly on to the reins, and my jaw is clenched as if ready to brace for the possibility of Florence suddenly bolting. Gareth clicks his tongue and tugs on Colin's reins while muttering a quiet command; breaking the circle, he heads towards the barn. The pace quickens slightly, but nothing as bad as what he had me imagining. I hold back on muttering 'bastard' as hilarity and relief take over, instead of shock. I shake my head as the race of my heart slows down to its normal rhythm, and my grip retracts a little. We bypass the barn and follow the carved-out path around the edge of the field. The same distant hillside with the quaint standalone cottage still stands unmoved, untouched, like it's part of a painting. I instantly recognise the grand tree on my left side with its overturned log seats.

The memory of our first passionate kiss springs to mind as I focus on the exact spot where we sat. My mind comes back to the task at hand when I realise Gareth is no longer in front of me. My gaze doesn't have to venture far until it falls on Colin's head. First, he's trotting alongside us and it doesn't stop there, my eyes keep scanning until they come across Gareth's face. That passionate kiss still floating on the surface of my mind, Florence stops as if she can read my mind, like she can sense the need in me. Colin stops too, maybe sensing something in Gareth the way Florence does with me. They both huddle closer together, urging for us to make contact. Our knees clash. I look down as they do, then to the space between Colin's neck and Gareth's groin; I wonder how easy it would be to jump across?

"I want to be closer to you," I murmur.

As our eyes lock again, I don't give him a chance to speak as I swing my leg over, now side saddling Florence, I stare at him, determination filling my eyes. Hooking my heel into the stirrup, Gareth offers both of his hands as he pre-empts my thinking; I gladly take them. I stand, shifting all my weight on one leg, my heart starts to pound against my chest. 'Don't think, don't dwell, just go for it' my inner spirit kicks in. I inhale an entire lung of air, as my inner spirit said, 'don't think'. Soon as I exhale, I pick my free leg up and swing, followed by shifting all weight onto Colin's back. The feel of my body slipping off forces my eyes to grow wide, my racing heart almost catapults out of my throat. Gareth lets go of my hands, and his hold scoops my underarms, pulling me closer to him. I cling to him as he holds me close, burying my face in his neck. The smell of his aftershave soothes me as my erratic breathing slows. It brings the memory back of our second date on the hillside walk. As well as his aftershave, the feel of his hand running through my hair calms my breath. I take one last deep inhale and my lips press against his neck as I exhale; warm breath travels right down his shirt collar, and I feel his goosebumps push up against my nose and cheek. I feel his neck twist, and his hand stops combing; I sense him searching for me. Picking my head up, I find his gaze then his lips, wasting no time in pressing all my need on to them; the sensation flies right through me like a rush. Cupping his face, I don't want him to move; I don't want the kiss to end. I feel his embrace move; an arm comes to rest across my shoulder blades while a hand caresses the back of my head. Parting my lips slightly, I feel his tongue brush against mine, leaving a thrill in its tracks. A gentle nudge from Florence makes us chuckle against each other's lips like she's saying, 'okay, that's enough now, you've had your fun.'

His tongue against mine was the briefest of touches, but something about it made me realise how much Gareth is warming to me.

Fifteen

A smart silver utensil set, a sizeable jolly-looking chocolate Father
Christmas, and a perfume box stare at me from my kitchen table. I
picked them up while I was shopping for my essentials on the way
home from work earlier. I brought two of them with Gareth's
Christmas present in mind. The perfume is one of Mum's floral
favourites, so that's her present sorted. My behind rests against the
counter as I sip my coffee, my bottom lip stays pressed against my
mug as my gaze drifts back to the other two items. Gareth's small,
sparse kitchen had sprung to mind when I came across the utensils. I
just hope he thinks it is useful, not patronising. It feels like Christmas
is fast approaching, even though we are only a few days into
December, but at least I am one step ahead in the preparations.

***

Fed and showered, I crash on the sofa in my pyjamas. Mr Grey lays
patiently waiting where I left him last night on the cushion next to me.
Just as I pick up the book to carry on where I left off, my phone buzzes
alive with a message. Putting the open book down, Mr Grey lays

splayed out across my lap. As I pick up my phone, my thumb flicks the screen to wake it.

'Hey Beautiful, hope you had a good day at work... I know Boxing Day is a few weeks away yet, but my parents have asked if you'd like to come to dinner? They like to plan ahead but no pressure though x.'

No pressure? Of course, there is; I feel it compressing my brain as it stares at me from the small screen. I fling my phone down like it's a hot piece of coal. The question has caught me by the throat, anxiety's fingers tightening, cutting off my air supply. My hands go to my throat as if they can physically unlock the invisible shackle like feeling. My inner spirit helps relieve my fears, 'meeting Cassie was fine... what's two more people?' She's right, constantly fucking right. The realisation throws me back against the cushions. I gasp long and hard when my airways release from the shackles. I grab and hold a cushion fiercely to my chest, closing my eyes as I bury my face and refocus on my breathing. The musty smell of age brings me back. Just my torso rolls to the side as I swing my legs up onto the sofa, shoving Mr Grey and my phone off as I twist. I feel like I'm crossing into unknown territory with no way back. Thoughts of Cassie's birthday enter, forcing me to do nothing but smile; she made me feel so welcome, instantly melting away the fears as she eased me straight into their conversations. I've triumphed that huge step, now I must conquer the next, I can do this. Confidence gushes through my body in a tidal wave overturning the anxiety and smashing it to pieces, giving me the power to shift myself off the sofa. 'Don't think, don't dwell, just respond, you've got this' my inner spirit's pep talk drives me to pick up my phone, sending Gareth a reply before the feeling totally diminishes.

'Sure... I'm staying at my mum's Christmas night, but I am free that day x.'

I hit send before I have a chance to think twice.

Sixteen

A deep satisfying sigh leaves my chest as I nurse a hot chocolate with marshmallows. The pace at work is starting to slow down this week as we prepare for the holidays. I peer at the night sky from the window seat in my living room, a place that I should use more often. I sit and watch the neighbouring Christmas lights twinkle in the darkness. This season is the best time of the year, my favourite season. I like nothing better than an oversized thick baggy jumper, cosy slippers, and a mug of hot chocolatey goodness. Don't get me wrong, I love summer and its heat, but I think I'd rather be cosy than sweltering hot. I bet poor George would rather be in warmer climes at the moment though, hope he's not suffering too much with his hip in this chill.

I rest my head against the window wall. As I continue to look up to the night sky, I notice the first flutters of snow starting to fall in the streetlamp glow, which gets me thinking of Christmas and the traditions that go with it. It dawns on me that I haven't gotten a tree yet and my eyes look away from the window, over to where the tree usually stands, typically next to my TV. I always buy a real fir tree; I love the fresh, natural scent and how that adds to the festive excitement. Back to the dilemma of the non-existent tree; maybe Gareth can help me out. I take a picture of the vacant space along with the caption:

'Umm... I seem to be missing a Christmas tree.'

After I hit send, I don't have to wait long for a response to my crisis.

'This will not do... don't worry, I will help you with your dilemma ASAP... how has your weekend been so far? I'm sorry I couldn't see you today x.'

I rest my head on the wall; my inner spirit mirrors me against the grey matter. I take another sip of hot chocolate, and I get a mouthful of sweet mush, forcing me to grimace as I feel it slide down my throat before I have a chance to chew, shuddering as it passes through. I bring my knees up to my chest, my latest read resting on my legs slides down and bumps against my stomach. I have finished with Grey; I am now onto the spinster that is Miss Jones and her unflattering big knickers. Balancing my mug on one knee and my phone in my other hand, the bump from Miss Jones reminds me to reply to Gareth's message.

'My hero! ...you are the best! I've had a rather uneventful weekend so far... Saturday night in, it's just me and a hot chocolate and a book... so rock n roll... no plans yet, probably the same again tomorrow x.'

Turning my attention back to the window, I'm not sure how long I have been sitting here, but the snow is falling thick and fast now; at least half an inch lays on the ground, making everything beyond these panes of glass seem so beautifully serene.

**

I shuffle around my kitchen in my pyjamas and fluffy slippers, and rub my hands frantically together to banish the new morning chills. Hopping from one foot to the other as if this prancing ritual will magically heat the house quicker, I feel my messy hair bun wobble as I go. There's an excited knock at the door; they tap several times like they can't wait to get in. Who on earth could that be this early on a Sunday? Soon as I unlock and open the door, the first thing I see is his huge childish grin.

"Oh my... umm hi... sorry I'm still... ah."

With a half-smile, half-grimace, I gesture up and down at my pyjamas. As if my appearance can speak for itself. Gareth waves away my concern.

"Don't worry, Beautiful... I thought I could help you out with your tree crisis this morning... early bird catches the worm and all that."

I can't help but smile at his enthusiasm as excitement swims through every feature. How can I say no to that face?

"Sure... just give me a few minutes...."

I gasp at the beauty; excitement rushes through me as I feel like a child walking through a winter wonderland. Fresh, crisp snow lays glistening everywhere you look. Hundreds of fir trees line each side of the walkway. Gareth watches me as I grow more and more excited the farther we go. Christmas songs pipe out of a nearby hut, where the owner (I assume) is standing and tucking into his breakfast sandwich, giving us a nod in mid scoff. I wander in awe of the beauty that surrounds us. Venturing a little further ahead of Gareth, I start stealthily scooping up handfuls of snow off the branches as I go. After all, I need payback for the orange veggie mush that hit me in the face on Halloween; my inner spirit chuckles mischievously, tapping her fingers together with the cunning plan. As soon as I have enough for a good size snowball, hiding it behind my back, I turn around to face Gareth, and I start to walk backwards. He catches sight of my impish glee, his expression growing warier and warier as his pace slows.

"SNOWBALL!"

I holler, followed by quick reflexes delivering the frozen ball like a baseball bowler; he clocks it right at the last second, leaving no time to react.

"Ha... payback!" I hoot.

A real belly laugh escapes from me, as I watch the freezing shock shoot across his face and crumbled snow fall from his hair. He shakes the excess snow off. His eyes snap back to me, with a game face on. A playful smile is etched on his features as he lowers his body into a stance like that of an Olympic runner. Uh oh, I am definitely in trouble now.

"You'd better start running," he hollers back.

I let out a shriek, a mixture of excitement and alarm. I do as Gareth says, looking behind me in mid-run. Gareth scoops up snow off the branches as he runs, forming it into a ball. The next thing I know, something hits the back of my knee, forcing my legs to buckle. My feet find no traction as I lose my balance and before I know it, my face meets the cold hard ground. I groan and squirm as the mixture of cold and impact registers. The chilling sting ricochets up my nose, making my eyes water. Rolling onto my back, I see Gareth through tear-streaked vision.

"Charly... I'm so sorry... are you okay?"

I wriggle my nose to try to shake off the numbingly cold pain; feeling it move reassures me that it isn't broken. I touch my nose, phew, no blood.

"I'm fine... really... it's okay... it was my fault... I think it's more shock than anything."

He helps me to my feet, eyeing me closely like he's assessing the damage.

"You look fine... Rudolph."

Oh dear, it must look worse than I first thought. Covering my nose with both hands, I peer at Gareth over my fingertips. He gently peels my hands away and smiles full of affection, reassuring me that I have nothing to fear.

"Honestly... I'm only joking."

He tenderly brushes away strands of hair that wriggled free from my ponytail as he says it, his eyes searching my features.

"Still beautiful."

A gentle kiss meets my nose; it feels good to have warmth on the injury, however brief. Taking my hand, Gareth leads me back down towards the fir trees. I halt in my tracks as one, in particular, catches my eye.

"Gareth... look."

I jog towards a fir tree standing tall on its own; for some reason, it draws me in, urging me to give it a home; I admire its grandeur. Probably a bit too big for my living room, but I'll make it fit. I turn and smile at Gareth, full of childish glee as he approaches.

"I have to have this one."

As he nears me, the thrill fills me from head to toe.

"Isn't she beautiful?"

I murmur under my breath, wide-eyed and astounded at the sight of it. Gareth looks at me fondly, holding my gaze.

"She really is."

Seventeen

We wrestle this way and that, both of us grunting and gasping, then finally getting it in. The floor is littered with a trail of green needles, all the way down my hallway to the living room. I'm surprised there's any left on the tree, as we gently set it free from its netted jacket. As the tree takes its natural shape, the branches bounce, releasing their fresh Christmas scent. We both stand back to admire it. Yep, I was right; far too big for my rather snug living room, it overshadows the TV slightly, but it's bearable. I head for the cupboard under the stairs, deep in the depths, nestled at the back, the box marked, 'Christmas Things'. It takes a bit of wriggling and shifting, but I manage to pull it out. I have everything in here to dress my tree. It's the only tradition I have, really; the rest of the house stays pretty much the same. I suppose it would be different if I had children. I carry the box over to the sofa. Gareth looks at me with his eyebrows raised in an 'is that all you got?' kind of way. I begin taking things out carefully one by one, placing them in a row, secretly in my usual order; jeez, I sound like a total control freak.

"Now the biggest question... lights first or last?" Gareth asks.

He shrugs as he holds the string of lights aloft.

"Always last... without a doubt," I respond.

I shrug away my overbearing answer and grin as I take the lights from him, placing them carefully to one side.

"Okay, Boss," he jokes.

He salutes me with one hand. I don't think I have ever let anyone help me dress my tree before, so Gareth's rather honoured, I smirk to myself. I must make sure my bossy Monica Geller side doesn't rise to the occasion since I like my tree to look, just so.

***

Admiring our hard work makes me smile contentedly. Gareth hardly bats an eyelid at my bossiness, although I did curb it a little. If my full-blown Monica side rose to the surface, I think he would run for the hills. It's a shame he had to leave earlier than he was hoping. An emergency down on Ted's farm needed his specific attention, leaving me here with a glass of wine and Miss Jones waiting to be read. I'm sitting cross-legged on my sofa, at the opposite end to where I usually sit, as the tree partially blocks the view for the TV. A glass of wine in hand and my thick baggy jumper back on, I glance from the TV back to my book, contemplating on what to do next. The newsreader is trying desperately to let me know the latest headlines, but my gaze is on the book. The silhouette of Miss Jones and her wine in hand almost mirrors me, except I'm missing a cigarette. I grab the TV remote and switch off the noise. Homework for the interview comes first. I take a large gulp of red wine then place the glass back on the table, letting the redness slip slowly down my throat, savouring the flavour. As I uncross my legs, they stretch across the sofa instead. Bringing a cushion round to my back, I melt into it, letting go a deep sigh. Now I'm ready for you, Miss Jones.

Eighteen

Standing on the doorstep, I can hear the familiar chatter and Christmas cheer coming from within. Mum lives by herself, and without fail, she holds a Christmas Day gathering and that joyous day has arrived. Friends, family, neighbours, you name it, they are there, pretty much anyone who takes pity on her. Come on, Mum, I'm freezing my arse off out here. I try the knocker again, but give it a damn good bashing this time around. Ah-ha, it worked as the door finally swings open.

"Whoah... someone can't wait to get in."

I notice the shoes, and they are definitely not Mum's unmistakable Rudolph, red nose flashing slippers. Yes, you heard me right; what the fuck indeed. Back to the unfamiliar shoes, my eyes scale up the body - dark wash jeans and a plain black jumper, sleeves rolled up to the elbows, revealing ink work of a snake trailing down one forearm, looking like it wraps right around the arm. It seems like it carries on up the arm as I notice the ink on his neck, but the rest is hidden from view. I finally meet bright emerald eyes, a sheer white grin and dark brown cropped hair; stubble completes his look. The sight of this stranger makes my heart nervously thrash against my ribs, blood thrums against my eardrums. I gulp hard to try to decelerate every frantic rhythm.

"Who are you?" I snap.

Oh crap, I wince at my demanding tone and look away. This isn't a great start to meeting someone new.

"Ethan... and you must be Charly."

It wasn't until I heard him say his name that I realised how deep and velvety his voice was. I peer back at him puzzled, 'how on earth does he know my name?' He gestures over his shoulder with just a thumb.

"I'm a friend of Alex's...."

The confused expression doesn't seem to want to budge from my face, even though the connection registers with my inner spirit.

"... you know, Harper's other half... they told me about you."

He continues along with a patronising circular motion gesture of his hand. I'm not confused by the connection, but I wonder why this stranger is in my Mum's doorway. 'I hate to admit but a rather good looking stranger,' my inner spirit adds. I shake the thought off; no, I'm with Gareth.

I force back the urge to be coarse again and my confused twisted features break into a smile instead. Half of a laugh barges out of me, doing its best to diffuse the tension.

"Sorry... I just ahh... I wasn't expecting to see a new face open my Mum's door."

I mentally grimace at the only thing I could think of. Holding my forehead as I sigh and shake my head, embarrassed, but it's no good trying to hide it. As I look up, I find him smirking at me as he finally stands to one side and gestures for me to come in; the doorway is narrow, but he doesn't move. I gulp hard as I sidestep past him with only an inch between us, close enough to smell his bourbon and cigarette-stained breath, catching a hint of aftershave underneath it all. I make a big mistake of making eye contact as I momentarily pause; his gaze goes to my mouth, and he smirks. I squeeze my eyes shut briefly and carry on, heading down the hallway. The tension lifts with every step I take towards normality.

Mum is in full form in her traditional but tacky Christmas jumper. I have never been so glad to see those garish Rudolph slippers of hers. She smiles, making the laughter lines more prominent, her brown wavy hair meeting her shoulders, the flicks of silver bounce through the waves. Her grey-green eyes glisten and sparkle with alcohol and glitter. She pulls me in for a big bear hug, and her merriment-soaked voice greets me.

"Merry Christmas, Char-ah oh... oh where is your boyfriend?"

As she lets go of me, she eyes me closely, well as close as she can through her beer goggles. I knew that question was going to come, but I still wasn't prepared for it.

"He couldn't make it, Mum."

I lie a huge twenty-four-carat lie. The truth is, I didn't breathe a word about the gathering to Gareth because I knew full well, he would want to come, and I'm not sure if I'm ready to introduce him to my Mum yet; her flamboyance is quite hard to handle at the best of times. Her current attire is not exactly something you'd wear for the first meeting with your daughter's new beau anyway. I hate lying to her, though, especially when she looks so disappointed.

"MERRY CHRISTMAS, CHARLY!"

The merry shriek comes from Harper, I watch her bound up to me, and for a split second, she looks like the excited six-year-old when we first met in the school playground all those years ago. She mirrors the same excitement now as she did back then. I snap out of the reminiscent moment when she grapples me into a bear hug. I am kind of glad for the break in the interrogation, though. Blimey, what time did everyone hit the bottle today? As she squeezes me harder and my chest crushes, I gasp for air when I'm finally released.

"Hey girl... where's this NICE fella of yours then?" she teases.

Oh fuck, not you too. Harper's excitement diminishes as her eyebrows furrow, trying to suss me out, intrigued by my long pause and my hesitant wide-eyed stare, no doubt.

"Gareth couldn't make it."

My voice is shaky as the lie sticks. Harper squints her right eye, along with the furrow; yes, she's definitely not convinced. The squint doesn't last long, as the alcohol (no doubt) flutters it back open.

"We're beginning to think he's all in your head," Alex teases.

He playfully elbows me as he swings round to take hold of Harper by the shoulder, pulling her close and planting a kiss on the side of her head. I force my face to smile, shadowing a grimace trying to break free.

I go to open my mouth to respond, but luckily Mum swoops in and pulls me to one side, out of the firing line, chatting at hundred miles per hour. She doesn't even stop for air; I don't know how she does it. I try my best not to glaze over as soon as I get the gist of her work and colleague's dramas, 'focus Charly 'my inner spirit prompts.

"You'll never guess what happened to Gertie...."

My brow furrows, trying to remember who the hell Gertie is. Who, what, why, when, exactly? She carries on, overtaking my silence.

"...Poor dear had a fall at work... had to call out an ambulance and everything... her leg is in a plaster cast... imagine that on top of Christmas."

She chatters on like I know her, I've maybe met the woman once (if ever), but just the once qualifies us as friends in Mum's eyes. Whatever pleases her, I guess. My inner spirit prompts me again, reminding me to nod along as her story continues to unfold.

"... She can't come back to work until the new year... she can't even have a drink either with the pain medication they've given her... so that's all her plans cancelled... poor love... shall I tell her you send your regards?"

My concentration and gaze seem to sidestep Mum's question, as my eyes drift across the room to where Harper was standing, but they meet a completely different pair of eyes. Those same bewitching emerald eyes that greeted me on the way in are on me. I stare at the snake trailing up his arm as he holds a pint glass aloft full of his drink of choice, beer, no doubt. Nodding his head, expressing a silent 'cheers', his mouth curls up into a smirk.

"S-s-sorry Mum... I'll be back in a sec... I ah... I need a drink."

I give Mum's question a total wide berth. Tripping on my own words as I squeeze my eyes shut for a brief moment to sever the tension before it gets too much. Oh boy, do I need a drink or maybe even a dozen to get me through the next couple of hours.

***

A Rudolph flashing nose and a bottle of unopened Rosé sit opposite me, on the coffee table next to my large JD and cola. Without fail, Mum has to give me a joke present; I smile at her nutty gesture. It made my box of perfume seem so humdrum.

I was supposed to stay at Mum's tonight, but I made excuses that I didn't feel well and needed my bed. At least it was half true; there's nothing better than hitting your hay. Hopefully, my mind will be a lot clearer after tomorrow. Dinner with Gareth's parents isn't the only thing that has got my inner spirit in a spin; those emerald eyes keep barging their way through every time I try to get my thoughts in order.

Nineteen

Black ties and ballgowns surround me; masks shield their true identities. They dance in sync; you could mistake them for duplicates. Tall windows instantly catch my eye; almost mirror-like, my reflection is so vivid. My dress is baby blue; it skims all the way down my body, hugging every one of my curves beautifully, a split in the leg to just above my knee. My lips are a light shade of pink, like an angelic version of Jessica Rabbit. There's so much striking detail and embellishment on my dress; it sparkles. My long hair cascades down with a slight wave. As I look down at myself, I notice I am holding something; bringing it up to my face for a closer look, it is a silver masquerade mask that glimmers as the light catches the embellishment. It looks just like the ones the strangers are wearing as they continue to waltz around me.

"Hello, Beautiful."

The voice makes me jump; I turn to face him. Another mask like mine greets me. Just by his hair and his big kind brown eyes, I instantly know it's Gareth. My eyes trail down his body, admiring his handsomeness. He's wearing a clean-cut black suit with a baby blue shirt; he looks pristine and perfect. He comes closer to me; at that point, I notice he is drifting, not walking. I look down; he's standing on a cloud. I take his hand as he offers it to me. I pause as something catches the corner of my eye and I let my gaze follow it with intrigue. A man stands alone, the only one without a mask, surveying us from the sidelines; his eyes glow an emerald green, making his features hard to decipher. With haste, I step onto the cloud with Gareth. He holds me close, but I can't take my eyes off the mysterious man as he watches us float up towards the ceiling. I turn back to Gareth, gazing for a moment, then reaching up, I lift the mask off his eyes, his smile warm and familiar.

Along with mine, I throw the masks to one side; they float down out of sight. I turn my attention back to Gareth; he smiles heartily as his lips find mine, his kiss so soft and gentle. The cloud shifts as if punctured beneath my feet. I slip from Gareth's hold. I am pulled away from him with some force. I try to scream as my body free-falls through the air. I hold my hand up in the hope that Gareth can catch me, but his actions come too late. I fall in slow motion; but I don't hit the ballroom floor. A black hole opens beneath me; it sucks me right in. I keep falling, but I can still see the room above me as I fall deeper and deeper into the darkness. The only light is coming from the room above me; it barely lights up my path. Closing my eyes, I try my hardest again to scream; my voice box vibrates, but there is no sound. I am caught. By what, I don't know. Feels like solid arms around me. I am too afraid to open my eyes, my heart races, my breathing comes short and sharp. I notice there is gentleness from the hold. I gingerly squint my eyes open; they widen. My mouth gapes when the mysterious man from above greets me. My body has frozen in shock. The glare of emerald from his eyes is blinding. I look away just so my eyes can recoup.

"Charly... look at me."

He knows me, and yet the voice isn't familiar, but no ounce of meanness, more pleading than anything. My gaze cautiously finds him again. The light from above dimly shines down on us, but it's just enough to see his features. As the green glow slowly extinguishes like fires, he sets me down then steps away. He buries his hands in his pockets as he upholds a confident stance. He's wearing a black suit and white shirt, but looks more dishevelled than the rest of them, up above. He has a black bow tie, but it hangs around his neck undone, along with two open-top buttons on his shirt.

"Ethan?"

My voice echoes and bounces on the nothingness. His unmistakable sheer white grin appears as I say his name. He steps closer to me, towering over my being. His expression turns serious as his mouth forms a hard line. My eyes drift along the length of his mouth to his neck, where the python ink licks his neck. I find myself biting my bottom lip as I admire the detail. I am drawn back to his eyes; they are fixed on my bitten lip.

"I know you can't resist me, Charly."

His deep, delicious tone sucks me right in; his roughness and readiness is everything I want right now. I know I really shouldn't, but I left the angel on my left shoulder in the ballroom; all that remains is the devil on my right, and he's whispering unthinkable things in my ear. With his lips so close to mine, he's right; I can't resist him. His lips find mine, hot and heavily, only for a moment. As he pulled away, my lips were an innocent shade blending from pink to red, a sexy hue of crimson. My long blonde hair was tousled from the fall. He steps back to admire me from afar. He starts to pace in circles around me, slipping off his jacket, edging closer and closer to me as he does so. At arm's length, his hand brushes against my waist and round to my behind. He keeps circling, his touch never leaving me. As I look down, the light shade of blue bleeds into black until my whole dress is consumed in the dark shade, a look that matches his roughness and readiness. He stops in front of me; we lock gazes. I smile at him, hoping that it's enough to give him some indication I want him here and now. In swift succession, just his torso pushes me backwards; my body dutifully follows until my back hits something like an invisible force field. He towers over me still, his body moulded with mine. Just his waist backs away, as his hand finds the split in my dress. His gaze never leaves mine as he rips the fabric; it tears willingly like paper. Biting my lower lip as the action fuels the fire of need burning within me. His gaze breaks for only a second as he tosses the handful of redundant fabric to one side. He grabs hold of my hands, bringing them up to either side of my head, forcefully pinning me against the darkness. Face to face, his warm breath pants heavily against my mouth. Ethan slams one foot against my inner ankle, driving my legs to part, his groin now pinned against mine. His chest suppresses my heaving breasts.

"Fuck me."

The two words leave my lips libidinously, a tone almost unrecognisable. Ethan smirks at my lustful expression, relishing the fact that he's tormenting me and my sex. His gaze drifts from my eyes to my lips, down my neck to my breasts; they heave with the prospect of Ethan's mouth on them. I am on the verge of begging as I watch him stare at my cleavage, watching them bounce with the heave. Is that what he wants? Do I need to beg? At that thought, his eyes snap back to mine, his mouth meets mine hot and heavily once again, yanking his hands away, releasing me, my hands free to wander. Just as he undoes his belt and zip, my hands find the buttons on his shirt.

I bury my fingers in between them and in one swift motion, I pull the fabric apart. It explodes like I have superhuman strength; shreds of white shirt and buttons flurry around us, falling to the ground gracefully. I lose myself in the splendour; the feel of Ethan's hands on the top of my thighs brings my attention back to him. He pulls me up onto his waist, the remnants of my dress willingly rise, revealing a black thong. Ethan's hand comes round to it, swiftly ripping it away from my behind. Excitement ricochets through my chest, up through my mouth, throwing my head back as I cry out. Holy shit, that was hot. Groin to groin, he pins me against the darkness; his hold on my thighs tightens as he drives himself into me, again and again. The thrusts come harder and faster; my arms and legs cling to him as he pounds into me. Ethan lets go of my thighs one by one as each of his hands finds mine, welding each one to the shadows, on either side of my head; my legs still wrapped around his body, the pace never ceasing. His signature smirk full of smugness resurfaces as he watches the satisfaction ripple through my features and flood my body. His emerald eyes start to burn once more, igniting into green flames with the pleasure. Throwing his head back, he roars into the darkness; it pulses through his chest. He lets go of my body; nothing stops me from hitting the floor. I keep my gaze set on Ethan as I watch him shift from human to something else; I don't know what. I watch as his hands furl into fists; the tension runs through every single muscle. His head looks down to find me, flames flickering in his eyes. It burns brighter and brighter, forcing me to half shield my eyes. His whole being combusts into green flames.

***

My eyes snap open, wide-eyed, literally out on stalks. My lungs desperately gasp for air as I wake, handfuls of the duvet are caught up in my white knuckled grip. I don't stir; I feel like I have been pole-vault-ed out of the dream world.

"HOLY SHIT!"

Beads of sweat trickle in between my breasts as I sit up, shifting my legs under the sheets, bringing my knees up to hug them.

"It's just a dream... it's just a dream."

Twenty

I find myself just staring at the row upon row of hanging fabrics. Last night's dream is being too stubborn to shift from my mind. 'Just let it go... it's just a dream'. My inner spirit's voice is soothing and helps ground my fears.

Okay, deep breath, I need to sort out this outfit, but what the fuck do you wear for such an occasion? 'Bloody hell, it's not a gala dinner and fancy frocks,' my inner spirit sighs. I back away from my vast wardrobe, holding my head in my hands. The backs of my legs hit the bed frame first, flinging myself onto my bed like some teenage drama queen. My arms and legs splay out in mid star jump.

***

As we park up outside his parents 'place, I can feel the nervous tension rising throughout my body and down to my fingertips, triggering them to tremor. Gareth places his hand on top of mine; his touch is enough to help fizzle out the tension.

"You've got nothing to worry about," he reassures.

He scoops up my hand; a soft kiss meets the back of it. I try my hardest to gulp away the nerves that are forming a hard lump in my throat, and do my best to paint a smile on my face. As we climb out of the car, the front door swings open, and Cassie comes bounding out, along with a small white dog who looks just as ecstatic as she does.

"So good to see you again, Charly."

I wince at her pitch; it makes my eardrums painfully quiver, flurrying like a mini-tornado. She hugs me fiercely, then let's go and bolts back through the front door with the little white dog following suit. Jeez, it was all so fast that if it weren't for my ears ringing, I would doubt if it ever happened.

I want to run. I want to hide when I hear the chatter humming from the open door. My torso freezes on the doorstep, but somehow, my legs keep moving. I am greeted by several faces as soon as I set foot through the door. I am introduced to every aunt, uncle, cousin, grandparent and then finally Gareth's parents. Although his Mum is just as lovely as Cassie, I am so dumbfounded; my inner spirit can't even process any of their names. I start to feel the fret of anxiety creeping up my body; the shadowy fingers trail up from my stomach to my chest, my lungs begin to feel suppressed as the sensation coils around me. I feel airless, yet I can still breathe. I clock an open door at the back of the living room. I desperately need some air; I need to feel the chill fill my lungs. I have no idea where it leads to, yet I find my feet heading straight for it.

The anxiety shatters like glass as soon as the cold air hits me. I rest my back against the wall of the house to my left, closing my eyes as I pinch the bridge of my nose to centre myself. A sharpness drags down my bare legs; I stupidly didn't throw on any tights when I opted to wear my purple a-line dress this morning.

"Fu... ah..."

My inner spirit mentally zips my mouth shut as soon as I recall where I am, best behaviour and all that. The strange stinging sensation forces my eyes to fly open. Peering down, I meet a furry white face and a pink tongue half hanging out as it pants. The cute little thing begs for my attention.

"Sammy... Sammy... leave Charly alone."

Cassie shoos the dog away. She rests her back against the same wall, mirroring me. She looks up and closes her eyes like she's trying to bask in the winter's sunshine.

"You look like you could do with a stiff drink," she muses.

That's not the only 'stiff' thing I need, my inner spirit smirks; I purse my lips to halt letting anything slip. I turn just my head to face her and just like Gareth, her skin appears luminous and flawless as the rays shine down on all the right places.

"Is it that obvious?"

She nods and smiles sincerely.

"Afraid so," she responds.

She looks away, up to the sky again, inhaling a deep breath, pouting her lips on the exhale; her breath clouds before her eyes. It was almost like watching the way you used to pretend to smoke a cigarette when you were younger, trying to act like a grown-up, or maybe it's just something Harper, Ashley and I used to do.

"To be honest... I was only prepared to meet your parents... it's all a bit overwhelming in there, you know... so much so I can't even remember their names... I don't think I'm ready for a huge step like that ye-et... ah so-sorry."

The words catch in my throat when I realise what I just said. Shit, I let my mouth get carried away again, totally forgetting whose presence I am in. My eyes grow wide along with my mistake.

"Ah-ha... so this is where you two are hiding."

Gareth's voice makes both of us jump, totally unexpected. I give him my best smile, fighting back the urge to grimace with all my might as he comes round to stand in front of us. I dread to think how much he heard of that.

"Just shooting the breeze, bro."

Cassie pulls away from the wall and glides around the back of her brother, slapping him on the shoulder as she winks at me like she will withhold my confession like it's her best-kept secret, then heads inside. Gareth waits for her to disappear. I feel his attention return to me, but my gaze is on his waist, where his dark grey jumper overlaps his dark wash jeans. Feeling like a naughty kid caught red-handed, my heart thrums in a panicked frenzy. A thumb and forefinger gently take hold of, and lift my chin; I meet a concerned face. Gareth's gaze flicks back and forth between each of my eyes, trying to figure me out.

"Everything okay?"

I can hear an ounce of worry in his question. 'Just be honest,' my inner spirit suggests. I suck in my dry lips like I just tasted the bitterness of lemon. His thumb firmly but gently runs across the width of my mouth, releasing my bottom lip. As he watches my lip intently break free, my inner spirit starts to wonder, is it so wrong to want him right now? You know, every inch of him, every inch of him inside me; the thought sends thrilling shockwaves through the deep muscles within my stomach, like a bolt it shoots straight to my cheeks, feeling them instantly blaze. I almost forget to answer his question, but the feel of his hand cupping my cheek helps ground me.

"I ah... just needed some fresh air...."

His thumb strokes my cheek, I close my eyes with the calming sensation. The warmth of his lips meeting mine fuels my being with the buzz of serenity instead. His touch slides away, but the warmth of his arms embraces me instead; my nose pressed against the crook of his neck, I inhale the scent of him deeply.

"Sorry, I should have given you a heads up that there was going to be more people here... but you're awesome to handle this bunch... I think they love you."

Love me; they've only known me for five minutes; how is that even possible?

Twenty-One

I think 'traumatised' is a little too strong of a word to describe me right now, but my inner spirit can't determine anything less intense. As soon as we step into Gareth's apartment and the door closes behind us, I finally feel like I can breathe.

Jeez, it felt like such an interrogation as soon as we stepped back into his parents' house earlier. They wanted to know everything about me except for my bra size and PIN number; quite literally I felt verbally stripped bare. Just as I place my bag down in the hallway and kick my heels off, Gareth immediately takes me by the hand and leads me straight to the bistro table, where a little white gift bag sits.

"I really didn't know what to get you for Christmas... so I ah... I asked Cassie for her help... I hope you like it."

He gingerly passes it to me. Reaching into the bag, I pull out a small white boxed perfume, an awfully expensive perfume. The french word for 'I adore,' or 'I love,' I can't remember which one. My gifts suddenly seem so minuscule in comparison to his generous gift.

"This is so thoughtful... thank you so much... I haven't tried this one yet."

I slide the little white box back into its bag and place it back on the table. I mirror his smile; Gareth looks somewhat relieved.

"Okay... now it's your turn... close your eyes."

I wait until they are shielded by his hands and head over to my bag to retrieve the gifts. Nerves try their best to break my smile, but as I look at Gareth and all that's on display is his childish grin, I can't help but let out a quiet giggle.

"Now you can umm... you can open them... sorry it isn't much... I didn't know what to get you either."

Mentally grimacing as I place both of them on the table in front of Gareth, his hands fly away from his face as soon as I give him permission.

"Aww, thanks! Beautiful... that's something I kept meaning to buy for the kitchen... and you can never go wrong when it comes to chocolate... but I may need help eating it," he chuckles.

As soon as I hear the sweet sound of his laugh, it feels like a tonne of weight has been lifted off my shoulders. His gaze takes hold of mine, and I instantly notice something different about his eyes, I noticed it earlier today in the garden, but I brought it down to the fact that the brightness of the sunshine was making them glisten and dewy. Right now, that same look is back, but no ounce of rays can be the culprit. It brings his handsomeness to a whole new level, a look that screams at me to say four meaningful words, 'I love you, Gareth.' I go to open my mouth, but my voice abandons the ability to speak. Why can't I bring myself to say it? His kindness and generosity are fucking huge signs that he adores me, and yet my feelings are refusing to surface from my chest. His eyes are like headlights, with me as the stunned rabbit caught in them. I look back at the little white bag then back to Gareth; I still can't bring myself to say it. I need a moment.

"I just need to use your bathroom."

I don't wait to be excused, heading straight for his bedroom, then through to the bathroom, immediately closing the door behind me without turning on the light, instantly plunging me into darkness. I know the sink is immediately to my left. Stretching out my hand, I feel the cool hard surface of the basin. I recall seeing the light above the mirror, so my fingers carefully trace the edges of the sink and then up to the cabinet; they come across the familiar texture of cord. I pull it down and the light dimly switches on, filling the mirror with a ghostly looking version of me. I rest my hands on the edge of the sink only to see an unamused expression twisting my features. What the hell is the matter with you? I want to scream. At times like these, I usually call Harper, but without my phone, it's just me; I can't even think of what she'd say to me right now. Probably something along the lines of 'stop being such a fucking jerk and get back in there'. I smile as my inner spirit lets me recall her voice. Shaking my head as I look down to find the taps, I let the water run through my fingers until I feel the warmth. Cupping my hands together, they scoop and fill with water. Leaning right over, I chuck the contents up into my face, and then pulling the towel off the hook, I pat my face dry, being careful not to smudge my makeup. My reflection is now looking a little brighter. 'You've got nothing to worry about' Gareth's kind words spring to mind; surely he must be right? In swift succession, I inhale deeply and satisfyingly, pushing myself away from the sink, not giving myself a chance for second thoughts.

As I make my way down the hallway, I notice the voice of Ellie Goulding first. I notice just the uplights are on; I can't say I noticed them before. Gareth beams as I reappear; his grey jumper gone, he's wearing a black shirt with a few top buttons undone and a white t-shirt peeking through the gap, teamed with his dark wash jeans instead, and I can't help but wonder if that was the same shirt that I had slept in. He draws me in and holds me close, linking my hand with his; my other hand finds his shoulder in the same stance as we were in the club.

"Charly... you haven't got anything to worry about... all my family loves you just as much as I-I...."

I silence him with a deep kiss; I could sense what was about to leave his lips. For him to say that he must have noticed the look in my eyes before I darted to the bathroom. I can feel him relax into me as I part his lips with mine, my tongue searches for his, but they don't meet before he pulls away. 'I Won't Give Up' by Jason Mraz starts to play. Gareth holds me by the small of my back as we begin to sway to the slow rhythm. I can't help but listen and take in the lyrics. I'm trying, Mr Mraz, believe me, I really am. Resting my head on his shoulder, my nose pressed against his neck, I want to love this guy more than anything. I inhale the scent of him deeply. It's evident that he adores me, and it pains me that I can't reciprocate. Don't get me wrong, I feel something for him, but I'm not sure what it is; I have never felt this close to someone before. I feel his mouth brush against my hair, just above my ear.

"Would you like a glass of wine?" he asks.

As the song comes to an end and fades into the next track, he releases me and eyes me intently.

"Sure," I smile.

He disappears into the kitchen, and I take the brief moment to distract myself from my thoughts and feelings. I walk over to the fireplace, where I notice a pile of logs ready and waiting to be set alight. A plush looking cream rug runs along the floor in front of the fireplace; I don't recall seeing it the first time around. Gareth reappears with two generously filled glasses of red wine.

"Ready to get cosy?"

He nods towards the fireplace as he hands me one of the glasses. Now that he's pointed it out, it does feel chilly in here. He kneels in front of it, placing his glass on the hearth before I even answer, making me doubt whether it was a question in the first place. I sit down beside him, my legs tucked round to my left, leaning on my right arm. I peer over my glass as I watch him unbutton the cuffs on his shirt, then roll them up to his elbows. My eyes keep drifting up to his body, wishing I could undress him with my eyes, drinking him, and the wine, in as he gets to work. The next song starts to play, I instantly recognise the guy's voice, but I'm not familiar with the song.

"I like this song... I can't think who sings it, though."

The fire comes alive just as I ask, and I place my glass down on the hearth. Gareth's body relaxes before he responds. In a position similar to mine, leaning to his left, we are almost shoulder to shoulder.

"It's 'Far Away' by Nickelback."

I watch his lips intently as he says it. I know he's a gentleman, but there's a tiny part of me that is begging him to throw down the chivalry gauntlet, push me down in front of this roaring fire and fuck me with every inch of his cock. I find myself mindlessly running my fingers up and down his bare forearm.

"Sorry... I just ah."

Words fail me as my actions dawn on me, but my fingers don't leave his arm, even though I feel the embarrassment set in; my cheeks red hot. Leaning over, grabbing my glass of wine instead, I take a large swig, swallowing it too hastily; the wine slips down the wrong way, forcing me to cough, jolting and sloshing the contents. Tears sting my eyes, and the liquid runs down my hand and my forearm. The glass is taken from me, just as well; I don't want him to wear it too.

"You know... you didn't have to share your drink," he chuckles.

Light from the flames shows up the wet patches on his shirt. My inner spirit shakes her head in dismay. The whiteness of his t-shirt underneath prompts me to help.

"Ah, I'm so sorry... you might want to take your shirt off before it gets to your t-shirt."

Watching his eyes shift from bright to panic, he hastily starts undoing the buttons. I see the redness first, like puncture-less stab wounds, ah that t-shirt's definitely ruined. Bundling his shirt on the hearth, he kneels to peel off the wrecked undergarment. Mirroring his kneel, I hold the wetness away from his body, helping him slip it off over his head. Staying close to him as his face reappears, his hair is ruffled from the drag of fabric. A yearning urgency rises within my chest; all my doubts swiped to one side as I see the same look of need in his eyes. With my hand on the back of his neck, I pull him closer to me until our lips lock, kissing him like I've never kissed him before, thrusting my breasts against his now bare chest.

I break the lock for a moment as my eyes drift along his neck, all the way across his collarbone, settling on his chest, noticing the smattering of hair; my fingertips graze against it. Peering down at my touch, without breaking his gaze, he flings his t-shirt to the side. The voice of John Legend takes me by surprise as the track changes; I didn't think that 'Stay With You' was his kind of song, judging by the rock band posters that line his hallway. Come to think of it; all his song choices have been a little out of the ordinary. He's been setting the mood all along. The running of his fingertips along my arms brings my attention back, they are tingling my skin under the fabric of my sweater until they disappear underneath; they find the bare skin on my shoulders. I peer through my lashes, his eyes glimmer with coyness and need. I let my arms fall to my sides. His touch encourages the fabric to slip off my shoulders and down my arms. I find my place of comfort, the crook of his neck, inhaling the scent of him first; my lips kiss and brush their way up to his jaw as his fingertips search my neck to my hairline. Cupping my face, he brings me up to face him, his eyes flit between mine - in search of permission, perhaps?

He lets go as I scoop up my hair and drape it over my shoulder, turning just my torso, revealing my zip. Turning my head, eyes level to his shoulder, I feel his presence come closer. His warm breath and fingertips graze down my bare neck, goosebumps prickle as his mouth brushes under my ear. His gentle touch glides down in between my shoulder blades to my dress. Holding onto his biceps, I pant heavily against his skin, my grip tightens as he finds and takes hold of my zip, my breath hitches as the juddering is teasingly slow. His fingers run down the gap, caressing my bare skin. As he hits the end, I lift my head to find him, just my torso backs away, freeing my straps. I let go of his biceps and find the hem of my dress, pulling it up and over my head, my hair falls messily over my shoulders, flinging it on top of Gareth's bundle of clothes. Our gazes lock, and I admire the bronze tint from the fire reflecting in his eyes. He moves his hands over the back of my neck, brushing my hairline with his fingertips, then kisses me lightly on the lips. Without breaking my mouth from his, my fingers run down either side of his back. Blindly curious of the shapes of his muscles. They fall upon his belt, they run along the edge to the front where the buckle sits. Pressing my lips deeper against his as I slip one finger into the strap, tugging and freeing it, swiftly undoing the single button and zip, using the buckle to yank the whole belt free, I let it fall to the floor with a quiet thud. His hands caress my shoulders, his fingers slip under the straps of my black lacy bra, tracing the shape of me underneath. My fingers continue their journey up the centre of his chest, blindly exploring every shape of him.

His breath comes in quiet pants, but I feel the warmth thrusting against my mouth. The anticipation fills his body, furling his whole grip around each of my bra straps, holding me firmly against him. For a moment, I wish he had enough strength to tear the fabric in two. The excitement of the thought shoots right through my core down to the deep muscles within my stomach. I pull away slightly, breaking our lips apart, my eyes flit between his, his face is flush. I feel the softness of the faux fur beneath my bare skin as I lay down.

He suddenly springs up to his feet. The jumping action forces his jeans to slide down his legs. I pull a blanket off the sofa, drape it over myself, peering over the edge of it. Sniggering all the while, I watch him shuffle with trousers around his ankles as he retreats to his bedroom for a rubber, I assume. He returns trouser-less moments later with a more confident swagger. I bury my face into the soft fabric as my giggling fails to cease. Alongside my body, I feel him lay, my face still covered, I clear my throat, halting the chuckling as the blanket glides down over my face, but my grin doesn't fade. The backs of my hands instinctively lay on the floor on either side of my head instead.

As the fabric continues to slide down my body, softly tickling its way over my breasts, stopping just above the edge of my panties. His body shuffles closer to me; half of him hovers over me, resting on his left elbow; I feel myself beginning to unravel under his kind but hungry gaze. My lips willingly part as his palm meets my cheek with a gentle caress; he watches my bottom lip quiver as his thumb runs across to the middle of it. As he drags it down, the anticipation runs through my core, down to those deep muscles, making them pulse and pinch so deliciously. Moving his head tantalisingly close to me. His mouth hovers over mine as he lets go of my lip. His fingertips run down my chin, over the curve of my neck, down the middle of my chest. I gasp against his mouth as I feel the warmth of his palm against my breast, teasing me at the edges of the lace. My arms feel like they are pinned to the floor as the thrill takes over, filling my body from head to toe.

His hand disappears under the blanket, his touch runs across the edge, in one swift movement, his hand slips right under the fabric of my panties, my back arches, my hands clench into fists, and my toes curl as he cups my sex, I let out a breathless moan. 'Oh fuck!' I want to cry out; I pant short and sharp, wondering what move he's going to make next.

His fingers find my clit, kissing me intently as he works it in circular motions; I am breathless against his mouth as waves of pleasure break through my body; my hips writhe with this notion. I feel my deep muscles contract, spiralling them in an arousing whirlwind. The blanket slips off me as I bring my legs up, my feet curl uptight, and my toes point to the floor. One touch, hits me in the right spot, sending me right over the edge, falling into climatic oblivion. I cry out against his mouth as I cum hard against his touch. Gareth breaks our kiss; he watches me intently as my body calms after the stormy whirlwind. I lift my behind, bringing my hands down to hook my panties and slip them off, kicking them to the side as they meet my ankles. I hear the tear of a foil packet; Gareth slips it on as he lays by my side. His body shifts, and my legs automatically part for him as he comes to lay on top of me. He meets my gaze as he drives himself into me; he stills, as a gasping moan escapes from me. Worry fills his eyes, but it soon disperses as I pull him closer to me by the back of his neck. Leaning all his weight on me, he finds my hands and brings them up to lay either side of my head. Our fingers interlock, he grips tighter and tighter with each thrust, pinning me to the floor. I want to let loose with my unruly mouth as he plunges deeper and deeper.

He lets go of my hands; they slide under me to grasp my behind, pinning my groin to his in a slow grind. I moan breathlessly, arching my back; my hips start to roll as the arousal buzzes through me; the feeling intensifies as he mirrors my movements. Our bodies feel like they are rolling on the ocean. Wriggling his hands free, they come up to my shoulders; they slide underneath, his palms to my blades and lips find mine. He pants heavily against my mouth as his pace quickens to deep thrusts. I hold him close to me as his body trembles as he slowly comes to the brink. He groans louder as a climax rips through him; he thrusts one last time, and then his head hangs breathlessly. He rolls off me onto his side but keeps me close.

While we catch our breath back, I lay in his arms. Goosebumps prickle their way up my body; I reach for the blanket that slipped off me, he helps me drape it over us both. We lay watching the mesmerising dance of the flames in the fireplace.

Twenty-Two

Shit, shit, shit, I've totally fucked it up. I couldn't leave the interview room quick enough without impairing the look of professionalism. Leo Nelson Osmond was my interviewer. Even though I have worked here for over a year now, I have never met or even seen the sandy blonde and clean-shaven CEO of this publishing house. I think he was away on business the first time around. Although he was intimidatingly handsome, his arrogant nature outweighed any of these qualities. He was lounging in his expensive leather office chair. His fingers pressed together, giving the impression he was listening, but intensely eyeballing me with his deep blue eyes in front of his floor to ceiling windows. I tried to relay my experience and fake joy working for his company so far, but I kept tripping over and stuttering my words, probably giving him the wrong impression. Way too many 'umm's left my lips, utterly unprofessional.

I fly with frustration down the four flights of stairs down to HR's level; he had given me some letters and a file to put on Miranda's desk. Pushing one of the double doors with way too much aggression, it swings open and flies back with just as much anger as I showed it. I manage to sidestep out of its way before it knocks me flat out. Before heading to the doors of HR, the voice of Billy Joel catches my ears.

Curiosity draws me closer to the sound, but someone else's awful rendition of 'Uptown Girl' takes over and I cringe at the attempt; it's like nails dragging on a chalkboard. I peer through the glass panel of the door; the karaoke attempt is coming from a woman standing on a desk. She's dressed in a navy skater dress, her long brown hair cascades down her back, silver tinsel drapes over her shoulders like a boa. I can't see her face, but her enthusiasm makes me smile. I watch her shimmy as she tries to sing. Maybe this is why Mr Osmond looked so disinterested with my interview, he possibly had a sneaky visit to the belated office Christmas party punch bowl or is waiting to attend it. My smile fades as my interview dominates my thoughts again, my inner spirit sighs when I realise I probably won't get the chance to join in with this merriment next year. Turning heavily on my heel, woefully continuing the instruction given by Mr Osmond, I slovenly place the pile in my arms on Miranda's neat and tidy desk. Straightening them up before I leave, I try to avoid them looking like they've been placed there by a petulant child.

Without urgency, I stroll out of HR, just as the doors across the way fly open. I recognise the blue and white checked shirt and the glasses straight away; long time no see. With a young brunette woman, dressed in navy, by his side, I realise then that I'm staring at the face of the 'Uptown Girl' destroyer. Ben stumbles over his own feet and she swoops in to try to hold him up. She, too, has glasses, and as she grimaces, the light bounces off the silver braces that line her teeth, her look reminding me of the TV show 'Ugly Betty.'

"I think we... we better... f-find you a... cab, Ben," she grunts.

Her voice strained as she does her best to prop him up, one of his arms around her shoulder. Setting my feet in motion, I hurry over to them.

"Hey... hey... can I help?"

The sound of my voice snaps Ben's head up like it brings instant sobriety to him. He straightens up and lets go of 'Betty,' her strained features turn to a frown, and she folds her arms like she's been played for a fool. He tries to resume his stance casually, and I can't help but smirk at his best efforts; he's not fooling anybody; he's still pissed as a fart.

"H-hey Char-arly... h-how you doing?"

He stumbles over his words instead. Ignoring the fool, I turn to 'Betty,' offering my hand for a shake.

"Hi, I'm Charly... not Char-arly...."

It takes her a moment to register my mockery; she finally breaks her frown into a broad smile, displaying her braces in full view and takes my hand, shaking it enthusiastically.

"Hi, Charly... I'm Kelly... and this mess here is Ben."

She lets go of my hand to grudgingly waft it towards Ben instead, along with a brief scowl; it fades as quickly as it comes.

"I know... we've met before...."

I jut out just my chin in his direction, without making eye contact. Her eyebrows raise, and her mouth forms an 'O 'like she suddenly remembers a distant thought. She looks at him as she goes to say something, but the crooked glare from Ben halts her words. I glance between them, waiting for some clarity. I feel like I am intruding on some sort of war of unspoken words; it hangs in the air. I have to break this uncomfortable silence; it's deafening. I clear my throat in a bid to sever the tension. It seems to have done the trick as they both focus on me instead.

"Umm... I'll take care of this dickhead if you like."

I playfully wink at Kelly. I watch the humour soften her features. It's a shame I won't get to work with these guys, I think we'd all get along.

"H-hey... I-I'm standing r-right here."

Doing my best to hold back another smirk as I watch him trying to regain a confident stance, his legs wobble like a newborn foal.

"You call that standing?" I tease.

Kelly bursts her gates that were holding back her laughter; she grabs hold of my shoulder as she turns, steadying herself on me for a moment before she continues to head back through the doors to the party.

"Believe me... he's all yours... nice to meet you, Charly."

She calls over her shoulder just as she disappears. Ben sheepishly half-smiles at me as he waits for us to be alone. I smile back with expectant eyes. When no words leave his lips, I head over to the lifts and press the 'call 'button. He comes to stand by my side as we wait for the familiar 'ding 'and 'whoosh 'of the lift's arrival.

Our backs rest against the wall, how we stood before his heroic act several weeks ago. Reaching over, I press the 'G 'for the foyer. I stand back and watch the doors angrily bang close. I glance out of the corner of my eye, although I don't know him very well, I can tell he's holding something back, watching his throat bounce with a deep gulp, or it could possibly just be embarrassment, I have caught him in a soused state after all. 'Who knows?' my inner spirit shrugs. For once, I have nothing to say to try to fill the ever-increasing void. The notion makes me feel uneasy; it presses down on my chest. We finally land on the foyer floor and when the doors finally bolt open, it feels like my chest does too, releasing all the pent-up tension. Ben follows closely behind me. I'm not sure whether it's the lack of people in here or the uncomfortable silence hanging over us, but the expanse of the foyer seems much vaster. The click of my heels against the tiled floors bounces off every wall, trembling my eardrums.

Cold December rain hits our faces as soon as we step out onto the pavement. If this doesn't sober him up, then I don't know what will. I wait with him by the curb, trying my best to hail a cab. He turns to face me, raindrops trailing down the lenses of his glasses.

"You could do with some window wipers for them," I joke.

Smiling coyly, as he takes off his glasses, the rain hits his lashes, encouraging his eyes to squint, making his smile seem crooked.

"I do indeed," he replies.

Probably the only three most sobering sounding words he's said all afternoon. The chill starts to settle into his body as I watch his blue-tinted bottom lip tremor and I bet he wishes he brought a coat. A cab finally pulls up alongside us. Although he'll probably appreciate the shelter of the vehicle, he seems reluctant to part ways with me. Opening his mouth, he readies himself to say something, but it closes again. I hug one side of his body, half a hug; I guess you could say.

"Happy New Year, Ben."

My words fill the void for him. He nods and half-smiles as he looks down briefly. Appreciation is what I thought it was, but when he doesn't make eye contact with me, it makes me think otherwise. I know that look, that moment when you acknowledge you are in the 'friend zone' and nothing more.

"Thanks, Charly... you too."

***

Finally, home in the dry, my hair in a damp messy bun, trying to chill out on my sofa, the only light dimly filling the room is the TV. Soon after I stepped into the house earlier, my inner spirit butted Ben out and replaced him with Gareth.

It's been a few days since I slept with Gareth or even spoke to him, in fact. That night couldn't have been more perfect if it tried. There's just something missing in me, a huge black hole in my chest where all the feels should be, but I can't put my finger on what should be in that space.

All my thoughts are scattering across the grey matter in one fucking huge complicated mess. I'm pretty sure that this is definitely not how you should feel when you finally jump to the next level or base of a relationship. I'm too stumped to think straight right now; not even the trashy soaps on TV are making any sense.

It's supposed to be instant, isn't it? Falling in love, I mean, you just know, don't you? I've heard it only takes just one look, and that's it, you fall, *hard*. I'm just not getting that, I know everyone is different, but that doesn't stop me from thinking that there's something not quite right here. Something not quite right with me. Maybe I just need to give it more time? But what if I do that and still nothing comes? What then? I sigh and groan heavily with that lingering thought, burying my face deeper into the blanket.

My phone buzzes with a text message; I peer at the name on the screen. The name that used to fill me with such joy now fills me with the jitters instead. There are several unread texts from the last few days:

'Last night was phenomenal... I miss you, Beautiful x.'

'Evening Beautiful, how was your day? x.'

'Hope you're not working too hard x.'

'Miss you Beautiful x.'

'Good luck with your interview tomorrow, Beautiful x.'

'Everything okay? How did it go today?'

I draw my knees and the blanket up to my chest, as an upset toddler would. I bury my face into the soft fabric and breathe in the scent of comfort as a single tear falls. I hate blanking him, but what can I say to him? I don't even have a reason for my silence. Clearing his messages from the screen, I tag Harper and Ashley in a single message.

'SOS agony aunts... can I see you guys tomorrow? x.'

Any relationship crisis always starts with our codeword 'SOS'. You just instantly know that shit is about to go down. A glass of straight whiskey is waiting for me on my coffee table. Leaning over, I grab it and knock it back in one bitter gulp. I don't know why but I keep the rim of the empty glass pressed against my bottom lip, the remnants of the bourbon aroma linger. It sparks a recent memory that I thought I had buried.

Twenty-Three

"Hey... hey Charly... Charly this way... hey Charly."

The shouts seem to come from all directions. Flashing lights blind and disorientate me; I close my eyes, but I still see the flashes. I take a deep breath and on the out-breath, I summon the courage to open my eyes. Everyone is chanting their love for ME; they've all come to see ME. As I look down at myself, I'm wearing the same black dress as before; it glints as the cameras flash. Beneath my feet is a plush red carpet. As I take in my surroundings, I realise I'm on a celebrity walkway for an award ceremony... BAFTA's, Emmy's, Golden Globes? I have no idea which one it is. There's no indication. I very much doubt it's the music awards, with the way I sing. A broad smile stretches across my face. I wave to my supposedly adoring fans; they go wild.

"OH MY GOD... THERE HE IS..."

I watch as a stranger points and yells at a pristine white limousine pulling up; the door opens, followed by smart shiny black shoes stepping out onto the red carpet. My gaze flows from the legs all the way up to the face. That unmistakable sheer white grin of his, along with those emerald eyes, he doesn't give anyone a blind bit of notice; the only thing he's focused on is ME. Strangers are desperate for his attention, but they may as well not exist. His body fully emerges from behind the vehicle's door, straightening his black tie and adjusting his jacket as he goes, his shirt as white as his teeth. Locking eyes with me all the while, he means business. Just like the movies, he strides in slow motion. I gaze up and down his body as he aims towards me, every inch of him immaculate this time.

"So, we meet again."

He says it in that deep hypnotic tone that suits him so well. I can't help but fixate on his mouth as he comes to stand next to me, then I turn back to the crowd.

"You'd best be on your best behaviour this time," I playfully murmur out the corner of my mouth.

He firmly puts his arm around my waist as I continue to wave to the crowds.

"I believe it was you that asked me to fuck you."

I watch his mouth from my side view as the words roll out so deliciously. He has a point there; I bite my lower lip at the memory.

"Then I must apologise for my rude insistence... it won't happen again."

I shuffle out of his hold and continue to sashay down the red carpet, looking like I am following through on my apology and vow. My hand is grabbed. Before I know it, I'm spinning to face him again. I gasp as he pins me against his chest, holding my arm up against my back. His mouth almost brushes against mine. I only have to utter the words, and he'll be mine; he wouldn't hold back, he wouldn't be afraid to be balls deep in me right now, even with these spectators surrounding us. I can feel his other hand run down my back; it seems to be searching for something, then it suddenly stops, he tugs the fabric of my dress. A vibration ripples down my back, my zip; he's undoing my zip and undoing ME. I gulp hard, trying to keep it together.

"Are you sure about that?"

A question so intense against my mouth, he is my deepest darkest desire, and I think he knows it. He knows exactly what he's doing to me, but I'm trying not to make it look apparent that he's slowly unravelling me into submission. His hand slides into the gap of my dress, down the crease of my behind; his fingertips are doing their best to tease me into giving in. Stay strong; you mustn't give in this time 'the angel on my shoulder appears, begging me not to succumb to his charm. She bursts into a puff of smoke and glitter when I defy her. The scenery and all the surrounding people follow suit, just like our emotions; sparks fly from exploding camera flashbulbs, then fizzle out, plunging us into darkness. A spotlight flicks on like we're part of a stage show. As my eyes follow it, it lights up the white limo that Ethan just rocked up in. I look over my shoulder, but Ethan has disappeared too. I search all around me. I slowly walk over to the limousine; my eyes still search from left to right, but they still don't come across Ethan. My heels audibly click as I walk; the sound echoes; it bounces on the nothingness. Reaching the vehicle, I walk around it just once, thinking Ethan is lurking inside or behind it, but I don't see him anywhere. Walking round to the front, I rest my backside on the bonnet, and my palms rest behind me, flat on the metal.

"You're not very good at keeping your word, are you?"

The voice seems to boom from all directions, and my eyes frantically search the darkness beyond the spotlight. Just like the voice, I hear footsteps all around me, making me think more than one person is advancing towards me. Movement catches my eye right in front of me and I see a shadow of a person, but there's not enough light to make a true judgement.

"Well, what's it going to be? Are you staying, or are you leaving?"

Ethan steps into the light; his tie and jacket have vanished. A few top buttons are undone on his shirt; he looks just as dishevelled as the last time. He unbuttons his shirt cuffs and rolls up his sleeves to the elbows as he walks closer to me. I really should be leaving, doing whatever I can to encourage myself to wake up. Instead, I find myself sliding my legs apart, forcing the slit in my dress to tear even further up my thigh. He places his hands on the bonnet, either side of me; I find myself voluntarily leaning backwards as he leans into me. He cocks his head to the side as he watches me unravel; my breasts heave with anticipation. I watch him watching me, seeing how my body responds to his presence. His groin pressed against mine is almost too much to bear. I just want him to rip my clothes to shreds and fuck me till the middle of next week. He nudges my nose with his; it was the slightest of touches, but it was enough to surrender to him. I tip my head back as I feel him hover over me. My breath hitches as I feel his mouth brush along my jaw and over my mouth, *but he doesn't kiss me. My body writhes as he teases me with the briefest of touches down my neck, in between my breasts. I feel the tip of his nose drag down my navel, and my throat catches my breath as he reaches my sex. My breaths come in short sharp pants; my lungs struggling to gasp for air. Within his chest, I hear a deeply buried laugh, almost wicked; it rumbles right through, and I can feel the tremors.*

"Sorry, princess, not today."

He lifts his hands, then slams them back down on the bonnet. I watch the strain rip through his face and body as he uses all his strength to propel the limousine away from him, shooting me right into the darkness.

***

I bolt upright, catapulting out of the dream version of me. I wake in a cold sweat and I struggle to get my breath back, like I just experienced actual velocity. I feel the lump of raw emotions rise within my chest; it spills out through my eyes. I'm shedding ugly tears as guilt and the feeling of holding up the weight of the world on my shoulders washes over me. I hold my head in my hands, and the tears run down my palms and arms. I can't do this anymore, I'm sorry.

Twenty-Four

'Commitment phobes: have problems committing to anything, not just relationships'. Harper had branded me with a new label earlier. I think about it now. Everything makes much more sense with how I have been feeling. Harper and Ashley wanted to stay with me tonight, but I lied and said I was okay. I stare at the ceiling through tear smudged vision, pressing my iPod earbuds into my ears to numb the silence as 'Thursday' by Jess Glynne starts to play. I close my eyes as more than just a tear falls.

Rewind: four or so hours earlier...

Harper and Ashley stand on my doorstep waving bottles of Rosé and chocolates, their half-smiles weighed down with compassion. I sit at my kitchen table while Ashley fetches some glasses and Harper pops the cork on the wine. She fills the glasses generously as soon as Ashley places them on the table. Soon as their behinds touch down on the stools, my verbal and emotional floodgates burst open.

"I think I am in too deep... I am not ready for this... I've met all his family now... it's all going way too fast...."

I relay every thought, feeling, date, and word shared between Gareth and me at one hundred miles per hour. I don't stop until I'm gasping for air and tears have soaked my cheeks. Ashley sits there gawking like she's still trying to process my jabbering, or she just doesn't know what to say.

"Commitment phobe."

Harper's short but not so sweet evaluation comes like a verbal slap in the face, an invisible punch to the chest and an almighty blow to the stomach. A total body pow that leaves me emotional and weak.

"Harper! You can't say that," Ashley hisses.

Harper snorts and folds her arms at Ashley's retort. I know that look all too well; she's hardly ever wrong when she looks that self-assured. My face is still frozen in trying to process my new label; I think I have heard of it, but my brain is too stunned to think.

Harper hops off her stool and fetches her phone, taps something on the screen keyboard, and slides the phone across the table. The description lays right in front of me. Reading it two, three times over before it begins to sink in, I mutely say it the fourth time, my mouth chewing on the words. When the realisation hits, my bottom lip starts to tremor, and my eyes begin to brim again. She has to be right; it feels like the only reason for the ever-increasing doubt and lack of emotions that keep beating me up inside. I shakily take hold of my glass of Rosé and down the contents, not stopping until the last drop forces me to grimace and hiss. I need the alcohol buzz for what I am about to do. As I hop off my stool, they both do the same, taking me into their arms and holding me close. A 'cuddle sandwich 'we used to call it when we were kids.

"Cuddle sandwich," I mutter.

The scent of both of their perfumes comforts me, one floral, the other one fruity. I feel a quiet, almost inaudible giggle ripple through both of them as they stroke my hair.

"Cuddle sandwich," they both whisper.

I wriggle out of their reassuring hold with a heavy heart, knowing it's now or never.

"I know now what I must do... I can't... I can't keep Gareth stringing along like this... I-I have to do what's right."

As I turn to walk out of the kitchen, I feel a firm but gentle grasp on my arm; turning slightly, I see that it belongs to Ashley.

"Are you sure about this?" she asks.

I give her a forged half-smile and nod. She stares back at me wide-eyed, looking like she's desperately searching for something from her own inner spirit to say, but nothing comes. Her gaze moves to Harper, probably hoping she'll have something helpful to say.

"We'll be right here for you... won't we, Ashley."

Harper raises her eyebrows at her, willing for her to agree. She reluctantly nods in agreement after Harper's stare has burned a hole in her. I'm probably making the wrong decision, but I need to put Gareth first; he's better off without me.

Heading out into the hallway, my hands start to shake as I reach into my pocket for my phone. My eyes begin to brim when I see Gareth's name in my contacts. Inhaling a shaky breath, I hit the icon to call. Nausea grips my stomach as I hear the monotonous dialing rings; the wait is torturous. The emotions form a rock-hard lump in my throat. I do my best to gulp it down when I hear the familiar break in tone and the sound of his kind voice.

"Hi, Gareth... umm... we need to talk...."

Twenty-Five

"Please, please, please, come to our party... it is New Year's Eve after all," Harper begs me.

I hold the phone away from my ear for a moment as her high-pitched whining starts to hurt my ear. Lucky for Ashley, she had a prior engagement with a few of her close family, much more peaceful than what Harper's probably got planned, I'd imagine. I would rather be in my pj's, curled up on my sofa, surrounded by a mountain of snacks and wine, watching trashy rom-com's until I fall asleep, but I know I'm not going to win this fight, not if I want my eardrums left intact.

"Okay, okay, I will come, jeez," I sigh heavily.

I am perching on the edge of my bed, with the brand new short red dress hanging on the wardrobe in front of me. I did buy it for tonight's occasion, but right now, I just want to be comfy in these tatty old sweatpants.

"Yay, Girl! Thank you, thank you, thank you...you won't regret this, trust me...you can stay too... by the way...I don't want to see those tatty 'break-up sweatpants 'of yours either...I bet you are wearing them as we speak," she teases.

I look down at my 'break-up sweatpants 'and smile; she does indeed know me all too well.

I am standing at the kitchen counter. Alex and Harper's balcony spreads out opposite me. Their friends are standing with them in a line outside, waiting for the clock to strike midnight. I'm thankful for a moment of peace to myself; it was so crowded with everyone in here a moment ago, stifling even. I'm pretty sure that most of them are Alex's friends. I think that's why Harper begged me to come; she needed a familiar face. The sounds of excitement echo through the windowpanes. My bare feet pad across the kitchen floor tiles as I retrieve my half-drunk bottle of red, bringing it back to my original spot. No lights are on except for the dull glow of the light above the cooker, but it's enough to see my way around the open plan kitchen. I watch the red liquid slosh to the bottom of the glass as I fill it just to the halfway point. I hear someone shout that there is only one minute to go, so I raise my glass.

"Cheers," I say to the nothingness.

I take a large glug of wine. I guess I should join them for the countdown. Turning on my heel, I meet a sheer white grin and arms folded in a confident stance; I gasp and my glass slips from my grip with the force of my fright. My heart leaps so much, that it feels like it hits my ribcage. I stare in shock at the floor, my bare feet surrounded by a red sea of shards. I snap out of my shaken-up state when I feel strong arms scoop me up and carry me out of the danger zone.

"I've been looking for you," Ethan says deeply and smoothly. He sets me down, but the deepness of his voice has captivated me; I gaze at the lips that just seeped out those suave words. Taking my chances, I hastily kiss him, but it lands on the corner of his mouth; his expression is unreadable. Oh, shit, did I just misread him? I turn away to conceal the embarrassment. Chanting and shouting echoes from everyone outside as my neck is grasped and before I know it, I am whirled round to face Ethan; his towering over me is a little intimidating. His lips hover over mine and the emerald burns brightly in his eyes.

"Don't you know what time it is?" He says in deep hushed tones.

The rush of his breath hits my lips as he speaks. His grasp on the back of my neck is firm but not hurting me; it's kind of hot, actually. Cocking his head to one side, he watches me intently; his eyes explore each of my features and assets. Maybe he's waiting for me to crumble into a begging mess, just like how I felt in my dreams. At that moment, I feel the excitement rush from my stomach down to my sex. I hear the chant of the countdown in the background, but it sounds distorted as the rush of blood thrums against my eardrums. My body aches to know if he's just as rough and ready as my dreams, so much, so the thought leaves me breathless. My demeanour switches when his eyes lock with mine from wondering to pure hunger, hunger for something rock hard that is purposely grinding against me. My hand mirrors his grasp, digging my fingernails into his neck, forcing him to hiss the pain through gritted teeth, fuelling his need for me too.

"3...2...1...happy new year!" everyone bellows except for us.

Way before the sound of '1', my mouth is on Ethan's. We steal each other's breath in between each kiss; the coarseness of his stubble on my chin sends my skin singing with the rawness. I feel all the frustration rising to the surface, especially after him unknowingly leaving me high and dry in my last dream. I pull him closer to me, digging my fingernails in further, I hear him grunt the pain, but he doesn't break the kiss; if anything, it makes him kiss me harder. He willingly follows me as I walk backwards. A hardness clamps down on my bottom lip as we blindly hit a wall; it stings across my shoulder blades, but the lust fuelled adrenaline overtakes the need to hiss the pain. Ethan yanks his hand free from my neck, grabs hold of my hips, and spins me round to face the wall. Bringing my hands up, he pins them against the wall. Goosebumps prick up across my skin as his hands trail down my arms to the hem of my dress. His hands disappear underneath it, grazing down each side of my panties, skillfully slipping one under the fabric right on the button. The other hand comes up to sweep my hair to one side as I feel his mouth hot and heavy against my skin. The stubble on his chin is harsh against my neck.

"Oh fuck."

I cry out as he nips and bites meet my skin. I press my back against his torso as he holds me close by my sex. My hands snap away from the wall, one of them overlaps his, and the other cups his cheek as his head hovers right over my shoulder. He holds me in that teasing position, watching me untwist and pulse beneath his touch.

I slam my hands against the wall as his fingers start to work me in such a way that my entire body grinds in the mounting excitement. He edges me closer to the wall just as we hear the sliding door to the balcony creak open and the rush of booming voices.

"Ssshh."

He presses a finger against my lips but still works me. The fear of being caught seems to thrill me rather than scare me. So much so I shatter against his fingertips. I suppress the need to cry out at the top of my voice. I push my back against him sharply, and he frees me just as we hear footsteps coming in from the balcony. He rests his palms on the wall for a moment. He looks over his arm at me as I duck out of his way.

"Catch me if you can."

I don't give him a chance to say anything; I turn on my heel, fly out of the living room and down the hallway. I take the steps two at a time as the excitement pounds in my chest. I almost close the guest room door, but barely leave it ajar instead. Quickly, I slip off my dress, but my lingerie remains. I turn on the bedside lamp just before I peer around the door's gap, and I see Ethan open the first door, looking inside, then closing it again. I wait for him to open the second one before I open my door fully. I lean on the doorframe with one outstretched arm and the other on my hip. He closes the second, and I finally catch his eye.

"Looking for something?"

I watch as he saunters towards me, casually stripping off his t-shirt and flinging it to one side. Oh my, I search him up and down. Now I can see the full extent of his snake ink as he comes closer to the glow of the light. He's ripped beyond compare. I turn and rest my back on the doorframe's edge as he steps up to the threshold. He towers over me without touching me, holds onto the frame above our heads with both hands and leans right in. I peer up through my lashes at him; I meet dark eyes hooded by the dim light. He cocks his head slightly, and his lips brush with mine, but he doesn't kiss me. Instead, he looks down at my breasts, watching the anticipation rise and fall in them.

"Have you found what you are looking for?"

My voice is breathy and quiet against his lips. He smirks but doesn't answer my question. He drags his lips across mine; his bottom lip pulls at my top lip, then he cocks his head the other way and teases me again. My throat catches my breath at this briefest touch. He watches my lips quiver with the torment of his toying; I am one more tease away from going crazy. I let the frustration tear through my features as he continues to smirk at me. He drags at my top lip part way, then his tongue swoops in to resume the drag. I try to kiss him, but he pulls away, and my head falls slightly forward. I look up as he gives me a flash of his eyebrows. Okay, enough is enough; I cup his cheeks and hastily pull him against me until our lips meet. I push him with all my might against the frame edge behind him. I hear him grunt the pain, but he doesn't shove me away. His hands let go of the frame; they come down as one cups the back of my head, and the other pins me to him by the shoulder blades. He parts my lips with his, swiftly followed by his tongue, brushing and teasing me again. He grabs a fistful of my hair and tugs my head to the side as his mouth finds my neck. I grasp his upper arms as nips and kisses trail down my neck and shoulder. I gasp and hold on tighter as my body leans back in response. He swiftly pinches my bra strap-free, but my chest keeps it pinned against him.

As I bring my head up again, I meet his gaze, and the emerald glow seems to blaze brighter. I smirk as I slip my arms out from my straps, but I don't throw it away, and now I see the frustration swim through his eyes. Ha, two can play that teasing game. I willingly follow as he steps forward, twisting our bodies and backing me into the room. He kicks the door shut. His fingers graze all the way down my back until he finds my hips. Ethan's hands grasp them, using them to spin me around and pin me against his torso. My hands cling to my bra covered breasts until his hands peel them both away. The curtains are still open as I look up, and the full moon beams right into the room.

"Oh fuck."

He growls against my ear when he feels the softness of my breasts as he cups and squeezes them. Keeping me cupped, he manoeuvres towards the bed, and my feet willingly follow. As soon as my knees hit the frame, he pushes me down, and I let out an excited giggle as I fall. I look over my shoulder as I hear a zip. Sure enough, he retrieves a foil packet from his pocket before letting his jeans fall. I can't see him sliding on the rubber, but I hear the familiar foil tear and latex snap. I part my legs as I feel him climb onto the bed, his knees between mine. His hands deeply caress my shoulders as if he's massaging them, but they don't stay. His fingertips graze down my back, deep enough to leave red trails. The grazing fingers swiftly slip off my panties as I raise my lower-legs up. Soon as my legs drop, I gasp as he grabs and pulls my behind up and slams himself into me.

"OH FU-UCK."

He stills as I feel his entire length buried in my sex. I feel his body come down over me, his hands on the bed on either side of me. One of his hands slides up underneath me; it settles between my breasts; scooping me up, he holds me tightly against his torso. As I steady myself on the bed, his scooping hand lets go. My head falls between my shoulders as he starts to thrust into me gently but deeply. A breathy moan escapes from my chest, and I close my eyes, relishing the molten hot desire that has engulfed my entire body. With a scoop, twist and a pull, he has a lock on my hair. He keeps winding it around his fist until my hair is as taut as a rope, and my back bows with the tug. All he needs now is an arrow to fire. As my head tips back, I meet carnal eyes in my side view that seem more grey than green, and lacking in lustre. They are dark, focused, full of intent and one intent only.

The lock on my hair releases; before my head can fall, it is grasped and pinned up just under my chin. I am held by the snake tattooed arm, and I have visions of it coming alive, coiling around my neck and constricting me in the same way as his hand. A moan gurgles around in my throat, trying to break free as he nails me harder, deeper but unrushed, allowing me to feel every inch claiming me. His breath pants hot and heavy against my jaw, and his stubble scrapes at my skin.

His hold abruptly releases me, grabbing my hips instead as he continues to pound into me. A dizzying euphoria rips through my body as my lungs gasp for air. It makes my head feel weightless, yet it falls against the bed with some impact. Holy shit, that was something else. My focus snaps back to Ethan as he buries his fingernails into the fleshiness of my hips, keeping my behind pinned to him. I grasp handfuls of bed-sheet and bury my face as his hammering picks up the pace. My breathy moans are clammy against the sheets. I hear his pants shift to groans; I feel him stiffen through his grip.

"Fu-uck... Charly."

He growls through gritted teeth. He thrusts once, twice, three times before he releases me and his climax. He collapses by my side, drawing me in as he rolls onto his side; Ethan has me in a grappling hold like he doesn't want to let go or want the euphoria to end.

Twenty-Six

The blackout curtains in Harper's guest bedroom certainly do their job. If it weren't for the slight gap where they came together, I could have easily mistaken it to be still nighttime. As I and my senses wake up, my shoulder blades and hips twinge painfully, forcing me to grimace. My bottom lip feels tender and swollen. I let my body stiffly roll over to see if Ethan is awake. As my eyes focus, I find that his side of the bed is empty, and my heart sinks. I carefully climb out of bed to find my backpack with my overnight things inside. Luckily, I packed a pair of flat pumps, jeans and a sweater; I change into them as quickly as possible. I yelp as I sling my backpack over my shoulder; it hits bang on the soreness. Carefully, I keep one strap over my shoulder, then grab my phone and head downstairs.

The place is deafly quiet. I walk into the living room, searching up and down. No one is out on the balcony either, hmm. The front door makes me jump as someone bangs their way through it. As I walk out into the hallway, Alex is hobbling on one foot and the other is bandaged up.

"What the hell happened to you?"

Harper comes bundling in behind Alex with a face like thunder.

"Someone left broken glass on the kitchen floor... he sliced his foot open... I'm surprised you didn't hear the commotion... we've been in A&E for hours."

Just when I am about to make a confession, I look at Harper's face again and think twice about it.

"I was going to head home, but do you want me to stay a little longer and help out?"

Harper shakes her head and points with just her thumb towards Alex.

"I think he's milking the sympathy... the doc said it looks worse than it is... but there is something you can do for us on your way home."

She walks over to the kitchen counter and retrieves something silver.

"We found this in the hallway... pretty sure it's Ethan's... he doesn't live far from you... can you drop it back to him?"

I gulp hard as she drops a shiny, expensive-looking watch in my hand. Before I can agree or disagree, she rips a piece of paper off a notepad and scribbles on it.

"Here's his address... it's not far from Green Grove Park."

I look down at the piece of paper and take in the address, pretty sure I've seen those apartments, quite plush from what I can remember.

**

I look up at Grove Place Apartments, and my heart beats ten to the dozen with the nerves. He took off for a reason this morning, and I'm not sure if I'm ready to know as to why. A smart looking woman hurries out of the entrance, and I manage to dive into the doorway before it slams shut. Three lifts are immediately in front of me.

I take the lift to the fifth floor. As I step out and look left to right, I notice a floor to the ceiling glass window, intrigued to see what view lies beyond it. It's a little disorientating as I peer out. It overlooks the whole of Green Grove Park, but as the trees are so tall, you can't see anything inside, not even the white Victorian bandstand. It's a breathtaking view nonetheless. I grab the piece of notepaper out of my pocket to refresh my memory of the apartment number. I stand in front of apartment number '23', and my heart continues to panic. I take in one deep, shaky breath and let it out slowly. I press on the doorbell before I can think twice. My eyes still fixed on the piece of paper even though I hear footsteps. As the door opens, my eyes are drawn to a pair of bare feet. Unless Ethan enjoys painting his toes red, I'm pretty sure that these aren't his feet.

"Who is it, Babe?"

I hear the familiar deepness of his voice, and I look up. I come face to face with a beautiful brunette, slim-framed woman with flawless skin, pouty lips and dressed in a skimpy negligee. I see Ethan's face over her shoulder, fresh from the shower, but looking like he's seen a ghost. The woman stands up straighter and folds her arms, waiting for more clarity on 'who, what, when, why.' Silver on her finger catches my eye and a diamond glints at me. Oh shit, I swallow my feelings hard; so hard, it feels like they fall right through my body.

"Ethan, umm... left this... left this on my nightstand...."

I feel awful as soon as it leaves my lips and I watch her face fall when I hand her the watch. Shock soon turns to anger as I watch it come down like a shutter over her features. My inner spirit hides behind the grey matter, waiting to feel the force of her hand or her words. She grabs hold of the door and slams it in my face. I feel the air shift as it slams, like the air being punched back into my lungs. As soon as I hear the slam, I suddenly feel like I can breathe again. Raised voices bellow at each other inside, loud enough without having to press my ear against the door.

"Babe... she meant nothing to me... just some slapper who threw herself at me... please, Babe, you've got to believe me... I just needed to vent my anger after our fight yesterday... that's all she was... a huge fucking mistake...."

I have no idea why I am still standing here listening to this while my battered ego lays at my feet. My inner spirit soothes me 'just move on, Charly... just move the fuck on'.

Seven months later...

Twenty-Seven

I stir as blissful vibes engulf my body, passion flooding through my veins. I hug my duvet with a smile stretched from ear to ear, my eyes still sealed shut as I relish the warm fuzzy glow feeling of devotion. I am in love with Jack Whitehall; at that moment, my eyes snap open. Seriously? Jack Whitehall? Realisation and disappointment set in when I finally take in my surroundings. I am not in my room or Jack's (unfortunately), but I have woken up here many times before, far too many times in fact. As I recollect my dream with Jack, visions of last night's drinking session come tumbling into my head, ending with the usual fling, who just so happens to be sound asleep next to me.

I slip out from under his sheets as stealthily as I can, being careful not to wake him. He stirs slightly as my weight shifts off the bed, forcing my heart to leap and my breath to catch in my throat. Relief calms the panic of my racing heart as it's not enough to wake him. I tiptoe across his bedroom floor, scooping up my abandoned clothes as I go. I close the door, to a one inch gap, behind me. My handbag is slumped on the floor just outside the bathroom. Coins and keys still jingle and clang together, even though I pick them up slowly. I pause in mid bend as I hear a body shift between the sheets; when no sound of footsteps come, I straighten up and head into the bathroom to freshen up. Rummaging through my bag, I find my phone. A new message from Harper reminds me I have a coffee date with her and Ashley this morning at eleven. Checking the time, I have half an hour to get myself down there. I quickly freshen up and throw on yesterday's clothes. I do my best to comb my hair with just my fingers and reapply last night's lip colour. I mentally grimace at the reflection staring back at me as late nights and drinking are starting to darken my eyes.

I open the bathroom door just a fraction to see if the coast is clear.

I carry on, tiptoeing down the stairs, finding my stranded heels on separate steps and remembering previous experience to wait until I am standing on the doorstep outside before I slip them back on. The first time I was here ended in a somewhat awkward breakfast when the noise of my clip-clopping heels on hard floors had woken him up. As I start to make my way down the road towards town, I fish out my iPod and press the earbuds in. Just as I make my way across City Bridge, the voice of Otis Redding starts to soothe me. I pause midway across the bridge and take in the view as 'Sittin' On The Dock Of The Bay' sets the thoughts in motion. I pick at my worn nail varnish as I lean on the edge. This side of the river overlooks grand all-glass-windowed office buildings that look like they touch the clouds. You don't get a good view of the sunset on this side, but I can't bring myself to stand on the other side.

The last six months have been far from easy. I have numbed the pain by falling in and out of a particular guy's bed and drinking way too much alcohol. Truth be told, I don't even recognise myself anymore. When Harper and Ashley picked me up from my hallway floor back then, I left ME on that floor, and I think she's still there somewhere; I just haven't found her again since. The track changes to 'Best Fake Smile' by James Bay. Hmm, how appropriate, I can't help but grin as I listen to the lyrics. July's heat is starting to rise and I look up to feel the rays on my face until the song comes to an end.

I look down, checking the time on my iPod. I have six minutes left until eleven, so I carry on strolling across the bridge as 'Shoop' by Salt-n-Pepa starts to play; my feet naturally pound the pavement in time to its catchy beat. My heels seem to be a staple of my wears these days; something about them makes me feel good, like I can conquer anything the world throws at me. Most things anyway.

As I approach the café, I hear some familiar voices shouting in my direction. All I can see at first amongst the busy heads is bobbing foreheads and waving hands. As I draw closer and the crowd thins out, I can see Harper and Ashley waiting outside the café for me.

"Whoah... sexy lady! ...look at you strut in your heels... scan-da-lous!"

I feel my cheeks blaze as their hooting turns some heads of passerby. I bashfully gesture for them to 'stop it.'

"So good to see you, gorgeous ladies!"

We hug as a threesome, just before heading inside for much-needed coffee and gossip. We manage to catch our usual seats by the window, armed with coffees and muffins, oh, and an extra pastry for me to compensate for no breakfast. As I place my tray down on the table, Ashley gawks at the number of calories lying on my plate.

"Charly, you're so lucky to keep your figure with the food you eat," Ashley digs.

Looking at her plate, even she's got a triple chocolate muffin sitting in front of her; with her jealous tone, you'd think she's about to tuck into a lettuce leaf. In the politest way, I ignore her remark. Harper shortly follows us carrying her skinny latte and skinny blueberry muffin; she's counting every single calorie and the days until her wedding at the moment. Harper eyes me closely as she sits down; she leans over and smooths down my hair at the back of my head. Ahh, my fingers must have done a useless job at combing.

"Somebody didn't sleep in their own bed last night then," Harper broadcasts.

I lower my head as if everyone around me knows me. After a glance, luckily, everyone surrounding me are strangers, but I still don't want them to know my business. I awkwardly try to straighten my shabby yesterday's look.

"Went out for a few drinks with work people... and then... I fell in and out of a certain someone's bed."

They both slump back in their chairs and groan as I shrug like the outcome of last night was inevitable.

"Not you and Ben again?" Ashley sighs.

I straighten myself up in my chair, retaining the ounce of dignity I have left intact. I take a bite out of my pastry while I wait for Harper's remark to slap me in the face.

"Since you got that promotion, all you seem to do is fuck that guy... Girl, he's not good for you... he's just using you... you've got to bin that guy."

Harper doesn't tell me anything I don't know already. I know he isn't someone I'd want to settle down with. It probably doesn't sound very good, but he's just there to itch a scratch if you know what I mean.

"We want to see you happy and settled, Charly... at this rate, you'll be our very own Bridget Jones," Ashley chuckles.

I gasp and pretend to look horrified as I clutch my chest over my heart, before I break into laughter.

"Hey... less of the big knicker talk, you... I'm not there just yet," I joke.

We all laugh together until the moment passes over us. Harper has a sudden outburst of excitement, like a lightbulb moment going on in her head.

"Oh... Oh... guess who I bumped into the other day... remember Joe?"

She winks at me, but I am too stunned to react. Of course, I remember Joe; he was my first boyfriend, but I didn't exactly treat him well. Just when you thought you locked away the memory in the deepest depths of your memory bank, Harper comes along with the key. Now she's unlocked it and the memories come flooding back.

"Oh yes... the boy you made me go out with at school... you forced us to hold hands in the playground... then ran off giggling."

I cringe at the vivid memory like it happened yesterday. As Harper looks at both me and Ashley, she just shrugs.

"He was my boyfriend's best friend at the time... it just made sense."

Harper automatically defends her actions with pretty much the same reasoning as she did back then.

"It only lasted for like a couple of weeks... anyway, he probably hates me... I wasn't exactly nice to him, was I?"

She bats away my comment with her hand and then with half a wolf whistle, she shakes her head while pretending to fan herself.

"Trust me, Charly... you wouldn't say no to him now... oh boy... or oh man, I should say now... he is hot... and I mean HOT."

Ashley bounces slightly in her chair like she too has a lightbulb moment.

"Oh... but didn't you say... he's got a girlfriend, though?"

Harper shrugs her off and turns her attention back to me. She rests her hand on top of mine, with her serious face on display.

"As we said... we just want you to be happy, Charly," Harper says.

She squeezes my hand gently as unbearable pity, instead of the humour, hangs in the air. Well, it's easy for them to say; they both have found themselves good men.

"We'll find you somebody... don't you worry about that... look at you, you're bloody gorgeous... any guy would be a dumb arse fuck not to snap you up," she continues.

I laugh as the old Harper steps back into the room. She lets go of my hand and continues to drink her coffee.

"Or... why don't you give online dating another go?" Ashley adds.

I grimace and shake my head at the thought of having to sift through another lineup of potential James Bond wannabes.

"I've heard through work... that there are apps... where you can swipe left and right on who you like or don't like... it's as easy as that," Harper suggests.

If only it were 'as easy as that.' I smile as I take note of Harper's suggestion.

"I'll definitely look into that...."

***

Joe and his curtain styled brown hair showcases in my mind's eye as my inner spirit flicks through the memory bank like she too is reminiscing. He was a little on the chubby side but still good looking. I'm lying on my stomach, on my bed, flicking through an old diary that I found in the loft. The little book of memories is mainly the shenanigans of Me, Ashley, and Harper. Until I come across the summer of 2002 and the day Harper placed Joe's hand in mine.

'I looked at his hand like what the hell do I do with this? Then I looked up at Joe, and he looked just as confused. I'm glad I'm not the only one....'

I smile as I remember that day so vividly. I'll never forget the stunned look on Joe's face; my expression mirrored his. It was the first time I ever had laid eyes on him, let alone spoke to him and there we were holding hands. Even though he mirrored my expression, he still didn't let me go. Maybe he feared Harper's wrath if he did.

'Joe wants me to go hang out at the park after school tomorrow... I'm bricking it! Like what the hell am I supposed to do with him?'

'He pushed me on the swings, then we went and sat on the park fence and chatted for ages... He hugged me; it felt nice.'

That was the very first time I had properly spent time with him— just the two of us. I can't for the life of me remember what we had talked about. I remember him smiling a lot, though, so we must have had mutual interests.

'He's nice. He brought me a rose from his mum's garden... it's white and pretty!'

'He tried to kiss me! I didn't know what to do! I was scared, so I ran away....'

'He keeps texting me, but I don't know what to do. I don't know if I fancy him.'

A pang of guilt hits me the more I read. Joe was such a kind boy, and the fourteen-year-old me treated him like shit. I can't bring myself to read the excerpt of when I dumped him. I was a coward and did it by text. I think I was too young to understand what a boyfriend or relationship was.

I wonder what he looks like now. Would I still recognise him if I saw him in the street? Harper reckons he'd be my cup of tea these days. Even so, I doubt he'd have time for me after everything that I had put him through.

Twenty-Eight

The silver embossed fancy lettering 'Plus One' on the crisp white card of Harper's and Alex's wedding invite stares back at me every time I go to my fridge and it's forever pinned on the grey matter. A constant reminder that I need to sort myself out. I took Harper's suggestion of dating apps and pretty much spent the whole of yesterday swiping left and right, so much, so I think my thumb has seized up. Yes, I have started to clutter my phone; it was inevitable to keep up to date with everyone.

I sit at my workstation as I feel someone's gaze on me. My first thought is that it's my boss, Stanley, as he's been breathing down my neck all morning for dragging my heels. I blame Monday. My head is still at the weekend. Before I know it, the unknowing gets too much; I have to look, even if it means another confrontation. I let my gaze drift to the person who the stare belongs to and it falls upon Ben; my inner spirit does the groaning for me. He's waiting for a pile of papers to go through the printer; he gives me a wide accomplished grin, then pouts along with a wink as he starts scooping up the printed stack. As I look away, I try to stifle my laughter, but it comes out in one long embarrassing, snorting sound. Judging by the heat of my cheeks, I bet they've gone the deepest shade of pink, probably giving Ben totally the wrong idea.

Kelly's head snaps up in the workstation next to mine, her eyes searching out the commotion. I meet her glazed stare while pointing with just my thumb in Ben's direction.

"Ben... being a dickhead."

She gives me an 'oh I see 'double nod; the glaze doesn't shift from her eyes. I can tell she's in 'work mode'.

"Do you fancy a coffee?" I ask.

She looks at me, but clearly, her mind is still stuck on whatever she's working on. I point to my own empty mug with raised eyebrows while waiting for her to compute the question.

"Oh... oh... yes please... coffee please."

Oh man, she's hard work sometimes, silently sighing as she hands me her mug. I rise from my chair and turn, focusing on the staff kitchen as I head towards it. I really don't want Ben to follow me.

Luckily, we have one of those hot water dispensers, so no hanging around for a kettle to boil; in and out, in no time. Two pours and stirs later, my mission is complete. My body whips around to put the milk back in the fridge, almost colliding with Ben. I leap out of my skin, followed by a weird shriek noise. The milk slips out of my clutches; it bounces and then explodes as it collides with the floor. I jumped back as soon as it slipped and narrowly missed the spray. Ben was not so lucky; as I look down, I notice a fountain mark of splashes up the front of his trousers. I hold my chest as my heart beats frantically against my ribs.

"You shouldn't sneak up on people like that," I snap.

I look down at the floor to survey the mess; on the plus side, at least it was a plastic bottle. I quickly fetch a bundle of paper towels before anyone slips. On my hands and knees, I start clearing up the soggy mess. Ben joins me on his hands and knees with another pile of paper towels.

"I was hoping to talk to you on Saturday morning... but you had already snuck out..." he says under his breath.

I meet his eyes, trying my best not to look horrified at the following sentence about to leave his lips. I watch as he adjusts his glasses and pushes back his crop of hair. His Adam's apple bounces as he gulps hard, and then he lets out a shaky breath.

"I... I really like you, Charly."

He breaks eye contact and looks at the floor instead; the nerves consume each and every one of his facial features. He takes in another deep, shaky breath.

"Can I ah... take you out sometime... on a proper date, I mean... just the two of us... no work outing?" "...and sober of course," Ben adds.

Somehow, he's morphed back into his old coy self. I feel like we've been transported back to December when he was too shy to look at me, after I pushed him into the 'friend zone'. He's not a bad fuck, but I think the alcohol played a huge part in the euphoria. As Harper said, 'you have got to bin that guy'. I rest back on my heels, removing myself from the kissing danger zone.

"Ben... I am flattered... I really am... you're a lovely guy... sorry, but... I just ah... I just don't see us in that way."

I have never seen such a wounded look before, like I have just shot his heart into a thousand-and-one pieces. If I had known how he truly felt, I wouldn't have let it go any further than a few friendly drinks on a work outing. Jeez, I feel absolutely awful as I watch him from under my lashes as we clear up the last of the milk. He scoops up the pile of soggy towels as he gets to his feet, and chucks them in the bin on his way out, dragging his wounded ego out with him.

Blimey, one minute I am making coffee, and the next I'm breaking hearts. Oh shit, yes, coffee, I forgot about that. I pick up Kelly's mug; luckily, I can still feel the heat coming through the ceramic. I take it over to her desk.

"Sorry... I had a bit of a milk accident... I need to run out and get some more... I won't be long."

I might as well be talking to a brick wall as she nods vacantly. I assume she heard me. Keeping my head down, I quickly grab my purse and bolt through the double doors. I ignore the lifts, flying down the flights of stairs instead. My lungs are in urgent need of fresh air. As my feet hit the foyer floor, I dash as best as I can in chunky heels on the tiled floor, passing the security guard.

"Everything okay, Miss?" he calls.

I don't stop to speak; for some reason, I feel the need to hold up my purse, just glancing over my shoulder.

"Milk emergency!"

I burst out of the doors, almost tripping over my heels. The fresh warm air filters through me, giving my lungs much-needed relief. My back rests against the same pillar that I smacked into when I thought Harper was a mugger. I laugh at the memory now, but I was shit scared at the time. I hold my side as the pain of a stitch kicks in. I feel so unfit; I need to exercise more often. I look up to the sky, taking in full lungs of breath as I let the stitch subside. Instead of the stitch, guilt now weighs down heavily on my shoulders. Why only now? Men are so bloody complicated. My brain hurts trying to decipher where I went wrong; how could I have missed it? I gently massage my wrinkled forehead for a moment. Then I look back to the sky, hoping it will hold all the answers. Something about the rotation of white clouds on the blue canvas is soothing; it helps my inner spirit organise my life. A car horn shatters my tranquil state of mind. It prompts me to carry on with my milk mission.

Back in the office, I head straight for the staff kitchen to put the milk in the fridge. I pause as I hear Ben's voice inside.

"... yeah, I totally blew her out."

I didn't have to catch the whole conversation to know that he was talking about me. I felt like I wasted time feeling sorry for him, even if it was only ten minutes—what a lying bastard.

***

It is just me, a large glass of red, a notepad, pen and this dating app, sitting cross-legged on my sofa. My 'plus one' search has finally narrowed down to three. Date number one is Mark, thirty-eight years old, five foot eleven, black hair, brown eyes and clean-shaven. Date number two is Ollie, thirty-two years old, five foot nine, blonde hair, blue eyes and clean-shaven. Date number three is Liam, thirty-one years old, six foot three, brown hair, green eyes and a little stubble. As I list them out loud, I feel like a dating game show host. 'Contestant number one, come on down'. I can't help but giggle at my appalling attempt. I write down each name on my notepad. I have never had three different dates in the space of one week before. With Harper's wedding just around the corner, I need to try my best not to go empty-handed.

Twenty-Nine

Mark reserved a table at the pizzeria in town tonight at seven. He was a gentleman to let me choose where to eat, and I love pizza. I root through my wardrobe for something to wear, picking out a pair of dark wash skinny jeans and team it with a blush pink blouse with a white camisole underneath. I let my hair down in a relaxed style. I slip my feet into a flat pair of pumps that are virtually the same colour as my blouse. One last look in the mirror; okay, I am good to go.

***

I arrive at the restaurant a little after seven, in the hope that he'd already be there. As I check myself in, I get told one of my first date fears.

"You're the first to arrive."

Why me? I mentally grimace as the waiter shows me to the table anyway. He takes my order for a glass of wine and scuttles away.

Ten minutes go by, and there's still no sign of Mark. As the minutes carry on ticking by, my seated position goes from polite young lady to a fed-up slouch. Every so often, the waiter comes over to ask if I'm okay and would I like anything to eat, and each time he gets the same answer 'no, thank you, I'm fine'. The other diners are starting to notice, throwing pity glances in my direction. Ah, I really can't bear this anymore; this is torture. When the long hand on my watch reaches half past, that's it, I have had enough. I gulp down the last of my wine and leave a more than a generous tip. I wait for him to come back to collect my payment and as he makes his way towards me, he's grinning profusely.

"This way, sir."

A guy follows on behind him. When I can see him fully, my heart sinks; it's not him. I stand to gather my things and throw my handbag on over my head.

"Charly?"

I freeze when I hear my name. I look up to meet the guy who the waiter just brought in; he's standing at my table. Huh? I take a moment to process the face in front of me. His smile is virtually the same as his profile picture, but he looks more like sixty-something, not thirty-something. He has salt and pepper hair, not jet black. Oh, and crow's feet wrinkles; they were definitely not in his picture. I try to hold back the shock while the realisation settles.

"Hi... I just ah... I just need to go to the ladies' room."

A cringing notion ricochets through my body, and it was the only thing my inner spirit could pluck from thin air. Without another word, I quickly turn on my heel, my eyes frantically searching for the familiar sign, the panic starting to rise in my chest. A passing waitress points me in what I assume is the right direction. I don't have to ask; she must have recognised the look in my eyes. I follow where her finger is pointing. The 'ladies' room' sign is right at the end of a tucked-away corridor, but that's not what I need. I need a moment to think, out of sight. I need an escape plan. Resting my back against the wall, head in my hands, c'mon c'mon think, I'm mentally pleading to my inner spirit for a way out.

"Are you okay there, madam?"

A gentle voice and touch on my shoulder encourage me to pick my head up; I find the waitress who had just helped me.

"I'm in a huge dilemma... and I don't know what to do... my date has lied about his age... and I just can't... I just can't stay like nothing is the matter."

I try my hardest to keep my voice as low as a hum as I wrestle with the panic. Her touch leaves me as she heads over to the door to the kitchen and opens it slightly.

"Follow me."

She beckons with her hand for me to come forward; I do as she asks. We walk right through the bustling kitchen, weaving in out of animated swearing chefs, their arms flying around in frustration and steam. When we manage to get to the other side in one piece, I notice a door to the outside propped open. This woman is an angel; I could kiss her.

"Turn right out of this door... walk all the way to the end... then you'll be back on the main road...and don't worry... I'll make an excuse for you."

We exchange smiles, mine is full of immense appreciation, and hers is full of understanding. It makes me wonder if she's done this before. Relief kicks into overdrive as I pull her to me, hugging her fiercely as I overdo it on the thank you's.

Thank goodness I decided to wear my flat pumps tonight; I must have known deep down. As soon as my feet step out onto the path, I run, following the waitress's directions to the main road, but I don't stop, my feet keep pounding against the pavement until the restaurant is nothing but a dot in my vision. I slow to a walk as guilt starts to creep in. Maybe I should have stayed just to be courteous, but I don't think I could have sat there and ignored the fact that he lied to me. I just don't get it; why lie? Did he not think I'd notice?

As I head closer to home, my local chip shop is open. I can smell their freshly cooked food wafting down the street. Ah... smells so good, my stomach starts to grumble.

***

I am so looking forward to this, gazing at the neatly wrapped lusciousness sitting on my kitchen table. I fill and place a generous glass of wine next to it, as always, meal for one. My fingertips gingerly tear open the piping hot paper bag; the salt and vinegar strongly hit my senses. I gulp down some wine as I drop Harper a text, hinting at an improbable successful date. I demolish a few mouthfuls of chips by the time my phone starts to ring.

"Fuck... girl, what the hell happened?"

She never ceases to amuse me; thank fuck for friends like her at times like these.

"Oh, Harper... it was a bloody nightmare... I went thinking I was getting a young Pierce Brosnan or someone similar... but I ended up with... oh god... I don't know... I can't think of anyone with salt and pepper hair... he must have been at least forty years older than me... or so he seemed anyway... anyway, I feel bloody awful... as I just legged it out of there... without saying anything to him."

Her laugh rumbles down the phone and I let her have a moment at my expense. As I hold the phone away from my ear, I can still hear her. I scoff a few chips while I wait for her to compose.

"There I was, thinking you were a polite young lady on a date... girl... you badass! ... So, what are you up to now?"

I wash down my mouthful with more wine before I answer.

"Stuffing my face with chip shop chips... and washing it all down with a LARGE glass of wine... then maybe watch some trashy telly."

I hear her almost salivating down the phone when I mention chips.

"Nice... bon appétit and all that...catch you later... love you!"

Thirty

I am dressed in my recycled outfit from the other night, heading for The Garden Bar; fingers crossed, I have not just jinxed myself. I am hoping and praying that this time will be more worth my while. Tonight, is lucky contestant number two, Ollie from... oh god, I have no idea where he's from; how bad is that? I mentally grimace as I walk the last stretch in my flat pumps; yes, I opted for the safer option again just in case I have to get the hell out of there.

I have a vague idea of what this guy looks like; my inner spirit holds up his portrait. Okay, I'm looking out for a Chris Hemsworth lookalike or thereabouts; oh, wouldn't it be nice if he was actually the real deal.

I push open one of the doors to The Garden Bar; immediately the smell of body odour and perfume is just as offensive as the strobe lighting and thumping bass. Luckily, I have been here before, and I know the bar area is tucked away at the back, through another set of double doors. You can so easily get lost in this place. My ears struggle to adjust to the gentle background music that fills the bar.

Right at the end of the stools, there's only one blonde guy sitting; well, if you can call it sitting, he's hunched over. As I draw closer, I notice he's nursing one of many shots judging by the line of empties in front of him. He struggles to pick up his head like a ball and chain weigh him down; I automatically look down at his feet with the thought, definitely no chains or shackles. I look back at the line of glasses, then to the barman, who looks well and truly miffed as he stands behind the counter aggressively polishing wine glasses and glaring at the drunken wreck of a man in front of him. My stare drifts back to Ollie; he watches me through squinted, glazed eyes. I give him a moment to focus and register who I am.

"Oh... hey... Ch-arly."

He gets up, probably a little too fast and stumbles but somehow manages to grab hold of the counter. He should carry on propping up the bar, I think that's all he's good for right now. I have heard of 'liquid courage', but this is beyond a joke; this is quite literally taking the fucking piss. He staggers towards me, like a toddler learning to walk, but trips yet again. This time, he hits the floor. I can hear him groaning, his cheek squashed against the floor, forcing his mouth into a duck's beak shape. Before I can respond, the barman summons the security guards to assist, probably mistaking his stumble for a lunge. It doesn't take long for two burly men to come and scoop Ollie off the floor. He tries his hardest to wrestle out of their grip, but he's no match for these guys.

"I think you've had enough, sir," one of the men barks.

I stand motionless, too stunned to move as they both hold him up under his arms effortlessly like he's nothing but a sack of feathers. Ollie tries to call back to me as they carry him out, but I can't make sense of his jabbering.

"You look like you could do with a drink...."

When my inner spirit shakes some sense into me, my gaze follows the voice. Another server has appeared behind the bar; he flings a white towel on his shoulder and throws me a sympathetic look.

"Yes, please... a rosé please... might as well make it a large one," I mutter.

He acknowledges my order with a brief nod.

"Thanks... I'm Charly."

Might as well get acquainted. I take the seat where Ollie had been sitting, the barman kindly stacks and clears away the line of empties. I place my bag down on the counter as a long fed-up exhale escapes from me; I feel my chest deflate.

"Nice to meet you, Charly... I'm Simon."

As he steps under one of the spotlights to pour my glass of wine, I realise how attractive he is. I watch the concentration on his face as he focuses on his task in the dimness of the lights. I notice his style, dark brown hair in a short messy rocker style with a side parting and short beard. He's wearing a dark green t-shirt with 'The Garden Bar 'in tall white lettering, his top half covers a sleeve of ink work, but I can't see the detail clear enough in this light.

"Friend of yours?"

He nods towards the direction Ollie was dragged off in, just as he places my drink down on the counter. I suddenly feel embarrassed for someone I'm not even responsible for; it's almost like I need to apologise for his bad manners.

"Erm... no, not really... well, supposed to be our first date actually."

Simon does an inhaled whistle, pouting like he's just heard something painful, and shakes his head as he leans on one arm, like a ready to listen to pose. Yes, it might as well be painful; my luck has crashed and burned after two unsuccessful dates in a row. I'm not even sure if you can call them dates at all.

"Well... lucky escape if you ask me... I overheard the guy trying to flirt with the female staff earlier... a bit of a jerk if you ask me... and crazy for...."

He trails off; I wait for him to finish what he was going to say, but it doesn't come. I just about make out a smile as he looks down at the counter.

"A bit of a jerk?... more like a colossal wanker!" I respond.

He looks up at me as he tries to stifle a laugh, his eyebrows raised, slightly taken aback or didn't expect me to say that kind of thing. I feel my cheeks blaze with the possibility of either. I take a large gulp of wine, trying to mask the embarrassment. As I peer over the rim of my glass, he smiles like he's unfazed. My potty mouth is probably one of many that pass through here. He straightens up for a moment and reaches for something under the bar, his hand returns with a bag of chili peanuts.

"On the house."

He slides them across the counter to me and nods towards my glass before he returns to his listening pose.

"Thanks... Is that your pity basket down there?"

I nod towards where his hand had disappeared to. He laughs at my ludicrous statement as he locks gazes with mine.

"I guess you could call it that... so what do you do for a living?"

I am so glad for the swift change in the subject. Simon looks genuinely interested in getting to know me and seems unperturbed by my quirky personality. Maybe tonight won't be such a waste of time after all.

"I'm a publishing assistant for a shitty publishing house... I have a shitty boss... and I spend all day reading shitty manuscripts... it's not as glamorous as I thought it would be."

I wash away the distaste in my voice with some more wine. My job isn't as bad as I make it out to be; it sounded good in my head.

"You?" I ask.

I roll my eyes as I look away and grimace as soon as the question left my lips. My inner spirit shields her eyes in a mortified fashion, 'it's pretty damn obvious, isn't it?'.

"Well... I'm the manager of this shitty bar... I serve shitty drinks... and deal with shitty people... it's not as glamorous as I thought it would be."

He ignores the absurdity and answers with the same humour; he starts laughing before he even finishes the sentence. I almost spray Simon with wine as I hear his reply in mid-sip. I try to hold back the laugh and the liquid, but I end up making a long snorting noise. It makes my drink go down the wrong way, stinging my throat and eyes, and forcing me into a coughing fit. As the harshness subsides, Simon sets down a glass of water and a pile of napkins in front of me.

"Sorry, I didn't mean to make you choke."

His face and voice are full of apology as he wipes the condensation off his hands with the white towel and flings it back onto his shoulder.

I sip some of the ice-chilled water; it soothes the sting. I can feel tears clinging to the corners of my eyes so I use a napkin to gently dab them away.

"It's okay... I'm fine," I croak.

I clear my throat in a bid to try to sound more like a lady than a toad.

"Good comeback," I add.

I take in a deep breath and clear my throat once and for all. It helps ease the ache in my chest, the hilarity passes.

"You've smudged your makeup a little."

Oh crap, panda eye alert and for some reason, I suddenly have no idea what to do about it. Simon grabs a napkin and lightly dips it in my glass of water, then leans right over the bar.

"Here, let me get it for you... lookup."

I do as he asks, leaning forward and looking up to the ceiling. Even though I was expecting it to be cold, it still takes me by surprise. I look down before he gives me the okay to do so. My eyes on him break his concentration and the glint on his eyebrow catches my attention; it's a bar piercing in the shape of an arrow from a bow.

His brown eyes have me caught in a moment that I can't ignore. They are so mesmerising that I swear they seem more like a honey hue the longer I stare. He rests his arm back on the counter, breaking himself away from me before the temptation is too much. I half-smile as I feel a pang of disappointment pull at my chest.

"Thanks," I murmur.

My voice is breathy from the intense moment. Simon nods and smiles as he draws right back to his original listening pose.

"Charly?"

Simon straightens and steps back, away from the bar at the intrusion. I feel someone's touch on my arm and I turn to see who the hand belongs to; my eyes grow wide. Oh, shit, why me, why now?

One spotlight highlights his face; he's made a considerable effort, with a new cropped hairstyle, a clean shave and the most obvious thing - no glasses. I never realised how blue his eyes were, suddenly prominent even in this dull light, they pop against his deep blue shirt. Judging by his clean-cut appearance, I'm assuming there's a hot date on the cards.

"Ben?... what are you doing here?"

I can't hide the sourness in my voice; my inner spirit hasn't let me forget the overheard lie he let slip at work. Just when I thought he was just briefly saying hello, he takes a pew next to me. 'For fuck sake,' my inner spirit sighs agitatedly. I look at my wine, wishing it were almost empty, not nearly full; at least then, I would have an excuse to leave.

"Stood up! ... And you?"

He looks just as down beaten as me. I feel a slight pang of sympathy as he seems just as dispirited as he did when I turned him down.

"I'm kind of in the same boat, I guess... my date did show up, but... he was ah... he was pissed as a fart... so the security guards chucked him out."

The sympathy look is batted back to me; his big bright eyes are trying their best to draw me in. I take another large glug of wine, a bit too fast, ah that one tasted bitter. It forces my eyes to squint until the feeling passes.

"His loss... my gain," he says, a little optimistic.

I smile half-heartedly, but inside I'm screaming, 'someone get me out of here! 'He shifts his attention to Simon and orders a beer. I notice my barman friend keeping a watchful eye over me, maybe preparing himself for the next brawl or maybe earwigging at our conversation to see who this intruder is. Whichever it is, he snaps his eyes away as soon as I notice, giving Ben his full attention. I'd rather be getting to know Simon than having to sit here and endure Ben's sob story. I sneak in another couple of sips of wine; getting there, I lean back slightly to judge the level, halfway to the finish line and my ticket out of here. As Simon sets down a perfectly poured pint of beer on the counter, our eyes meet. I wish I could tell him telepathically how sorry I am. All I can muster is half a smile in the way of apology and hope he understands, but his expression doesn't give anything away. I think Ben has blown any chances I had. My inner spirit is hissing at Ben like a disgruntled cat flexing her claws, ready to swipe retaliation. I try to let my eyes do the talking as I glare at him, but he doesn't even seem to notice, too caught up in his drama.

The annoyance simmers down as talk turns to work; my inner spirit softens and retracts her talons. I take another big gulp of wine; oh why, oh why, did I order a large glass, but three quarters are gone. The conversation flows from colleague to colleague, from mocking Kelly's karaoke renditions to our boss Stanley. Rumours are starting to circulate that he has a bit on the side, who's much younger than his wife. Apparently, she's just a rather eager client who insists on having private one-to-one meetings twice a week. Why would anyone want to fuck that, let alone go near him? It's beyond me; he's hardly charismatic, and butt ugly... probably wealthy and has a huge cock, but it still makes me queasy just thinking about it.

Oh shit, I've just realised that my barman friend has disappeared. Squinting through the dimness, I search the bar, nope he's definitely gone; how disappointing. Thanks a fucking bunch Ben. I furiously knock back the last dregs of wine. I take one last look at the bar for Simon, but he's still nowhere to be seen. I sigh heavily and give Ben my excuses to leave. He looks at me a little disheartened; maybe he thought bumping into me would end in a pity fuck, sorry kid, not today, not ever, nice try. My bag slips off my shoulder as I get up to leave. A body blurs like a flash of lightning, swooping down to catch it before it hits the floor; that's some skill. For a moment, I hope it's

Simon coming to my rescue; as he stands up and hands me the bag, I realise it's just Ben meeting my gaze on the way up.

"Here..." he murmurs.

He places the strap of my bag right over my head, then untucks my hair from under the material for me; his fingertips brush my neck.

"Thanks," I mutter.

I make the mistake of making eye contact. An aching for something that is so out of reach, that's what I see in his eyes. I don't know why, but I don't care for him in that way. Yes, he's good looking with or without his specs on, but as Harper implied, he's just not good for me, and that lie he let slip pretty much seals the deal. I step backwards as I wave awkwardly.

"See you at work... bye, Ben."

I head straight for the door without waiting for him to respond. I feel like I am walking high, even without my trusty heels.

Thirty-One

Everything hangs on tonight; my luck has got to change somewhere, right? I walk high in my silver heels, taking in the warm summer breeze, the sun only just setting over the city. I have never set foot in the Pearl Lodge; it's a hotel with a swanky wine bar, one that calls for an LBD (little black dress). This little number was hiding at the back of my wardrobe, never worn from the day I bought it. Matched with a black clutch bag and my hair styled in a gentle wave, it's the first in a long time that I've actually felt good, looked good. I see the bold sign in the distance, and my heart starts to thump in my chest.

Okay, I've got this; my inner spirit holds on to the picture of Liam. As I walk into the bar, I survey the scene. Uplights line both sides of the navy walls, jazz music lingers in the background, setting a hefty price tag kind of mood. My eyes scan from left to right as I walk the length of the bar. I look down at my watch; I'm more than ten minutes late. My heart begins to sink in my chest; don't tell me it's going to be a 'no show'. I take one last look, and when my vision doesn't fall on anybody that resembles the picture stapled to my grey matter, I turn heavily on my heel to walk out. A guy standing at the end of the bar halts me in my tracks. He's dressed in a dark grey suit, white shirt with one undone top button, hands in his pockets, assure of himself. Whoah, just whoah, his smile is breath-taking, quite literally, my lungs feel airless. As he draws closer, I feel like I grow smaller; his self-confidence is quite overpowering. His hair is light brown and parts down the side, green eyes that aren't so bright in this light but inviting nonetheless, his look is finished off with stubble, so far so good. I'm glad I have worn heels, but he still somehow manages to tower over me.

"Hello, Charly."

His tone is smooth and charming. He kisses each of my cheeks before I can speak; as he leans in, I catch a spicy note to his cologne. I almost stumble forwards as my nose tries to follow the tantalising scent. 'Keep it together, keep cool'.

"Hi."

I just about manage to keep my voice calm and controlled; yes, I've so got this.

"I reserved a table over there... it's a bit quieter," Liam says.

He gestures over my shoulder, and my eyes follow to where he's pointing; they fall on the corner of the room. Liam boldly takes my hand and leads me straight to a circular table tucked away in the corner, surrounded by burgundy seating, very voluptuous looking. I place my bag on the table first, then take a seat. Not looking where I am going, my thigh lands on his. He's a fast mover; I don't know how he managed to get there unnoticed.

"Oh god... I'm so sorry."

A hot flush races across my cheeks as I shuffle my behind away. Our gazes lock, and his dark green eyes are unfazed as they bathe in his ego.

"It's fine, Gorgeous."

Just when I thought I had got my shit together, I can feel the wall starting to crumble under his intense handsomeness. How does one guy manage to hold so much power over a person? I try to concentrate on my breathing, but it's no use as my chest gets tighter and tighter. I excuse myself and hurry to the bathroom; I need to call Harper. Her phone only rings once, her voice thick with worry.

"Girl... what's up? Aren't you on your hot date?"

I place my bag on the sink; my fingers start to fumble with the fabric on the front of my dress as if it has a line of buttons to undo, and then I find myself easing the frustration with big deep breaths instead. I lean on the unit as my reflection stares back at me from the mirrored wall.

"Oh yeah... he's hot, alright... like Chris Evans kind of hot... I'm not kidding, Harper... it's so overpowering... I can feel the anxiety trying to step in and ruin it all."

She half-wolf whistles down the phone at me. Now she knows exactly what level of hotness I'm dealing with here.

"Whoah... Mr Evans, kind of hot, ay? ...Then why the fuck are you hiding away talking to me... and not out there blowing this guy's socks off... or blowing something else entirely...."

I hear a squelching noise, and I'm pretty sure she's using her cheek to mimic a lewd act. I should be cringing, but a laugh barges out of me as I envisage her doing it.

"... now walk back out there... strut like you've never strut before... with more sass than Beyoncé... Girl, you've so got this... now go get him."

I look down at the gap between me and the basin while Harper's pep talk sinks in. The silver embellishment on my heels glint in the restroom light; I smile as my body starts to fill with confidence that overrules the anxiety.

"Thanks, Harper."

I hang up before my newfound confidence fizzles out and bring my head back up to my reflection. As she said, I've so got this. The grin that stares back is one that's full of self-righteousness and borderline impishness; using my fingers to comb my hair, I push it upwards against the growth for a little volume and then touch up my fading lipstick. I roll my lips together to even out the colour, and straighten my dress. I take one last look; yes, I am good to go.

I take one long deep satisfying breath; on the exhale, I straighten up, chest out (not literally, of course), as fearlessness sweeps through my body, giving me the willpower to 'go get him'. I walk tall as I exit the restroom; I feel like I glide across the room, making sure I emphasise my strut with my curves as I go. Liam still sits in his casual manner, but I notice a slight shift in his body as I near him; I may have grabbed his attention. A few heads turn from neighbouring tables; it fuels the ego, when I already feel like I am touching the ceiling, but now I feel sky high.

Placing my bag back on the table, I sit with my knees overlapped and angle myself towards him, teasingly hiding my bare thigh from his clear view while he intently watches every move I make.

"Would you like a drink?" he asks.

Yes, a dozen shots of tequila should do the trick to keep my cool and keep the anxiety buried in the pit of my stomach.

"Sure."

I instinctively clench my stomach muscles as I speak just in case anxiety's shadowy fingers try to creep back up my body. Liam raises his arm and gestures for a waitress's attention like he owns the place. A woman dressed in a black pencil skirt and a white blouse, carrying a tray of empties, is eager to answer his beck and call. She fixes her gaze on Liam, totally ignoring my presence. Her hair is up in a tight ponytail, but she keeps going to tuck an invisible strand of hair behind her ear. I almost cringe for her; she couldn't be more obvious if she tried; she'd be kissing his feet next.

"Good evening... and what can I get for you, sir?"

As she over pronounces the S, it makes me wonder, can words actually lick you on the face? I swear that's what just happened. Liam orders a whiskey on the rocks, then gestures to me with raised eyebrows.

"And my date will have...."

Her face falls like her feelings have just been shot down in flames, ouch. She reluctantly takes my order of a glass of red wine and mopes away, all her enthusiasm zapped, leaving her demeanour in tatters.

Liam's gaze drifts back to me; his features alone have the ability to render any woman speechless. That's exactly how I am right now, wordless, my inner spirit clutching at straws on what to say. How is he still single with such power?

"I love this kind of music."

My gaze drifts to the ceiling as if I could see the notes, not just hear them. 'What are you doing?' my inner spirit squeezes her eyes shut with embarrassment. Movement in the corner of my eye catches my attention; his body has slid closer to mine. We are almost knees to knees, his elbow leaning on the back of the seat, his furled fist supporting his head, an ankle over his knee.

"What scent are you wearing?" he quizzes.

His body curves towards me, and for a moment, my mind has gone blank.

"It's erm... it's Vivian... uh."

A tingling sensation cuts me off; it brushes across my cheek to my earlobe, I hear him inhale my skin, almost inaudible, but I feel the shift in the air.

"You smell divine."

The compliment smoothly rolls off his tongue, so smooth in fact, he has me mesmerised. I turn my head as his green eyes seem to cast their own spell. A throat clears; the sound belongs to the not so enthusiastic waitress. I peer out of the corner of my eye and notice that she doesn't make eye contact with Liam as she sets our drinks down. He thanks her and tips her generously. I feel a dryness tug at my throat. I sip some wine to soothe the scratchiness. There hasn't been much conversation flowing between us other than being pretty forward, so I desperately search for a subject starter.

Too late, his hand overlaps mine on the table. I look for those enchanting eyes, but I am caught in a lip-lock before I can find them again; he presses his lips against mine, demandingly claiming them. As he breaks away, my head almost falls forward, his kisses just as spellbinding as his eyes. The notion makes me quietly laugh, almost giddy. Oh god, what is this guy doing to me?

Something catches my eye, his hand catches my eye, and I can't ignore it. I gulp hard when I realise what it is. There's a dent on his finger, like it's missing a ring. It dawns on me that he may have done this before. My inner spirit starts chewing on the facts. Rewind to the beginning of the evening; he knew precisely which table was the quietest. You would only know that from previous experience, and now this mark. Ah, I feel nausea grip my stomach and my head whirls with the facts. My gaze falls to my lap, unwilling to meet his. I take a deep breath to ready myself.

"Does your wife know you're here?"

I feel his hand on mine stiffen; I pluck up the courage to look him in the eye. He doesn't have to say anything; his face is ashen, drained of all blood, guilty as charged. I find myself waiting for affirmation of my suspicions, even though his face says it all. I hold on to the hope that he may say that he is recently divorced, separated or something, anything to make me feel less ridiculous, less cheap, less dirty right now.

"I... I... umm... I work away a lot...."

Of course, a HOTEL wine bar should have rung massive fucking alarm bells. I've never felt so utterly stupid. His hand suddenly feels heavy with the shame, and so he should be fucking ashamed. I am too disgusted to look at him as I yank my hand free. I have heard enough, so I grab my things and get up to leave.

"I'm sorry, Charly."

I've barely made two steps away from the table, as his pitiful apology forces me to stop short, like someone has just thrown a screwed-up paper ball at my head, like in a school canteen scene. The feeling flicks on like a light switch; I am furious and my body whips round as anger fills my veins. I slam my hands down on his table.

"It's your wife you should be saying sorry to!"

I spit the words out like they are venom. I don't recognise the growl I just released, like it came from somewhere deep within my stomach, not my chest. Liam's whiskey catches my eye. I snatch the glass and chuck the contents in his face, but the glass slips out of my grip and shatters across the table, narrowly missing him. Without another word, I turn and head for the door before he has time to react. I don't look back; he doesn't deserve my concern. I stride with what dignity I have left intact. I keep my eyes fixed on the door; I don't want to look at the gawking spectators. My confidence slowly crumbling, I hold the back of my hand against my mouth as if that will help restrain the feelings from spilling out. I burst through the door. That's when his spell officially breaks, and the misery hits, shattering my spirit into a million pieces.

"I am DONE!"

I roar at the dark night skies above me, and my head drops after the force. My shoulders shudder with the comedown of my outcry.

"I am so done with men," I breathlessly mumble.

Onlookers hurry past me, probably scared I am about to lose my mind.

The pavement is soaked from recent showers and a car speeds past, right through a deep puddle, spraying the contents up my bare legs, as if I wasn't humiliated enough right now. My feet slip and slide with the wetness; I have no choice but to take my heels off. Despair weighs heavily on my being as I just keep walking, until I realise I have reached City Bridge. The moon seems especially bright tonight as its reflection ripples on the water. I lean over the edge to watch as a tear falls. Why me?

Appearing like a fairy godmother, an elderly lady is standing right next to me, enjoying the same view. She wears a brown faux fur jacket, her red nails match the colour of her lipstick, her blue-grey eyes glint in the light of the moon and grey hair hangs smoothly at her shoulders.

"No man is worth your tears, Sweetheart."

She kindly offers me a tissue. I gratefully take it as I form a smile.

"How do you know that I am crying over a man?"

She turns to me and gestures up and down my body.

"You're bearing the look of a stood-up date."

Her observation is the obvious choice and yet seems almost laughable. I think even being stood up would be less humiliating right now.

"Oh no, he did show up."

I let out a disheartened laugh as I say it. The woman's expression forms an intrigued arch to her eyebrows. No doubt, she's going to wait for an explanation.

"Oh?"

She's willing for me to continue. My shoulders slump, wishing that what I am about to say wasn't true. This is all a dream, right? I pinch the skin on the back of my hand. Nope, this is real.

"He's married."

I watch her shoulders bounce as she lets out a big huff with the news. She shakes her head, and I just about make out a tutting sound.

"Bastard," she mutters.

Her remark brings a stunned smile to my face. It was so unexpected as she doesn't come across as someone who swears. She looks at me with an accomplished grin and winks, like she's succeeded in helping me forget my woes for a moment.

"A good man will go out of his way to make you feel special, Darling... It isn't about fancy dates, fat bank balances and expensive gifts... It's the simplest things that matter... like what Mother Nature has given us...."

She turns back to lean one hand on the ledge, and the other gestures to the moon. My eyes follow. That's when I realise what side of the river I am on. The side I have been avoiding for the past six or so months.

"...what is more heartfelt than that," she continues.

I find my eyes mindlessly drifting along the buildings that run along the river bank. I see The Victoria Hotel first, then the small building of the vet's office nestled in-between. The sight almost makes me choke on the rising emotions in my chest.

"I ah... I umm... I once knew a man who loved this kind of thing... nature, I mean... I let him go... I wasn't ready then... I let my head overrule my heart."

I blink when I realise how dry and gritty my eyes are from staring at the building for so long. The feel of the woman's hand overlapping mine brings my focus back to her. She smiles so warmly when our eyes meet again.

"You should listen to your heart more often then, my dear... and don't worry... keep searching... you'll know who's right for you... something within you just ignites, and then you just know...oh and don't be too disheartened... we all meet a few pricks before we find the rose."

I listen to her intently until I hear the word 'pricks' and then I fail to hold back my laugh. She's so full of wisdom and yet still so young at heart.

"Thank you," I murmur.

She gives my hand a gentle squeeze before letting go, dipping her head in acknowledgement. As she steps back, she turns to the moon and blows a kiss. I wonder who it's for.

"Good luck, Sweetheart... I hope you find him."

Before I can ask or say anything more, she shuffles on her way. I watch as she disappears into the city nightlife. My eyes willingly drift to the vet's office; without the old lady to keep me distracted, my eyes begin to well as the memories come flooding back. My eyes continue to drift back to the moon and the images in my mind start rolling like an old-fashioned film reel, my own personal cinema. Someone pass me the popcorn; sadly, I know this one will be a tearjerker that hasn't got a happy ending.

Thirty-Two

It's almost midnight, as I stand in my bathroom with a tough decision to make. Do I want a bath or a shower? My inner spirit is in such a daze, making the most straightforward decision seem impossible. I look down at my bare legs, the remnants of the dirty puddle splayed across them; hmm, a bath seems like the better option. I perch on the side of the tub as I watch the bath fill, watching the water turn into foam as I pour in some bubble bath liquid. My fingertips make figures of eights as they skim the water.

The air was blue when I finished filling Harper in over the phone; I called her on the way home. All I heard was 'fucking bastard this' and 'fucking bastard that'. To be truthful, it did bring a smile to my face. The water has almost reached the top, so I lean over and turn the taps off. I stand to peel off my mess of a dress and slip out of my underwear and now I can see the full extent of the messy splattering. I dip my toes in first, then slowly immerse myself into the bubbles; my head bobs on the surface.

I am officially dateless for Harper's wedding. With that wretched thought, I push the bubbles to the leg end of the bath and close my eyes, fully immersing myself. They usually say 'third time lucky', but I think I was dealt the 'bad things happen in three's' card. So, judging by that theory, the next man I lay my eyes on will be 'the one.'

The visions of me as a middle-aged spinster pounce on me; I am surrounded by twenty or so cats and wearing an oversized unflattering cardigan. The thought forces my torso to bolt upright, like a catapult. I send waves of water across the room. I need to vow to myself, right here, right now, THAT is not going to be ME. I sit hugging my knees, picking the sticky clumps of mascara off my lashes.

How can guys like Liam, Ollie and Mark live with themselves? A cheat, a drunk, and a liar; it's exhausting just thinking about those labels. I sigh heavily as my mind tracks back to tonight's events. When I first laid eyes on Liam, I thought I had struck gold. As he showcases in my mind's eye now, his once handsome face now repulses me. My inner spirit would rather shudder than fall at his feet. I'd hate to think how much devastation his behaviour will cause in the long run. I wonder how many women he's managed to dupe so far. Somewhere out there is a wife none the wiser; I feel sorry for her to have such a slimy, lying, cheating dickhead for a husband.

***

I can't sleep. It's a humid night, but that doesn't usually get in the way of my falling asleep. I lie on my back; the ceiling fan is in its highest setting. I thought watching the blades rotate at full speed might hypnotise me into falling asleep. I don't usually fall asleep facing my window, but I find myself rolling over, the shadows of tree branches stand still in the glow. The spare pillow next to mine lays untouched for so long; I rest my palm in the middle, where a head should be. I close my eyes, but I still picture that side of the bed in my mind. I stroke the pillow with my thumb when Gareth's face appears as clear as day, and my eyes fly back open. They stay fixated with the space. I pull the pillow over to me and hug it against my chest; the comfort soothes me until my eyes finally get heavy.

Thirty-Three

'Bang, bang, bang'.

We all freeze mid-sip; Harper's eyes dart around the room, looking like she's mentally counting heads. The knock at the door sounds more urgent than a guest wanting to come in and join in with the fun. 'Bang, bang, bang,' it's louder and more insistent sounding this time. Ashley turns the volume on the music right down to hear the commotion.

"Open up, please... this is an emergency."

Harper's eyes grow even wider as the panic sets in. She looks like she's frozen to the spot, so I go and answer the door for her. Two uniformed men stand on the doorstep, two very handsome uniformed men, I might add. One looks a lot like Tom Cruise, back in his Top Gun days but with stubble. The other guy looks a lot like Channing Tatum, with short dark blonde cropped hair, he's standing just behind 'Tom.' I step to one side to allow them in, giving 'Channing' a cheeky wink as he passes me. I think the champagne has already gone to my head. I quickly close the door and follow closely behind them, watching Harper's face through the gap between their shoulders as she comes forward to greet them. She has a thing for guys in uniform, especially this kind of uniform... firemen. I can't say I blame her, judging by this rear view.

"Sorry to interrupt your evening, ma'am... but we received a call that someone can smell something burning from this house," 'Tom' says.

Harper looks over their shoulders at me, puzzled, probably hoping I hold the answer to this problem, but I just shrug and shake my head. For once, she is lost for words which is so unlike her, a cocktail of panic and lust, I think.

"I'm so sorry, gentlemen... I think someone has wasted your time... there's definitely no fire or smoke here... but thank you for checking in on us anyway."

She did well at keeping her cool; I'm impressed. My inner spirit does the smiling for me.

"Are you sure, ma'am... or maybe it's these pants that are burning up..."

Within nanoseconds, all you can hear is velcro and ripping fabric as their jackets fly off. It was cheesy as hell, but Harper is hooked. If only I could frame the look on her face right now, it's priceless. I walk over to Ashley and we share a high-five.

I should explain that tonight is Harper's last night out as a single lady, but you probably already guessed that. The big day is just a week away. Ashley and I have been plotting this for a couple of months. All Harper knew was the date and time that everyone would meet at her house; everything else about this has been TOP SECRET and sealed with a CLASSIFIED stamp. Harper's two soon-to-be sisters-in-law have joined us tonight, as well as our other friends. The sis-in-laws,

Anna and Stacey, seem easy-going enough; and by the looks on their faces right now, frozen in gawking amazement, they are quietly thrilled as the rest of us hoot and holler. Well, these guys are here to please, and I think we've definitely gotten our money's worth so far. Ashley grabs a chair while I go over to the stereo and play our requested song.

'Too Close' by Next. I can't for the life of me remember what these guys names are, so let's just call them Tom and Channing. Tom backs Harper up without touching her until the back of her legs hit the seat that's waiting for her. She falls with enough force that the chair tips back, but Tom puts his foot on the frame, slamming it back down just as the beats start playing. Towering over her, he scoops up her hand, and places a single kiss on the back of it. Then he kneels by her side, like it's a proposal; he whispers something in her ear as she nods, looking and smiling a little bashfully. He stands again, straddling her only for a second, as he steps over her lap. His hands never leave her body as he walks round to stand behind her.

Meanwhile, Channing is teasing the other ladies with his hip rolls and body rolls, lifting his t-shirt just a smidge giving them a cheeky peek at his goods. Back to Harper, Tom has her arms in the air, her palms on his chest; she grins profusely, loving the attention. His hands guide hers down his chest then down her own, right over her breasts. Biting her bottom lip, she squeals through her closed mouth, briefly closing her eyes, almost like she shouldn't be enjoying this, but it's the best time of her life, all at the same time. Tom turns her head to look up at him straight in the eye. His hands come to rest on the back of her chair. He leans all his weight on his hands and his legs lift off the floor in a semi handstand, then they swing around Harper, straddling her once again. The crowd around Harper shrieks in amazement. He hugs her as he grinds on her lap. For once, Harper has no idea where to put her hands. Channing comes over to join Tom as he dismounts Harper. The look on her face is off the scale priceless; flustered doesn't even cover it.

As I watch their dance routine unfold, all I can concentrate on is how their fitted black t-shirts cling to every toned muscle on their chests, abs and arms, oh my indeed! They slowly and seductively slip their arms out of the grip of their suspenders, letting them drop to their sides. Within seconds of that drop, the shirts are ripped from their chests. It was expected, but still took me by surprise. The action forces my chin to hit the floor at the same time as the fabric. I stand with my arms semi folded. I bite one of my thumbnails while I admire every step, every thrust, every fist pump, every ripple of muscle, every single hot dance move they make, drinking in every minor detail. Channing catches my eye and winks just as he steps up to Harper, and turning his attention back to her, he grabs hold of her hand as he straddles her, guiding her hand to glide down his chest and abs. I watch those firm buttocks of his grind round and round, back and forth, again and again. It's not even happening to me, but I feel like I am burning up. Oh boy, his hose can put out my fire anytime. The thought makes me snicker out loud. Yes, the champagne has well and truly taken over my mind and body; another large glass full, and I'll more than likely be joining in with the show.

Meanwhile, it's Tom's turn to thrill the bystanders. He turns to the sis-in-laws, grabs Anna's hand and glides it down his chest; the look on her face, she's so thrilled I won't be surprised if she passes out. Both gals look like they don't get out much, but I bet they're glad they came now. Back to Harper, Channing stands mid-straddle, running his fingers sensuously through her hair, grazing her scalp, turning her head full circle as he goes. As he tips her head back, their eyes meet, his fingers still locked in her hair. She breaks the eye contact first, turning her head to the side as his fingers unhook themselves, her cheeks blazing red hot. He finds her hands, holding them firmly as he steps back, he pulls her up with him in swift succession. With both of their arms stretched above their heads, he unhooks his hands from hers. His hands glide down her arms, down her sides, then to her hips. Within a blink of an eye, he has her wrapped around his waist. She clings on round his neck like her life depends on it. Shock soon turns to delight as he turns, then stealthily kneels to lay her down on the floor. She half covers her face with her hands, mumbling while trying to keep it together. It sounds like she's saying 'oh my god' over and over again. He straddles just one of her legs, as he holds her other one upright against his shoulder, and grinds right on her groin. She shrieks with so much delight, so much so I think she's going to burst; burst in more ways than one if you know what I mean.

"Well... what do you think?"

Ashley almost has to shout the question against my ear to compete with the music and the cheering. I am assuming she means the price tag on these guys' performance - not how hot they are.

"Worth every fucking penny."

I shout back to her, along with a wink, and oh boy, it is true. Ashley rolls her eyes as she nudges me with her bony elbow. Channing helps Harper get back on her feet; looking a little shaken up (in a good way, of course), she struggles to regain her balance. He doesn't let her go until she feels steady. Harper hugs him and speaks closely to his ear, more than likely thanking him a million times over. Harper staggers over to us, looking like she's got 'just fucked' hair, with a grin much broader than a Cheshire Cat's. She looks at us both, so breathless and ecstatic, that she might as well have just been fucked.

"Oh my god... you guys... you are the best... that was so fucking hot... I think I need to change my underwear...."

She shrieks, like she's a teenager, again before we even get a chance to say anything to her. The excitement ripples through her body as she hugs us both fiercely and like a whirlwind she quickly disappears upstairs, to sort herself out I'd imagine. Ashley and I grin at each other and break into laughter. A good job well done, sealed with a firm high five, mission fucking accomplished.

**

Harper points to a large sign in neon lettering, REVERSE. Why does that name seem so familiar to me? My mental cogs try to whir through the champagne-fuelled haze. Oh, shit, I do know, Cassie's birthday. It suddenly dawns on me. I feel my anxiety creeping in; the shadowy fingers crawl from my stomach up to my neck where they heavily lay as they encircle my throat. The more I focus on the neon lettering, the more I'm filled with dread. I can't let this feeling overtake me; I need to keep it together, no matter what, for Harper's sake. The grip of fear slowly retracts its fingers as my inner spirit focuses on Harper. She pounces on me in utter excitement, pulling me closer to the club. The good mood from Tom and Channing's show hasn't fizzled out just yet. My fears melt away when I see Harper in all her 'bride to be' glory.

The look on her face takes me back to the first time we snuck out, when we were sixteen. Being sneaky gave us such an exciting rush. Harper, Ashley, and I have always looked older than we are. Somehow, we convinced the doorman to let us in. I can't for the life of me even remember what the nightclub was called. Harper and I were always the wild childs and Ashley was always the sensible one. But I'll never forget the tables turning that night. Ashley got so drunk on just two shots and a mojito that we were the ones who had to reel her in. We dragged her off a table before she had a chance to make a scene.

The burly bouncer, standing at the entrance of REVERSE is looking like a force not to be reckoned with; he eyes us closely, his stern exterior slightly cracking a crooked smile as he winks to Harper and detaches the rope barrier. He gestures for us to come forward, allowing us to jump in front of the queue. We comply. Moans and tuts stem from the line behind us as we move closer. Harper boldly kisses the bouncer on the cheek. We all giggle at the V.I.P. treatment and

Harper's forwardness. Judging by the bouncer's face, I think she just made his night a whole lot better. The alcohol keeps flowing as soon as we enter the club. We knock back shot after shot. I feel the buzz coursing right through me; my head starts to swim. We all make our way to the dance floor. The more my head swims, time and everyone seem to slow down. The lights seem to trail in smudged lines. My eyes start to refocus as my body gets used to the alcohol racing through my veins. As my ears tune in, I realise what song is playing. Something about this beat captivates me, seduces me. Harper and the others seem to have vanished. I'm standing in my own circle of space, unusual for a busy club. My eyes desperately search for them, until they fall upon him. Just beyond the first layer of bodies, circling me, surveying me, watching me, then he disappears.

Did I just imagine that? The track's bass overtakes my thinking. Niall Horan's lyrics swarm around me, sensuously licking at my eardrums. Before I know it, I am closing my eyes. I tune out the world around me and just focus on the music, envisaging 'slow hands' trailing up and down my body. My hips start to roll willingly in their spellbound state, swaying in broad sweeps. My arms follow, brushing the air in front of me. My whole body starts to circle along with my hips and arms. I open my eyes and there he is again, circling in the opposite direction, his eyes fixated on me, observing every move I make. My hands trail from my hips, up to my torso, all the way to my head, as if I'm taking off an invisible top. I brush the air above with fingertips, as the rest of me dances. He stops in his tracks and heads straight for me; his intentions are unclear. My inner spirit shouts at me to stop, but I mentally flick her away as my body refuses to listen. I close my eyes as if I know I'll be safe in his arms; I feel his presence in the darkness. A firm hold on my hips pulls me closer, and I open my eyes for just a second as his lips meet mine possessively; his tongue forces its way into my mouth in search of mine. This kiss is not how I remember Gareth; he was always tender and loving, not aggressive and forceful. His lips trail along my jaw, as I feel his breath on my ear. Cigarettes and alcohol have stained his breath. He inhales my hair.

"What's your name, baby?"

I freeze at the words, 'name' and 'baby'; it propels me out of my drunken dreamlike state. I am stuck in fight or flight mode as he pulls back to face me, waiting for my answer. His grin is soused and crooked, a fuck ugly version of Gareth, looking like he's struck gold with me. Vomit catches in my throat when I realise my mistake. How could I have gotten it so fucking wrong? A gross trail of saliva along my cheek feels sticky; the sensation makes my stomach flip again. My inner spirit yells at me to get the fuck out of here, but all I can do is stare at the mouth that has just violated me. When his hands come at me again, my inner spirit kicks the switch for 'fight' mode. With all my might, I forcefully push him away, making him trip and fall backwards. My cue to get the fuck out of there, but the rush makes my head swim again. I try to battle my way through the blockade of grinding and dancing bodies, trying desperately to find my way out despite my intoxicated foggy brain. I see neon lights above a door, but I have no idea what it says; it could be the men's room for all I know. I burst through the door and a warm breeze hits me; luckily, I have chosen the right way. A pounding sensation beats my head and I hear disjointed chattering all around me as the blood thrums against my ears; they seem to swarm around me in one buzzing hum. I try to focus, willing the scenery to stop seesawing; it's like trying to walk across a rocking boat. The motion makes me feel sick, seasick. Someone bumps into me, or I bump into them; either way, it forces me to stumble and fall, hitting my knees on the pavement. Our drinking session and the disgusting taste of a stranger force their way out of my stomach. I chuck up the contents across the ground; I hold my head as it pounds, hmm, classy.

"Charly... Charly, are you okay?"

Through the buzz, I hear my name as clear as day, but I grimace and groan at the sound of my own name. The voice is familiar; a male voice, not Harper or Ashley, coming to rescue me. Someone holds me under my arm as I stagger to my feet. I try to focus on who's helping me, but it's just no use.

"Hey, you... it's Ben... are you okay?"

Do I look fucking okay? I want to scream, but all I can muster is a long rumbling groan, yelling internally when I register his name. At this moment in time, I need all the help I can get. I mentally grimace as Ben is my only option. I misplace my feet and my ankles buckle; I feel his arms grapple my waist, saving me from hitting the floor, bringing me close to his body.

"Don't worry, Charly... I got you."

I feel him scoop me up into his arms and I cling onto him as best as I can. Peering up, I just about make out that he's back to wearing his old glasses.

"Th-tha-thanks Ben... you are th-the b-b-best."

All grievances pushed aside for the moment anyway. The rhythm of Ben's stride is soothing and I close my eyes as it rocks me into soused unconscious oblivion.

Thirty-Four

Clicking my tongue as I come to, my mouth is dry like sandpaper. As I sit up, my head feels like it's stuck in a vice. I focus, noticing a glass of juice and painkillers staring back at me. The room seesaws, so I lay back down for a moment. Recognising these bedsheets, I realise where I am—the place where I've woken up many times before. By now, I would be on my way out the door, but not today. I am held captive by my own head. When the room slowly draws to a halt on the seesawing, I rest up on my elbow and reach over for the tablets and juice, swallowing them one by one. Even at room temperature, the drink soothes my raw, desert-like throat. Gently placing my glass back down, I turn over. Ben has his back to me, still fast asleep I assume. I gasp as I realise he's naked, an inch of his behind peeking out from under the bedsheets. The sound makes him stir, oh shit. He rolls over to face me and sees the shock etched on my features. He tiredly squints and smirks at my alarm.

"Don't freak out...we didn't do anything... I just undressed you and put you to bed... you were so out of it."

I note the baggy band t-shirt I'm wearing as I look down. Ben gestures towards his wardrobe, where my last night's attire is hanging.

"You chucked up all over your clothes... I had no choice... I washed them for you, though," he beams.

He waits for me to say something for his thoughtfulness or reward him with a medal or thereabouts. I could have sworn I aimed for the pavement as the memory drifts back. I lean over and peck him on the cheek.

"Thanks, Ben... for rescuing me... and for the clothes... but I really need to go... my friends are probably worried sick about me."

I shift my body away from him to slide out, but he grabs my elbow.

"Wait, Charly... please don't go... stay for once... I told Harper you are safe."

I stare at him dumbfounded; Harper? How does he know her name?

"As I carried you home... you kept muttering her name... so I just assumed that's who you were supposed to be with... so I found her on your phone contacts... she knows you're with me and safe."

I'm not sure whether to be grateful or cross; the thought of him scrolling through my phone fills me with dread, not that there's anything to be ashamed of on there, just feels a little intrusive. I focus back on his anxious features and remind myself that he did put himself out for me. I ruined his night too. Oh shit, I feel awful; it tugs at my stomach, or is that the remnants of alcohol? I'm not really sure. He looks at me with those big blue eyes; they seem to dance in the morning rays that beat through the gaps in the blinds.

"Please stay a little longer... at least have breakfast with me."

Uh, food. For once the thought is unappealing. Both his eyes and his voice plead with me. I close my eyes as the lie he let slip clouds my mind. I want to be annoyed with him, but the second heroic act ever done for me, punches through and gratitude falls in its place instead. He lets go of me and opens his arms, gesturing for me to lie down with him. But then I suddenly remember the 'no boxers 'situation, and I smirk.

"Put some shorts on first."

I laugh as he rolls his eyes, then he swiftly pulls me into his arms anyway.

"Hey!"

An arm holds me against his bare chest.

"It's not like you haven't seen me naked before."

He smirks suggestively, then holds my gaze, the hilarity pushed to one side, his eyes try their best to reel me in. I try to fight back the urge, but I don't resist the pull, like a foolish magnet. As he pushes my hair away from my face, my body wakes up under his touch. It feels good to be wanted and to have someone hold me. Hell, it's been a long time. It won't be a drunken fumble this time around; I want to know what it feels like, I mean what he feels like. When I let those thoughts overrule my head, I take the plunge and kiss him first. I feel he's stunned under my embrace and pull my head back to assess the situation.

"Are you sure about this?" he asks.

His tone is hushed, almost like it's a secret. I know I'm going to regret this later, but right now I am sure. Curiosity prevails over my common sense.

"Definitely."

I reciprocate his whisper; letting the word linger on the end of my tongue, it licks the backs of my teeth. Ben drinks in my suggestive manner. His hand pushes my hair right back, then sweeps round to take hold of my chin. He lifts my chin, and our eyes lock momentarily before his lips avidly claim mine. Whoah, all my senses ignite as the sensation sweeps across my body. I feel alive... I feel sexually alive; there's no other way to describe it. My skin tingles and prickles under the caress of his stubble. He rolls me onto my back as his lips trail along my jaw and down my neck. His kisses line the way down to the hem of the t-shirt; it's sensual even through the fabric. He doesn't stop there; his head almost disappears between my thighs, and I suddenly feel embarrassed that he's down... you know, right down there.

I gasp so hard it sounds like I am crying out, as I feel his mouth brush against my pantie covered clit. My thighs twitch with the urge to slam shut; he pushes the fabric to one side just as his palms firmly pin my thighs down. His warm breath teases me; the feel of his lips curve around my clit as he sucks me in then releases, to kiss me. I cry out with more enthusiasm this time around. My arms fly up and grasp hold of the bed frame railings above my head; my back arches, pressing my groin deeper into his face. I close my eyes as the intense teasing sensation ripples right through my deep muscles, down to my sex. He watches my body respond to each kiss, each touch that he plants down there. He suddenly shifts up onto his knees. For the first time, I see him all, well, without my beer goggles on anyway. Ben reaches over to his bedside table and I hear a rustling. When his hand comes back to view, he's holding not just one packet but a whole strip of condoms. They eagerly unravel, I'd estimate half a dozen in a row. It's not even funny, but I find myself giggling anyway.

"Blimey... you're a bit presumptuous, aren't you..."

My laugh turns into a full-on snigger and he finally sees the funny side of the moment.

"I don't have that much stamina... I'm good but not that good," Ben chuckles.

He is one cheeky son of a... he distracts me as he tears into a packet and I watch him slide it onto his erected length. Ben slips his hands into the sides of my panties and pulls them off. His head comes down to my navel; I feel his nose trail first, then a kiss. He repeats the action for both sides of my stomach. I am still holding on to the bed railings, my grip getting tighter and tighter as the teasing accelerates and they rattle against the wall with my squirming movements. The t-shirt gently rises along my skin as his kisses replace where the fabric once was; the fabric trails over my nipples, sending them sensitively throbbing under the sensation, followed by his tongue circling and nipping each one.

My feet draw up the bed, closer to my behind. Letting go of the railings, I sit up, allowing him to lift off my top to reveal me in all my natural glory. As I go to lie down, I notice Ben's eyes widen as he hovers over me, like he's seeing me for the first time too... I mean really seeing me... with the clearest of vision. He lowers himself gently onto me, coming to rest on his elbows. My arms come to rest on the small of his back. I gasp as he glides himself into me, and for the first time in a long time, I feel everything, I feel him, deep inside of me. It feels ... it feels so good to be skin to skin. It takes him a moment to find a rhythm, but once he finds it... he has really found 'IT'. He grunts and pants as he drives into me, again and again, and again. I moan loudly as he pounds into me deeper and deeper. The bed rails clang noisily against the wall, a moment of sympathy for his neighbour, on a Sunday morning as well. I bat away the thought before I start laughing; he might think I am mocking his performance. He lowers himself right down, tucking his hands under my head, burying his face into my pillow; his back stiffens like a board. There's a look of disappointment on my inner spirit's face; I try not to mirror her expression. She's yelling, 'oh no... no...please... please, don't stop... not now'. His grunts accelerate, followed by a howl like a cry, sounding more painful than anything. My wide-eyed gaze is fixed on the ceiling, but I'm not sure whether I should be stunned, shocked, disappointed, but it was good while it lasted, I give him that. He wasn't kidding on the stamina part. The weight of his body winds me as he collapses, forcing me to make an 'oof' sound. Ben doesn't even seem to notice as he rolls off me. What on earth do I say or do now? I have no idea what prompted the thought, but it just dawns on me, doesn't he have a girlfriend or is seeing someone? Our conversation at The Garden Bar comes flooding back. I feel the colour empty from my cheeks. Oh shit, poor girl, whoever she is. Ben is still lying on his back, catching his breath. I waste no time scrambling out of bed.

"Whoah, whoah... Charly, what's the rush?"

His voice is sluggish, like the blood is still drifting back to his head.

"I'm so stupid... so fucking stupid."

I mutter it under my breath as I collect my panties and slip them back on.

"What are you talking about?"

Worry starts to thicken his voice; he leans on his elbow, watching my every move. Grabbing my clothes off the hanger in silence, I just want to get out of here. Yesterday's clothes are still slightly damp, but no time to be fussy.

"What's wrong, Charly... why aren't you talking to me?"

The panic in his voice is getting thicker and thicker. Once I have everything on, I grab my heels, then my bag and phone off the dresser, and make sure I have everything before saying anything more. Ben starts getting out of bed, and I catch sight of the sorry looking knapsack hanging off his dick. Automatically looking away to hide my mortified expression, I can't meet his eyes.

"I'm so stupid... because... you have a girlfriend, Ben... I should have realised that... before... before what just happened...."

I can't think of anything else to say, so I just turn and head for the door. Ben follows me to the stairway; not that he could follow me out into the street. Just as I take the first step, he grabs my arm; it catches me off guard and I almost lose my footing. I glare at Ben as I steady myself again.

"Let me go."

I hiss just like my inner spirit; she flexes her claws, ready to pounce.

"I...I... I'm sorry, Charly."

It's beginning to be a common phrase thrown at me these days. I shrug him off as he looks at me with big sorry eyes, a look that would usually halt my anger. No point-blank denials of him having a girlfriend come; I must have been right. He hovers over the bannister as I hurry down the stairs and bolt out of the door. Slamming the door, I vow that this will be the very last time I close this door behind me; I'm making no more reckless decisions, and that's the very last time I get that wasted.

***

There are dozens of messages flooding my phone from Harper and Ashley. I send them both a message to reassure them that I am fine and on my way home. A slight hangover still hovers over me, but I'm feeling less pained as I deeply inhale the fresh air. Knowing Harper, she's going to have a few choice words for me when I speak to her, especially when she finds out about this morning. Hopefully, it won't be soon; I don't think my head could take it right now.

As I walk through the streets towards home, I can't believe that I let myself fall into Ben's trap yet again. When will I ever learn? As I approach home, I mentally grimace, trying my best not to show it, as I notice Doris tending to her garden with a friend. She eyes me up and down as I draw closer; deep breaths, here we go, ready for the interrogation.

"Good morning Doris... how are you this morning?"

I am trying to keep my voice cheery through the ache. I bring my pace right down, but I don't stop, just inching my way across the length of her garden, faking my pleasantries as I go. Why, oh why does she have to be out on what is possibly the worst morning for me.

"Good morning Charly... lovely morning."

I can feel her scrutinising my last night's attire. It aches even to smile, let alone keep a conversation flowing.

"It is indeed... your garden is looking beautiful... it puts mine to shame."

I force half a laugh as I gesture to my bland and boring flowerless garden; it actually looks quite depressing.

"Thank you, my dear."

She nods and gives me a brief wave as I continue on my way. As I reach the path to my house, I pick up the pace again, eager to get away from prying eyes. Phew, not so bad this time around, probably because she has company with her this morning. I put the key in the lock, overhearing Doris as she mutters to her friend,

"That's the one I was talking to you about."

It was an awful attempt at a whisper. I heavily sigh as I open and close the door behind me. If I'm not careful, I'll be the talk of the whole street next; if I'm not already, I wouldn't be surprised if news travels fast with that one. I sling my bag down on the hallway floor along with my keys and kick off my heels. I go into the kitchen to strip off and chuck all my clothes into the washing machine. I know Ben cleaned them for me last night, but they seem dirty again, dirty with my shame. My bare feet pad across the wooden flooring and up the stairs, grabbing my iPod on the way through.

I head straight for the bathroom; I need to wash off any trace of Ben. I turn on the shower and steam quickly fills the room. Placing my iPod on the edge of the sink, my playlist loud and on shuffle, it decides to play Corinne Bailey Rae's cover of 'The Scientist'. Opening the shower door, I step in and gasp at the almost blistering heat of the water. I close the door on the world behind me and stand right under the pour, letting it drench and redden my skin from head to toe; the hotter, the better to kill and wash away the shame. I close my eyes as I face the flow, smoothing down my hair and then placing my palms on the tiled wall in front of me.

Letting the wall take my weight, I hang my head to feel the warmth and patter on the back of my neck. Opening my eyes, I watch the water pool around my toes before flowing on its journey down the plughole. I wish I could go right back to the beginning and rewrite all my wrongs. Despair weighs heavily on my shoulders. I close my eyes, trying to halt the rising emotions within my chest, but as the song plays out and the lyrics continue to resonate, it sets everything free. Recent events have finally got the better of me; my tough exterior starts to crack under pressure. What sort of person have I become? I don't even recognise myself anymore. With that thought, my hands slide down the wall along with my body until I am on my knees, holding my head in my hands. My façade breaks as the old me rises to the surface and I sob like I have never sobbed before, with so much force that my chest feels like it's on the verge of tearing open at any second. It's an ugly feeling that I wouldn't want to wish on anyone. The more I cry, the more it slowly frees the burden; the ache slowly eases. I shed every last tear until my tear ducts are squeezed dry, and it's just a noise escaping my chest. My body slumps to one side, my head against the tiles, I peel my hands away and look at them, watching the mascara-stained water run through my fingers. I am drained, empty of energy and emotion. From here on in, no more chasing, no more searching, I'm going to let love find me. No way am I destined for Miss Jones's big knickers.

Thirty-Five

Ben unsurprisingly has been off sick from work all week, probably too ashamed to show his face. So, he should be; I did not think he was the kind of man to do something like that. I've been beating myself up all week for instigating the sex, but Ben's as much to blame as I am; he could have, and should have, said no. What on earth was he thinking? I'm sitting at the tall table by the window at the back of the staff kitchen, poking around the cherry tomatoes in my shop bought bland pot of chicken salad. Harper had allowed me a couple days of peace and quiet before she gave me a full-on lecture about Ben. I was hoping she had forgotten about it when I didn't hear from her straight away; I thought last-minute wedding stuff was keeping her busy. My ear ached for ages after that phone call; it was red, hot and throbbing. But it was the wake-up call that I needed. Even though I had always known deep down, that he wasn't right for the long term, her few choice words that day, made me think differently, feel differently. I gave her my word that I would not set foot in Ben's house again. The only exchanges we'd be making between us from now on would be polite conversations. I am never going back on that promise; it is signed and sealed, tucked away at the back of my heart. I prefer that to the usual saying 'cross my heart and hope to...'. It sounds too morbid to me, so I never use it. With all that said, I will never go back on it.

Tomorrow is the 'big day' for Harper and Alex. I wonder what is going through their minds right now. Much to Ashley's dismay, Harper decided not to have any bridesmaids or maid of honour. I think she's asked a couple of her soon to be nieces to take on the roles of flower girls, but that's it. I don't blame her; it's one less expense for them and judging by the pictures of the venue they chose, they probably don't have much money left to spare. I don't think I have ever attended a wedding, or any function in fact, without a date. A first for everything, I guess.

Thirty-Six

I Instantly regret wearing heels as I make my way up the gravel driveway, cursing myself for not getting the taxi to stop closer to the venue. The huge stately home is absolutely breathtakingly beautiful. I pause momentarily, halfway up, to take it all in. Tall windows are glinting gracefully in the sun's rays and ivy trails down each side of the building. On the top floors, there are balconies. You could almost imagine Romeo and Juliet kind of romances unfolding here back in the day. 'Romeo, Romeo, wherefore art thou Romeo.' Yes, Romeo, where the bloody hell are you? This Juliet is right here waiting for you; I want to laugh out loud. Focusing back on the glorious sight in front of me, they definitely have a perfect day, and not too hot for a summer's day, just right.

Harper's parents, Stella and Nick, are standing out front to greet the guests as they arrive. Stella clocks me and tries to run to greet me, but it looks like she has opted for the same footwear. I hold my hands up in a bid to halt her; it's okay, I am coming. Once we meet, she plants the daintiest of kisses on each of my cheeks. Her jet-black hair is shaped in a perfectly straight bob. She's dressed in a plain but still beautiful burgundy fitted dress and matching short blazer with Harper's flower choice in a buttonhole.

"Darling... wow... look at you... navy and silver are so your colours... how stunning... absolutely gorgeous, isn't she Nick?"

Nick is too busy talking to another guest to answer her. Then she playfully looks around each side of me. I think I know what's coming next.

"Where's your plus one?"

Bingo, and there it is! I shrug, trying my best to smile, but it ends up on the verge of being awkwardly crooked, not a good look.

"It's just little old me."

I shrug again, but more coyly this time. Nick catches the tail end of the conversation as he finishes with the other guest. He comes over and takes me under his wing.

"Now... now, this will not do... come along, Bridget, let's get you inside... there's someone I would like you to meet."

I don't know how much more pity I can take. I grimace at the thought of Harper gossiping about our 'big knicker chat' in the café to her parents. I really don't want my newfound nickname, Bridget, to stick; I shield my eyes with the embarrassment.

Music echoes through the halls as we enter, a live band of violins or cellos, I think. Nick lets go of me so I can walk in solo. Portraits from centuries ago line each of the walls, pristine red carpet laid throughout makes you feel like a celebrity; where are the paparazzi when you need them? Waiters float from person to person with trays full of welcome tipples, nibbles, sorry, canapés, correctly speaking. I gracefully take a glass, just as Nick calls and gestures for me to follow him. I wear my best fake smile as I approach him. He puts one arm around me, giving a slight squeeze for reassurance.

"Charly, I would like you to meet William. He lives and works in the city too."

He gestures towards a tall guy, sandy blonde hair and piercing blue eyes; he kind of reminds me of a surfer dude. I tingle with excitement at the thought of washboard abs hiding under that dark grey suit and my cheeks redden at the idea. William steps forward; his hand lightly meets my shoulder as he kisses my cheek.

"Nice to meet you, Charly... please call me Will."

My inner spirit sticks a pin in the image bubble of a surfer boy; it bursts loudly in my head, making me jump. Judging by his posh accent, we are two complete opposites. I know I should not judge a book before I have read it... or whatever the saying is.

I find myself zoning out as he rattles on about work, finances, or something along those lines. Keeping up a fake interest is tiring so I excuse myself to the ladies' room. I literally dash through the door, right into two women, who unamused, end up tutting at me on their way out. I grab hold of the basin to steady myself, almost smashing the glass that I momentarily forgot about. Using the unit for support, I take a few deep breaths as Harper's authoritative voice dominates my head, reminding me of her grilling from the other day. She told me to start letting other people in, letting other guys in. I need to find someone new. A flush sound behind me breaks my train of thought and Stella appears from a cubicle. She quickly washes and dries her hands before consoling me.

"Love... what's wrong?"

She puts an arm around me. I want to lean into her for comfort, but I know she won't be able to take the weight of me.

"I'm sorry, but that William, isn't for me."

We use the mirrored wall to look at each other. She looks at my reflection with relief, probably glad it is only William that appears to be wrong.

"Oh love... you had me worried there... you have nothing to be sorry about... when you finally find someone, you'll know in a heartbeat if he is right for you... if in doubt, listen to your heart."

Hmm, yes, that whole 'listen to your heart' chestnut again. I nod and smile in agreement; Stella gives me a dainty squeeze, fully satisfied with her words of wisdom, she leaves me to freshen up by myself. Looking back at my reflection, I straighten myself up; she's right, when I find him, I'll know. I smile as I put my game face on. Okay, I am so ready for this, Harper's big day, here I come.

It feels like I am walking much higher than everyone as I sashay through the hall. After Stella's pep talk, I suddenly feel newfound confidence coursing through me. Luckily, we all get ushered into the ceremony room before William gets a chance to speak to me again. I eventually find Ashley and her husband amongst the sea of guests. We hold hands as we wade through to get the nearest seats to the front.

"Someone has their eye on you" Ashley whispers.

She gestures with just her head towards the front, where Alex is waiting. Oh fuck, I gulp hard when I realise who is standing next to him. I had no idea he was going to be here. I know they are good friends, but I didn't think he'd be chosen for the Best Man duty. Ethan notices me staring and smiles at me; it's genuine, with no ounce of smugness, but I can't forgive and forget what happened on New Year's Day.

"Not a chance... never again."

I break my eyes away from Ethan and focus on Ashley as she gives me a look as if to say, 'I'll believe that when I see it.' It's true though, I am not going to cave in to him.

Everyone stands as music fills the room. Harper's two flower girl nieces start the wedding march, chucking the petals in a not so graceful fashion. They are swiftly followed by Harper with her dad by her side. She looks stunning as she glides down the aisle; her ivory ballgown and train match her big personality. She beams like a Cheshire Cat. The love in each other's eyes is priceless as she and Alex come together. Ashley and her husband stand next to me, wrapped in each other's arms, totally engrossed at the moment, reminiscing about their wedding day, no doubt. As I watch Harper and Alex exchange their vows, it fills me with the need to be loved, even greater than before. Adoring faces, all caught up in the moment, surround me as I glance around the room. My eyes drift back to the front of the aisle and Ethan catches my eye again; he's glancing out of the corner of his eye, I wonder what game he's trying to play.

I focus back on Harper and Alex as they say their 'I do's' and a mixture of emotions starts forming a lump in my throat. I am so done with the single life now. This is what I want, love, commitment, and everything that goes with it. I am ready to settle down.

Thirty-Seven

Today is flashing by in a blur. The reception is set up in a huge gazebo on the grounds, lit up by twinkling lights in a spiderweb-like fashion above our heads. Familiar faces surround me, a mixture of old and new friends, mostly coupled with their partners consumed in the romantic atmosphere. It makes me feel so out of place and alone. I think I'll get some fresh air. As I turn, I am caught; my hands fly up onto his shoulders to steady myself, he holds me close in his arms, I don't have to look up to see who it is. His snake ink creeps out from the edge of his shirt collar. I find myself drifting with him back to the dance floor; he keeps me close as he encourages us to sway.

"Don't you know what time it is?"

His tone is as smooth and deep as I remember it to be. Is that supposed to be funny? I pluck up the courage to meet his eyes and just like earlier today, I meet genuine kind eyes and a smile; no trace of arrogance, but I feel like he's trying to lure me into a false sense of security. His eyes are slightly glazed. I smell sweet wine on his breath, not the usual bourbon and cigarettes. I wonder if he's given up on smoking; why am I even thinking like I fucking care?

"I fucked up big time, Charly."

He looks down like he's fighting some inner battle, or he's trying to make me feel sorry for him. Either way, these heartstrings are staying well and truly taut. He looks up when I don't respond. My lips remain sealed; a part of me wants to see him down on his knees begging for my forgiveness, and the other part doesn't give a shit. Once someone has burnt me, my faith in them has charred beyond recognition; the trust is nothing but ash. I don't want to hear what pitiful excuses he has for me, so I wriggle out of his hold and head for the exit. A hand grabs my arm and before I know it, I am spun to face him again. His jaw clenches and tremors with the rising displeasure within him; his eyes darken under his glare.

"I need you to hear me out," he demands.

His voice is low but still has an angry bite to it. I feel the panic rise within me; I try to back away to free my arm, but his grip on me tightens, forcing me to yelp.

"Ethan, you're hurting me... please let me go."

I plead with him. My voice cracks, tears prick my eyes as my arm stings in pain under his grip. I have no idea how he thinks this will convince me to hear him out. I meet his eyes to show him the fear in them.

"You hurt me big time... I heard every damn word you said about me... how I was the biggest fucking mistake... I can't... I can't... just... forgive and forget... you cheated on your fiancée... how... how... can I trust you... knowing you did that to her... I would never trust you... just let me go."

His eyes are glistening, but his nose is flared. I can't tell if he's hurt or I've just given his irritation more fuel to thrive on. My voice trembled as some of the things were hard to admit; I do like him, correction... I did like him. The outcome could have been different; we could have been standing here dancing as a couple. Any hopes I had were blown out of the water when I came face to face with his 'wife to be.' I don't think I'll ever be able to erase the look on her face when I handed his watch over to her.

I raise the arm he has hold of, and I give it one last attempt to yank it free, but it's no use. Suddenly, William appears from nowhere and steps in. He must have noticed the rising conflict and panic in my body language.

"I think the lady isn't interested, mate...."

Ethan quickly retracts his grip as William puts an arm around his shoulder and steers him away from me, but it doesn't stop Ethan from glaring back at me, talking in hushed tones on the way to the other side of the room. William looks over his shoulder, and I mouth him a 'thank you.' He nods in acknowledgement.

I take a moment to nurse the soreness that burns my arm. I feel my eyes start to well as I take in a shaky breath to halt it; I will not let Ethan get the better of me. I'm still standing on the sidelines of the dance floor, focusing my mind on my surroundings instead. I watch Harper and Alex drift from table to table; she glides with so much grace, it suits her. They thank their guests for their presence with broad aching smiles. I bet their faces will hurt tomorrow. As I look from left to right, there is a mixture of events going on: kissing, smooching couples, nagging wives with husbands who have had a little too much to drink, excited children high on sugar (no doubt) chasing each other, more smiley boozed-up faces, Joe...

My gaze sweeps across the rest of the room as I take in who I just saw. Did I just imagine that? My eyes revert to where I thought I saw him; they frantically scan each face. It must have been my imagination, playing tricks on me. I look back to Harper and to whoever has caught her eye. I shuffle along a bit more to see better. Whoah, my heart tries to pole vault out of my chest when I see who it is; I see Joe. He briefly stops now and again to acknowledge greetings from our friends. As he comes into full view, yes unmistakably Joe, just much taller and trimmer from what I can remember of him from high school. I had no idea he was coming. Then I see Harper spring on him, talking closely to his ear, she then looks and points in my direction. He follows where she's pointing, and for the first time in years, our gazes meet, his schoolboy smile remains unchanged, and my heart lifts. I reciprocate his smile as he makes his way to me. He shyly looks down, for just a brief moment, then comes back up to find me. Why can't real time slow down as you see in movies, giving you more time to relish the moment. His dark brown hair is styled much shorter, and he has a neat short beard to match. I can't help but notice how well the royal blue colour of his long-sleeved shirt suits him. My knees suddenly feel weak and my heart thuds so hard against my chest, blood thrums in my ears; I feel a little on the giddy side as he approaches me. My inner spirit does the jaw-dropping for me; I feel my cheeks blaze.

"Shall we?"

He speaks in a dreamy deepish tone now; the last time I heard his voice, it hadn't broken yet. He points to the dance floor; I look to the crowd to see if anyone is watching us, still wary of Ethan. Harper has resumed her table greetings.

"Love to."

Smiling, I head to the dance floor first. Arriving, I turn around, he is right in front of me, only a couple of inches separate us. I gasp with a mixture of fright and delight at the encounter.

"Sorry, too close?"

He smiles apologetically. 'Definitely not' I so want to say out loud. As I look up to meet his gaze, a feeling within me starts budding. Those deep hazel brown eyes still feel so familiar. They draw me right in, sending the butterflies into a fluttering frenzy; but I need to remind myself of what Ashley mentioned in the café, there's a chance he has a girlfriend. I must keep the urges at bay unless he tells me something different. He draws me in just as 'At Last' by Etta James starts to play. I smile as the lyrics resonate; she somehow manages to sing the words that I feel. I can't help drinking in each of his features as I listen. My eyes fall on his lips, and I can't resist seeing them like they are forbidden fruit; I bite my lower lip to fight back the urge.

Oh, how I wish now that I had kept holding his hand all those years ago. Today would be a different story; my whole life would be a different story. I gingerly place my hands on the edges of his shoulders, but he takes hold of them and draws them closer to his neck. Then his hands hold me by the small of my back.

"It's been a while... It's good to see you again, Charly."

He says it so smoothly, holding my gaze, I don't want to break it.

"It's so good to see you too, Joe."

Thoughts track back to our school years; his smile is unaltered, even after all this time. Now I am kicking myself for running away when he tried to kiss me goodbye after walking me part of the way home after school. I take deep breaths trying to empty out the regrets;

I want to enjoy this rare moment. It will probably never happen again. We start to sway, then he takes one of my hands and holds it in mid-air. Stepping away slightly, he whirls me around on the spot; my dress flies with the motion. He places his hand back on my hip to end it; we still continue to sway. In a swift, bold move, he dips me back. It was unexpected, and my ankle decides to buckle on my nimble heel. Joe's hold tightens to stop me from hitting the floor. Our faces are so close; the hint of peppermint on his breath is deliciously mouth-watering.

I see a flicker in his eyes; temptation is written across his features as he holds me, lingering there longer than necessary. I break the tension by looking away, pretending to be embarrassed. I don't want him to make any moves that he shouldn't be making.

"Where did you learn to dance?" I ask as he brings me to my feet.

I cling to his upper arms to steady myself, and the side of my head rests against his shoulder. My nose so close to his neck, I smell his aftershave. I feel him shrug halfheartedly.

"Too many wedding receptions, I guess."

I sense a hint of heartache; it reverberates through his chest. I hope my caress on his shoulder brings him some comfort. Something to do with his girlfriend, maybe? Or his fiancée? I gulp at the thought; it pulls at my chest. Ah, this is all too overwhelming. As we continue to sway, I turn my head the other way and catch sight of Harper. She winks with a slight nod and signs, 'Okay'? I shake my head just the once, her shoulders sink in an 'oh no' reply.

The song draws to a close, and I abruptly excuse myself from Joe. My chest suddenly feels tight as my pace tries to quicken. I need air. I feel my feet start to wobble in my heels, almost tripping over. Soon as my feet hit the grass outside, I kick my heels off and scoop them up in mid-run. I ignore the evening's cool dewy grass. I keep running up the green to its highest point. I bend over to catch my breath after the sudden athletic outburst. The night's sky almost swallows up the sunset. Clutching my heels close to my chest, I suddenly realise what this reminds me of... Gareth. My eyes start to well as I hear Harper's voice chasing after me. Her touch on my arm brings my attention to her.

"Hey, you... what's going on?"

As I turn to face her, she sees the sadness in my eyes and grabs hold of me in a bear hug, then releases me to hold me by my face instead.

"This isn't about Joe, is it?"

My eyes start to drown in the rising welling, but I hold back the tears; this is Harper's wedding day, after all. I forge a smile.

"I'll be fine... honest... I just needed some fresh air... you go... enjoy your party."

My inner spirit is screaming, 'I'm torn,' but luckily, Harper can't hear that. I can't get into something deep like that now. By the unconvinced look on her face, she knows it is a twenty-four-carat lie, but she lets it go.

"Girl... you have got to track this guy down and tell him how you feel... it kills me to see you like this."

I wish it were still just about him; as I glance back to the gazebo with a heavy heart, it's not that simple anymore. Harper gives me one last squeeze before heading back. As she walks away, I call back to her.

"Harper... you were right about Joe... he is bloody gorgeous."

She grins and gestures in a 'what did I tell ya' kind of way, then carries on her way. Oh boy, isn't he just something else? The thought stirs up the butterflies once again.

My gaze comes back to the sun-kissed landscape; the scenery looks ablaze with the remaining orange, red and yellow glow. As I take in deep breaths, I let the warm air soothe me, the tightness in my chest slowly eases.

When the memories come knocking on my grey matter, I mentally open the door to let them in. I close my eyes as the images rotate like they are on a carousel. I see every fling and failed date, every infatuation and relationship I've ever had rolling on a continuous reel. Joe, Gareth, Ben, Ollie, Liam, Mark and Ethan. A voice in the darkness makes me jump; my eyes fly open, and I turn slowly, but I didn't meet their gaze.

"You know that's the second time you've run away from me...."

His tone is light-hearted and humorous, but I still feel my cheeks redden, feeling small and sheepish. I pluck up the courage to look up, and his expression drops to a serious one.

"Who's the lucky guy?"

My brow furrows with confusion... who, what, why, when exactly?

"Harper briefly mentioned it to me just now as I passed her... I wanted to see if you were okay."

He gestures towards the gazebo in confirmation. I instinctively wipe away any evidence of tears. Joe automatically steps forward to comfort me but hesitates at the last second, and still lingers close by.

"Any guy would be crazy not to want to have you, Charly."

His gaze manages to pick mine up all on its own; I so want to tell him how I feel. He's close enough that I can smell his scent. I can't tell you enough how inviting it is. If only he weren't so out of bounds.

"I am so sorry for just now, and back then... you didn't deserve any of it."

I look at his lips again; I'd do anything to kiss him right now, even if it was just this once. In second thoughts, I will dive straight in! Dip my toes in to test the water. What have I got to lose?

"I think I owe you something... probably long overdue."

I look from his lips to his eyes, then back to his lips. It doesn't take him long to twig what I am suggesting. He raises his eyebrows in an 'oh I see' kind of look. I close my eyes, and we are right back there, at that moment after school. Now both of us are rewriting history. My breath hitches as I feel his presence edge closer, and he cups my face; there's a moment of hesitation, so I open my eyes momentarily. I give him a reassuring smile, and my hands overlap his, filling us both with confidence that this will not go any further than a friendly kiss. A gentle warmth caresses my lips. It was the briefest and friendliest of kisses, but still stole my breath away.

"That's for back then."

I pull back, opening my eyes as he releases my face. He jumps back, holding his hand out.

"Shall we resume our dancing?"

I laugh as I chuck my heels to one side. I can barely see Joe as the ever-increasing darkness of the evening draws in. Taking his hand, we drift together. I almost hear the lyrics of 'Thinking Out Loud' by Ed Sheeran drifting from the gazebo. Oh, Mr Sheeran, if only I could do that right now. Joe's hand rests firmly on the small of my back, bringing me close to his chest, closer than before. I gasp as he touches my bare skin, where the back of my dress dips. My hand comes up to rest on his shoulder. I look over to our other hands laced together, then back to Joe, and my heart hammers to a different beat. The feeling makes me smile coyly.

"Relax... and just follow me."

His words are such a low smooth hum, almost hypnotic, and I fight back the urge to passionately kiss the mouth that just said them. I didn't realise how tense my body was; I take a deep breath in, and on the out breath allow myself to relax into Joe. He steps back, and my feet follow as we box step at a gentle pace.

Joe gradually picks up the pace and we move in more graceful circles, less boxy. I feel the joy ripple through me as it feels like we fly. I could be on cloud nine for all I know; it feels like floating. It's amazing what you can achieve when you put your mind to it; I'm not so left-footed without heels. Joe lets go of my back, raises his arm to spin me around, and my dress flies with me. He brings me back to him and dips me back in swift succession. My chest heaves as I come down from that cloud, taking a few deep breaths to calm from the pace. He lingers over me for a moment, just like before. I make the most of this moment as it is the last repeat. His features look like they are readying themselves to say something; I can see it in his eyes.

"I... I don't...."

Bangs of fireworks interrupt him; we both jump, forcing us to laugh nervously. He brings me back to my feet but keeps me close, his eyes still fixed on mine. His mouth opens, I assume to continue what he was about to say, but howls and cheers from the advancing crowd behind us cut him off yet again. He quickly releases me from his hold just as Harper, Alex and all the other guests ascend the peak. Was he embarrassed, maybe? What did he want to tell me? The unknowing taunts me. Joe and I get separated as everyone joins us.

As the fireworks boom, hiss and crackle above us, we all stand in a line, old school friends reunited, linking our arms together. We look up and down the line at each other, taking in this rare moment. I then concentrate on Joe; he's sporting a look much like disappointment, but it's hard to tell in this multi-coloured glow. Fresh firework smoke fills the air, along with the oohs and aahs from the crowd. Harper stands next to me; I feel her hover close to my ear.

"Nice to see you smiling again."

Oh, Harper, you have no idea how elated I feel right now; the woes a distant thought. She cheekily winks and nudges my shoulder with hers. I look back to Joe; something within me is flourishing; it's not something I've felt before. I catch his eye, and his mouth breaks into his old schoolboy shy smile.

Thirty-Eight

Ice cubes clink merrily in my rosé as I swirl my glass around like I am some sort of professional wine connoisseur. However, I've probably wrecked everything exquisite about it by putting ice cubes in, oh well. I take a sip; it slips coolly and soothingly down my throat. Resting my head back on the edge of the bath, I hold my glass up towards the window; the wine looks almost translucent. The condensation droplets run the length of the glass, resembling a window on a rainy day; it's mesmerising. Reaching up, I place my drink on the window ledge, then rest back on the bath edge. It takes a moment or two, but I watch as the droplets run off the glass and down the wall; it reminds me of tears this time. I close my eyes, willing for myself to relax.

Harper and Alex are jetting off on their honeymoon today; sunny Jamaica here they come, lucky sods. The wifey thing seems to suit Harper, as visions of their wedding yesterday bombard my thoughts. Her dress was phenomenal. I'm not sure what I'd choose for a wedding dress, maybe something vintage with lace trailing down the arms. I don't think it'd be big and bold. I think I'd be too clumsy in a ballgown type dress. I envisage me tripping over down the aisle, which makes me chuckle. That vision gets cut short as I see someone picking me up and holding me close. Then I'm looking up into the gaze of Joe as he makes sure that I am okay, the boyish charm etched in his smile. My breath hitches as I watch it all play out in my mind. He's wearing a charcoal suit with a white shirt, no tie, but there is a flower in his buttonhole that seems to match the bouquet I am holding. As I straighten up, my dress has switched for the one I just described; it's vintage, fishtail, ivory, open in the back, and lace skims down my sides and arms. We adoringly gaze at each other; oh wow, we look so good and happy together. The kiss that we share, is so soft and gentle, almost real.

My phone buzzes alive, launching me out of my daydream. I scramble out of the bath, sending the water cascading down all sides of the tub like a mini tidal wave. I quickly drape a towel around me and look at my phone. Harper's name fills the screen; I answer the call without hesitation.

"I thought you'd have a honeymoon to get to?"

My tone is playful, even though no pleasantries pass my lips.

"Yeah, I know... we've got a few minutes before we have to board... I just had to know you were okay before I stepped on the plane... you looked so sad last night... promise me, you'll do some soul searching while I am away...."

It's been a while since I heard her sound so true, sincere and apprehensive.

"Harper, I am fine... don't worry about me, okay?... I've still got Ashley here... and yes, I'll get in touch with my inner self. I promise... now run along... you've got a nice hot sandy beach waiting for you to be glamorous on... go... go have fun... don't worry. I am not alone."

'Alone.' The word hangs in my mind and the air around me, but I am alone, aren't I? My bathroom suddenly feels huge and daunting, like it will swallow me up. I lean my behind on the sink as I take in my surroundings and I hear the announcement of their flight in the background.

"Okay, that's good... I'm glad... you had me really worried for a moment... I'll see you when I get back."

I feel awful that I caused her some anxiety. Hopefully, I have said enough to put her mind at ease for now. What I have to confess can wait; the last thing that I want is for her to be miserable on her honeymoon.

"Have fun, Girl... see you soon... take lots of pictures... love ya."

I keep my tone light and upbeat. Harper hurriedly hangs up as I hear the final call for her plane again. My arm drops to my side. My wrist bashes against the sink, nearly knocking my phone out of my grip, while my other hand comes up to rub my forehead. Everything in my head seems to be in one jumbled up mess. Harper's right. I do need to get my shit together and do a little soul searching as well.

I wish that thought of me and Joe together had lasted a moment longer, or better yet, that it was more than just a fantasy.

Thirty-Nine

Damn it! My inner spirit yells back at me; I'm angry at my empty hands like it was all their fault. As I approach my work building, I realise I have forgotten my lunch. Then again, the thought of a café cheese and tomato toasted sandwich seems more appealing anyway. I sigh heavily; thank goodness it's Friday.

Luckily there hasn't been much awkwardness between Ben and me since he's been back from his supposed sick leave. I couldn't be bothered to confront him about the rumour mill he started, or the one morning stand. Judging by the smitten look, he's patched things up with his mystery woman or moved on to another one anyway. Good for him, I guess; I don't think I could get past that if I were her, but each to their own, I guess. I watch him smiling all gushy at his phone; he catches me staring at him and quickly hides his phone in his pocket, all embarrassed. He bears a look of an infatuated teenager, rumbled. I keep watching as he shuffles off to the staff kitchen.

"Someone jealous?"

I look over at Kelly, her eyebrows raised, her cheek resting on the palm of her hand. She is entirely in her, 'ready to hear some gossip' pose. I'm going to have to disappoint her.

"Rumour has it, you've got a little crush on him."

She gives me a double flash of an eyebrow. She's fucking kidding me, right?

"WHAT?"

My outburst comes out like a high-pitched screech and throws her back, not at all what she was expecting.

"Pah... it's more like the other way around... he's chasing me."

I lean a little closer towards her, beckoning for her to come forward. She does exactly that, my mouth next to her ear.

"Between you and me... he was a lousy fuck."

As we both pull away from each other again, she bears the look of a stunned goldfish. I don't give her a chance to say anything to the revelation; I just get up and announce,

"I think I'll go and grab an early lunch."

I don't wait for her to grant me permission, grabbing my bag and phone, I leave. Hopefully, that'll alter the rumour mill, once and for all. My inner spirit shouts, 'whoah, girl, you are on fire!'

I don't feel very active today, so I think the lift is the better option. Pressing the button, then tucking my phone into my bag while I wait, something scratches my fingers. I peer into my bag first. There's a small piece of card, a bright green business card. I carefully take it out to view it closer. In bold white lettering, it says 'The Garden Bar' with their contact details underneath. Turning it over, it has a plain white backing, with black biro scrawled across it. A name and number, Simon? Hmm, who's Simon? I hear the lift announcing its arrival. The name Simon doesn't mean anything to me. As much as I screw up my face trying to figure out this mystery, it's no help. When no bells ring, I chuck it into the bin as I enter the lift.

The sandwich shop isn't that busy, considering the time of day. I stand at the chiller cabinet, trying to decide upon cheese and tomato or brie, bacon and cranberry toasties.

"I'd choose the brie and bacon."

The smooth polite voice startles me, and I end up dropping both of the neatly wrapped toasties back onto the chiller shelf. A hand picks up the brie and bacon for me. My eyes follow the arm to see who it belongs to and he smiles as I meet his gaze.

"Nice to see you again, Charly."

I just about manage to paint on a smile, but my stunned expression is stubborn at disappearing.

"Sorry, did I startle you?"

My face finally becomes animated as it wakes up from its stunned state.

"H-h-hi... umm... no, it's okay."

I cannot tell you how awkward I feel right now; I am facing the guy who almost bored me to death, who I fled from not even a week ago. His kind smile doesn't seem to be fazed by my said actions. As the sun beats in from the window, it brings a healthy glow to his blonde hair. His appearance seems more relaxed even in his work gear.

"Do you come in here often? ... You seem to know a lot about sandwiches."

I cringe as soon as the question leaves my lips. Thank goodness it made him laugh. There's only one person in front of me in the queue.

"I do actually, most lunchtimes... the best sandwiches I have ever tasted."

I notice he picks up the same sandwich. My turn comes up to hand over my sandwich to the barista; I ask her to toast it for me and order a cappuccino. I was tempted to get a takeaway, but intrigue about this guy starts to set in for some reason. Hopefully, he'll join me. He comes to stand right next to me.

"Here, let me get that for you" he murmurs while he adds his lunch order to mine before I have a chance to say anything. The kind gesture takes me by surprise. Surely, I should be the one buying his lunch, as a way of apology.

"Umm... thank you."

It comes out slightly on the coy side, and I feel my cheeks start to redden under his charm. I turn around to look for vacant seats. Luckily, there are some by the window. I take one while I wait, my back towards the door. The world is on display through the big windows, with everyone going about their everyday business, so many lives, so many different stories. Do you ever wonder, when looking at passers-by, what kind of day they are having? Or find you make it up on the spot judging by their facial expression, or is that just me? William heads over to me with my mug of cappuccino.

"Do you mind if I join you?"

I smile sweetly while my inner spirit shouts, 'yes, I win.' I'm thankful for his company, actually. I gesture to the empty seat opposite me.

"Sure."

It's the least I can do in return for his generosity anyway. As he takes his pew, a pang of guilt for prejudging him last weekend hits my chest. The way he's speaking today is more upbeat, more laid-back. Maybe it was the fact he was put on the spot to talk to me? Or the company we were in? Who knows.

"Thank you for coming to my rescue."

He cocks his head slightly to the side as confusion sweeps across his face.

"At Harper's wedding, I mean... the guy that wouldn't leave me alone... thank you for stepping in and steering him away."

Judging by the nod and half of an accomplished smile, I think he finally twigs what I was trying to say.

"You are most welcome, Charly... I can't stand cocky men like that... it's no way to treat a lady... I hope he didn't hurt you."

He holds my gaze on the last few words. Hurt me? Like you would not believe. You might go vigilante on his ass if you knew exactly what he said and did.

"Was he an ex?" he continues.

I swallow hard; it tugs at my dry throat, and I shift in my seat, uncomfortable with the direction this conversation is heading. I can't tell if it's the lack of food or the subject matter that has got my stomach in a nauseated twist. How on earth do I begin to explain what we had or didn't have?

"We weren't an item as such... just a one-time thing... but I didn't know he had a fiancée... I would have never gone near him if I had known... it still makes me feel nauseous...I really don't understand how someone can be that cruel... he wanted to talk it through I think, but I really didn't want to hear what he had to say."

I pause, suddenly feeling like I'm waffling on, but he's actually leaning forward and concentrating on my every word.

"I can assure you, we're not all like that... I was going to ask you to dance after I managed to steer the guy out of your way... but someone else beat me to it."

Oh yes, Joe. So fucking out of reach, Joe. I feel amazing vibes gush right through me as I retrace the events of the reception. The train of thoughts is disturbed by the clash of plates on the table; I was mentally so far away that I nearly jumped out of my skin.

"Oh god... I'm so sorry... for then and now."

I say it without thinking it through. I squeeze my eyes shut briefly and open them to find my toastie. I take a bite; the sweetness of cranberry, creaminess of brie, and the smoky taste of bacon is indeed a match made in heaven. It's so delicious. William was right; he really does know his sandwiches.

"You both looked very close... are you two an item?"

Oh, if only. William observes me closely, his jaw clenched with anticipation, as he waits for me to answer. I kind of got a feeling where this was heading. I know that as soon as I say what he probably wants to hear, I'll be immediately faced with the dreaded question, 'do I or don't I.' If he ever asks me out at all, that is. Going back to his question, it's a bitter pill to swallow, admitting there is no chance for Joe and me.

"Unfortunately, no."

Hope flickers through his eyes, and his features relax. The thought of Joe being with someone else, or talking about him in general, is too much to bear.

"So, how do you know Harper's dad?"

It's the only thing I could think of to redirect the conversation. I take another bite of the toastie while I wait for William to answer. He doesn't seem fazed by the rapid change of subject; I've probably just allowed him to buy more time.

"Our fathers work together within my company... I haven't known Harper for very long."

I nod in between bites of my toastie. Mmm, oh wow, this does taste so good. I realise then that I'm making the 'mmm' noises out loud.

"Are you enjoying that?"

I don't look at him when I sense a slight sternness to his tone. Uh oh, I've been rumbled; for a moment there, I thought I had gotten away with it. I feel my cheeks flush red hot, oh crap.

"Erm... yes... it's lovely... thank you."

I feel so small as my voice comes across so timidly.

"Good."

I still can't bring myself to meet his eagle-eye gaze as again his tone sounded so sharp. I feel like I'm going to be held accountable for my improperness. I need to watch what I say and do. Picking up my mug of cappuccino, I try to hide my embarrassment behind it. I find myself peering over the rim; I realise he's not scary at all, observant, yes, but nothing more. The way he sits is so relaxed and carefree, along with his expression. However, there's a hint of a smirk as he runs a hand through his hair. His accent doesn't reflect his personality; at this revelation, I start to unwind.

"How long have you known Harper?"

His tone is more attentive this time around.

"Erm... pretty much since preschool... we've always been more like sisters than friends... I don't know what I'd do without her sometimes... well, all the time really."

Every word rings true; I'd be so lost without her. The last few bites of my toastie are waiting to be eaten. I take a cautious bite, reminding myself to savour each mouthful without making a sound and then wash it all down with a large gulp of cappuccino.

"You're right about these sandwiches... the best I've had in a while."

I hide my mouth behind my mug again as I quietly chuckle; it wasn't even that funny. Peering at the clock over William's shoulder, I realise I've only got five or so minutes to get back to the office.

"I'm sorry, but my lunch break is over... and thanks so much for lunch."

I feel awful for eating then leaving straight away. If I were more prepared for this meeting, I probably wouldn't have been so skittish.

"Same time next week, maybe?"

He stands as I get up to leave; I meet his eyes as he asks, the blueness of his eyes shines full of optimism. How can I say no to that look, far from pity? I am intrigued to get to know him better.

"Sure... that'll be lovely... it's a date... bye William."

I smile sweetly as I watch his face light up.

"A date it is... and please call me Will," he calls after me as I open the café door and I peer around the frame to answer him.

"Okay... William."

Forty

Time has passed surprisingly quickly this week; Friday has come around again. I tried to leave for lunch a little early, like I did last week, but ended up about ten minutes later. I dash down the flights of stairs and bolt through the foyer; the security guard looks up, but doesn't question me this time, probably used to me flying around the place by now.

I almost bulldozed into the café with a little too much eagerness. I realise William's not here, oh shit, have I missed him? Continuously glancing at my watch and the door, the minutes tick by, and I begin to lose hope.

"Hi... is your name Charly?"

As I look in the direction of the voice, I see a hand waving a piece of paper just above the tall counter. The barista's head just about peers over the top of the counter. I step forward to acknowledge her.

"Yes, that's me."

I head over to the cashier's side of the counter to see who the voice belongs to. Pretty sure this is the same girl who served us coffee last week.

"A tall blonde guy, Will, left you this note...."

Hmm, okay, why do I get the feeling I've been stood up. I smile appreciatively at the barista gal and reach over to retrieve the piece of paper from her.

"Thank you."

I turn my back away from the counter like it's top-secret. I carefully unfold it as a business card slides out. The neat handwriting on the piece of paper reads:

'Charly,

I'm so sorry that I can't make lunch today.

Reschedule for dinner tomorrow night?

Will x.'

Reschedule? It sounds so formal and business-like. My smile doesn't fade even though my hopes have been dashed slightly. I glance from the note, then back to the door, then back to the piece of paper in my hand, like he's still going to waltz in at any moment. Peering at the sleek black business card, I see his name in full for the first time in bold white lettering.

Will Anderson, CEO of Anderson and Freeman Investments LTD.

Just his email address sits at the bottom of the card, no telephone numbers - that seems a bit odd. Then my eyes trackback to his title, whoah, CEO? I remember him talking about something along the lines of finance at Harper's wedding, but I kind of switched off; I should have paid more attention. Oh, and last week he said something about Nick working alongside his father within his company. It kind of makes me feel unaccomplished.

Along with a sigh, I slide the note and the card into my bag. I think I'll let William stew for a little bit, because I have a brie and bacon toastie with my name on it right now.

***

From: Charlotte Bay
Subject: Your note...
Date: 31st July 21:04
To: Will Anderson

Dear Mr Anderson

Thank you kindly for your dinner invitation, but I'm afraid I will be washing my hair tomorrow night.

Charly Bay x

My finger hovers over the button on the mouse; the arrow lingers on the send icon on my laptop screen. I don't know him well enough to know if he'll get my sense of humour or not. Then again, his body language was quite laid-back last week; I think I'll take my chances as I gingerly click on send. I nervously start to bite on my fingernails and luckily, I don't have to wait long for that familiar new message ping and for his name to appear in my inbox.

From: Will Anderson
Subject: Re: Your note...
Date: 31st July 21:09
To: Charlotte Bay

Dear Miss Bay
Thank you for your RSVP. That is a huge shame, Miss Bay; I was hoping to get to know you better ;)
Will Anderson x

I smile broadly at the message displayed on the screen in front of me. The winking face fills me with enough reassurance that he gets my humour. That being said, I think I'll tease him for a little longer.

From: Charlotte Bay
Subject: Good things come to those who wait...
Date: 31st July 21:20
To: Will Anderson

Dear Mr Anderson
I think I may be able to squeeze you in after, but I must warn you it might take a while. So, if you're happy to wait...
Charly Bay x

From: Will Anderson
Subject: Re: Good things come to those who wait...
Date: 31st July 21:25
To: Charlotte Bay

Dear Miss Bay

Trust me, I have all the time in the world to wait... you will definitely be worth it. I'll book a table. Shall we say after eight tomorrow night?

Will Anderson xFrom: Charlotte Bay
Subject: Mint chocolate...
Date: 31st July 21:32
To: Will Anderson

Dear Mr Anderson

After 8? Hmm... does that mean I'll be rewarded mint chocolates if I'm a good girl and show up?

Charly Bay x

From: Will Anderson
Subject: Re: Mint chocolate...
Date: 31st 21:40
To: Charlotte Bay

Dear Miss Bay

I guess there is only one way to find out...

Will Anderson x

From: Charlotte Bay
Subject: You tease...
Date: 31st July 21:51
To: Will Anderson

Dear Mr Anderson
Hmm... okay, then I'll have to think about it...
Charly Bay x

From: Will Anderson
Subject: Re: You tease...
Date: 31st July 21:55
To: Charlotte Bay

Dear Miss Bay
I was not kidding when I said that I want to get to know you better... I do hope you can fit me into your busy schedule.
Will Anderson x

From: Charlotte Bay
Subject: Like I said...
Date: 31st 22:02
To: Will Anderson

... good things come to those who wait.

Charly Bay x

From: Will Anderson

Subject: Re: Like I said...

Date: 31st July 22:15

To: Charlotte Bay

I'm sure they will, Miss Bay. If you can make it, I'll meet you on City Bridge at 19:45 tomorrow. Goodnight, Miss Bay.

Will Anderson x

From: Charlotte Bay

Subject: We'll see...

Date: 31st July 22:24

To: Will Anderson

... goodnight William.

Miss Bay x

Forty-One

Luckily, I didn't throw out my 'little black dress'. I have no idea what William has planned for me. If we are going to a restaurant, then more than likely, it'll be one of those where you have too many forks, knives and spoons.

I decide to walk to City Bridge. The sun is on the verge of setting over the city as I make my way alongside the embankment; rays from the last ounce of sun colour the water in orange and yellow as it bounces and ripples. It's simply beautiful. I breathe in deeply, relishing the warmth of the glorious evening. Scanning up and along the bridge, squinting through the brightness, he doesn't seem to be here yet. Following the path alongside the embankment, I then turn left to join the bridge. Just before I get to the midpoint, I see him walking towards me on the same side of the bridge, dressed in a light grey ultra-sharp suit, pale blue shirt, no tie, his blonde hair combed back and sleek. My inner spirit's mouth gapes open. Hmm, yes, quite handsome, actually. I slow down as he comes to a stop halfway, and I notice he has one arm behind his back. As I near him, he has the broadest appreciative smile I have ever seen.

"I'm so glad that you managed to fit me in, Miss Bay... you look stunning tonight" he murmurs, swiftly followed by a peck on my cheek. The sensation is soft and friendly, even sweet.

"Thank you, Mr Anderson... well... after careful consideration I decided... that I wanted to get to know you too."

I smile warmly with an edge of amusement. William brings out his arm from its hiding place; I see the familiar dark green box and, of course, the logo. My smile broadens at the thoughtfulness.

"Oh damn... it isn't eight o'clock yet... but thank you, William... that's really thoughtful,"

playfully peering down at my watch-less wrist as I say it. I look up to meet William's gaze; his smile hasn't ceased.

"I've booked a table for us... it's just a bit further this way," he murmurs.

He points with a thumb over his shoulder without turning an inch or taking his eyes off me.

"Perfect" it leaves my lips a little too enthusiastically, but it doesn't seem to faze him. He turns to stand by my side and offers his arm. I quickly place my chocolates in my bag and gladly accept his arm. We stroll across the rest of the bridge, admiring the colours of the evening sky as we go.

Yes, just as I thought it would be. I look up at the grand building in front of us. I have passed this place many times, but I would never have guessed it was a restaurant. Maybe something along the lines of a museum or a theatre, but never a place to consume food. William has no idea how much pressure I am under right now to look and act a certain way. Not to mention that my dress doesn't even meet my knees. I try to gulp away the anxiety that's lurking within me.

We're a little early, so we are told to wait in the bar. William opens his mouth to speak, but is immediately distracted by voices behind me. I watch as his cheerful face turns to a slight grimace.

"Darling!"

I watch William greet a middle-aged couple. He reluctantly hugs the woman and kisses her on the cheek. She is well-groomed with flawless skin, her glossy dark blonde hair done up in a fancy up-do, built like a rake, dressed in a navy dress suit like she's off to a wedding. William turns slightly and gestures in my direction as he introduces them to me.

"Charly, this is my mother, Fiona... and this is my father, Richard."

You've got to be kidding me. I try my best to soften my stunned expression. I was about to step forward to greet William's mother first, but I notice her smile rapidly disappears, and her top lip curls up in the corner like she's disgusted. Just her eyes scan me up and down. Clearly, she's made up her mind about me already, probably thinking I'm not good enough for her baby boy. Not that we are even an item anyway, technically speaking. Oh boy, first impressions are not good.

"Charly? Ha, isn't that boy's name?" she scoffs.

Can I run now, please? I try to keep my body in neutral, forcing back the urge to be spiteful in retaliation.

"Yes, it is...."

I respond in my deepest tone, and the blood in her cheeks runs half dry. She obviously can't take a joke. A roar of laughter comes from Richard, while Fiona, on the other hand, looks a little miffed that I outwitted her. Richard steps forward, his large round belly just about stays within the confines of his white shirt, to kiss both of my cheeks as he greets me enthusiastically. He's just as smartly dressed, in a navy suit, but seems more down to earth than she is.

"Ignore her; I do... so, William... this is the young lady you've been banging on about... beautiful and witty... I like her already."

Richard grabs and shakes my hand vigorously, then turns to plant a heavy pat on William's back, which makes a few strands of his hair fall out of place. William quickly smoothes it back as I notice a glimpse of redness flush across his cheeks. It takes me by surprise, and I instantly raise my eyebrows at him like I am searching for an explanation. It sounds like someone has been bragging. I let it lie... for now anyway.

"Table for Mr Anderson."

Thank fuck for that. I see a waiter searching for us, and I automatically put my hand up; he smiles and gestures for us to follow.

"Lovely to meet you both."

It comes out slightly sarcastic, I can assure you that it was unintentional. I don't wait for his parents to say anything more. I head towards the waiter.

People like her sadden me; she clearly doesn't believe I belong in their world. In hushed stern voices, William says goodbye to his parents and soon catches up to me.

"I'm so sorry about them...."

Judging by his expression, he seems genuinely agitated by the way they just spoke to me. Hopefully, he stands in my corner.

"... Especially my mother, she always seems to jump to defence mode if she suspects I'm seeing someone."

Jeez, someone must be so bored of her own life if she insists on meddling in his. Talk about overprotective; he's thirty-odd, not a three-year-old. Who says we even see each other? As we sit, I notice the cutlery; I mentally grimace when I realise I was right.

"Don't worry... I'll help you as we go."

I suddenly feel embarrassed, like a child who needs their food cut up into tiny pieces. I sit in awkward silence, feeling so out of place as I glance around the room at the tall daunting ceilings with their centuries-old engraved patterns. How can something be so beautiful and yet so intimidating? This is definitely not my scene; come to think of it, I don't think I belong to a 'scene'. I feel my body curve inwards, my hands frantically playing with the tassels on my bag.

"Excuse me, madam."

Out of the corner of my eye, I see a flash of white, that makes me jump, as the waiter shakes out a crisp white serviette, or napkin; I have no idea what the correct word is. He gestures to lay it on my lap. It's something that you'd expect in these sorts of places, but it still seems alien to me. He hands me a menu and at first glance, I have no idea what I am looking at; it's like trying to read a different language. The words become jumbled as I try to make sense of it all, like trying to read through beer goggles but sober. I mindlessly rub my forehead. William leans closer to me.

"Do you want to get out of here?"

A mischievous grin stretches across his face as I look up at him over my menu. He doesn't wait for me to answer; just like at the reception, I think he can sense what I'm feeling. Standing up, he fishes around in his pocket for his wallet, and puts down a more than generous tip. I don't know what for; we haven't even touched anything. He offers his hand, and I gladly take it. Following his lead, I dash with him, giggling all the way out to the entrance, like naughty children. Diners are expressing their disgust on our way through.

Soon as our feet touch the pavement, we don't stop; we weave through the streets—the thrill of it buzzing right through us.

As we finally slow to a stroll, I realise how sore my heels feel; my legs go into automatic limping mode. William is still clutching hold of my hand as he looks down at my feet, then back to my face. William leads me straight to a wall and insists that I sit down. He kneels in front of me and carefully slips off my heels; I wince at the action; it tugs at the soreness. He mirrors my wincing face and half-smiles apologetically. Once he has both of my heels, he tells me to stay here. Intrigued, I watch him jog off, as he heads straight for one of the late-night market stalls we had just passed. Moments later, he comes jogging back with a blue and white striped carrier bag and takes out a flat pair of pumps, a rather garish sparkly pair of pumps. I mentally grimace at the sight of them, but what a kind gesture nonetheless.

"I'm really sorry about the colour... they only had these in your size ... here... let me help you with them."

He kneels back down on one knee in front of me, gently cupping and lifting one ankle. Slipping on the first shoe, he glances up at me as he lets go; it feels like a real Cinderella moment. He gently cups my other ankle, lifting it and slipping on the second shoe. As he lets go, I feel his fingertips brush a little above the back of my ankle as he gets back to his feet. The sensation tickles and tingles all the way up my leg. Offering both of his hands to me, I take them and shuffle my behind off the wall. He locks eyes with me as my feet land on the ground, but he doesn't let go of my hands.

"How do they feel now?" he asks.

I feel like I am still lost in the Cinderella moment, captivated by the thoughtful and romantic gesture.

"They feel a bit better... thank you... that was really kind."

His face turns bashful again, a hint of crimson across his cheeks. Holding one of my hands up to his mouth, he pauses.

"You are most welcome."

As a gentle peck meets the back of my hand, I feel myself warming to him. The butterflies lay dormant though, maybe a tiny flutter but hardly noticeable. Letting go of my hands, he retrieves my heels and places them in the market bag. He comes back to stand at my side to offer his arm, I gladly accept.

We stroll further down the cobbled street as we near more market stalls. Freshly cooked food wafts in our direction, making my stomach growl like crazy. There's so much to choose from. As we draw nearer, I let go of William's arm and head straight for the hotdog stand. William follows closely behind me. We order two, with heaps of fried onions, lashings of mustard, and ketchup. I grab a handful of napkins before we walk away; I've got a feeling this is going to be messy.

We walk and eat until we reach near the end of the street; that's when we hear stringed instruments. We instinctively follow the sound, round to the right where we find a band of violins and cellos, in the middle of the square. I stop abruptly, admiring the sight and appreciating the sound echoing around the square as I finish my last bite of hotdog. A few random couples are making the most of the free entertainment as they sway and box step around the set-up. I can feel William's eyes on me; as I turn to face him, he starts chuckling.

"You've got a bit of sauce... here; let me help you."

Placing my bag of heels down first, he takes one of the napkins; he moves closer to me and tells me to look up to the streetlamp, wiping away the incompetence of my eating. After a couple of wipes, his hand pauses just in front of my face, an action that instantly catches my attention. I look down from the streetlamp to find his face.

"There you go," he murmurs deeply.

So hushed, you could mistake it for a whisper. William lowers his arm to put the napkin in his pocket, but he keeps his eyes fixed on me. He seems hesitant, but I can see the yearning in his eyes, so I step closer to him; I look to his mouth, then back to his eyes. I stand on my tiptoes and peck him just once, hoping it will give him the courage to kiss me back. In nanoseconds, both of his hands come up to cup my face, bringing me in for a passionate but tender kiss. As we relax into each other, his arms come down to hug me, his palms resting just above my behind. Resting my palms on his shoulders, I feel the warmth from his chest as I huddle into him; it's far from a cold night, but it's comforting.

As he breaks away, he gives me a shy smile, keeping me close; he scoops up one of my hands off his shoulder. He moves back towards the band, joining the other couples. I'm so glad he keeps to a slow sidestep-and-rotate on the spot, like embarrassed teens slow dancing at a school disco. Well, I don't think my sore feet could handle anything more vigorous than this. The long, drawn-out notes of the violins remind me of Joe; no matter how much I try, however much I curse at myself, it's simply impossible to erase that evening from my memory.

Forty-Two

From: Will Anderson
Subject: A more than satisfactory night...
Date: 3rd August 20:35
To: Charlotte Bay

Dear Miss Bay

I am writing to inform you that Saturday night was the most enjoyable time I have had in a long time. Thank you again for squeezing me into your busy schedule at the last minute, much obliged.

If you're not busy washing your hair again, can I cook you a meal? Possibly Wednesday night, around 7?

I hope you have had a good start to the week.

Mr Anderson x

Wow, he sounds so formal and yet so eager; it doesn't fail in making me smile. My feet still feel a bit raw from that evening. It didn't help that I had to run all the way to work this morning. I think my body was still stuck in weekend mode or la la land and I ended up over sleeping. My back rests against the cushions on my sofa so I bring my legs up, until I sit cross-legged beneath my laptop. My elbow rests on top of my thigh as my finger taps against my cheek in thinking mode; hmm, what to write back? I sit and stare at the screen until something springs to mind.

From: Charlotte Bay
Subject: Re: A more than satisfactory night...
Date: 3rd August 20:47
To: Will Anderson

Thank you, I too had the most enjoyable evening. I think you may be in luck; according to my diary, I have no prior engagements or the need to wash my hair that day. So, I gratefully accept your invitation.
Miss Bay x
P. S. I like you addressing me in that manner.

From: Will Anderson
Subject: Much obliged...
Date: 3rd August 20:59
To: Charlotte Bay

Dear Miss Bay
I am ever so grateful that you accept my invitation.
I know I told you that night that you looked so stunning, but I would like to take this opportunity to compliment you again. There's only one problem; I can't seem to think of anything greater than stunning. No words seem to come close to express how beautiful you looked.

Mr Anderson
P. S. Your postscript has been clearly noted ;)

From: Charlotte Bay
Subject: Code of conduct breach...
Date: 3rd August 21:14
To: William Anderson

Dear Mr Anderson

May I also take this opportunity to say that it is strictly unprofessional of you to say so, Mr CEO, but thank you, it is much obliged. You didn't scrub up too badly either.

May I bring something to dinner, wine perhaps?

Miss Bay x

From: Will Anderson
Subject: Re: Code of conduct breach...
Date: 3rd August 21:29
To: Charlotte Bay

Dear Miss Bay

I am so deeply sorry if I caused you any offence with my previous message, Miss Bay; that was not at all my intention.

Please accept my sincerest apologies.

Just your company is more than sufficient, thank you, Miss Bay.

Mr Anderson x

From: Charlotte Bay
Subject: Your apology...
Date: 3rd August 21:34
To: Will Anderson

Dear Mr Anderson
After much careful deliberation, I will gladly accept your offer of apology; thank you kindly, Mr Anderson.
One is looking forward to dinner already.
Miss Bay x

From: Will Anderson
Subject: Re: Your apology...
Date: 3rd August 21:47
To: Charlotte Bay

Dear Miss Bay
I am thrilled to hear that you accept my apology.
I, too, am very much looking forward to dinner, more than you know. I enjoy every minute of your company.
Mr Anderson x

'More than you know'. Hmm, what is that supposed to mean? I know I started this formal banter, but it's beginning to feel tiring to keep up with this jargon; I don't know how much longer I can keep up with it.

From: Charlotte Bay
Subject: Good to know...
Date: 3rd August 21:54
To: Will Anderson

Dear Mr Anderson

I am so pleased that you enjoy my company.

Now, if you would excuse me, I need to get some beauty sleep.
After all, it is a school night, let me remind you.

Goodnight Mr Anderson

Miss Bay x

From: Will Anderson
Subject: Re: Good to know...
Date: 3rd August 22:05
To: Charlotte Bay

Dear Miss Bay

I'm so sorry to keep you from your beauty sleep. However, the
beauty part is not necessary.

I hope you have a great day at work tomorrow, sleep well.

Goodnight Miss Bay

Mr Anderson x

Forty-Three

Double-checking the address on William's message that he sent earlier today, and looking at the door numbers, I walk down his street until I come across his place. I have been looking forward to this all day, but at the same time, nerves have had a firm grip on my stomach. I'm not sure why, but I was half expecting to see a security conscience fortress, with CCTV cameras everywhere you looked and tall gates with intercoms. Right at this moment, I am pleasantly surprised, as from the outside, it looks like any other ordinary city dwelling.

From the top of his front garden path, I can see right in through the window, and I spot William. From afar, his rooms appear open plan. He looks like he's enjoying a good sing-song to 'I Want It That Way' by Backstreet Boys. The sound is muffled by the panes of glass, but the tune is recognisable. It's not something I'd ever imagine him to listen to. I was half expecting opera to be piping out full blast and him to be wearing a smoking jacket. Such a stereotypical mind I have, my inner spirit tutting at me and rolling her eyes. Instead, he's in relaxed attire just like mine, dark wash jeans with a black tee. I was so wrong about this guy, I realise, as I admire his blonde hair ruffled in a cool, sexy way. 'Sexy?' My inner spirit says it quizzically. What can I say? I have a little more warmth for him now. Safe to say, he's definitely growing on me.

Watching on in amusement for a moment, as he jigs around in his kitchen, it's a shame to interrupt the show. I carry on down the front garden pathway and ring the bell. Once, twice, then finally on the third ring, he hears it. Watching the shadow of his tall frame appear in the door panels, I see his brilliant white teeth first as he beams, even in the dimly lit hallway.

"Hello Miss Bay... please come in."

He stands to the side to let me enter; as I step in, I suddenly feel hesitant, like I'm lost with no idea what I should be doing or saying. My confusion is interrupted by a peck on the cheek, and I can't help but smile as the unsureness disperses.

"Mr Anderson."

I nod; my expression turns jokingly serious but only for a moment, then a smile breaks through. His eyes dance with the humour. He gestures to take my jacket. I feel him so close to me as I turn, allowing him to do so. He's barely left enough room for my jacket to escape; I feel his touch on my bared arms as the material slides off, my breath hitches at the gentleness of the briefest touch. I turn back to him, watching him place my jacket on the stairway post. As his gaze finds mine again, his eyes are drawn to a wisp of unruly hair that catches his attention, and he tentatively flattens it with a few strokes, his hand pausing on my hair. He looks far away as he gazes at me, almost like he's stuck in a daydream. William shakes his head just the once like he's telling himself to wake up, which makes me think that I'm glad that I'm not the only one who does that.

"Would you like a glass of wine?"

He heads straight through the curved archway, asking the question over his shoulder; I follow him as he goes.

"Sure."

I barely remember to acknowledge him as I take in his open plan living room; everything around me is so modern and stylish, exactly what I thought it wouldn't be. I was half expecting it to be all high ceilings, grand fireplaces, a butler waiting on us hand and foot; it leaves me pleasantly surprised. To the world outside, he probably feels he must look like he's keeping up with the Joneses, but behind closed doors, all he probably wants is to be like any other guy. Every wall is washed with a deep burgundy hue, sensual yet cosy.

I place my handbag on the black leather sofa that sits along the bay windows at the end of the room, facing the entrance to the kitchen. I notice the absence of a TV.

"Don't you have a TV?"

William effortlessly pops the cork on a bottle of wine, then fills two glasses that are almost goblet sized.

"Of course... it's in my drawing-room, my dear."

He exaggerates his posh tone; his pretend seriousness breaks into a grin.

"I bet you do."

I mutter it mockingly under my breath. Maybe that's where the butler is hiding; I quietly chuckle to myself.

I head towards the kitchen. I see a worktop first, looking like it's been converted into a seating area. As I walk through the threshold of another curved archway, the kitchen seems to suddenly expand; it is deceptively large. It must be his pride and joy. It's immaculate, every side is lined with top of the range gadgets. I take a pew on a stool at the kitchen table.

"What's cooking?"

I ask as I look over to the cooker top, where a pan is simmering full of rich tomato sauce. The richness of the tomatoes wafts its way over to me. It puts my 'fresh out of the jar' efforts to shame. William hands me a goblet of wine, then leans on the corner of the kitchen table next to me.

"It's Bolognese... all homemade... my speciality."

He grins as he blows a chef's kiss.

"Oh... so not fresh out of a jar of Dolmio then."

I pretend to look disappointed, followed by a grin just to tease him a little. His bemused expression finally merges to amusement as he notices my mocking expression. Oh no, he really thought I was serious.

He's standing close enough that I catch a hint of his cologne, even over the top of cooking tomatoes. I lock eyes with him; the blueness seems to dance, yet I still sense a shyness. I am drawn to him. I feel the magnetic pull to get up and pull him close to me, for my hands to search what's hiding underneath his t-shirt. Every thought that passes sends a tingling sensation through my core.

I grab a handful of his t-shirt as I hop off my stool and he smiles softly at my yearning expression; I pull him close to me, locking our lips immediately. He follows as I take a few steps back until my behind bashes against the counter, forcing me to yelp under his embrace. Abruptly he pulls away.

"Sorry... did I hurt you?"

Concern tears through his features as he surveys me. My jaw clenches, and my eyes squint at the sting that spreads across my lower back. I just about shake my head.

"No... I'm okay."

Relief relaxes his features as mine soften. Jeez, his counters have some sharp edges, that stung like a bitch. I take in a deep breath as the sensation subsides. William lingers close to me, not moving an inch from where I pulled him to. His waist is pressed against mine and peering up, he seems more relaxed tonight, like he can finally be his true self with no judgements. His eyes stay fixed on mine as his hands come up to cup my head; his thumb brushes back and forth across my cheek, then over my bottom lip; his gaze watches his own thumb. The torment is agonising as the sensation ignites a tiny fire of desire deep within my stomach. I want nothing more than my legs wrapped around his waist right now. Both hands trail across my cheeks, his fingertips brush their way up to my hairline, they drag right through my hair until each hand almost meets at the back of my head. He swiftly draws me towards him as our lips find each other again. As he caresses my head, goosebumps prickle their way down the back of my neck and tingle my spine. I keep my lips slightly parted, but our tongues don't meet; it's passionate nonetheless.

A high-pitched buzzing sound makes us both jump. William breaks the kiss but presses his forehead against mine as he exhales with frustration, like he's annoyed that his cooking has beaten us to it. He gives me a long deep kiss and then pulls away, returning back to the cooker. He seems to float around the room as he gets things ready. I can't help but smile at this domestic god; I'm in awe of him. I linger near to him in the hope that I will be of some assistance. He grabs a saucepan from one of the top cupboards, turns towards the sink and fills it with water and places it on the hob. He turns his attention back to the Bolognese, picking up the spoon to stir when the doorbell rings. Judging by William's expression, it's a little unexpected; he starts to stir, but the sound rings again, more impatiently this time. He grunts and huffs at the intrusion. Maybe he has an annoying, nosy neighbour like mine. He gestures for me to stir the sauce instead and smiles apologetically.

"Please excuse me."

William swiftly disappears through the two archways and round to the front door.

"Darling... what took so long!"

I freeze mid stir as the shrill voice sends goosebumps of fear prickling up the back of my neck. Oh shit, shit, shit! This cannot be happening right now. My heart kicks into panic mode as it beats frantically against my ribcage, like a caged animal trying to break free.

"Mother, this isn't a good time... I have company."

I hear the door shut, so heavily that I swear I just felt the walls shake. Maybe they, too, fear the presence of this judgemental cow. I look down at myself, cursing the fact that I opted for a low cut, plain, deep-red maxi dress. No problem with ordinary folk, but to her, I'm probably standing here like a red flag to a raging bull. A piercing sensation digs into my palm; that's when I realise how tightly I'm holding the stirring spoon. Taking a deep breath, I try to relax my hand. I angle my body, so I can see the entrance to the hallway, but at the same time, try to remain out of sight.

"Nonsense darling... I uh..."

Soon as she barges past William, she waltzes into the living room like she owns the place. Her eyes immediately clock and lock on me.

Her body is frozen in a rigid state, like a cat who has just encountered a rival feline on her turf. Staying quiet is luckily all I'm capable of right now, but my inner spirit is silently flexing her claws, ready to scrap. She stands there, in a hideous floral blouse and pencil skirt, her hair down, her hands clutching onto the strap of her handbag, hanging off her shoulder.

"William! ...what is that trollop doing here?!"

My body jolts as her words practically shoot through my chest and obliterate my heart. The spoon slips from my hand and hits the cooker top, splashing piping hot sauce up my bare arm. Shit, it hurts, making my eyes water.

"Mother!"

I hear William yell as I push back the pain; I hurry across the room to retrieve my bag without a word. I have a particularly good idea how this is going to pan out, and frankly, I don't have the patience to endure it. I don't make eye contact with either of them as I barge past.

"Charly... wait, please don't go."

I don't acknowledge William's plea, ripping my jacket from the post, then immediately opening and slamming the front door behind me. Raised voices come from the house, but I don't wait around to make sense of it. I hurry down the footpath, doing my best to wipe off the red sauce before flinging my jacket back on. How can a lovely evening turn so suddenly sour? Not so long ago, I was practically skipping with joy up this path; now, I can't leave quickly enough. I hear William's voice chasing after me, and then I feel his touch on my arm as he catches up to me.

"Charly... please... please don't go."

I turn towards him, but I can't bring myself to meet his gaze. He cups my hand with both of his, almost like he's pleading with me.

"... My mother had no right to talk to you in that way... I'm so, so sorry... please come back inside... I'll tell her to leave."

I look up then, to meet his pleading eyes; a look of apology written across his face draws me in and convinces me it's genuine. But movement behind William's shoulder grabs my attention. His mother scowls at me from the doorstep, arms on her hips in defence mode, even after William's abrupt words. She wins; quite frankly, I don't have the energy for this kind of shit. My eyes break from her scowl to briefly look down at my feet. I take a deep breath, and on the exhale, I look up to find William again.

"William... let's face it... your mother will never accept me for me... no amount of convincing is going to change her mind... you know it... I know it... I shouldn't have to prove that I'm worthy of you... I think it's best if you let me go, William."

His grip on my hand reluctantly loosens, and my hand slips away from his. Genuine sadness fills his eyes, making me feel that I don't want to leave him this way, but with the sight of his mother looming in the background, I have no choice but to walk away. Otherwise, I'll be forever curtseying and kissing her ass for respect until the end of time.

"You know it's for the best... If we came from the same walks of life... it'd be a totally different story...you are such a kind-hearted man, William... I hope you find someone your mother will approve of."

Oh boy, what a mission on this poor guy's shoulders. With that, I move closer, putting my right hand on his cheek and pecking the other. His hand overlaps mine, securing my hand to his cheek. I can't bring myself to look in his eyes any longer; I feel like I'm the bad guy when really, she's standing right behind us lurking in the shadows. William's other hand comes up to my neck and draws me in even closer; he kisses my lips with such intensity, it breaks my heart. Breaking away, he rests his forehead against mine.

"I really don't want this to end... I really am sorry, Miss Bay."

His voice is cracked with grief, but the briefest of smiles flashes when he says my name. Wriggling my hand free and stepping back a little, I keep my eyes locked with his.

"I know you are... I don't want this to end either... trust me... but I think it's the right thing to do."

I nod in his mother's direction.

"... you better get back to your darling mother."

It was a low blow, and I curse at myself for sounding so patronising. Then again, isn't it about time he starts listening to his own heart, fulfilling his own desires, not his mother's? He winces at the word 'mother', his jaw tight and teeth clenched. His features soften as he glances at me one last reluctant time before turning and walking away. My eyes don't leave him until he walks back indoors. He never looks up, totally ignoring his mother. I scale back to her, her features twisted with smugness and victory. She uses her fore and middle finger to form a walking motion along her arm and then points down the street. She is basically telling me to jog on. I raise a cocky eyebrow at her, my inner spirit jumping up and down, egging me on, yelling at me, 'c'mon, c'mon do it, do it... go on, you know you want too!' Without further persuasion, my middle finger springs up as I lift my hand in mid-air, my face follows suit with a smirk full of attitude. Ha, I win this time, bitch. Shock consumes her face as I watch her jaw drop. Turning on my heel, I don't run... I don't walk... I strut, with more sass than Beyoncé.

**

Nearing home, I felt my cocky façade dissolving. I should have tried harder with William's mother, but then again, she clearly had already made her mind up about me; it would have been an immense uphill struggle to try to convince her that I'm not a bad person. I know for a fact she wouldn't have made it easy for us to have any sort of relationship. Sitting on the edge of my bed, I call Ashley.

"You're back early... how was it?"

No pleasantries, straight down to business just like Harper would have done, she makes me smile, and for a moment, I am happy.

"Ah... umm... not so good."

I hear her groan echo down the phone.

"What? ... What happened this time? ... He seemed rather charming."

Oh, just the usual overbearing bitch of a mother who can't help but stick her fucking huge conk into our business. Charming? Oh boy, yes charming, so charming in fact he could have been the prince himself.

"His mother hates me."

Sadness weighs down my voice; the sentence rolls heavily off my tongue. Fiona's scowling face clouds my mind; my inner spirit hisses at the image and claws at her face until the image bursts.

"What has his mother got to do with anything?"

Every-fucking-thing, unfortunately. She's a self-righteous old hag who loves to tear people down and tread all over what dignity is left, then spits her words out like venom all over your crumpled remains; how's that for a summary?

"She barged her way into the house and ruined our dinner plans... she even called me a trollop, Ashley... she's one nasty piece of...."

Ashley, too troubled by what I just said, couldn't wait for me to finish.

"Whoah, whoah, whoah, ... wait, what? ... She said what? ...What the hell? Who the hell does she think she is? ...I hope he told her where to go."

My eardrum was well underprepared; it ached and throbbed from her sudden outburst. I don't think I've ever heard Ashley raise her voice like that. Harper, yes, but never Ashley so I'm quite taken aback.

"I know, right... her mind was made up way before she even got to know me... or before I even opened my mouth to say anything... anyway, I'm so exhausted... I think I'm going to turn in early."

I hear Ashley exhale as she slowly comes down from her cloud of ferocity.

"Don't let that cow get you down, Charly... she was probably just overwhelmed by your natural beauty... just like the wicked old queen in Snow White, for instance... watch out for any huntsman... oh, fair maiden."

She giggles lightheartedly; I'm so glad I called her.

"Well, let's hope that doesn't happen... I've got to go now, Ashley... see you soon... good talking as always."

I hang up before I hear her goodbyes. My arms feel heavy, with what I don't know. As I slip out of my clothes and into my pyjamas, the garish sparkly market stall shoes stare at me from my dresser, accusingly; 'how could you do that to us?' That evening was full of firsts for me, memorable moments that I will never forget. I take one last look at them before tucking them away at the back of my shoe collection. Goodbye, Prince Charming; I will never forget you.

Pulling back my bedsheets, I clamber in and wrap myself up. Humiliation drifts its way in and weighs down heavily on my chest. I feel sad but relieved at the same time. The hunger growls are strangely quiet, considering the lack of food, probably suppressed by the unwanted notion. I roll onto my back and my gaze fixes on the nothingness. I'd be lying if I said I wouldn't miss the formality we shared in our messages. Sadly, I will never find out for sure if he had surfer's washboard abs hiding under his shirt.

I close my eyes, and Gareth suddenly springs to mind. I see his face so vividly, serene and smiling. Emotions form a lump in my throat as I mentally hang on to the image, but like a mirage in a desert, it ripples and disperses. My brain can't seem to fathom the meaning behind it, and just like reality, he's gone.

Forty-Four

Staring blankly at my home brought lunch, I sit at one of the tall tables in the staff kitchen. How on earth do I keep getting it so wrong? I'm not even referring to my marmite, pickle and cheese sandwich. Yes, you heard me right, but don't mock it until you try it. We're having a staring contest, my lunch and I, no prizes for guessing who falters first. The sound of someone clearing their throat disturbs my thoughts; the noise belongs to Stanley. He glances at my thigh area, then carries on over to the water dispenser to make himself a drink. Looking down, I realise that my pencil skirt has ridden halfway up, practically no wider than a belt. Shit, shit, shit, oh god, how could I not notice? I have no idea how long he was standing there ogling at my naked leg; the thought makes me shudder. Before he can make small talk with my thigh and not my face, I hop off my stool and scoop up my neglected lunch, slam-dunking it in the bin as I stride out. I tell Kelly that I need fresh air for the rest of my lunch hour. Grabbing my bag, I turn to walk out, just as my boss exits the kitchen. He gives me a brief nod, a semi smile and a hint of a wink. How mortifying. My thigh and I dash out of the office.

***

Just when I was contemplating visiting the sandwich shop, I see him; I see William. His blonde hair and tall frame visible through the window, recognisable even from across the street. A part of me wants to go and say hi and reconvene our lunch dates, until I see that he's with a woman. His hand resting on her shoulder, I can't see her face, but whatever she's saying, it's making him smile; it's like watching a silent movie. She's beautifully elegant from the back, smartly dressed in a straight electric blue dress, long straight auburn hair that falls past her shoulders. Definitely, someone his mother will, without a doubt, approve of. Well, at least someone got their wish. Good luck to them, good luck to her most of all. I reluctantly carry on down the street to the next café, hoping that their brie and bacon toasted sandwiches are just as good.

Forty-Five

'Fighter' by Christina Aguilera pulses through my earbuds as I slip into a new pair of running shoes. Yes, you heard me right. It's been just over a week since I saw William through the sandwich shop window. I'm so desperate not to dwell on it anymore. I've been putting off running for ages, and there's no better time than now. I grab a hair tie from my dresser, scooping my long hair into a tight ponytail and smoothing out any bumps. With hands on my hips, I give my reflection in the long mirror a look of determination. I am so ready for this. I jog down the stairs to the front door. I am standing on my doorstep, stretching to Christina's beat. Fuck yes, I'm a warrior; her lyrics empower me to wipe the slate clean.

Time for me, time for a new me. I inhale and exhale deeply, and the track changes to 'Shape of You' by Ed Sheeran. I look down at myself; I think I am a pear, will that pass, Mr Sheeran? I skip to the next track, 'Señorita' by Justin Timberlake. Honestly, Mr Timberlake, I'd be pretty happy to be your señorita, but not right now; sorry, skip. 'Love In An Elevator' by Aerosmith. Why the hell not, except not with you, I'm afraid Mr Tyler, but Mr Timberlake on the other hand? Yes sir!

Instead of the usual right turn towards town, I head left towards Green Grove Park. It's easily a mile away and I think that would be a good starting point. Ha, famous last words. I set off at a steady pace. The mid-morning sun beating down on my face, mixed with fresh autumnal air, feels exhilarating. Halfway there, I start to feel the strain in my calves, but I push on; I so need to do this. iTunes keeps banging out more upbeat tracks, keeping my feet pounding the pavement. Huffing and puffing, the cool air is stabbing and aching my lungs, but I must keep going. The familiar sight of the tall hedgerows that line Green Grove Park comes into view; the finish line is fast approaching. Just as I thought I had hit my limits, a sudden burst of energy surges through my legs, powering my feet to keep going. Bolting through the gates, I narrowly miss a walker and her dog.

"So sorry," I call back.

Oops, I think I frightened her. I keep to the same pace, following the winding paths. The beautiful white Victorian bandstand flashes past me, no time to admire its charm today. The winding paths come to an end, reaching the vast open green space instead. I keep running until I hit the furthest point, slowly coming to a stop once I see the city skyline. My arms feel like dead weights; I bend over and rest my palms on my thighs to catch my breath. My entire body throbs and aches, the tension pulses through my legs, but I feel alive. I slow my breathing by taking deep breaths and shaking out my limbs as I straighten up again. Resting my hands on my hips, I take in the view, the city still in its weekend slumber.

A small white dog comes bounding up the hill towards me; it looks delighted to see me. Someone not so far behind it is yelling its name.

"Sammy! ...for goodness sake... come back! ...Sammy... SAMMY!"

I freeze on the spot when I recognise the person chasing the dog. I gulp hard, my feet fixed to the ground; what the hell do I do now? Her auburn curls are flowing behind her as she dashes. As she comes closer, her face becomes more apparent; it's her. The little white dog jumps up to my legs, desperately trying to grab my attention. The woman stops in her quest, I think she's clocked who I am, or she's unsure whether to approach a possible stranger. I look down at Sammy.

"C'mon boy... let's take you back."

One of us needs to break the ice; I guess it should be me, so I set my feet in motion, and the cute little dog obediently follows my command. I swallow hard as I approach her; this is going to be an awkward reunion. I paint on a smile, hoping and praying it doesn't look false. Not that I have anything against her, it's just the possibility that she hates my guts. I wouldn't blame her. I broke her brother's heart after all, and probably deserve any anger she's got stored up for me. To my surprise, she gives me a broad smile, but there's still a hint of awkwardness to it. She's probably under strict instruction not to have any communication with me. That thought gets pushed to the side as she hugs me tightly. It doesn't feel as enthusiastic as our very first meeting but welcoming nonetheless. My eyes grow wide with a cocktail of relief and surprise.

"Charly... It's so good to see you... how you been?"

I can feel the tension in my body melt away as her kind words flow and release me.

"It's so good to see you too, Cassie."

I sidestep the 'how you been?', I really don't know how to respond to that.

"Don't look so worried... I'm not going to bite your head off... you had your reasons for leaving... and I respect that."

Whoah, is she a mind reader or something? I guess facial expressions can speak louder than words. We turn and walk back up the hillside, and Sammy dutifully follows. Cassie points over to the park café as it appears.

"Fancy a coffee?"

This woman is so unbelievably nice. I jilted her brother, and she still wants to be friends. My features melt into a softer, more relaxed smile with that thought.

"Yeah, sure, why not."

She shrugs and smiles delightedly as she links her arm with mine. I'm astounded that she doesn't want to rip me apart verbally. I don't think I could be so lovely and calm in her position.

We grab a coffee and take a seat outside. I'm surprised Cassie wants to be seen with me out in the open. I was half expecting to huddle in a corner inside, like some sort of covert operation, whispering behind the menus. The seating area nicely traps the warmth from the sun. Sammy sprawls out next to our feet, enjoying the rays on his belly.

"How's Gareth doing?"

Soon as I ask it, I regret it; it just slipped out without my giving it any thought. The prospect of hearing that Gareth's happy with someone else is almost too much to bear. Yet, it's something that inevitably is going to happen sooner or later. Cassie's smile turns a little crooked; the tables have turned, she's the one in the nervous corner now.

"He's... umm good... better than he was anyway... I'm not going to lie, Charly... you leaving... tore him apart... I've never seen him so distant... we barely spoke... and that's so unlike us... we're back on track now... he's back on track now... he's umm...."

For the first time, she can't look me in the eye; her gaze fixes on a nearby tree instead. This isn't going to be good news for me anyway, I can feel it, the tension squeezes my stomach into a tight knot. Dread washes over me as I watch her take in a shaky breath. Centring herself, she looks at me straight in the eye; her mouth opens but hesitates for a moment.

"He's umm... he's found someone else... he's happy... I mean really happy... I haven't seen him this way... well... since he was with you."

Her words push me back; I slump heavily against the back of my chair. It was an inevitable conversation, but I still feel like I have taken an almighty blow to the chest. A gaping hole remains where a heart should be. Cassie might as well be sitting there holding it aloft like some sort of victory trophy. I shake the image away, but as the emotions rise within my chest, my eyes start to brim.

"I take it you haven't found anyone else yet?"

All I seem to be capable of is a little head shake. I didn't think I was in love with Gareth, but the hurt that's dragging down my chest, tells me otherwise. Like the old lady on the bridge said, 'you should listen to your heart more often then, my dear'. If only our brief encounter were before it all went tits up, though. Ah, my head is buzzing into overdrive; I hold my head in my hands. I left the house with a clear mindset, determined to wipe the slate clean and come running back into my place as a new woman. I feel Cassie's presence; looking up, she's squatting down by my side, with her hand on my arm.

"Charly... do you love Gareth?"

It's the question I have been asking myself all along. My heart is torn in two, a piece for each of the men I care most about.

"To be honest... I-I-I really don't know... my head and emotions are all over the place... I'm so confused right now."

Her soft touch on my arm is comforting.

"Is there another guy in this confusion, too, then?"

Oh man, she's good; she must have the same power as Harper. Her words prompt me to think of Joe, and I can't help but smile.

"Erm... yes... his name is Joe... I've known him since school... my first boyfriend actually... I haven't seen him or spoken to him for years... until we were reunited at my friend's wedding not so long ago... it was so lovely... it was kind of like picking up where we left off, you know... but I'm pretty sure he has a girlfriend though... but I can't stop thinking about him."

With her brow furrowed, she's listening to and processing my every word. Her features soften as I finish.

"Do you really want my opinion?"

I have no idea which way she's going to sway. At a guess, it'll be Gareth, naturally supporting her brother. I give her a brief nod for her to continue.

"Well... this is just what I see... or sense... take it or leave it, but... I don't think you're in love with my brother at all... I think you may still have a little spark for him... but I don't think it's any more than that, to be honest... no more than lovely memories... I feel like you're worried about the wrong guy here... your face... seriously... it lights up so much when you speak about this Joe fella... you need to track him down and make sure he's definitely unattainable... in my honest opinion, he's the one you really want... or I'm just really crap at reading people."

She light-heartedly chuckles as she catches her breath from her long spiel. Her touch doesn't leave my arm as I take a moment to process her statement; my chuckle is a bit delayed and a little forced as my mind slowly comes back to the right track. In my head, in my opinion, my heart and my feelings are split, fifty/ fifty.

***

My earbuds are still chucking out tunes, but in my clouded mind, they all sound the same. Just like a sulking child, I drag my feet home, kicking at the fallen leaves as I go. As I near home, the track changes to 'The Climb' by Miley Cyrus. This song always seems to boost my morale, but not today. I open my front door; it slams shut behind me under my total weight, my back slides down until my behind meets the floor. I tug at my hair tie, ignoring the pulling pain as I yank it free, grunting as I chuck it across the floor in exasperation. Cradling my knees, resting my head on them, I feel numb, so numb. I stare at the hallway stretched out in front of me as tears well and sting the corners of my eyes; two single tears roll down my cheeks. Those two single tears turn to an ugly cry forcing my shoulders to shudder as my emotions spill out; they soak my knees. Miley sings at me to push through the ups and the downs, but I just can't; I can't gather the momentum to move on.

Forty-Six

An invisible 'vacant' sign is hanging above my head as I sit at my workstation. My brain is refusing to function; I'm distraught and stuck in weekend mode. As my mind comes back down to earth and my ears tune in, I realise there's chatter coming from Stanley's office; I stand to see what's going on. The small crowd parts and I realise what the excitement is about. I see his striking brown and copper hair. At first glance, you could mistake him for one of those Twilight vampires, Edward something, I can't remember his full name, but this guy isn't deathly pale like he is. His luminous blue eyes are mesmerising, there's an air of uniqueness to them. I slowly step out from my workstation as he's gradually introduced to everyone in the office. I am hypnotised by his eyes and his wickedly handsome features. I am drawn to him like Bella was to Edward. Is this how she felt, like a moth attracted to a flame? I don't particularly like getting burnt, but something about him makes me think I should take my chances. His slender frame towers over mine, I usually find this intimidating, but I can't put my finger on why it doesn't faze me.

"... and this is Charly... Charly, this is Robert."

Ha, how fitting; I can't help but smile.

"Hi, Robert... welcome... it's so nice to meet you."

Ah, it came out way too enthusiastically, oh shit. Robert smirks, with one eyebrow arched, slightly entertained, I think.

"Nice to meet you too, Charly."

Just like his whole demeanour, his tone is deep, powerful and hypnotic. Whoah, it feels like the air in the room has just shifted, so much so, the ground follows suit.

I look around the room. I am not the only one who this mysterious man bowls over. Every woman in this office is in awe; I may have some competition here by the looks on their faces. Stanley and Robert move on to Kelly, who looks just as captivated as the rest of us are. Once everyone has had their turn, the two men disappear back into Stanley's office. Kelly's jaw physically drops as she gawks at me, still stunned.

"Whoah... just fucking whoah... how hot is he?"

I don't think I've ever heard her curse, and yet I'm too lost in my thoughts to tease her about it. My face mirrors her gawking expression.

"Extremely," I murmur.

Forty-Seven

His eyes shift from a luminous blue to a smouldering topaz that burns deeply from the shadows, almost penetrating. He emerges fully into the light, full of intent, of what exactly I don't know.

My breath hitches at his frosty touch on my hips. His torso is pale and bare, just dark tatty jeans from the waist down, they hang off his hips. The copper in his hair seems to blaze in this spotlight glow. I am frozen to this spot as he circles me like a lion surveying its prey. Or a wolf in sheep's clothing. All the while, his glare never leaves my naked body. Only my eyes follow him; I'm too skeptical about whether I can move or not. The more he circles me, the more sinister his stance and grin becomes. Thirsty, bloodthirsty. I gulp hard, waiting for him to pounce and maul me to death. Or he'll sink his teeth into my neck and drink my blood; either way, I am fucked. The thought sends shockwaves through my core and down to my sex; oh no, no, no, I can't be aroused by that. That's not me, I'm not into that, but I can't stop the urges; it grows and grows within me under his dark presence. My thighs automatically clench together, almost crossing paths, trying to halt the arousal. His fingertips sweep away the hair from my shoulders one side at a time, unveiling my naked breasts. He changes direction of his prowl as he does so. Icy dagger-like fingers claw at my skin, across my stomach, round to my behind. I feel the presence of his tall frame behind me; his once warm breath is now cold and raw. As I gasp and pant, I see my breath cloud before my eyes, as it would do in the dead of winter. His fingers creep round to my stomach and linger at my belly button.

"Do you fear me, Charly?"

His deep hypnotic tone curls sensuously around my eardrum, his mouth is close to my ear, yet my eyes grow wide, stunned with the rising notion of fight or flight. My mouth moves, trying to utter the answer to his question, while the shivers consume my whole body.

"N-n-no."

A simple word so hard to utter through frozen lips, I have entirely succumbed under his spell. My lungs and chest are not functioning the way they should, while his fingers trail up my body. A deeply buried devilish laugh reverberates through his chest as he shifts to my other ear.

"You should."

Before I can react, my breasts are grasped in an icy lock; I throw my head back against his shoulder, gasping, waves of blue wash over my skin under his touch; it dazzles like diamonds in the spotlight. I am cold but alive; his grasp tightens and my nipples are clasped between his icicle-like fingers, sending lightning bolts of pleasure through my chest and down to my sex. Breathless pants escape from me as I squirm under the mounting pressure for release. I hear his wicked laugh once more as his hands let go of my breasts and glide back down my body until his palms rest just above my pubic hair. Fluttering vibes pulsate under his touch, invisible forces make my muscles pinch and clench. Heavenly sensations from a *devilish being blow my mind. The vibrations are getting stronger and stronger, his powers winding my insides into a tight coil. I grasp his wrists as I reach the brink; I moan as I try to hold back the release. I shimmer under the light as my blue diamond skin dazzles some more. My grip on his wrists tightens as my body jolts and squirms; it's no use; I'm not strong enough to resist. His fingertips press down on my sex; ice bolts send me into climax oblivion. I cry out as my whole being shatters into a billion diamonds; I fall through his fingers, glittering rocks of me clink and smash against the floor, while he stares into the shadows with wicked glee.*

***

I'm still crying out as I'm thrust out of my weirdly erotic dream into the world I know. Hugging handfuls of my duvet against my chest, I realise that it's still night-time, as the light from the streetlamp creeps in through the blinds. Rain suddenly pelts down on the windows, making me jump. My eyes dart from the window, over to the door, then to my wardrobe, then back to my window; I'm frightened in more ways than one. Whoah, what the fuck was all that about? I know my new colleague has something strangely hypnotic and sexy about him, but he's no vampire or any other supernatural being for that matter. My chest is paining; the gasps must have been genuine, rubbing my chest in the hope of some relief. As I shift my legs under the sheets, I realise I'm wet in-between my legs. Shit, was that a real orgasm? The whole experience weirds me out; oh Robert, what have you done to me?

Forty-Eight

Haunted by last night's fantasy, I was contemplating phoning in sick at work. But as no one knows about it except for me, I can do this. Keeping my head down, I enter the office. I know Robert will have no idea what I dreamt about, but how on earth will I be able to keep my cool today? With those dazzling eyes of his, I bet he could see right through me and figure out my dirty little secret. A copper flash catches my eye above my computer; I reluctantly let my eyes follow it. Stanley is pointing him in my direction. My cheeks blaze with possibly the deepest shade of crimson, impossible to hide. I am reluctant to rise from my chair to greet him with the most awkward smile.

"Nice to see you again, Robert."

He peers down at me a little intimidatingly; my nerves are just barely clinging on to the edge as I try to keep my cool. The corner of his mouth curls up into a half-smile. Is he mocking me? Maybe he's getting a kick out of putting me under immense pressure for no apparent reason.

"Likewise."

It rolls off his tongue effortlessly, sensual and smooth, like silk. Whoah, it feels like the air has been sucked from the room.

"Apparently, I am shadowing you today," he murmurs.

Oh boy, yes, you can shadow me anytime. My inner spirit suggestively licks a finger, points to Robert and makes a red-hot hiss sound. I try to suppress the urge to chuckle at the thought, resulting in a weird twisted smirk on my face. I look away immediately, trying desperately to clear my mind and throat. My eyes finally come back to Robert. He looks at me a little confused, unaware of my secret joke.

"Sorry... I'm just not used to telling people what to do... and you make me erm... it makes me nervous."

Fuck it; I have totally crashed and burned on this one. What a lame excuse, I redden with the embarrassment. Robert finally cracks his blank face into a broad, friendly smile. Eventually, the iceman breaks!

***

Like a lost boy, Robert has followed me all day. We've shared my desk; as I've shown him the ropes, he's been straightforward to talk to. Soon as the ice broke this morning, conversations have flowed easily. There has been the odd occasion when our hands brushed against each other, but I apologised and carried on. Besides, do I really want to get involved with someone I work with again?

"Have you enjoyed your first day with us, Robert?"

Kelly asks, a little over-enthusiastically, bounding up to him like an excited puppy. I almost laugh as I imagine her jumping up and licking his face to death.

"I have... thank you, Kelly... thank you for the warm welcome."

He murmurs, a little uncomfortable but still managing to crack a smile. Erring on the side of caution, I think. He hurries along towards the men's room, the poor guy. Kelly turns to me, absolutely gushing, totally smitten.

"Aww isn't he just... isn't he just... so dreamy... he makes me go all tingly... you know... down there...."

I don't know why she felt the need to point 'down there'. I think I have a fair idea by now where all those vibes come from. But I can't help not passing up on this chance to humour her.

"What do you mean... you mean... you know... right down there... down there...."

I tease her, placing my palm just above my sex, playfully gawping while going cross-eyed. She puts her hands on her hips, looking at me and pouting unamused. So, I do it again and her face creases up. As much as she tries to hold it in, her laugh barges its way out.

I think Robert caught the tail end of our shenanigans, smirking at us as he passes to go to the staff kitchen. I look back to Kelly; her cheeks are ablaze.

"Bow chicka wow wow."

I tease her, balling up my fists, thrusting my hips back and forth, my arms following the same direction, as I say it.

"Stop it... that's not funny."

She shrieks under her breath. I start roaring with laughter, so much so I lose my balance, hitting my thigh on the corner of my workstation.

"Ah fuck it!"

I exclaim, vigorously rubbing the sting. Now it's Kelly's turn to roar with laughter, not holding back on the obvious.

"Ha, that'll teach you."

Forty-Nine

Silk sashes in a deep crimson shade, delicately drape down my arms.
I am hanging by my wrists; I feel no force or pain from the knots,
almost like floating. I am dangling like something's or someone's
next meal. Peering down through the gap in my arms, I am naked
once again. The spotlight seems to shine brighter this time around,
dazzling even. I squint as I sense movement from within the
shadows.

"You look good enough to eat."

A deep voice snarls, taunting me from the cusp of the light. A
torso only partially emerges, shadows for every feature, but I
recognise those worn jeans and the pale skin of his chest. My
heartbeat is erratic, but strangely I am not scared; I pant through
anticipation.

He emerges fully into the light with the same wicked grin, his eyes
hooded and dark. Sexy, deadly sexy, it should feel so wrong, fucked
up even, but weirdly it feels so right.

"I'm not the man for you, Charly."

Only his lips move; he is statue-still like a fine marble sculpture,
frozen in a menacing stance. His eyes, the brightest shade of topaz,
burn into mine as he draws closer. My mouth moves, but I cannot
speak, like someone has just hit the mute button on my voice box.
'Untie me,' I desperately want to say.

Face to face; his glare never ceases; his expression is unreadable. I shiver and pant as his cold breath hits my skin. My neck is at his mouth height; anticipation shortens my panting. I freeze as his lips meet the crook of my neck. I gasp as it sends thrilling lightning bolts right through my chest and down to my sex. I am still uncertain of his plan for me, toying with me probably, for his own twisted pleasure. His icy breath leaves frost-like patterns on my skin; they shimmer in shades of blue, then disappear. Just my eyes peer down at him, watching every move he makes. He feels my stare on him; his eyes dart to mine. Taking two steps back, his eyes burning bright with that mesmerising smouldering topaz, they look warm but deadly as they fail to blink. Out of the corner of my eye, I see his arm fly up towards me. I close my eyes tightly, prematurely wincing, waiting for the impact, but it doesn't come. The air shifts above my hands as the silk is swiped free, gravity pulls me down for a split second, my eyes fly open at the motion. With my hands bound, I can't save myself. Snatched in mid-air, I feel the grasp of his arms around my waist, a chilling embrace. My legs swing up and around, but I don't quite make his waist. I feel his icy grip on my behind, hoisting me up. Bringing my reluctant arms down, my silk laced hands rest behind his head. Lassoing myself to him, I am his prisoner. It feels like cold hard stone encases me; goosebumps prickle their way across my body. The shivers are trying to wriggle their way through his firm hold. Our eyes locked on each other's stalemate; I refuse to blink, trying desperately to keep my wits about me. After a while, his features soften to be more human-like. The blazing topaz in his eyes *fades like an extinguished flame, the crystal blueness returns. The warmth from my body seems to fill his; I feel it travelling through his whole being. I let my guard down as my lips find him, his grip remains firm around me but warm. I pull away gingerly to assess the danger. The colour and warmth fill his cheeks too. With half a smile, he closes his eyes. Fragments from his right cheek peel and flutter away; gradually, his whole face follows suit. I watch on in stunned silence. His eyes stay closed all the while as his features fade; no more words leave his lips. The rest of his body follows the same pattern; before I know it, I have nothing to hold on to. Time slows, my mouth gapes, trying to scream as I plunge into the dark oblivion.*

***

I feel the hardness of the floor beneath me as I pant uncontrollably. I freeze in mid gape, my throat parched. My forearms are shielding my face like my hands are still bound together. Just my mouth is exposed to the world; I'm too afraid to open my eyes. Taking deep breaths, I realise the coolness of my room; it fills my lungs. The familiar whirring sound of the fan makes itself known as my ears tune in. Gingerly opening my eyes, peering through the gap in my arms, the familiarity of my streetlamp lit room brings me back to home ground. I slowly peel away and lay my arms by my sides, palms to the floor, feeling the hardness of the floor. The reassurance of reality sets in, and I start to focus on steadying my panting breath. I feel like I have just free fallen for an eternity, and yet all I have done is fallen out of bed. Eventually, I roll onto my side. I reach for the bed frame and pull myself up onto my knees, resting my forehead on my hands for a moment as my body adjusts to being awake. My tired eyes feel dry and gritty; my whole body is heavy with exhaustion. With one last effort, I shift my weight up onto the bed and lie down. The sheets are cold; I hate to think how long I have been on the floor. Facing my alarm clock, I have only a few hours left to sleep. My brain feels numb and too tired to fathom any meaning for this weirdness.

Fifty

Last night's dream is still fresh in my mind. It's the second one I've had this week, and I am worried that I am unlocking some sort of weird deep dark desire buried at the back of my mind. The thought makes me shudder; no, no, no, that's not going on here, it's just a fucking weird dream. Staring at my cold cardboard-like toast, I've suddenly lost my appetite. Hopping off my kitchen stool, I chuck my neglected breakfast in the bin. It's way too early to head for work, but I grab my jacket and bag and head out the door anyway. I need some fresh air to cleanse my dirty mind.

***

Sunlight hits his hair perfectly; just like in my dream, it looks ablaze. We approach each other from opposite ends of the street and Robert beams, his mysterious but sexy grin. A couple of people walk in front of him, but I just about see his features as he's pretty tall. He turns his head to the right, his lips silently moving; I wonder who he's talking to. The two people, slightly blocking the view, finally, cross the road. Another man, just as handsome, walks alongside Robert. They both stop just outside L.N.O.'s entrance. I slow down my pace as intrigue sets in. Robert glances my way so I wave, a little too enthusiastically;

he smiles as he raises one hand and nods politely. The mystery man follows Robert's gaze, looking at me quizzically. What's his problem? Robert turns his attention back to the mystery man; I freeze in mid-stride as Robert leans towards him. I watch as their lips meet affectionately. Forcing back my surprise, I continue on my path to work. As I approach Robert and his no-longer-so-mysterious man, he introduces me as his 'lovely co-worker'. Ha, if only he knew what my mind had been up to. I think there's going to be one or two broken hearts in our office, including Kelly's, when this revelation sets itself free.

***

Peering over my computer, I watch Kelly collect her pile of printouts. She crosses paths with Robert on the way back to her desk. He only says hello to her in passing, but she practically turns into a giddy wide-eyed teenage mess out of sight from Robert. Her mouth touches the floor, I turn, and my gaze follows her as she comes back to sit down at her desk.

"You have no chance."

I say it to her under my breath. Kelly sucks her gawp back in and holds her breath at the same time. She stares at me with big melancholy eyes, like I have just dashed all her hopes in one single blow.

"He's gay."

I continue, filling in the gap. Momentary relief sinks into Kelly's features when she realises it wasn't a personal insult. She finally exhales, long and hard, like a deflating balloon, slumping to the back of her chair.

"For fuck's sake... what a waste."

She groans with despair. I can get used to this new foul-mouthed version of Kelly, maybe she's hung around with me for too long, and I'm rubbing off on her. Our faces crease when we find the funny side, giggling quietly to ourselves.

"Sorry... no bow chicka wow, wow for you."

Fifty-One

The twenty-second of August marks my thirtieth year of walking on earth and the right side of spinsterhood. There's no better way to celebrate it than with my besties and a pyjama party. Yes, I know I'm not ten years old anymore, but it was a silly thought that entered my head, and I thought, why the hell not. It's something we haven't done since the three of us were kids. I was contemplating expanding my cooking skills and laying out a three-course meal, but I am no chef, like you already know. The only menus I will be laying out this evening are the ones neatly tucked away in my kitchen junk drawer.

With hands-on my hips, a huge exhale ripples through my lips as I face the pile of unopened birthday cards lying on my kitchen table. The task seems daunting, soon as these are open, it pretty much seals the deal that I will be officially one year older and on to the next decade. But unopened cards are never going to change that. I need a giant coffee to get me through this; it is way too early for something stronger, although it is lunchtime somewhere in the world right now. I better stick to the caffeine, for now anyway.

A click and a stir later, sitting on a stool, watching the steam dance off my mug, I find it quite mesmerising. It brings Harper's wedding to the front of mind, the events of that day, still fresh like they happened yesterday. As I close my eyes, I see Joe with his shy boyish grin, and I automatically smile back. Then Ethan's genuine remorseful eyes barge their way in, pushing Joe to the side. I was quick to judge him, I know that, but can people change? They must say 'a leopard never changes its spots' for a reason, right? As I said, if the circumstances were different, we'd probably be together right now. Besides, however much I try to forget about it, New Year's Eve was hot as fuck. Yet, for him, it was probably the biggest mistake he had ever made. With that thought, I feel nauseated when one of the best night's I've had, turns out to be someone else's worst. I think he was mad at me for not hearing him out, but what could he possibly have said to make that situation any better?

Enough of this train of thought; I have a mountain of cards to get through. As I reach for the one on top, someone else springs to mind. Gareth springs to mind; I see him in my mind's eye as vividly as I did in the ceiling mirage. My hand comes back to rest on the table without a card in its grip. I take a sip of coffee while I hold on to the image for as long as I possibly can.

***

There is an eager knock at the door. Soon as I open it, Harper and Ashley embrace me with shrieks of excitement. Bags of wine bottles clinking merrily along with us, I usher them into the kitchen and waste no time in lining up the wine glasses, ready for the fountain of bubbly. They cheer and shout 'happy birthday' as we clink our glasses together. Placing my glass safely down on the kitchen table, I start a drum roll with my hands on the table and start calling the shots.

"Okay... for tonight's cuisine, I have chosen... pizza and ice cream!"

Judging by the bouncing, hooting and clapping, I think they are happy with my choices. We swiftly order, then change into our pyjamas and start listening to some music. When Vanessa Carlton's 'A Thousand Miles' starts to play, we can't help but belt it out - singing at the top of our voices, just to annoy Doris, and giggling as we mimic the piano playing. The singing, laughter and bubbles keep coming until we hear the glorious sound of knocking on the door. Harper jumps up first to answer it and dances down the hallway to 'Run To You' by Bryan Adams, strumming on her air guitar all the way. Ashley and I watch in amusement as the delivery guy stares at the breathless, and bra-less under her pyjamas, Harper. We can't help but giggle at the poor guy's stunned face as she tips him generously. He looks reluctant to leave. He goes to say something, but Harper quickly closes the door with one foot. She turns gracefully with the stack of boxes.

"Well, this is mine... I don't know where yours is," Harper muses.

She struts down the hallway with pizzas up high, the bag of ice creams hanging off her hip like she's a saucy waitress. Just as she comes into the living room, one of the boxes decides it's had enough of the shenanigans and starts to slide off, but luckily, like lightning Ashley was there to catch the escapee; phew!

With our plates piled high, we sit on scattered cushions on my living room floor. Our wine glasses re-fuelled, we are good to go. The chat keeps flowing as Harper amuses us with tales from her honeymoon.

"So... are you going to tell us finally... what's going on with you?... seeing you nearly in tears at my wedding reception is making us worried."

I was hoping to have a few more glasses of wine before we switched to this subject. I drop my pizza slice back on my plate. In silence, I am trying to figure out how and what to say to that. Once it's out in the open, there is no turning back. I feel the emotions rising in my chest and forming a lump in my throat.

"I... I... I..."

By looking away from them, I hope it helps halt my tears that are rapidly filling up. But it's no use; they spill over, out of my control. Ashley leans over, and using a napkin she wipes away my tears.

"Have you told Gareth how you feel?" Ashley asks.

Big droplets fall off my eyelashes as I shake my head in response.

"I... I didn't tell you guys that... I bumped into Gareth's sister last Sunday... I went for a run and ended up at Green Grove Park... and she was there walking her dog... we sat and chatted for a while... she was actually surprisingly nice to me... erm...."

I hesitate. This is the first time I'm going to have to say it aloud; once spoken, it'll be official; there's definitely no way back now. They patiently wait for me to carry on.

"Erm... she said... erm... that Gareth is... umm... really happy...."

Old wounds are slowly prised open as the words leave my lips.

"He's umm... really happy with someone else apparently... she said... she hasn't seen him this happy since... well... since he was with me...."

My wound is well and truly gaping open as the truth seeps out. Ashley and Harper look at each other wordlessly and wide-eyed.

"Whoah... whoah wait... what?... you went running?" Harper teases.

Her stunned face breaks into a smirk, and I can't help but follow her lead.

"Why didn't you tell us any of this when it happened?" Ashley asks.

I just shrug in reply. Maybe I thought, if I could keep it locked away, then I could carry on believing that it wasn't happening.

"What am I going to do... if this is all true?"

The despair weighs heavily on my shoulders. Harper takes hold of my hands and looks me straight in the eye, her serious face on display.

"Then you can finally close this chapter and start a fresh one."

Ashley nods along in agreement with Harper.

"I agree with Harper... close this chapter... if he's moved on, maybe it's time for you to do the same...."

I wipe away the last few tears that stream down my cheeks. My thoughts take a sudden u-turn to Joe, and my sadness lifts a little. Only just realising that they have no idea how I feel about him.

"That's not the only problem."

I take them both by surprise; they gawp, gesturing and willing for me to fill in the gaps. I look down at my hands clasped together in my lap—another revelation for them, but something else hard for me to come to terms with.

"Joe."

I don't think they expected that name to fall from my lips by the looks on their faces. My feelings well and truly hanging off the end of my sleeve.

"When we were reunited at the reception... it was such... an amazing feeling... the butterflies could have burst out of me and swallowed me whole that night... we... erm... we kissed...."

If they were sitting on seats, I think they would have fallen off them at this moment, in amazement. I half-laugh at their expressions.

"He also wanted to tell me something... just as the fireworks display started... I have no idea what he wanted to say."

As I talk about him, it feels like it lifts me and my mood. My smile and my being feel like they light up; an ecstatic glow surrounds me.

"Whoah... whoah... hold up a second here... let me get this straight... you have a thing for Joe?"

I have no idea why I suddenly feel so embarrassed; I nod at Harper as I feel my cheeks flush red-hot crimson. I'm feeling like a giddy teenager again.

"Whoah girl... you've got it bad!" Ashley adds.

Ashley and Harper beam at each other like they are telepathically communicating. I stand by the fact that expressions do speak louder than words.

Fifty-Two

Harper and Ashley didn't stay long this morning, as they both needed to get home to their husbands. I nurse my morning coffee at my kitchen table, my running shoes staring back at me from where I kicked them off last week. They look somewhat neglected. I'm not in my running gear, just loungewear, but I hop off my stool and grab my iPod. Earbuds firmly in, I slip my feet into my trainers. iTunes wakes up with 'One Way Or Another' by Blondie as I do up my laces. Straightening up, I quickly do a few stretches, then set off. I head straight for Green Grove Park again. I think I'm getting used to this running lark; my feet pound the pavement harder and faster this time around. I fly through the gates and down the winding paths until I hit the green open space. I see the colour of her hair first. Her features blurred with the motion of my run, but I am sure it's her.

I slow down my pace as I reach the café. Sammy clocks me first and comes bounding towards me. Cassie goes to shriek after him, but then realises who he's saying hello to. Stopping for a moment to get my breath back, Sammy happily leaps up the side of my leg, begging for my attention again. I squat down to greet him. Surrendering himself to me, he rolls onto his back for a tummy tickle. I look up towards Cassie, she puts down her coffee and gets up to greet me with a smile, but there's something that I can't put my finger on. Her entire body language is different. Cassie stands with her hands clasped together, tense, her knuckles white. A part of me wants to turn, run away and never look back. My inner spirit gulps down the anxiety for me, mentally shrugging, I don't know what's happening here, but I'm not too fond of the vibes coming from her.

"Hi... I was hoping to bump into you again."

Her voice is edgy with the nerves that are consuming her body. Okay, I don't like this one bit; this doesn't appear to be a chance meeting.

"Sit with me."

It's not even a question or invitation; it sounds more like a polite command, too formal even. I do as Cassie asks and take a seat. I'm too taken aback for a moment to speak. I instinctively mirror her body language as the tension hangs in the air, creating an uncomfortable invisible wall between us.

"So... how has your week been?"

I'll hand it to her, she's doing her best to normalise the situation, but to no avail. This small talk charade is not going to wash with me.

"It's been okay, thanks... but please tell me... why are you really here... this doesn't feel like a chance meeting to me... I can tell something is bothering you."

I nod towards her hands that are nervously playing with the fabric of her top. I regret the sharpness in my tone when I watch her shift uneasily in her seat. She looks away, focusing on a tree as she bites her bottom lip and her fumbling fingers turn their attention to the strap on her watch instead.

"I umm... I can't tell you anything... he wants to talk to you himself... Gareth, I mean."

She murmurs under her breath; her gaze still doesn't find mine. When I hear her say that Gareth wants to talk to me, my eyes frantically scan the green, expecting him to emerge from his hiding place. Am I being watched?

"He's not here."

Her voice is reassuring enough, but I'm still not convinced.

"If you're free on Friday... when you finish work at five... he said he'd meet you... at the café where you guys first met."

Okay, shit, this is huge; I'm not sure if I should be worried or excited about this. Am I wrong to think that there's a hint of romance about the meeting point?

"Why didn't he just come along with you today?"

I can tell that there's something immense eating her up inside. For fuck sake, I just want to know if it's good or bad news.

"Sorry, I really don't know Charly... will you go?"

If I was feeling bitchy right now, I could leave the answer hanging unanswered. I can't do that to Cassie; when she's been so kind to me, she looks restless enough already. It's unfair of Gareth to use her as a go-between.

"Of course, I will, Cassie."

Soon as she has my word, I watch her whole body start to relax. Was she expecting me to make a scene or something? Whatever it is, I'm glad I have put her at ease, for now anyway.

"Fancy joining me for a coffee?"

I don't know how she can expect us to resume a normal conversation after that tense display.

"Thanks, Cassie... but I need to get going... I'm meeting some friends for lunch soon."

It's obviously a huge twenty-four-carat lie, but I just can't sit here and ignore the fact that she's got a top-secret fact hiding under her hat. I wouldn't be able to contain myself. I'd probably end up beating her over the head with my coffee cup until she surrenders the truth, hypothetically speaking. So, I gingerly rise from my seat. She looks a little disappointed, which makes me feel terrible, but I really can't stay.

"Great to see you again, Cassie... I'll see you soon."

She nods just once, barely cracking a smile. I set off before she has the chance to change my mind.

Fifty-Three

My chin rests on balled up fists, my stare is fixed on the wall clock at the other end of the office. Maybe somehow, I can conjure up psychic powers to speed up the last fifteen minutes. This week, I've kept to myself; it has been torture not knowing what today is all about. I'm surprised my boss hasn't dismissed me, as my attention has been elsewhere. It feels like my inner spirit has literally packed up her bags and left, no note, no explanation. I've been keeping small talk to the absolute minimum this week, so I know everyone has been worried about me. I won't be able to explain myself until I know more.

"Hey... hey, Charly... are you okay?... you look like you're a million miles away."

Kelly's voice brings me back, my eyes sting from the persistent stare. I lean back to rub my sore, dry eyes, then my aching elbows.

"I... umm... I haven't been feeling great."

My gaze eventually drifts to meet Kelly's. I blink away the wide-eyed stare that seems stubborn to disappear when I see her brow furrowed with concern.

"You've been quiet all week... everything okay?"

I don't want to answer that right now. I glance back to the clock, just one more minute until five o'clock. As I look back to Kelly, her brow still hasn't ceased the furrow.

"I... umm... sorry I... I need to go and meet somebody...."

Glancing at the clock again, finally, it's time. Springing up from my chair, I quickly stuff my phone into my bag and fling it on over my head.

"I'll see you next week."

I glance in her direction as I say it, but I don't make eye contact. I just desperately need to get out of here as quickly as I can.

"Have a good weekend" Kelly calls to me as I hastily make my way to the doors without acknowledging her. I'll apologise to her next week. I'm sure she will understand. Right now, I have somewhere I need to be. Quite a few people are waiting for the lift, so I decide to take to the stairs instead. I fly down the steps, two at a time, without giving it a thought. I don't stop even when I arrive in the foyer; it's full of people eager to get home for the weekend. I weave in and out; I'm excusing for my impatience as I hear quite a few tuts and curses as I barge through.

Soon as my feet hit the pavement, I begin my pursuit again. I bolt up the street, across City Bridge, narrowly avoiding commuters heading homeward. I don't stop until I see the familiar café sign.

***

I am standing solo, in the same place where I first laid eyes on him for real, willing to see him through the sea of faces. I should have worn my old faithful pink and white striped jumper, albeit a bit ragged around the edges now, but at least he'd know it's me. I see a flash of moss green fade into the mass, but my heart sinks when I realise it isn't him. The skies above start to rumble; I curse at myself for forgetting my jacket at the office. Again, I regret my forgetfulness when I feel the first few drops of rain on my face. But nothing is going to stop me from clinging onto every ounce of hope in this reunion. Of course, there is still the possibility that he hates me, but I ache to know what he needs to tell me. I shiver as the rain hits harder on my skin and as I notice the anxiety that has my stomach in knots. Passers-by look on in concern; they must think I have gone crazy, maybe I have? So crazy, in fact, that the white rabbit with his pocket watch might appear at any moment, willing for me to follow him instead. I shake away the bizarre thought and carry on, sifting through the faces in the crowd, but none of them seem familiar. I look down at my watch; it's almost twenty past; I sigh heavily; he must have had second thoughts.

"Charly?"

Just when I thought of giving up, I freeze at the familiar voice behind me. I know I was expecting to hear his voice again, but for some reason, it still takes me by surprise. Slowly, I turn around, looking a bit shy and sheepish. In silence, I try to assess his mood through his expression. I can't tell if he's grimacing at me or the rain. Instinctively I step forward to embrace him, but I hesitate at the last second. It's strange to feel him so out of reach and a pang of sadness ricochets through my chest. The stress of not knowing anything this week has finally risen to the surface as I feel my eyes start to brim. The tears stream down my face, but the rain disguises them.

"Cassie, let slip that you may still have feelings for me."

He looks disappointed rather than pleased with this fact. Looking to the ground, he shakes his head in disbelief.

"... do you have any idea how hard it was for me to try to get over you?"

His head and eyes snap back to mine as he waits for me to answer. But I am too stunned by the sternness in his voice to try to get my thoughts in order.

"I... I... I umm."

I pause for a moment to let the stammer slide; every breath is shaky. This meeting is not the way I had pictured it in my mind. Moments like these in movies are supposed to be romantic. You always see the gentleman sweeping up the love of his life into his arms, saying 'I forgive you baby' and snogging each other's faces before they walk off into the sunset. THE END, and the audience claps as the credits roll. I wish it were that easy.

"I'm so so sorry that I hurt you... I... I... I was scared that we were moving so fast... I had huge commitment issues... if only I had met you when I knew what I wanted... I wish things were...."

His hand flies up in a 'stop 'command which catches me off guard, but I quickly squeeze in what I wanted to say.

"... different... I know it's not enough to convince you that I've changed."

His grimace doesn't falter at all, even though my heart is hanging by a thread on my sleeve. His glare is still hard as nails.

"You're right... it's not."

His reply sounds so cold and bitter. I glance up at his stony exterior, and my heart sinks even deeper, practically into the pit of my stomach. He hates me, I can just tell. His grimace is for me not the weather. I have never felt so pathetic; the lump of emotions stuck in my throat feels like it's growing, fattening with every harsh word that leaves his lips. I try to shift the lodged feelings by gulping as hard as I can.

At that moment, I notice we are starting to draw attention from passers-by. I patiently wait for him to say what he needs to tell me. The long pause gives me a brief moment to brace myself. His stony exterior finally breaks as he hangs his head, refusing to look at me.

"Charly... I... ah... there is no... there is no easy way for me to tell you this... I'm ah... I'm getting married."

I feel the colour drain from my face as the shock consumes me. Where's the white rabbit when you fucking need him? I'm willing for the ground beneath me to open up so that I can tumble into 'Wonderland 'and away from this nightmare. My eyes grow wide, and my lips move, but words fail me. He reaches out for my hand.

"But..."

I snatch my hand away, turning on my heel and fleeing before he has a chance to add anything else. There's nothing he could possibly say to make this any better.

Fifty-Four

I race against the gusts of wind and heavy deluge, the cold wetness whips across my face. The shame weighs heavily over me; my dignity left behind at the scene. I mentally beat myself up until I reach my front door. I need to get inside quickly to my haven. Forgetting how saturated I am, I hurry inside. Soon as my feet hit the wood flooring, I slip and fall flat on my face, as if I could not be humiliated enough already. Rolling onto my side, I kick the door shut with both feet. My body curls up into a shape resembling the fetal position. I realise this was the exact spot where I made that phone call to Gareth. So stupid, so naive, I didn't realise how lucky I was, now I have officially lost him for good. I feel the sorrow weighing down on my chest. I have no chance with either of the men who each own half of my heart. I have lost all the energy to carry on crying; just the odd random tear falls as I stare at the wall. 'C'mon, this isn't you... you're stronger than this' my inner spirit gives me a gentle nudge. I peel myself up off the floor, leaving a puddle shaped version of me behind. I strip off all my soggy clothes and bundle them on the floor. The house is warm, but I'm chilled to the bone. Hugging myself as I look at my reflection in the mirror, I don't recognise the woman staring back at me. She is sporting the drowned rat look, with makeup trailing down each cheek, like racing stripes, and the most prominent panda eyes you've ever seen—a face of a crying clown, not half wrong there. I trudge up the stairs to get dried, fetching a towel and throwing on a clean shirt and panties. I do my best to wipe away the marks of the runaway makeup. Hunting for a clean pair of jeans, I realise they are downstairs in the tumble dryer. I wrap my hair into a towel, grabbing an extra one for the wet floor as I trudge back downstairs. The puddle is still in the shape of me.

I throw the towel over it, wishing it were that easy to disguise my own real shame. Making my way through to the kitchen, I turn the radio on. I grimace when I realise it's 'Someone Like You' by Adele. Anything is better than the silence ringing through my ears right now. I get as far as retrieving a mug, and a jar of coffee from the cupboard as the song takes over my train of thought. Oh, Adele, did you really feel this way when you recorded this song? I'm hearing her voice in a completely different way as her heart and soul drive through each note, each lyric. It's thick with the heartbreak; it ripples through her voice. The more she sings, the more I relate. Closing my eyes, 'I feel you, sister,' as her voice belts out in her sorrow. Now I understand why they call it heartbreak; my heart might as well be made of paper, as I feel each strip torn so easily. Just when the tears are about to fall, the radio DJ's voice interrupts and the song comes to an end. The coffee and mug are waiting patiently for my attention to return to them. I fill and switch on the kettle. I unravel my towel wrapped hair, rubbing the drenched ends while I wait. As I look down, I realise I hadn't done up the buttons on my shirt.

I only get to do up a few buttons when I hear a desperate rap on the front door. 'Tap, tap, tap.' I don't want to see anyone right now. I bet it's Doris, wanting to add something to her weekly gossip list, but then thinking about it, she probably wouldn't be out in this weather. There it is again, getting increasingly impatient. With a heavy sigh, I peer around the kitchen doorway, trying to stay out of sight. I see a tall figure in the glass panels; yes, definitely not Doris. With haste, I hurry to the door, skipping around the towel still on the floor. Just opening it a fraction to see who it is, my arms drop to my sides, stunned. I stand back and the door swings open entirely by the wind. It must be my imagination tricking me. His hands, on either side of the entrance, rest his exhausted frame, his head almost hanging. It looks like he ran here. Fat raindrops drip off every facial feature. I let him catch his breath, then, he straightens himself up to look me straight in the eye.

"I... I tried to stop you back there... I think the rain drowned out my calls... I couldn't let you go...."

The nerves seem to be getting the better of him. I stay quiet, intrigued by what he needs to tell me.

"I need to tell you what I wanted to say...."

He takes in a deep breath to ready himself. My throat has caught my leaping heart; the waiting is torture.

"... and I couldn't let you go through with it...."

Confusion twists my expression; I have no idea what he's talking about. I keep quiet, waiting for more clarity.

"Harper said you were meeting him... but I got there too late... then I saw you run...."

His expression is willing for me to say something. My lips are moving, but no words are coming out, then it dawns on me how little I am wearing, I wrap my arms around myself in a bid to stop my chattering teeth.

"Ever since Harper's wedding... since I held you in my arms... I haven't been able to stop thinking about you, Charly...."

This poor guy is pouring his heart out to me, but I still can't find the right words.

"... I was gutted that I didn't get to finish what I wanted to tell you... I umm... I don't... I don't have a girlfriend."

His mouth tremors with the relief, no doubt of finally being able to say it aloud. My prayer shaped hands spring to my face.

"Oh my... oh my god."

I mutter it between my fingers. Something within gives me a gentle nudge, telling me to act, to respond, do something at least. I join Joe on the doorstep, up close, ignoring the rain drenching me once again. Being this close again feels different, more intense this time.

"That is... that is the best news I've heard in ages."

My voice finally finds the right words. The relief in his face sends my heart racing as he breaks into his schoolboy smile. The atmosphere around us is electrifying. I don't care that he's soaked through to the skin, I rest my hands on his body, and I can feel his firm abs under his shirt. Oh my, now I am tingling from head to toe. Meeting his gaze, he looks at me intently, then he picks up and pushes away the soaking strands of hair clinging to my cheek. He holds me by the chin, pulling me in until our lips meet. I wrap my arms around the back of his neck. The sound of the rain is silenced by the mounting passion; it might as well not exist. He pulls back to survey my face, hoping that he recognises the longing in my expression. He draws me in, so I'm pressed right against him; he obviously can read me well. His hands try to run down the length of my body to my thighs, then firmly grabbing hold of them, he pulls me up onto his waist. I wrap my legs around him to secure my place. I take this moment to appreciate what I have in front of me; his handsome smile is infectious. I run my fingers through his beard, my eyes glance at each of his features as they, too, are stunned to see what I have. I cup his face with both hands, my lips meet his so wildly like they never want to let go. My shirt, now officially soaked, clings to my skin. His arms move up to my back to hug me. We break our embrace for a moment, and I rest my forehead against his. He pecks a light kiss on the end of my nose, then on my lips with the utmost softness. He carries me into the house before setting me down. I help him peel off his soggy jacket.

"You can use my shower if you like. It's straight upstairs."

He smiles and nods gratefully. I disappear into the kitchen to open a bottle of wine and fill two generous glasses; the coffee can wait. Carrying them through to the living room, I see a pair of bare legs and the trim of black trunks disappear up the stairs, oh my. I place the glasses on the coffee table and return to the hallway as the familiar sound of the shower echoes down the staircase. I notice he's piled his clothes on top of mine, so I scoop the whole lot and hotfoot it to the tumble dryer; it all gets thrown in. I return to the hallway again, my heart pounds against my chest as I bound up the stairs. I fetch him a towel before I knock on the door. I can just about hear him over the roar of the shower.

"Come in."

As I enter, I try not to peek, but I see his firm buttock out of the corner of my eye. Once I see it, I can't help but turn my full gaze on it.

"Oh my!"

The towel falls as I cover my mouth with both hands. I couldn't contain my unruly mouth. Joe turns and grins at me through the glass panel; oh shit, he heard me. He opens the shower door to reveal a third of his body, a sexy third no less. Clothes don't do him much justice as my gaze scans down his body, his cock still hidden from sight.

"Did you want to join me? You look cold."

He nods to my chest and grins cheekily. As I look down, I realise that my nipples are standing to attention, clearly visible through my pale shirt. I feel my cheeks flush red-hot with the embarrassment. He emerges fully out of the shower onto the mat. My eyes surprisingly fixed on nothing but his face. Whoah, my knees feel weak as he approaches me. He places his hands firmly on my hips to steady me and his fingertips graze the edges of my underwear. I stare at his lips hungrily, as they no longer represent forbidden fruit; they are officially mine for the taking. I bring his head down so our lips can meet in one long, smouldering kiss like I am savouring every movement. I gasp heavily against his lips as I feel his fingertips slip under the fabric and squeeze my behind. The touch wakes up my whole body, lust rushes; I feel it wash through like a tidal wave. In haste, I lean back and my fingers lose all senses to function as I fumble with the buttons on my shirt. His touch alone calms them down, overlapping them with his for a brief moment. My hands fall from my shirt as his fingers do the work for me. Slowly unbuttoning me, his fingertips graze my bare skin as each one opens. Joe comes closer to me, and I feel his heat. His head hovers over my shoulder as he peels away my shirt from my body. He lets it fall to the floor with a damp thud. As the fabric leaves my body, Joe's fingertips run down either side of my back until they reach and slide beneath my underwear and pause. Joe's gaze finds mine; he looks at me like he's seeking permission. 'Oh, please rip them off,' my inner spirit yells. I nod and smile coyly even though, internally the desire is impatiently waiting to be set free. He kisses my lips just the once, then moves to my chin, trails down my neck and the centre of my chest to my navel. My body wants to crumble at the sensation. I steady myself on the top of his head and my fingertips comb through his damp hair. He toys with my belly button, running his tongue round and round, then plants a single kiss before heading further down. He runs his nose along the edge of my underwear; I feel his warm breath through the thin fabric. I hold back the urge to pull on his hair as he loops his fingers around the sides of my panties. Slowly pulling them down, he lets them fall to my ankles. As he stands fully, our bodies relax into one another and his arms hold me close. I never thought I'd end up in his arms again, let alone standing here dressed in nothing but our emotions.

My groin presses against his, and I feel he's hard for me already. He holds onto my hands and as he moves back towards the shower I willingly follow. We close the door behind us. Still holding his hands, I rest my back against the tiles, then I bring our hands up to either side of my head in the hope that he pins himself against me.

"I want you so badly" I murmur suggestively against his ear, thrusting my hips towards his groin, wanting to feel his erection graze against me once more. The action, or the words, ignites something within Joe and he acts on my heart's desire, pinning my hands and his groin with mine. His mouth remains tantalisingly close, but I can make out a smile. I feel his lips brush teasingly against mine, but he doesn't kiss me.

"Oh, do you now?"

The rush of warm breath hits my mouth as he says it; it turns me on like a flick of a switch. He lets go of my left hand, to find and scoop up my knee, bringing my thigh to level with his hips and holding me in that teasing position until I almost beg. His eyes have mine; they never leave as he slides himself into me, inch by magnificent inch, then stills. He watches me as I gasp at his length. 'Oh fuck!' my inner spirit cries out. My breasts try to heave against him as I wait for his next move. I watch the rivulets of water run down his toned body, which alone sets my heart racing. His hand pinned with mine wriggles free, it comes down to my cheek. He brushes his thumb along my bottom lip, I give it a suggestive pinch with my teeth, before he gives me a more sensual kiss. I feel him withdraw his cock almost entirely in mid-kiss; for a split second, I think he's changed his mind, but one firm thrust changes everything. I cry out aloud this time, I couldn't help myself, my muscles pulse and pinch deliciously around him as he thrusts into me. So deep, so fucking deep. I hold on at the back of his neck, resisting the urge to dig my nails in. He rests his forehead against mine as his hips start to circle. I feel the rising sensation of release rippling through my core. Both of my hands move to his shoulders and my grip tightens with every circle and thrust he makes. I groan louder and longer.

"Uh... Joe!"

He starts to pant louder as my gasps and moans accelerate; it seems to excite him as he watches me unravel around him. I feel myself hitting the point of no return.

"Oh... Joe... don't stop!"

He buries his face into my neck, centring himself to my desires; my face mirrors his. On the last thrust, I explode, shattering into a million pieces, as I cry out. My muscles are pulsing and pinching at the amazing relief. Whoah, I'm a little starry-eyed; no guy has ever come close to making me orgasm mid-sex. My face remains buried in his neck as my shoulders bounce with my breath, my heart races like it wants to break free.

I pick my head up as I feel him do the same; he grins at me, accomplished. His cock continues to glide in and out but at a gentler pace as I come down from my intense orgasm. His body becomes rigid, the muscles in his arms more prominent. Resting his free hand on the tiles next to my head, he kisses me hard, then pulls out of me just as he reaches the brink. My hand finds his erection, I continue the same sliding action, making him grunt and pant copiously against my mouth until his pleasure peaks, and he climaxes. Our bodies relax into one another as he breathlessly kisses me, sensually but softer. His grip on my thigh releases me, and my leg slides down his body with pure satisfaction.

He clocks my shower puff and reaches for it. I feel his mouth brush against my ear.

"Turn around."

I do as he asks, resting my forearms and palms on the tiles. I hear the familiar sound of a bottle being opened and squeezed. He sweeps my hair to the side and works the shower puff into my shoulder blades, then along each arm. He teasingly glides it slowly down my right side first. He doesn't stop at my waist; the soapy gliding continues down the side of my leg, brushing over my heel, then up my calf. The tingling sensation still lingers on my skin from my orgasm. His hand comes up to my behind; his fingertips brush teasingly across the crease of my backside. My legs instinctively slide apart as I feel him graze deeper against my sex. I gasp as his hand makes one more teasing stroke before mirroring the same action down the other leg. But on the way up, he kisses all my weak points. I squirm as his touch ignites my muscles to pulse and pinch in the mounting excitement. The kisses continue over my hip, and up my side, which tickles; I let out a quiet giggle. I angle my torso slightly, hoping his mouth will meet my breast. Instead of kisses, he runs his tongue and fingertips over it. Moving my chest further back, I release my breast entirely from the tiles. I feel his warm breath against my nipple; I groan as he circles and playfully nips me, my head tips back as I mentally beg him to touch me in between my legs again. Cupping my breast as he stands fully, the shower puff falls from his grip as he glides his hand back down my body to my behind. He watches my body react to his movements. The feeling is so intense that I could shatter under one touch. Sliding his fingers along my sex teasingly, slowly, my entire body shudders, longing to release again. His stroking finds my clit, with his finger right on the button, the pace quickens until I can't contain the pleasure any longer. A long throaty groan escapes from my chest as I cum on his fingers. I peel myself away from the tiles and fall into Joe's arms in satisfied exhaustion.

Fifty-Five

I hope it wasn't just a dream, a cruel mind trick to cope with bad
news. Lying on my back, with my eyes still closed, I'm afraid that what
I am thinking is true. But as my senses gradually wake up, I realise my
face is tingling in a sensitive way that only happens when I kiss
someone with facial hair; I touch the area lightly as I grin like a
Cheshire Cat. Opening my eyes, I turn my head just a fraction, and
there he is, lying on his front with his arms tucked under the pillow.
How on earth can anyone sleep like that? He's facing my way, his lips
slightly parted in quiet slumber. I gently turn from my back to my
side. He stirs slightly as my body shifts, but it's not enough to wake
him. My gaze drifts along his arm; the leaves of his tattoo seem to
wrap around and hug each muscle, as they reach down his forearm.
It's hard to believe that those were the arms holding me last night.
Wow, and what a night it was, two sensational orgasms, my insides
tingle with the memory. His hair is ruffled from sleep and our
shenanigans. I could so fall for Joe; the butterflies stir at the thought.
Or maybe I have already? My face aches when I realise I have been
wildly smiling since I woke. Sliding my hand under my pillow, so I can
hide my grin in my upper arm, he stirs. One of his eyes peeps open
and squints in the morning rays that are creeping in through the
blinds.

"Hey, you" he murmurs; his voice is gruff, thick with sleep, he finishes with a huge boyish grin.

His deep hazel brown eyes dance as he smiles; they seem to shimmer in the sun's glow. He shifts onto his side to face me and for some reason, I go shy, as if my alter ego was the one in the bathroom with him last night.

"Hey, you" I whisper back through the crook of my arm.

Joe's fingertips trace along my arm, up to my wrist, where my long hair has fallen. He fishes for my hand that's hiding under the pillow and brings it out towards him, revealing my coy smile.

"That's better," he murmurs.

Our fingers interlock as he shuffles closer to me. As I lay here and take in his features, my heart lifts. A bud of something is blossoming within me; I feel it every time I look at him and that signature grin of his.

"I'm not going to run this time... if you don't want me to, that is."

Even though I say it teasingly, I mean every word. He gives me a playful 'I'll think about it' expression that breaks into a cheeky grin. In blurred moves, the duvet flies up, and he swiftly pulls me almost on top of him. My left leg falls in between his thighs, and the other just drapes over his side. The duvet falls right over our heads, shutting the world out and I rest my hands on his hips. A strap of my silk camisole slips off my shoulder as his hand brushes up my arm and over my shoulder, revealing half a breast. Even my clothes fall apart under his touch. It doesn't bother me; nothing is secret anymore, he's seen me in all my glory, and he's still here. Joe sweeps away a few dangling strands of my hair and tucks them behind my ear.

"I don't want you to run either... and I don't want anybody else... I need you, Charly."

His grin turns to a serious expression as he says it. The words make my heart melt, and my arms feel weak. I playfully gasp in shock as I feel him harden against my thigh.

"Down, boy!"

He smiles and shrugs like it was out of his control.

"What can I say... I can't help it... you drive me crazy... even with bed hair," he starts giggling before he even finishes and I give a playful slap on his chest in retaliation. I smile as he brings me down, hugging me briefly before rolling us both, ending with him on top. His waist is neatly tucked in between my thighs. I pull the duvet away from our heads so I can get a better view of his face. He comes down to rest on his forearms as I take in his features. His beard looks rough but is soft to touch as I run my fingers through it. Scooping up and holding my hand, he kisses my palm and places it back on his cheek. He feels new to me and yet so familiar.

"I want to take you out... on a proper date, I mean... as we kind of skipped that part last night... what do you think?"

It's the daftest question he could possibly ask, but at the same time, I'm over the moon that he asked.

"Sure... where to?"

His thinking face tells me he hasn't thought that far ahead yet.

"Don't worry, I'll think of something."

He looks deep into my eyes while he says it, brushing my cheek gently. Our lips meet in a slow, steamy kiss, parting my lips with his, as our tongues seek each other out. One of my hands rests on the back of his neck, not wanting him to part from me. We're rudely interrupted by the loud growls of hunger bellowing from my stomach. Joe starts chuckling mid-kiss and I feel my cheeks flush with embarrassment. I feel him pulling his head back, so my hand reluctantly releases him.

"Breakfast?"

Fifty-Six

Slipping a clean white shirt over my camisole and shorts, I head downstairs. Joe wanders around in my kitchen in nothing but his fitted black trunks, and I can't help but notice that they hug him so well. He insisted on making me breakfast, and I am not complaining. I take a seat at my kitchen table, as Joe sets down a mug of coffee for me, with a wink, then turns to carry on cooking; the gesture makes me smile. I pick it up and take a sip, mmm, and he even makes good coffee. I peer over my mug, watching him, hungry in more ways than one. Oh my, I watch his toned back flex with his movements. My bottom lip brushes against the rim of my mug flirtatiously. I can't believe we've both spent the last few weeks secretly pining for one another, but what's done is done now. This must be my brand-new chapter; our brand-new chapter. The notion fills me with such immense delight that I simply can't put it into words. I can't wait to see where this goes.

My phone buzzes alive with a different tone, disturbing my blissful thoughts. Puzzled, I look at the screen; Harper is video calling me; that's odd, I don't think we've ever done that before. Just as I answer it, I purposely ruffle up my hair for a talking point, and her face fills my screen.

"Hey, girl!"

Her voice is thick with so much excitement, almost like a shrill. No one should be allowed to be this ecstatic this early on a Saturday morning. She eyes her phone closely; I think she's clocked my 'just fucked 'looking hair.

"Sorry... did I wake you up?"

Or maybe not. I give Harper the widest mischievous grin.

"Not at all."

It comes with a flirtatious laugh and Joe catches my eye; he turns around and rests his backside and palms behind him on the counter opposite me, smirking at my coquettish glee.

"Aww, good... I have something to show you...."

She holds up a small white stick and shrieks with off the scale delight. Her movements make the object blur, but I think I have a pretty good idea of what it is. I can't help but mirror her excitement.

"OH MY GOODNESS... that's bloody amazing!"

I see Alex hovering in the background, probably waiting for some recognition for firing bang on target.

"Well done, Alex."

I laugh as he waves, then takes a bow. My window is small on my phone, but I just about make out Joe's waist and trunks over my shoulder as he gets the milk out of the fridge. I smirk at the sight and then at Harper's reaction.

"Oh... you have company."

She doesn't sound as shocked as I thought she'd be; maybe she knew already. Joe sets the milk down, then comes round to my side of the table, dragging over a stool behind me, pushing it right up against mine. His face comes into view of the camera when he sits down on the edge of the seat. Feeling his groin pressed against my lower back, I'm lucky our waists are out of view from Harper. His arm comes round to hug me; his fingertips graze along my inner thigh. Oh no, no, please don't turn me on in front of her. I clear my throat trying to hold back the sensuality.

"Joe!"

She shrieks his name; it sounded more like genuine surprise this time; maybe she was half expecting Gareth's face to appear.

"Oh my god... you guys!"

She coos at us like she's gushing over a couple of adorable kittens or something. She drops her little white stick as she jumps excitedly.

"So, does this mean... are you guys official?"

I lean slightly to the side so I can see Joe's face in full view. His brown eyes dance at the thought of me being his, I assume.

"Fuck yes... I'm not letting her go this time."

Even though he answers Harper's question, his eyes never leave mine. My dormant inner spirit falls to the floor, like she's fainted, which makes me feel a little giddy, in a good way, of course. I hold back the urge to kiss those gorgeous lips of his. I don't want to give Harper a cringing public display of affection; even though she probably wouldn't even bat an eyelid. She'd probably cheer us on. I look back to Harper, who's looking like she's on the verge of squealing with delight again.

"Yay!"

She fist-pumps the air as she shouts it. It dawns on me that we have totally stolen their thunder, so I quickly think of something to turn the tables back round to them.

"Congratulations! ...so... so excited for you guys, though... that's great news! ... we're just about to have breakfast...."

I'm in a hurry for Joe's lips, not food, but I do my best to keep the urge to escape subtle, and I bet she can see right through me like she always does.

"I bet you are... you filthy pair."

She playfully winks at us. Joe's fingers still lingering on my inner thighs, they start grazing up and down the length of them. 'This isn't fair,' my inner spirit wants to protest. I squirm under his touch, trying to keep the arousal to myself, but I bet Joe can sense it. We quickly say our goodbyes and hang up. Placing my phone back down on the table, Joe doesn't move an inch, his fingers still grazing. I lean to the side again and fix my gaze on his, but raise my eyebrows to quiz him.

"Oh, so... we're official now, then are we?"

His mouth moves so tantalisingly close to mine, so close I can feel his breath on my lips; they part, ready for his embrace. My breath hitches as his lips brush against mine teasingly, without leaving a kiss in their tracks.

"Why... don't you want to be?"

If I weren't seated, I'd be on the floor right now. Whoah, that sexy, husky whisper could have easily encouraged my shorts to drop to my ankles by themselves.

"Of course I do," my whisper is breathless from the mounting anticipation of his next move. His hand comes up to sweep my hair away from my face. Cupping the back of my head, he searches my expression with the slightest of smirks. My chest is heaving; he makes me breathless with just the thoughts of what I'd do to him and what he'd do to me. I have never felt this way with anybody. His thumb brushes along my cheek, then across my bottom lip; I gasp as he pulls it down with his thumb tip, my breath hits against his mouth. His lips finally find mine in the slowest, most meaningful, long sensual kiss. Joe breaks the embrace, but keeps his forehead on mine.

"I better finish cooking this breakfast," he murmurs.

Judging by the quiet grunt that followed, I'm pretty sure he also has other things on his mind. I think we've worked up quite an appetite already; I know I have, and my stomach gives me a not-so-subtle reminder. He reluctantly peels himself away, getting up to carry on preparing the tomatoes that sit whole on the chopping board.

I turn back to the table and take a sip of the not so warm coffee. I feel like I should be doing something to help, so hopping off my stool, I come up behind Joe just as he starts frying the tomatoes. Wow, he's a fast chopper; it puts my cooking skills to shame.

"Can I help?"

Lightly touching his upper arms as I peer up to him from the side, he turns his head just a fraction.

"Sausages and bacon are under the grill... maybe make some toast if you'd like."

Okay, I can deal with that. I turn and sashay to the other end of the counter where I retrieve my iPod and a hair tie from the corner. Setting my iPod to shuffle, I place it next to me. It chooses 'Cry To Me' by Solomon Burke. The music entices my hips to rock from side to side without a second thought while I sweep my hair up and secure it in place with the tie. Ready to begin, I fill the toaster as my hips continue to rock. As I wait for the familiar ping of the lever, my hips decide to dip mid-way, letting my shorts rise just enough for a cheeky peek. My shoulders bounce with every flick of the hip, in tune with the song. I can sense being watched, but I don't turn; I just carry on like I'm in a world of my own.

The toaster pings up, and I take the slices out and lay them down on the plate. I start spreading butter on each piece in time with the music. My hips slow down, but don't cease their movements, they turn to a hip roll, no rocking, just rolling and then I feel Joe's presence behind me, mirroring my moves. His hands move in a circular motion on my shoulders. His body edges closer as his hands glide down my arms and brush over my hands that are trying to spread butter. He places his palms down on the counter, either side of me, he's cornered me, and it feels so fucking hot. I press my back into his chest as he presses on me, his hips mirror my rolling. His head hovers over my shoulder, his mouth angles close to my neck and I feel his warm breath travel down my collar. Joe pulls out my hair tie, which makes my lips part in a silent gasp as his fingertips drag on my strands, and my head tips back with the tug. The action forces me to drop the butter knife. He places his left hand on my stomach, sliding his fingers in between the buttons on my shirt; his touch finds the bare skin hiding beneath my camisole. I willingly step back as he pulls me away from the counter. His right leg slips in between my thighs, and I lean all my weight on Joe's torso. I feel his groin grind against my behind; my body responds eagerly as I feel the sensuality ripple through my core. His free hand lays on my waist just above the other one, brushing against my breast as it slides across. My arms overlap his as rolls merge to broader sweeps. It feels like we lose ourselves in the music, just the two of us creating such a sensually electrifying atmosphere. Joe's hands slip out from under mine to hold my hips; stepping back, he spins me round to face him, slipping his leg back in between my thighs, his hands still firmly grip my hips. My eyes stay fixed on our entwined bodies. Lifting my arms above my head, I lasso my hands together and they circle with the same motion as my hips and his. Joe's fingers drag up my body, lifting my shirt slightly to graze my skin.

After a moment, my left arm comes down to rest on Joe's shoulder, the other rests on his chest, feeling the thrum of his excited heart. My gaze trails up his bare chest until our eyes meet.

"Hey, you," he murmurs.

Joe's whisper is deep and bewitching.

"Hey, you too."

I keep my lips parted to welcome his, but he just brushes my top lip teasingly with his. Whoah, whoah, wait, I'm not having that.

"Hey, come back."

I hear him quietly chuckling at my frustration. He eyes me closely as he finally gives my lips what they were waiting for; our tongues unite between each kiss. Joe pulls away a fraction, but still rests his forehead on mine.

"Trust me?" he asks.

Soon as I give him a brief nod in reply, his hands glide up to the middle of my back. I have an inkling of what he wants to do and I lean my weight back onto his hands. He dips me back and sweeps me round to the other side of him; my hair floats down, almost touching the floor as it glides with my body. Bringing me up slowly again, I feel a little rush from the notion. A high-pitched beeping sound grabs our attention, and Joe's eyes grow wide when he realises he's left the tomatoes frying. Letting go of me, he dashes over to the cooker to switch off the frying pan. How could we not have noticed the smoke-filled room? It tickles the back of my throat, forcing me to cough. I turn and lean over the counter to open the windows. We turn to face each other again; the panic morphs into amusement. I rest my behind on the counter as the adrenalin rushes over me.

"See, you're a bad influence on me."

His smirk breaks into nervous laughter. I cover my mouth with the back of my hand to try to suppress the urge to giggle, but it manages to wriggle its way out.

Fifty-Seven

I don't think I have ever been in such a good mood on a Monday morning, like ever, with the exception of bank holidays, of course. So much so, I feel like dancing and skipping my way to work. I seem to be surrounded by this glow, a glorious feeling that fills my whole being. The thought of the weekend makes me smile; who knew I'd end it with a new man—of course, not forgetting Harper and Alex's big news. I inhale a deep contented breath, letting the cool air fill my lungs. Joe pretty much spent all weekend at my place, although we did do some catching up, it was mainly... talk, fuck, eat and repeat. Well, less talk, less eating, more fucking than anything else; I instinctively blush at the thought.

I don't think I have walked into the office in such a good mood either. Kelly is already sitting at her desk. Usually, she's knees deep in her work before it even hits nine. Today, she's patiently waiting for me, looking like she's teetering on the edge of her chair. Oh shit, I forgot how rude I was towards her on Friday. I clock my jacket, which's still sitting on the back of my chair. Her anxiety eases when she notices the delight written across my face. She leans on the palm of her hand, elbow on her desk, gossip stance at the ready, as I sit down. Her big bright expectant eyes shine at me as I look away, trying to stifle a laugh. For once, I have something juicy to tell her.

"Somebody had a good weekend."

She gives me a double flash of her eyebrow as she says it, then sticks her tongue out at the corner of her mouth. Balling up my fist, I let out a long sniggering sound against it, which makes Kelly break into a giggle too.

"Yeah, you could say that... I have a new man... well, I guess he's not new really... more like an old flame, I guess you could say."

Looking at Kelly's face, she looks like an engrossed teen, listening to her best friend's relationship triumphs or latest crush.

"Oh really... is that Gareth... you were talking about him a lot last week... well, muttering about him... you looked so caught up in him."

Huh? I know it felt like I breezed through last week, but maybe I didn't. I don't even recall mentioning Gareth's name at all. As Kelly said, I must have been so caught up with the pending meeting, but I must have just erased it all.

"Ah no... it isn't... It's an old flame from school... my first boyfriend at school... we were reunited at my friend's wedding recently... I was totally blown away... but I didn't make any moves at the time as I thought he had a girlfriend."

She's hooked on my every word. Her features gushing at my sweet-sounding story, she'd soon change her mind on that if she knew what we had gotten up to.

"So... so how... how did you guys end up together? I... thought you were supposed to be patching things up with the other guy."

Oh, blimey, it all seems rather complicated now that I think about it. I take a moment to try to simplify it all somehow.

"Erm... I did see Gareth... he wanted to tell me he's getting married... I don't know why he couldn't just get his sister to tell me that... He probably wanted to humiliate me after how I treated him... I ran home before he could say anything more... then I get a knock at the door... Joe was standing there... apparently, my friend told him about my meeting with Gareth... he came to try to stop it, but got there too late... he saw me run... it was raining... and boy, did he look hot all wet on my doorstep... and then... you know... one thing led to another... I'll let you fill in the blanks."

She nods and mouths a 'wow' here and there as my story unfolds. It's the first time I properly talked about it, making it feel less of a dream and more of a reality.

"Oh wow, Charly... oh, it sounds so like... it sounds so like a love story destined for Hollywood... I wonder who'd play you...."

Kelly squeals like it is set in stone. She bounces in her chair and claps as she leans back out of her gossip pose.

"Eh hum... ladies... time to do some work, I think."

The booming voice makes us both jump. We look up sheepishly to meet the glare of Stanley, tapping on his watch. Oh crap, busted.

***

I am sitting crossed-legged on my sofa, catching up on the last week's TV, with a mug of hot chocolate. Yes, you did hear me correctly; I opted for chocolate, not wine, shock and horror. Although, it probably is just as calorific. Messages have been flying back and forth between Joe and me every day without fail. Picking up my phone, I can't help but keep reading the last message he sent to me. It was just about date plans for Saturday night, but I can't seem to stop staring at it, like I can't believe it's from him. Like an illusion of letters and numbers. I wonder what he has planned for me. All I know is what time to be ready. It's only Thursday and I know you shouldn't wish the days away, but I really wish I could.

Fifty-Eight

It seemed fitting to opt for the same navy dress I wore to Harper's wedding, but then again, probably a bit too dressy for a date night. So, I settled for a navy sweetheart neckline, A-line dress instead, still smart, though. Harper and Ashley enlisted themselves to help me get ready. Ashley loved the idea of wearing a sweetheart dress. Harper rolls her eyes at our gushing conversation. Harper offers to do my hair, and Ashley offers to do my makeup and nails. I accepted their help gratefully. Sitting in my dressing gown, Harper spins me around, away from the mirror.

"No peeking."

She flurries around in a blur as she gets to work, armed with something resembling a tool belt full of combs, brushes, hairspray and straighteners, or they could be curling tongs. Ashley starts with my nails, choosing a nude colour with flecks of glitter. I watch as concentration overtakes her features. I can't remember the last time I could relax like this, and it feels so good. Ashley wiggles with excitement for the finishing touches to my hair.

"You're going to look fab-u-lous!"

Harper gives Ashley the green light to start applying my makeup. She won't tell me or even let me see what colours she's using, but I can trust her. My nerves gradually turn to excitement as the time ticks on. Ashley grins wildly as she completes the finishing touches. With broad aching smiles, they both step back to admire their handy work, high fiving each other. Spinning me around in my chair to face the mirror, I can't believe my eyes. My hair is styled slightly wavy with a bit of volume for added sass. The black eyeliner, false lashes and mascara frame my eyes perfectly, with a tiny flick in the outer corners. They chose a nude shimmer for the eyelids and baby pink lipstick that is virtually nude as well. Grinning wildly, I jump up and grab them both for a group hug.

"Thanks, guys... you two are the best!"

Disappearing downstairs, they leave me so I can get dressed. My outfit is hanging gracefully on the wardrobe door. Okay, this is it dress, time to wow. Firstly, I rummage through my underwear drawer for the black lacy bra matching set, reserved for such moments like these. Big knickers are definitely out of bounds this evening and very much for the near future. I find the black set tucked away at the back. Tonight, without a doubt, deserves the fancy ones, just in case my dress meets Joe's bedroom floor. I blush at the sexy thought. I step into my underwear; the bra is a plunge style; it adds a little lift and va-va-voom to the situation. I carefully undo the side zip on my dress and slip into it, then gently pull the zip back up, praying the fabric doesn't get caught. I stand in front of the full-length mirror, smoothing the fabric down; I double-check that everything is in place.

"Okay, girl... this is it."

I quickly slip on my trusty heels and head down the stairs. Harper and Ashley wolf-whistle and hoot as they watch me sashay down.

"Girl... if he doesn't fall head over heels in love with you... I'll slap him myself."

She blurts out the statement as she hands me a small glass of wine. I quickly down it as I peer at the hallway clock; it's nearly showtime!

Fifty-Nine

In the car, my heart is thudding as I mindlessly fiddle with the tassels on my clutch bag. Ashley sits in the back seat next to me and puts her hand on mine to calm me down.

"Don't worry... you'll be fine."

Her voice is gentle and reassuring. I have never been so anxious about a date in my life. It hit me as soon as I climbed into Harper's car. I feel the need to chew my nails, but then I remember not to ruin Ashley's hard work. Harper pulls over next to Green Grove Park. I look out of the window, confused.

"Why are you stopping here?"

Harper turns in her seat, her elbow leaning on the back of her seat.

"I am under strict instructions from Joe to bring you here... I don't know any other details... promise."

She half-smiles gleefully. Hmm, I bet she hasn't told me everything; her smile looks slightly on the shifty side. I look to Ashley, hoping she can enlighten me, but she just shrugs and raises her hands in an 'I don't know' kind of fashion. I look back to Harper; she's looking through the windscreen and glances at me through the rearview mirror.

"Looks like he's waiting for you... good luck, Girl!"

Ashley unbuckles her seatbelt and throws herself at me, hugging me fiercely as she squeals.

"Go get him!"

I push past the nerves and give them both my best grateful smile before I climb out of the car. Sure enough, he's waiting for me at the entrance, with the sun slowly setting behind him. He's dressed in a lush burgundy long sleeve shirt, that hugs his muscles just right, loosely tucked into a pair of dark wash jeans. One of his hands is obscured by his back. I suddenly feel shy, which forces me to look at the ground as I approach him, clutching my bag nervously with both hands. As his shoes come into view, I look up to find he's grinning with adoration.

"Wow... Charly... you look...."

Pushing my nerves to one side, my mouth spontaneously cuts him off. I just couldn't wait to taste him again. The sound of a horn, hooting and cheering makes us jump; we look to the road as Harper and Ashley slowly drive past us. The noise soon disappears and then it is just us. Joe brings out his hidden hand into view; he's holding a big white rose; I'm in awe of its size.

"It's huge!"

I was about to say thank you, but his brow distracts me, giving me a suggestive double flash.

"I know."

I give him a playful elbow at his cheekiness. That doesn't stop me from flushing at the memory of his naked body and his perfectly sized manhood. All joking aside, he takes hold of my free hand.

"I want to show you something."

He leads me through the park gates, following the winding path. The white Victorian bandstand comes into view, looking like I've never seen it before. It's been adorned in twinkling lights, and red rose garlands line the pillars on either side of the entrance. I notice a bouquet lying on the top step. Joe releases my hand to retrieve the flowers. This is so amazing; I think I could cry. Joe takes the single rose from my hand and replaces it with the remaining dozen. He snaps the stem on the single one and slides it through a wave of my hair, tucking it behind my ear.

"This... all this... is so amazing... no one has ever done anything like this for me before... thank you."

I am so lost in awe right now. My eyes flicker to the roses, to the bandstand, then back to Joe. He tips my head up by my chin and I watch his eyes glimmer with adoration.

"No... YOU are amazing."

He steps round to my side, bending his knees and I squeal as he swiftly scoops me up into his arms. My side lines his torso, and the bouquet lays across his shoulder blades. He doesn't miss a step as he carries me onto the bandstand floor. Gently releasing my legs, they slide down his body; he cups one thigh before my foot meets the floor, holding me in the same position we were in, in our bathroom rendezvous. If he's not careful, I'll rip his clothes off, right here.

There's a twinkle in his eye; maybe he's thinking the same thing. After a long teasing moment, he reluctantly releases my thigh.

"I had a little help setting this up."

He turns and holds his thumb up to someone on the other side of the park. It looks more like a shadow in the rapidly disappearing sunlight than an actual person. Moments later, music fills the air around us.

"My song choice this time."

He murmurs profoundly and sincerely. Etta's voice brings the wedding reception back to life and I quickly place my roses to one side. As I turn, he is right there, just like the first time.

"Sorry... too close?"

He muses as his hand finds the small of my back; the other finds mine and brings it up to mid-air. Our fingers lace together, more like lovers than friends this time.

"Definitely not."

It feels so good to finally say those two exact words out loud.

"Remember... relax... and follow me."

Joe takes the lead as we drift back into the middle of the bandstand floor. He holds me firmly against his torso as we start to sway. I swear my heart races even faster each time Joe looks at me; it thuds so hard you probably see the imprints on my chest. I close my eyes as I bury my face in his neck, just as I hear Etta sing the very first line.

"He has," I murmur.

I flinch with embarrassment as I say my inner spirit's thoughts out loud. It was a quiet slip; maybe he didn't hear me. I refuse to look up until I am sure my cheeks have stopped burning.

I am more prepared for his dance moves this time. He steps back to spin me around, and my dress freely moves with me. To finish, he dips me back. Phew, no heel wobbles this time.

"She really has."

He utters it almost wordlessly. I see a flicker of emotion in his eyes, and my heart lifts. It seems to flutter in a different rhythm every time he looks at me, every time he touches me, every time he whispers sweet nothings in my ear. Is this what 'love' feels like? They say, 'you just know', and I think I do, I can't help but smile, and he mirrors it back to me. Actually, I do know. My heart gives me the confirmation that I needed. I am a little anxious to use the 'L word' out loud, but looking at his expression right now, I have a feeling that he feels it too. This whole romantic gesture screams, 'I love you,' doesn't it?

Joe frees his hand from mine and it comes up to rest on the side of my face, his thumb brushes my cheek. He slowly brings me back to my feet. Our lips meet tenderly on the way up. We refuse to part ways; in one swift motion, he pulls me up onto his waist and I wrap my legs around him as the song draws to a close. It changes to 'How Would You Feel' by Ed Sheeran. Is he trying to tell me something? Communicating his feelings through his song choices. He walks with me over to a ledge, where he sets me down and our lips part ways. His waist stays in between my thighs, his hands on my waist.

"Just in case you decide to run away again."

I laugh sheepishly; I don't think I'll ever live that one down. I run my hands up Joe's waist, feeling the ripple of abs under the fabric; my eyes follow the trail that they make, all the way up to his neck, then his cheeks. He responds to my touch on his face, leaning the weight of his head on me.

"Trust me... I won't... ever."

I know 'ever' is a strong word to say, as our first chapter plays out, but it feels so right; our first juvenile relationship was just the prologue. By the look on his face, I don't think he 'ever' wants me to go either. It's crazy to think I first laid eyes on him half of my life ago, yet it feels like nothing's changed. We were too young to know what we wanted back then. In fact, I didn't realise it until Harper's wedding. Seeing her in that stunning ivory ballgown and the love that consumed everyone in the room. I wanted it too; I still want it. I look deep into his hazel brown eyes for an answer. Do I see Joe waiting for me at the end of the aisle?

"Can I tell you a secret?"

His whisper immediately pauses my train of thoughts. My arms suddenly go stiff with the unknowing of what he's about to tell me. The feeling melts away as soon as his fingertips trail down my arms. Resting my hands on his shoulders, he overlaps mine with his and I nod for him to continue.

"You haven't strayed far from my mind over the years... even after you ran away from me... the first time around... I was young, but I knew I wanted to fight for you... but I was too afraid to do anything about it... when I saw you run home that day... so distraught... I couldn't pass the chance to try to fight for you... even if it ended up with you slamming the door in my face... at least I tried... you deserve to be happy... and I want to be the man to make that happen... I guess what I am trying to say is... I... L..."

He looks down, and in seconds, he looks like the shy schoolboy from back then. I patiently wait for him to gather the confidence to carry on. I cup his face; I bring his head up to face me; nerves are swallowing him up.

"It's okay... you can tell me anything... even the 'L 'word...."

Leaning my cheek on his, my mouth whispers it against his ear like it's a secret; I'm not sure why; it's not like anyone else is here to overhear us. For a moment, I thought I misread him as I pull back. I give him a moment to process it. I watch his features as the realisation sets in. His smile quite literally stretches from ear to ear. Without another word, he whisks me off the ledge and spins us both round in playful joy. I squeal and hold on to him tightly. The velocity pulls the rose out of my hair. Joe gradually slows to a stop and our foreheads meet while we wait for the scenery to stop rotating. Tipping his head back slightly, his eyes read each of my features before settling on my gaze.

"I... I... I love you, Charly."

Just those few words alone fill my body with so much elation that we're floating on air. For a brief moment, I thought he would tease me by just saying 'I like you', but no, he dove straight in. He patiently waits for me to respond.

"I love... the roses... I love... the song... and I love...."

The tables have been spun round to me; now, I'm the shy schoolgirl. I gulp down the nerves as this is my first, my everything.

"... and... and I love you, Joe."

I watch as the anxiety lifts from his features. He looks astounded; maybe he set himself up to be knocked back or something.

"Am I worth the wait?" I muse.

He looks at me a little perplexed, like it's the most absurd thing he's ever heard.

"Fuck... yes!"

It rolls off his tongue divinely, dragging out the 's 'for dramatic effect. It's enough to reel me in; I kiss him deep, hard and full of need. The need drives right through me, from my lips right down to the pit of my stomach, sending goosebumps prickling up my arms. It makes me shiver in a warm fuzzy way, if that can be possible. It catches Joe's attention.

"Are you cold?"

I smile flirtatiously and shake my head, followed by a silent double flash of my eyebrows. I keep them raised, and he does the same.

"Oh... I see."

He chuckles at my suggestive manner. He brings a hand up into view and glances at his watch, then looks back to me.

"We've missed our table reservation... do you want to come back to my place?... we can grab some food on the way...."

Do I want to go back to his place? Now it's my turn to look a little perplexed. My stomach growls loud and clear for both of us to hear. His face creases in amusement; at least he sees the funny side while I'm mortified inside.

"I better satisfy your hunger monster... before I feed the pony."

I playfully act shocked at his statement, but deep down, I love how bold he can be amongst the kindness. Equal parts naughty, with equal amounts of nice; he's everything I need and want in a man.

Sixty

Joe's apartment is on the top floor. As we walk in, I gawp at the beauty. There's no hallway; it's all open plan throughout, grey and white walls alternate around the room, very stylish. The kitchen is tucked away on the left-hand side and I watch Joe disappear into it with the bag of Chinese take-out that we grabbed on the way here. The huge dark grey sofa takes centre stage to the right, with cushions scattered across it. My gaze carries on, sweeping around the room. A single armchair sits near the other end of the sofa in the same colour; they both face a massive flat-screen TV. My eyes meet the wall opposite the couch, charcoal coloured brickwork surrounds the fireplace, which seems a bit dramatic compared to the rest of the room's decor. As he reappears, I point to the brickwork.

"That's a moody colour compared to the rest of the room."

I gesture to the other walls as if that'll prove my point.

"Maybe I am moody."

He smirks. Somehow, I find that hard to believe. A couple of steps catch my attention; they lead to a vast sliding door, looking out to the dark sky. I wonder what view is beyond it.

"I want to show you something."

Joe takes my hand and leads me up the two steps, then slides open the door. Stepping out onto the balcony, I shiver as the cool air rushes at me. He leads me closer to the balcony's edge, and the city skyline comes into view. The dark night is lit up by the city lights, the colours pool into the clouds. We're so high up, but you can still hear the hum of traffic in the distance. I catch sight of City Bridge; it's bizarre to think that such a simple structure holds so many memories, good and bad ones.

A flash of warmth surrounds me as Joe drapes me in a blanket. He smiles intently as I turn to face him, then he holds both hands up in a 'stop 'kind of way, still smiling.

"Wait here."

My eyes follow him as he disappears back into the apartment. Moments later, music pipes out from nearby speakers; the tune is familiar, her voice is familiar, the lyrics are familiar. My eyes widen and glisten as the feeling of nostalgia sweeps over me, making the emotions rise within my chest. Alanis Morissette's album, 'Jagged Little Pill' was the soundtrack of our youth. 'Head Over Feet' plays out, but it sounds different, like it's been stripped bare, an acoustic version, maybe? It seems to sound more spiritual this way. Lights spring up around me in mid-thought, and he's lowered the indoor lights too. My heart melts when I see his face reappear through the glow. I feel my eyes well at this whole thoughtful gesture, he stops with his hands in his pockets and admires me for a moment as I sing a few song lines, albeit a bit out of key.

Joe gestures for me to spin; I smile at his bonkers request. The blanket slips from my shoulders as I lift my hands straight up into the air, sweeping the air as I spin as graceful as I can in heels, combing the breeze like brushing snowflakes in winter; my dress follows suit as I turn. Coming to a stop, he's right there to catch me. With one hand on my back, he draws me in, offering his other hand in mid-air, I gladly take it. My nose settles at his jaw, I inhale the scent of him, he's all body wash and peppermints. He sways with me nestled in his arms and I close my eyes as my ears zone into the voice of Alanis; her mesmeric tone is so powerful that I'd give anything to be transported back to our youth.

"Take me back to 2002," I murmur.

My eyes remain closed, but I feel his head tip downwards. His nose buries into my hair and I feel him inhale me deeply.

"What... so you can run away from me again?"

I feel his chuckle, against my head and through his chest. Yes, I'm definitely not going to live that one down, am I? He's never going to let me forget.

"No, not that... because knowing how I feel now... I would never have let you go... then I would have never known the meaning of heartache... let alone experienced it."

I hold back the tears that want to break free; the feeling shudders through my chest and breath. Joe lets go of my hand, and cradles the back of my head, delving his fingers into my hair. A hold that tells me that he never wants to let go.

"It doesn't matter where we've been... it doesn't matter who we might have loved before... all that matters to me now is making you happy Charly...."

I open my eyes to the sweetest statement I think I have ever heard and Joe's hand releases my head as I look up. Now his eyes are glistening, and the budding feeling within me flourishes a little more.

"I don't want you to look back and be full of regrets... I want you to look forward with hope... and dance with me."

He smiles down at me as he says it and kisses me, just the once on my forehead. Looking to my side, he fishes for my hand; holding it aloft and stepping back, he spins me around twice, then draws my back into his chest. His arms wrap around my torso as we move from side to side. The song draws to a close, and silence fills the air, but we continue to sway to our own rhythm of contentment.

Sixty-One

Caught up in the moment, we almost forgot about our food. Eventually, we sit at the dining table with platefuls of Chinese, delving straight into the sweet and sour chicken with some rice. I grimace as soon as it hits my tastebuds; it's stone cold. As if by mutual distaste, we look up at each other simultaneously with the same distorted expression.

"I made some chocolate brownies earlier... do you want to try some?"

My stomach grumbles with hunger and delight for a chocolate dessert, my one and only favourite chocolate dessert.

"Absolutely."

I help him clear away the plates of Chinese. The tray of brownies sitting pleasingly on the kitchen side catches my eye, and I fight against the urge to salivate.

"Get comfy on the sofa... while I throw something together."

I don't need telling twice. I could skip to the sofa, but I play it cool. Sashaying through the room, I collect my glass of wine, take a seat on the sofa, kick off my heels, and then bring my feet up to rest under my behind. Resting my elbow on the headrest, I support my head with my palm so I can watch Joe effortlessly flitter around in his kitchen. Although I can't quite see what he's up to, I can definitely smell fresh coffee and chocolate.

Moments later, he brings a tray over to the coffee table in front of me. He takes my glass of wine and replaces it with a bowl. A generous portion of brownie sits in the middle, with whipped cream, strawberries, and chocolate sauce drizzled in fancy lines, all finished with a chocolate heart.

"Wow, this looks amazing."

My eyes feel like they are on the verge of popping out of my head with amazement. A neat stack of napkins lays next to two frothy coffees. I don't waste time; I get stuck straight in before my stomach embarrasses me some more. Soon as the richness of dark chocolate hits my tastebuds, I moan with satisfaction at every mouthful, savouring every bite. As he takes his bowl, he sniggers at my appreciative noises and relaxes next to me. His foot comes up to rest on his opposite thigh, his knee points in my direction. I am officially lost for words; my gaze fixed on the nothingness above me, something cold and wet lands on my nose. I refocus to find Joe giggling.

"Hey!"

It comes out more like a yelp, as it startles me. Touching my nose, I find cream on my fingertips. Picking up the heart-shaped chocolate in a flash, I plonk it on the end of his nose. Ha, he didn't see that one coming; I can't help but giggle until my sides hurt, as he gawks with the coldness. For a moment, he reminds me of a Care Bear, which entices me to laugh even harder. He picks it off and eats it, then picks up the one sitting on his dessert. He gestures for me to open my mouth; I gladly welcome it; it melts in the middle as I chew. Ignoring the mess on our noses, we carry on, delving into our desserts until every mouthful is gone.

"You've got some chocolate there...."

He points to just above the corner of his mouth. I use my tongue to try to reach the corner of my mouth, but to no avail.

"Here, let me get it for you."

His foot comes down to the floor briefly so he can reach for a napkin and as his foot returns to its rested position, he leans in to wipe the corner of my mouth; his eyes lock with my lips. I bite my lower lip as I observe him help me. From the corner of my eye, I can see the napkin float down. His hand cups the side of my head, wasting no time to pull me in closer until our lips meet; steadying myself, I put my hand on his chest. In swift succession, he rolls me into his arms, my back across his lap. Breaking the kiss for a moment, we laugh at each other's cream smeared faces. I reach over to the tray for another napkin and wipe Joe's face, and he returns the favour. Screwing up the napkin into a ball, he lobs it onto the tray. Pleased with his accurate aim, he punches the air.

"YES," he bellows.

The brush of excitement soon dissipates and he returns his attention back to me. He pushes my hair away as his hand glides up and over my shoulder. His eyes widen as they survey my chest; judging by the look on his face, I'm assuming my plunge bra has done its job. I peer down and laugh, the result of laying slightly on my side, plus the bra pushing them up considerably, reveals the black lace edging. My cleavage resembles rolling hillsides; it might as well be my own personal chin rest.

"Hello there."

He murmurs, captivated by the hills. From my shoulder, his hand and eyes glide back down to the black lace, his fingertips tracing the patterns, gentle and featherlike. They glide all the way along to the crease of my cleavage. My eyes stay on his chest area, remembering his toned body, the rivulets of water trailing down it and the way his muscles flexed as he wandered around practically naked in my kitchen. I quiver in between my legs at the invited memory. Joe's hand trails down my side and the length of my thigh, towards my knee to rest. I can feel his gaze back on me, I look up to meet him, and our eyes lock. His hand on my knee sweeps up the side of my thigh, encouraging my dress to slide out of its path, revealing part of my lace panties. Brushing up and down, his fingertips have found the seam on my underwear. He watches my body intently as my breasts heave and my hips roll back and forth slightly with the ever-increasing eagerness under his caress. I bet he enjoys teasing me in this way. The sensation is too much to bear; I raise myself onto the arm I am laying on. Taking the lead, I cup his face with my free hand, drawing him in closer, I brush my lips against his without leaving a kiss behind. I pull away as he tries to kiss me, see how he likes to be teased. He grins, but it's a little twisted with frustration.

"Hey, you... come back."

His hand on my hip swiftly comes up to the back of my head. He draws me in and pins his lips against mine, our tongues deliciously entwine.

I briefly break away as I feel his foot come down to the floor, allowing me to swiftly take a seat on his lap facing him, my breasts almost at his chin level. I cup his face, running my fingers through his beard, he steals my breath away when his lips lock with mine; wild but tender. Without breaking the embrace, one of his arms come round to my back, holding me tightly; he uses the other for support as he shuffles us off the sofa. I wrap my arms around the back of his neck, and I let out a squeal as he stands fully. I giggle at the sudden motion; my stomach leaps with the movement, making me hold on tighter. I gasp as Joe finds my behind, squeezing both buttocks in a firm caress. He carries me across the room with little effort. As soon as we cross the threshold of his bedroom, he has my back pressed against the wall. Just as Joe lets go of my behind and his hands slide to my hips, my legs slip down his body one by one. Before the last leg meets the floor, I gasp as he catches it, cupping my knee. His groin is pressed against mine so that even through his jeans I can feel that he's hard for me. My arms relax and glide down to the top button on his shirt. The feeling in my fingers is far from clumsy this time around. As I undo each of his buttons slowly down to his belt buckle, he leans his torso back, so my hands have room to pull out the ends of his shirt from his jeans. Peeling each side away, I bite my lower lip as the glorious sight of his flawless body is revealed. I help him slip the shirt off; it swings around and hangs from the arm holding my knee. Admiring him with hungry eyes, he really does take my breath away.

As he towers over me, a playful grin appears and he lets go of my leg, allowing the shirt to fall, and my leg slips flirtatiously down his body. I feel for the zip on the side of my dress; my fingers find it and gently pull it down all the way to the bottom. The straps, now loose, fall from my shoulders but stop not so far below. The tumbling fabric catches Joe's attention; he helps my dress finish its journey to his bedroom floor.

The featherlight touch of his fingers tingles my skin. Holding me firmly by the hips, he steps backwards, and I dutifully follow, allowing me to step out of my crumpled dress fortress. Tip-toeing so my hands can reach his hair, I comb my fingers through it, he groans under my dragging touch. I lean all my weight on Joe, forcing him to take more than just one step backwards, but his build is rock steady. His arms swiftly come down to my waist and sweep me off the floor into a fireman's lift over his shoulder. As he straightens, I squeal at the surprisingly sudden motion. He playfully spanks me on the backside and I yelp with astonishment.

"Hey!"

I let out half a giggle, which entices him to do it again but harder, a proper spank. I let out a short sharp moan; whoa, the sensation is smart, yet hot. His hands glide, one by one, from my thighs up to my backside. I gasp as his fingertips brush along the crease of my behind, feeling along my inner thigh and up to the lace patterns of my panties. My arms dangling down his back, my hands hold onto the sides of his waist as his teasing accelerates. Slipping into the waistband of my panties, he gives one cheek a squeeze before he peels them right off and lets them float down my legs. Another spank meets my behind, but harder and smarter this time, the clap sound reverberates across my bare skin. It forces out a more exciting gasp from the deep depths of my chest. He feels and hears my excitement, encouraging him to do it again, harder, smarter, sexier, making me cry out in complete satisfaction.

Walking over to the bed, he flings me down, making me let out a delighted shriek. As I land, my long hair splays out in all directions, a real mess. Joe's head stays at my waist, planting sensual kisses along each hip bone, then across my stomach, heading north up my body and over the rolling hillside cleavage. His beard sends goosebumps popping and prickling their way across my skin. He suddenly springs up to his feet. Sitting up onto my elbows to get a better view, I watch as he unbuckles his belt and pulls it tantalisingly slowly from the loops, then with a whip sound, he tugs out the last section like some sexy cowboy. How can something so ordinary drive me so crazy? The belt falls to the floor with a thud.

Biting my lower lip, I watch his teasing display play on. He's undoing the button and unzipping his jeans in a way that has my inner spirit almost exploding with longing. Pulling down and shimmying out of his jeans, unveils snug navy trunks, that seem to hug his bulge perfectly, accentuating his size. Oh boy, the muscles deep within my stomach go into overdrive, pulsing and pinching in an unbearably lustful way. I bring my feet up to rest on the bed, trying to disguise my arousal for a little longer. Over my knees, I watch intently as the waistband on his underwear slips down and disappears out of sight. My eyes are fixed on the way his muscles move as he steps out of his trunks, that same flex that I love so much. Lowering myself to lie flat as he turns and reaches over to the bedside table, all I can hear is a drawer opening, the sound of foil packaging rustling and the pinging of latex. Resting my hands on the bed above my head, the anticipation rises within me; the sensation makes my body roll like waves crashing through me. My sex is still buzzing from the brief encounter with his fingers. I feel his presence towering over the height of my knees. Without asking, each of my feet slide back down the bed, my legs slightly part. His eyes, full of desire, intently watch every move I make. As he climbs onto the bed, my thighs automatically part ways, granting him full access. Lowering his total weight onto me, I feel his erection press against my groin; it torments me for being so close and yet so far. His hips start to roll gently back and forth, teasing me even further into oblivion. Covering my eyes with the backs of my forearms as the arousal intensifies, all that's exposed is my quivering lips that gasp with every rolling action.

"J-o-e"

His name struggles to break free from my lips, almost groaning between each letter. His weight suddenly shifts, and my body feels exposed to the world. Before I can uncover my eyes to see what's going on, he flips me over. I feel him hovering over me; his hands are on the sides of my behind, inviting it to arch up ever so slightly. The strap on my bra is pinched and freed from its clips, allowing it to slip off my shoulders. I reach under myself, pulling my bra-free, then give it a flying lesson across the room. Joe's hand glides from my right shoulder blade down to my right knee, bringing it up the bed, almost level with my hip. His hand slides back down to cup my buttock. I bury my face into the bedsheets as another deep throaty groan escapes from my chest. His hand circles in all directions on my behind, everywhere except my sex; he comes teasingly close, but seems to skip across it. It leaves me breathlessly panting and wanting. Grasping handfuls of sheets, I'm almost at the point of no return. I know he's intently watching me unravel under his touch. I roll my head to the side to try to peer over my shoulder.

"Please... Joe..."

I breathlessly moan his name. I don't have to explain myself. The sensation in my muscles keeps winding into a coiled spring, on the brink of letting go at the slightest touch. His fingertips slowly brush along my buttock; they drag at my skin, to my clit, almost pinching me in-between his flushed fingers. My grip on the duvet gets tighter and tighter as he glides up and down. I didn't realise how wet I was until that motion. He stills and presses down firmly, right on the button. I gasp with all that's left in my lungs; they feel empty, yet I can still breathe. My whole being is teetering right on the edge of the peak. It only takes a few strokes from Joe's skillful fingers, and I shatter; not just in a million pieces but a million fragments. Letting my grip soften slowly from the sheets, the wound-up spring finally releases, and my whole body feels alive but frozen as my muscles pulse and pinch in a delicious way. I'm still panting; my heart thrashes against my ribs. Joe's body comes down to lay half across mine, scooping me into him with one arm, holding me close as I float down from my euphoric cloud.

"Whoah."

He brushes my hair away and my neck is exposed to his mouth, his warm breath travels down my neck. I hear a faint triumphant inner chuckle.

"You're welcome."

He kisses behind my ear, which sends tingling shockwaves down my neck and back. Every inch of my body feels alive with desire; it makes me shiver, in a good way, of course. As I land fully from the cloud, feeling totally exhilarated, I wriggle out of his hold to roll towards him. I could quite possibly lay here forever looking at his handsome face, but need prevails. Joe must have mistaken the shivers for a chill as he reaches around the back of him to pull up the end of the duvet. Just when I thought he was just going to drape it over us, he mischievously giggles as he swiftly rolls us both into a duvet sausage roll. I shriek with the surprise, but soon end up laughing with him as we wrestle to free our arms, but it's no use. Shifting our weight back the way we came, I land on top of him; the giggling subsides as we focus on each other instead.

"Hello again," he muses.

He brings me down to kiss me, but I teasingly brush my tongue on his top lip; I feel his cock harden even more. He tries to kiss me again, but sure enough, I tease him once again. A little frustration tinges on his smile.

"Hey, you."

Joe's arms come down to my lower back, holding me close; encased in his muscles, I feel secure and safe. Gently he rolls us again, his waist slides to be neatly tucked in between my thighs. No teasing escape routes from his lips this time. His features soften from playful to loving as he admires every feature of mine.

"I love you, Charly."

The four words roll off his tongue sensuously, sending the butterflies into a delighted spin. I can't help but smile as it fills every part of me with immense joy.

"I love you too, Joe... so much."

So much emotion runs through his face as I say those words back to him. Almost like all his dreams have finally come true at once. I give him the kiss he's been eagerly waiting for, fuelled with so much love and passion. My hands run wildly through his hair, all the while our lips are locked. His hips start to roll slowly against my sex, sending it into another tingling frenzy. I let go of his hair as I feel him slide into me, our fingers lace together, as he pins my hands down on the bed and drives himself further into me. My back wants to arch with off the scale delight as I feel his entire length. Exposing my neck to him, his tongue glides from the crook up to my jaw and over to my mouth where he kisses me so deeply, so longingly, oh my!

He squeezes my hands tighter and firmer as he drives his entire length into me, again and again. It's slow and passionate but deep, oh so deep; I wrap my legs around him, not wanting him to stop with the slow deep grind. His eyes burn brightly, watching me closely as the moans tremble through my lips; he nips and sucks at my lower lip.

His mouth stays close, just hovering above mine, I feel his warm breath as he pants. Joe loosens his hands from mine, and my palms sting from the numbness. Using one to cup my face, his thumb traces along my lips, dragging down my lower lip, parting them with ease, his tongue strokes mine in a steamy tangle. Joe buries his face in my hair as thrusts merge from deeply penetrating to a vigorous rhythm; he groans deeply like he's teetering on the edge. My arms come round to his back; I want to hug him as he climaxes. His back forms a rigid arch like he's going to let go at any moment; his breath is clammy against my neck.

"Oh fuck."

He grunts against my ear; I feel him tense up and shudder as he ejaculates, then his body gradually relaxes under my touch. Releasing my legs from his waist, I play with his hair as he lays in my arms while I wait for him to come down from his own euphoria.

Sixty-Two

The sun's rays beating through the gaps in the blinds arouse me from my slumber; my senses are slow to wake up. Joe's side of the bed is empty and cold. Sitting up, my bleary eyes sleepily search the room. As I shift my body between the sheets, I realise that I am still naked. I clock a black cotton bathrobe hanging on the back of the bedroom door. Slipping out from under the sheets, my bare feet pad across the wood flooring. Lifting the robe off the hook, holding it close to my face, it still smells of Joe, a hint of his aftershave and peppermint lingers on the fabric. Sliding my body into it, I tie the belt into a loose knot. I scoop my hair out from under the material and then smoothe it down. The smell of cooked food lures me out of the bedroom. As I walk around the corner, sure enough, he's effortlessly flitting around his kitchen, once again. The kitchen island is masking his lower half, so just his bare torso is on display. Standing and surveying him from afar, I loosely fold my arms, keeping one hand near my face, biting on my thumbnail. As he turns in my direction with a piled-high plate of pancakes, I startle him. He almost drops his hard work, but manages to steady himself just in time. He clutches his chest with his free hand, his features twisted with humour and fright.

"Ah fuck."

As the moment passes, he eyes me up and down while I remain standing with my arms folded; I smile against the thumb pressed to my mouth.

"Wow... Charly, you look...."

He wolf-whistles, and gives me a double flash of his eyebrow. As he places the plate down, I notice he's wearing a pair of black sweatpants that hang off his hips. My inner spirit barges in with a thought, 'wouldn't he make an excellent naked butler?' He comes over to me, leaning in for a good morning kiss but pauses, barely leaving an inch between us, looking at me quizzically.

"What are you thinking about, Charly?"

I thought I was succeeding at hiding my raunchy thought, but obviously not. I feel my cheeks flush, but I'm not sure if it's embarrassment or because of the insanely hot image running through my mind's eye; I think I'll go with the latter.

"Umm... I was just thinking... how hot you'd look as a naked butler."

I murmur it breathlessly as his mouth teases me, so close to a kiss, but yet so far. His features are a little out of focus, but I'm pretty sure I sense one of his mischievous grins.

"Oh... did you now?"

His tone is so deep and smouldering that it has me in a trance instantly. Before I can say anything more, he holds me by the hips, pulling me close, then lifts me up onto his waist. He carries me over and places me on the kitchen island; the bathrobe slips down my thighs as I'm seated.

"I'll remember that for next time."

Oh my, what a statement full of promises. The sliding fabric catches Joe's attention; he grunts in a way that tells me he wants me. As he looks down at me, the robe decides to part ways around my chest too, and it makes me wonder if he possesses the power to do that with his mind; my clothes seem to have the habit of falling off when I'm around him. He holds me firmly by the hips as he wriggles his waist in between my thighs. Visions of him whisking me off, back to his room, start the whirring of my internal sexual cogs. His hands come up to hold my face, and he starts kissing me with such intensity. His fingertips trace up to my hair and as he is running them across my scalp, pushing my hair back, dragging at the strands, the sensation makes me gasp. No one's touch has ever ignited my body in this way. Leaning his torso onto mine, pressing me backwards slightly, gives the impression he's going to take me right here, right now. The cogs are in full power pumping mode now. The bathrobe can't stand the mounting sexual tension either; it slips right down off my shoulders as my back arches slightly, thrusting my chest outwards. The robe just barely clings to my breasts. Joe's grip on my hair loosens, but our lips are still locked in their steamy rendezvous. His hands trail back down to my thighs, sweeping away the fabric, so he has access to my bare skin; his fingers graze up and down my hips, pushing the fabric even further away, as he grips me with such longing. As he starts to draw me in, my behind slides willingly on the fabric towards Joe's waist. The belt around me clings on for dear life. As our groins meet, I feel his erection even through the thick fabric of his sweatpants. He leans into me further, forgetting the kitchen island has breakfast items laid out; we nearly flatten his hard work.

"Watch the pancakes."

I murmur along with a playful tutting noise. As I look deep into his eyes, the connection between us is so powerful; the world around us might as well not exist, it's just him and me in our own universe.

"Fuck... the pancakes," he murmurs.

Hastily he sweeps me and my behind off the counter, my arms leap up to hold on around the back of his neck. An exhilarated shriek escapes from me with the sudden motion and the insanely hot possibilities that are waiting for me just around the corner. I wrap my legs around him to secure my place. I can't take my eyes off his handsome face and as the excitement dances in his dark but glimmering eyes, it makes me wonder what his inner spirit is saying. We cross the threshold to his bedroom; I could get used to this, and my inner spirit squeals with the thought of sex on tap.

He's gentler this time, placing me down near the top end of the bed. As he lets go, I shuffle up and lay down on the pillows. Before he lays down, he wrestles out of his sweatpants and kicks them off, then grabbing hold of the duvet, he pulls it over us as his body lays over mine. My legs automatically part ways to allow him in. His knees rest on the bed, but he leans over me like he's in mid-press up. He eyes my body up and down, almost like he's wondering what to devour first. I squirm under his watchful gaze; just making me wait is teasing enough; he hasn't even touched me yet. My breath hitches as he lowers himself down towards my pelvis, planting deep sensual kisses from the top of my hip down to my pubic hair. I gasp, with his mouth so close to my sex; I close my eyes as my back arches, my breath ragged with anticipation. My hands grip each side of the pillow with the rising thrill of wondering what move he'll make next. He heads north over my belly button, untying the belt, what's left holding on. Using both hands, he glides the ties outwards, pushing away the fabric to unveil the rest of my bare skin for him to caress. My grip on the pillow tightens as his head drifts further up towards my breasts. His mouth lingers over my nipple; all I can feel is his warm breath teasing me deliciously; just his bottom lip brushes against it, followed by the prickling of his beard. Joe's mouth ventures over to the centre of my chest, brushing and kissing his way up to my neck.

Leaning back, he beats away the duvet to see better, then stretches over to his bedside drawer and the familiar sound of foil packaging rustling. He rests back on his heels as I watch him tear open the packet, then retrieve the rubber inside. Even watching him glide it on is so freaking hot. He smirks as he notices my gawking expression. He uses his index finger to push my jaw back up into its rightful place. Laying his hands down on the bed on either side of me, he leans all his weight on them, using them to walk his torso up to my body until we're lying face to face. My hands leave the pillow to find his hair, his oh so sexy bed hair, or soon to be twice 'just fucked' hair. Running my fingers through it, feeling the textures, it drives me crazy. The good vibrations circulating around every inch of my lower body, are making me almost come apart at the seams.

He swiftly scoops me up and rocks backwards, bringing me up to take a seat on his thighs. The robe flies off my arms, splaying it out behind me. Whoah, this is new and so unexpected. I hear a chuckle caught deep within his throat as if he can read my thoughts. Lifting myself up slightly to reposition, he quickly grabs his cock; as I come back down, I slide right onto him. I throw my head back with rapture as I feel his entire length fill me up. He holds onto my behind tightly, using all his strength to guide me up and down; he makes it look so easy. The closeness, deepness, sensuality, and electricity are all so overwhelming as it builds. There are no words to describe such a feeling except for 'OH BOY!' I tip so far back at the sexiness that I almost fall back completely, but Joe's arms catch me. He brings me back face to face and I wrap my arms around him, one hand on the back of his neck, the other resting across his shoulder blades. I bury my face in the crook of his neck, breathing him in deeply; the fragrant body wash and peppermint have long since faded, unmasking the true scent of Joe. I breathe him in deeply again, relishing the natural scent of him as my lips, then my teeth graze the crook of his neck. Is it so bad that I want to bite him? At that thought, a hardness nips my shoulder; I gasp as the sensation tingles down my shoulder blade, instinctively I dig my nails into his skin. He does it again, harder, sexier, oh my! It's as if he sensed my hesitation, almost like he was giving me permission to do it to him. I graze my teeth against his skin, running them back and forth across his shoulder. I hear him groan deeply as I come back to the crook of his neck, and I giggle mischievously; it's muffled by his skin. A stinging sensation raps across my backside, forcing me to bite down hard as I flinch; a shot of guilt flies through me, but when I hear him grunt and chuckle against my mouth, instantly the feeling melts away. His skin looks red raw; I kiss it softly, hoping it soothes the sting. I pick my head up to find his lips and press mine with his. I break away to rest my forehead on his as I continue to grind on his lap; like an electric current, I feel the arousal buzz and ricochet through my core. His arms move to the centre of my back, hugging me fiercely as he buries his face in my hair and his body stiffens. His arms release me for a moment until I feel his hands clasp my buttocks, making a loud slap sound. I let out an aroused yelp which encourages him to tip over the edge, his grip tightens on the last thrust, and he shatters into his own ecstasy; his groans rumble through his chest on release. We bring down the pace until I'm just sitting on him; I watch his shoulders bounce as he pants.

After a moment, Joe's eyes finally meet mine, his cheeks so flushed and his expression still lost in satisfaction.

"Whoah... fuck me."

It leaves his lips in a breathless whisper. A smirk appears on my face that soon turns into a triumphant giggle.

"I think I just did."

Sixty-Three

Seems a bit disappointing to finish a sublime fuck with a bowl of cereal. The pancakes were obviously stone cold by the time we came back to the kitchen. But it was oh so worth it; being deep-seated on Joe was more than freaking hot. I feel myself redden with the not-so-distant memory as I play around with my 'O 'shaped cereal. We're sitting on the same side of the dining table. Joe turns towards me, sideways in his seat just as he finishes his bowl; he notices my flushed cheeks, his touch on my inner thigh makes me jump at first, then excitement ripples through my sex. For a moment, I feel embarrassed, and I try to hide my coyness from him as I look away. I feel his touch on my opposite cheek; he brings my face back to meet his and catches my lips in a deep and meaningful embrace. As his lips caress mine, he strokes my hair, pushing it back and tucking it behind my ear.

"You make my band t-shirts and trunks look sexy."

His remark has my features in a twisted smirk. Looking away slightly as the back of my hand flies up to my mouth, still holding my spoon as a long snigger forces its way out. I can hear a muffled chuckling against my ear; his humorous remark is enough to break the tension. I put my spoon in my bowl and let my gaze drift back to him. His features have softened to a thoughtful but serious expression.

"It's bizarre to think I've known you pretty much half of my life...
yet you've barely been a part of it... I don't feel like I've been apart
from you, though... like we're picking up from where we left off...
there doesn't seem to be any words good enough to express how I feel
about you, Charly... when I saw you at Harper's wedding... you... you
blew me away... you looked stunning... gorgeous even... it was like
stepping out of a time machine... you looked no different from the last
time I laid eyes on you... then I thought I had lost you all over again...
loving you doesn't seem enough... but I do love you, Charly... so
much... always have... then and now...."

He pauses a moment to catch his breath; it's shaky with his
emotions.

"... and I... I think... I always will."

If his heart was physically hanging off his sleeve, I think it'd be on
the floor by now or exploded with the immense love and devotion that
fills it. I feel my eyes well, and my heart swells with every word that
just left his lips; I'm hanging onto his every word as tears pool in the
corners of my eyes and then find their way down my cheeks. I long to
be closer to him, just sitting next to him feels too far away. I take a
seat on his lap, sideways; as I sniff back the emotions, he notices the
tears and using his thumb, he wipes them away, but his touch doesn't
leave my face.

"Trust me, Joe... everything you just said... fills my heart with so
much joy ...that you feel the same way as I feel about you... I thought I
had loved before... but nothing has ever come close to this... I feel like

I am so lost in you... that the world outside may as well not exist...
you've lit up my life in ways I never thought possible... I love you so
much... and it feels so fucking amazing."

So. Fucking. Amazing. Out of this world even. Especially the sex,
whoah yes, even describing it as mind-blowing feels like an
understatement. Joe keeps my face close to his as I say every word. I
watch the emotions swim through his features when my heartfelt
words settle in. I press my lips against his deeply, not in lust, but
fuelled with so much love, adoration and fulfilment.

All the time I was with Joe, I didn't look at my phone once until I got home. Both Harper and Ashley had left message after message. Each one filled with the ever-increasing urgency to know how well our date went, right down to the nitty-gritty details. There are only two words that I can think of that will sum it all up nicely. I go to my inbox and open a new message, tagging both ladies to it, and just those two words I type...

'FUCKING AMAZING! XX'

And send.

Sixty-Four

I inhale their fresh scent, and I smile, arranging each stem of Joe's white rose bouquet in a neat display. Stepping back to admire my handiwork, while I take a sip of rosé, I should really get out of these work clothes. I take another sip, just as my phone buzzes. My heart leaps when I see his name fill my screen. Setting my glass down, I read the message.

'Miss you, Baby xx.'

The word 'Baby' takes me back to our first morning together. Oh, Joe, boy, you can move. His body so close to mine as his fingertips grazed my bare skin through the gaps of my shirt. I touch where his fingers had been; the thought heats and prickles my cheeks.

Lost in thought, I almost forget to reply to him. Hmm, something lovely, witty or filthy? I peer around the room as if seeking inspiration. Smiling broadly, my eyes fixate on the corner where the dancing took off. My bare feet pad against the floor tiles as I walk over, and I rest my behind on the edge of the counter, then pull myself up to sit. Switching my phone's camera into selfie mode, I take a picture. I send it to Joe, along with the caption:

'Hmm... I am missing something too, in this corner... xx.'

I don't have to wait long for a reply.

'Hmm... you know what... I have no idea what that could be... xx.'

With my smile never ceasing, my fingertips tap against my mouth in a way that I hope helps me to think of what to say next.

'I'm not sure why but... I really, really fancy some ridiculously hot toast right now... xx.'

Almost immediately after I hit the send icon, a new message pings back.

'Do you need some help with that? xx'

I automatically bite my lower lip at the thought of round two in this corner. Surely, Joe doesn't mean coming here now, does he? Or is this just something else to tease me with? I feel myself overheat even more with the possibility. I bet he's just toying with me; after all, he's probably only just finished work.

'I think I can just about manage... but thank you anyway... xx.'

I hit send, then take another sip of wine while I wait for his next reply. A few minutes tick by, but nothing comes back. Hunger starts causing havoc with my stomach; I really need to eat. My old faithful, quick and easy pasta dish is in the cards, I think. I sweep my hair up and secure it with a hair tie. Retrieving a saucepan from the drainer, I fill it with water and place it on the hob. I grab a tub of sauce and some pasta from the cupboard; I should really make an effort to make my own sauce from scratch one of these days. My dish quickly comes together and all gets sloshed into a bowl then finished off with a generous helping of grated cheese. I turn on my iPod to shuffle, setting it down next to the toaster. 'Come Away With Me' by Norah Jones starts playing as I sit at my kitchen table with my dinner. I love this song; the sound in the background makes me think of waves crashing on a shore; it's so soothing. I could do with a holiday, a nice beach holiday. Preferably with Joe, in nothing but swimming trunks. A James Bond beach scenario plays out in my mind, and I nearly drop my fork. I shovel a forkful of pasta, as I hear a knock; it sounded like just the once, but my heart leaps anyway. I peer around the kitchen doorway. I sigh heavily with a bit of disappointment that it was just letters falling onto the doormat. I retrieve them, then return to my dinner. I demolish a few mouthfuls as I listen to Norah, closing my eyes for a moment as my eardrums and my inner spirit sail away with the music and the softness of her voice.

'Knock, knock, knock'.

My eyes fly open, was that a proper knock this time? I was lost in Norah's voice; I'm probably just hearing things.

'Knock, knock, knock'.

Pretty sure that sound wasn't part of the song this time. I drop my fork; it clangs noisily against my dish as I spring up from my stool. Excitement and anticipation start racing through my veins. Could it be? My heart thrums as it beats frantically in my chest. I quickly put my dish in the sink. I hear the knocking again as I walk through the hallway, yes definitely not Doris this time either.

Opening the door just a fraction, I see his grin first. He's dressed in his work gear and I eye him up and down. Charcoal coloured suit, white shirt, and a charcoal tie with faint silver stitching in diagonal lines. Let's just say if we worked together, oh boy, I don't think we'd get any work done. I step back and open the door fully. He stands casually with one arm resting on the door frame, the other tucked in his pocket.

"I just wanted to make sure you spread the butter correctly."

He emphasises the word 'spread' in a rather suggestive manner. I try to hide my amusement by covering my mouth with the back of my hand, but I soon give the game away when I let out a long-stifled giggle. I clear my throat and step to one side to let him in.

"You best come in and check then."

With that, I turn and sashay down the hallway and through the kitchen. I hear the front door close and the sound of fabric slipping off. His footsteps are silent, but I feel his eyes on me. Then I realise that iTunes has decided to play 'Crazy in Love', but the slowed-down version. My mind centres on the fact that Joe's wearing a tie. I hold on to the counter, feeling the overwhelming heat coursing through me at the possibility of his tie around my wrists. I shake away the thought with a quiet giggle. I reach up to retrieve a wine glass from the top corner cupboard. I must admit that I overstretched a little, lifting one foot off the floor, allowing my skirt to rise, feeling it skim my buttocks. Joe's touch on my hips makes me jump; luckily, I hadn't touched a glass yet. He brings my outstretched arm back down on the counter and my body brushes against him as I come back to my feet, his hands overlap mine.

"What's so funny?"

He murmurs deeply against my ear. Pulling my collar away from my neck, he kisses me so softly there, then I feel his hand trail down to my breast, teasingly caressing me while he waits for me to answer. I gasp and feel the urgency to bite onto something, anything; I look down at my free hand, bringing it up to my mouth, bending my forefinger, my teeth clamp down on it for a moment. I almost fall forward, but I swiftly put my hand back on the counter to support myself.

"This song... made me think... of your... your tie... your tie around my... around my wrists...."

I gasp in each pause; his breath and his caress have me in a hot mess.

"I didn't think you were into that sort of thing...."

I almost crumble completely as it rolls sensuously off his tongue; his breath rushes against my skin with his words. I'm not into that sort of thing as it happens, but then my mind tracks back to the smarting when Joe's palm met across my bare buttock. I must admit that I did get off on it; maybe I am a little kinkier than I thought.

"I... I... uh."

I can't finish as Joe's fingertips run up the back of my left thigh. I lean against the counter and gasp with the ever-increasing arousal that's fuelling the desire for him to fuck me even more. His other hand comes round to join in; now both hands graze up the backs of both thighs, encouraging my skirt to rise fully. He loops his fingers around the sides of my panties and stills.

"May I?"

He whispers the question against my ear. Oh my, a question that deserves a million yeses, yet I can't even seem to find one. It wreaks havoc with my inner spirit, turning me and her into putty as his fingertips graze my skin while he waits for my answer. I am his putty to play with and he can mould me into any shape he pleases, preferably around his cock.

"Oh my... oh my god... y-ye-yes... fuck yes."

I feel Joe bend slightly as he tugs the material over my behind and lets them float down my legs, instinctively I step out of them; as they meet my ankles, my legs remain parted. His body brushes against mine as he stands, cornering me once again, my behind pressed against his groin. 'Jitterbug 'breaks the sexual tension almost completely. I laugh at the happy, bouncy tune of 'Wake Me Up Before You Go Go' playing merrily. Hastily, I grab my iPod before it totally turns Joe off, but I hear a muffled giggle against my ear. He takes the iPod from me and scrolls until he finds what he's looking for. He places it back down on the counter as the voice of Solomon Burke fills the air.

"We've got nothing to burn this time."

His voice is smooth and delectable; that alone turns me on. I close my eyes as his fingers pull back my collar again, and his lips meet my neck, sending a prickling sensation down my spine. I feel my hair being wound around his other hand; I gasp as he finds my hair tie; his grip loosens slightly as he pulls at my hair tie, and my head willingly tips back with the drag. I bring my head back down once I feel him let go of me and my hair falls messily around my shoulders. Peering at Joe from the corner of my eye, my lips part suggestively, my hips start rocking slowly from side to side, pressed right against him. He fits around me snugly, but I manage to slide round to face him. My gaze fixes with his, his deep hazel eyes dancing as he smiles. I reach up to undo his tie, but I don't take it off. Winding each end around my hands, I use it to slowly reign him in, until our lips meet with kisses fuelled with off the scale heat and passion. Our lips don't part, even when Joe swiftly lifts me up and places my behind on the counter. My grip on the tie tightens, as I reel him in closer and wrap my legs around him. Fuck me, I want him so bad. A great urgency to see those abs of his rushes over me, so hurriedly I unravel my hands; Joe watches me intently, as I yank the tie free, his eyebrows rise with my eagerness and momentarily his features soften to a smirk. I let the tie fall to the floor. I swiftly find the buttons; I don't think I have ever undone a shirt so rapidly before. The feeling of the fabric pulling out of his waistband is so satisfying. My inner spirit squeals when his shirt is peeled away. 'Oh, hello there!' my eyes widen with delight; I relish the thought that he's all mine. Leaning against him, I pull the material down his arms as he shakes the shirt off his wrists. I drink in his flawless body as I run my fingertips up and down his arms, tracing each and every curve etched in his muscles. I feel my blouse being pulled out of the waistband of my skirt, instantly drawing my attention back to his touch. I look down and watch him undo the first few buttons.

"Lift your arms," he murmurs.

His tone is deep and stern; without hesitation, I obey his sexy command. The light fabric tingles my skin as it floats up my torso, revealing my deep red satin bra. As he pulls my blouse up and over my head, my hair well and truly becomes ruffled, falling back down freely.

"Red suits you" he purrs.

My inner spirit takes a mental note. One of my straps falls as he says it. I release Joe from my leg hold as he turns slightly to kick off his shoes; his hand goes down to his pocket and fishes out his wallet. Putting it on the side next to me, I'm impressed that he's come prepared as I notice a foil packet poking out of it. Going back to his waistband, I lean back on my hands and watch lustfully as he undoes his belt. Joe notices my expression and smirks, purposefully dropping the speed a peg or two just to tease me. We look at each other and giggle when we hear the intro to 'Let's Get It On'. Well done, iTunes, good pick. Joe shimmies out of his trousers and turns his attention back to me.

"Well... how appropriate."

He must have read my mind. He chuckles deeply as his eyes burn into mine. I'm still leaning on my hands, as Joe pulls just my hips, and my behind happily slides on my skirt, closer to him. Leaning closer to me, he cups my face, brushes my lips with his, then embraces them so intensely deep that it steals my breath away in between each kiss. My left hand frantically tries to find the foil packet while our lips are still locked. I grab it as soon as my fingers come across it. Joe pulls back to take the packet from me; he rips it open with his teeth; whoah, that was hot. Within a blink of an eye, his trunks are down, and the sound of latex pings. He brings my hips even farther forward; I am literally teetering on the edge. He cups my face again to reunite our lips. One of his hands glides down my neck, down to my chest. His fingers run along the edge of my bra, yanking the cup down freeing my breast. As he grips it with his whole hand, I gasp hot and heavy against his mouth. My head tips back, forcing me to break our embrace, but his mouth finds my neck instead and I groan so loud that I feel it rumbling through my chest. My back bows, thrusting my chest out as I feel him drive himself into me. Holy shit, that's deep. I gasp. He stills, with his full length inside me; my back relaxes slightly, and I bring my head back to see his face; peering through my eyelashes, my lips are still parted from the gasp. I pant through the anticipation of his next move. He withdraws almost entirely, firmly grabbing onto my hips, as he drives into me again, forcing me to cry out, that was deeper than deep. Holy crap, I think I'll come apart sooner than I expected.

"Whoah... fuck me, Joe."

My inner spirit seems to have let my lips loose as the thoughts manage to wriggle their way out through my mouth. Feeling my cheeks blaze, I look away to hide it. Joe cups my cheek, bringing me back to look at him, his eyes full of amusement, not appalled or shocked with my runaway mouth. I think he knows it wasn't a command. His thumb grazes along my lips, parting them as he drags down my bottom lip, ready to receive his. He almost pulls out of me again; our lips meet as soon as he thrusts his way back into me; I cry out under his embrace. No teasing this time; his thrusts keep coming. I break off our kiss as my head flies back again, and my hair sweeps the counter. Joe lets go of my hips to hug my waist instead; his mouth finds my bare breast, his warm breath and tongue sweep across my nipple. He hugs me fiercely as he pounds into me harder, faster, deeper, hotter, again, and again. My toes curl with the thrill that shoots right through me like they to need something to hold on to. Joe semi lets go of my waist; his hold moves further up my body, bringing my head back down, face to face. The pulsing feeling in my muscles is so divine that I don't want it to end. He starts to circle his hips; I almost forgot how fucking hot that was in the shower. It sparks an amazing feeling through my sex; it buzzes all the way through me. I reach the peak, but my body refuses to let go, my deep muscles quivering on the brink. Lifting my arms off the counter, I grip onto Joe's shoulder, my fingernails digging into his skin; I think he takes that as a cue to fuck me harder. He goes deeper than I ever thought possible. I pull Joe into me, hugging him so fiercely as I cum so hard around him. My cry roars out of me as I explode; stars dazzle and then fade in my eyes. My deep muscles splinter a billion times over and over.

My arms slip down his with a sudden weighted feeling as I come down from the exhilaration. Joe scoops me up into his arms, holding me firmly, as my arms hang loosely around his shoulders. Turning around, he pads across to the island, kissing me deeply as he lays me down gently, but my arms don't leave his shoulders. My sex is still buzzing with delight. Resting his forearms on the table on either side of me, he kisses me again but with more softness, featherlight even. Bringing my legs around, I lock the top of his thighs to me as he starts to glide in and out of me, slowly, deeply; the glorious sensation hums right through me. Our lips are still locked as his pace quickens slightly, but is still gentle. I feel the muscles in his shoulders tense. Keeping one of my arms locked around his shoulders, the other comes up to his hair; my fingers attentively play with the strands as I feel him reaching the peak, his panting quickens under the embrace. Joe pulls his lips away to bury his head in my hair, my fingertips never leaving his hair. He groans as his body quivers; the thrusts slow as he climaxes. His breath beats heavily against my neck, warm and clammy. He lifts his head to find me, no words are exchanged, but his eyes say it all.

Whoah, fuck me indeed.

Sixty-Five

I stir to the sound of running water. Sleepily, I peer at my alarm clock, a whole hour left before my alarm sounds. Rolling onto my back, rubbing the sleep out of my eyes, then my gaze meets the ceiling. The water turns off, and I hear the creak of the shower door opening, shortly followed by damp bare feet padding their way down the landing. I sit up and rest back on my elbows just as Joe appears in the doorway, wringing wet, his towel just about clinging on to his waist. Droplets of water cling to his hair and fall freely down his chest. He leans on the door frame with his arms folded.

"Hey, you... sleepyhead."

He murmurs along with a broad smile.

"Hey, you."

I murmur coyly and sleepily, throwing back the bedsheets. Unfolding his arms, Joe pads closer to me before I get up. He climbs onto the bed, I wince prematurely as he leans right over me; his palms rest on the bed and I notice the droplets hanging on his hair are about to fall. He smirks at my expression, mischief written across his face, and I get an inkling of what his next move is going to be.

"No... no, please don't wet me."

I giggle and shriek as he shakes his head very slowly a few times, grinning all the while. I squeal and squirm as cold droplets fall; they hit my chest and roll down my camisole in between my breasts.

"You are so mean!"

I just about manage to exclaim through the giggling. Joe kisses me deeply just the once and pulls back slightly.

"Shall I get off you then?"

No way! He kisses me again with even more firmness, but still just the once. My hands slide up between his shoulders, round to the back of his neck, bringing him with me as I lay back down; our lips ardently meet, increasingly steamier with every kiss, so steamy in fact I can feel my deep muscles starting to wake up with the excitement. Joe pulls back to speak.

"I take that as a no, then."

He murmurs deep and husky while his eyes gaze at each of my features one by one. I lose myself in the deep hue of his eyes, ignoring the cold wetness from his hair and body. Deep in thought, I wish I could wake up to this face every morning; that's not something I'd ever imagined with anyone. Now I understand why they say it in movies; I used to think, 'Jeez, nobody is that perfect.' The early morning sun bounces off his features perfectly. There's that word again, but he is perfectly perfect in each and every way. I smile along with that thought, and Joe eyes me quizzically.

"I wish your mind had a window so I could see what you so often secretly smile about."

My smile remains broad. I can't explain myself word for word and the last thing I want to do is scare him away, although he could be thinking the exact same thing.

"Just thinking how handsome you are and... how lucky I am to have you... and I love waking up next to you."

There you go, half of my thoughts laid out there. As I whisper it, his old schoolboy smile appears and then he looks down at my neck like he's embarrassed. Hasn't anyone ever told him that before? If so, how can anyone not tell him that? It's something I want to ask, but I don't want to open up any old wounds he may have.

"You know what... it's crazy... I was pretty much thinking the exact same thing... looking at your gorgeous sleepy face."

He looks up at me as soon as he says 'gorgeous sleepy face', with a gaze so full of affection that my heart could burst. An expression that is so perfect that I want to frame and keep it. I am determined to do whatever it takes to make it happen.

To be continued...

Thank you so much for reading!

Enjoyed 'Like No Other'?

C Jaye would be grateful if you can leave a rating/ review on Amazon and Goodreads.

Come and join C Jaye's Facebook group for the latest news and teasers for upcoming releases...

https://www.facebook.com/groups/cjayeauthor

Printed in Great Britain
by Amazon